ONE BIG LITTLE SECRET

A SECRET BABY ROMANCE

NICOLE SNOW

ABOUT THE BOOK

I guessed wrong.

A little reckless fun with a stranger never hurts.

A drunken one-night stand doesn't leave you pregnant.

A savage twist of fate won't make your baby daddy your new boss.

Bad luck can't last forever—unless you're *me*.

Should we count the ways I'm cooked with Patton Rory?

He rocks the grumpy gene, dialed up to eleven.

He's so handsome the mirror winks back and his bank account has its own zip code.

He's also totally oblivious—*thank God.*

I'm not sure what he'll be if he figures out the little boy who trashed his fancy building and ruined his favorite tie is his son.

Maybe I'm becoming a human knot, but I won't make the same mistake twice.

If he starts acting human and making my munchkin laugh, I'm not swooning.

If his forbidden kiss tastes like pure temptation, I'll eat mud.

If he makes my heart sing, I'm still clinging to my big little secret.

Even if it's growing so massive I can't separate love from the lie.

1: TAKING A GAMBLE (SALEM)

Six Years Ago

The water glimmers from the riverboat's lights, spinning reflections into streaks of gold.

It's pretty in a distant way, but with how I'm hanging over the side, I'm feeling lucky I haven't fallen in.

The worn wooden railing feels warm under my arms on this balmy night and the water looks delightfully cool.

Oh, I'm tempted.

But a night of pure torture will make you consider the craziest ways to escape.

Of course, splunking down in the Missouri River *would* ruin my makeup and my best dress. Not good when Kayla Persephone, my so-called friend whose father rented the boat, spent *at least* twenty minutes bringing me oh-so-close to matching her rich-girl friends, so I'd feel a little bad.

I just wish I knew why she bothered inviting me.

I twist around, leaving the water to its shimmering silence, and face the rest of the riverboat scene.

The sunset stains the sky blood orange.

The music pounds away in the main cabin, so loud I'm pretty sure I'll have Adele's voice burned into my brain for life.

Kayla's giddy little hamster friends talk and gamble. I see them through the windows, exploring the many rooms of this boat, throwing away play money I can't even dream of.

To distract myself from the fact that I'm the only one here who *isn't* a high-class daddy's girl, I swipe a glass from a nearby waiter and turn back to the water. Against the backdrop of big money, the river looks more inviting by the second.

God, why are we still friends?

Sure, so back in ninth grade I shared my umbrella with Kayla once, saving her perfect makeup and designer outfit, but we're adults now.

We're total opposites socially and—well, every other way.

She left high school and went to Old Mizzou, partying it up like everyone else here. She had the time of her life husband hunting between chasing a degree in whatever her heart desired.

She's glamorous and successful and beautiful.

And I'm—I'm *me.*

The girl who turned down debt and her parents' pleas to go to a real university.

The clown who ditched the conventional college-first advice to work on my business plans back in Kansas City.

I take a long sip of my mimosa and try to savor it, but it just tastes like privilege.

I've had loads of businesses by now. Gobs of big ideas.

They've just never quite worked out.

The vending machines selling mints seemed like a

winner, but I didn't have the charm to win any amazing locations and the turnover sucked. Apparently, Kansas City isn't too worried about bad breath.

My eco-friendly cleaning business would've been lucrative enough if the market wasn't jam-packed. It's amazing how many folks are willing to clean toilets for a living and brandish their green chemical-free credentials, even here in flyover country.

And in this town, good luck charging premium prices for dog walking when there are ten new doggy start-ups every month.

But it's fine.

I'm fine.

My next big idea is out there, I just know it.

And maybe I'll even have a chance at finding it if I can get off this casino riverboat with Kayla and her rich friends.

"Salem!" Kayla's scream splits the air. Everyone turns to stare as she throws herself at me like an overdone kitten, her white-blonde hair curling around her ears. She's gone for a Marilyn Monroe look tonight and I kinda hate that she's nailed it.

Beside her, I look like I just clocked off a long night shift at the loser factory.

"Hey, Kay." I summon a smile from the tips of my toes. "Having a good time? Are you winning anything in there?"

"Lady, we're just getting started! But why aren't you playing with us? And why aren't you drunk yet?" She scoffs at my half glass of mimosa, jerking my arm until I follow her inside to the velvet interior and the longest bar ever.

A cute bartender glances at me for a second. He has a piercing in one ear and a dark tattoo curling up his forearm.

"Lemmy, loosen up! You could be having fun for once," Kayla croons in my ear.

I try not to shudder.

"I didn't want to go too crazy tonight. Long week ahead, y'know," I start, but she's already leaning over the bar, pushing her ample cleavage half out of her dress.

The cute bartender coughs and spills a big scoop of ice all over the floor, trying not to stare.

Presto boobo, I'm forgotten.

"Shots!" Kayla demands, banging her fists on the counter.

"Huh?" I look at her.

"Tequila. You're slamming it with me. Right the fuck now."

Wow. So this evening *can* get worse.

"...I dunno. I really do have an early morning and—"

"No, Lemmy. No. *We* have a double date with a top-shelf hottie made of glass and a lime and we're not standing him up." She leans back and laughs at her own joke. "You're gonna have fun here, babe. I promise."

Inside isn't much better than outside.

Worse, in here, I can't just mope around in a corner and imagine swimming home.

But maybe she's right.

Maybe I need to stop worrying and relax a little.

"Okay, okay," I tell her. There's not much else *to* say to Kayla.

She's got the rich girlboss vibe down pat with her big brown eyes and full lips and carefully accented face. Tomorrow, she'll be back to impersonating another celebrity, and doing it so well everyone around her will pretend to be impressed.

"Stop being so awkward. You look *gorgeous*." She runs a hand down my arm, laughing again. "Look at your dress. The red really suits you. I bet you never get to dress up like this much, huh?"

"I mean... you picked it out. And no, I don't get out enough," I say dryly.

"You're welcome, Lemmy. Didn't I tell you I'm a genius? Look at your *butt*." To emphasize her point, she slaps my ass. "Babe, you're going to pull tonight."

Holy mother of cringe.

I wonder if the security guy in the corner carries so he can shoot me right now.

"Hang on, I don't know about that. I don't know if I want to mess around like—"

Too late.

Kayla squeals as the tall tequila shots land in front of us with the usual salt and lime.

I knock mine back, trying not to grimace as a fireball goes down my throat.

"Remember Christmas?" she asks, reminding me of the last time we hung out. Although that's a pretty strong exaggeration for 'existing at the same party.'

Just like now, Kayla was completely smashed.

I was barely any better, and at the end of the evening, we wound up sitting together and ranking the guys in the room while I tried not to barf. Until I joked too much and Kayla threw up her drinks all over my shoes while she was laughing.

"C'mon. What's the score tonight? Just look at that stallion stable. Every dude here is hot *and* rich." She glances at the bartender again, biting her bottom lip.

Sigh.

"The guy by the door, he's pretty cute," I say. "I give him a seven."

"Security guy? Lemmy, he must be like *forty*. Do better." Kayla doesn't even spare him a glance. "What about him? Over there by the roulette table?"

She whistles obnoxiously.

The guy she nods at stands alone, this tall, dark silhouette who becomes the center of attention purely by existing.

5

Okay, yes.

He's hot, in a forbidden kind of way—the kind of sexy you see in moody ads for expensive colognes and watches. Those ads are always photoshopped, I think.

Only, unless he's a figment of my imagination, there are no edits happening here, not in the flesh. Just Hercules in a white button-down shirt, curled open a little at the neck, looking good enough to eat.

"Him? Jeez, Kay, he's a solid twelve out of ten."

She giggles and elbows me in the side. "You gotta go for it now. Don't make me drag you over."

My heart almost stops.

"Um, right. How many drinks have you had?" I ask her. "Remember that time in high school when you told me to ask the quarterback to prom?"

"And he made a *huge-ass* mistake by turning you down," she says, waving a server down for another drink.

"He didn't just 'turn me down.' He humiliated me in front of half our class. Then he asked you out for putting me up to such a dumb prank."

"Yeah, well…" She looks me up and down, wrinkling her nose. "You're prettier now, right? That dress, you're rocking it tonight."

I can't tell if that's an insult or a compliment.

You never can tell with Kayla.

Like any young Missouri woman from an affluent family, she's skilled in the art of insulting you with a sunny smile on her face.

But this doesn't *sound* like an insult.

"Thanks," I mutter. "But I don't think I'm enough for that guy."

Smiling, she jabs her fingers in her ears. "Nope, not hearing it! Stop putting yourself down. You could get

6

whoever you wanted if you just smiled more, Lemmy. And if you dressed aggressively, like now."

"You dressed me," I remind her.

"I know, but you have boobs. Use them."

"My boobs are *not* aggressive," I hiss.

Man, I can't believe we're having this conversation.

"Well, not if you aren't using them right!" She pulls the front of my dress to show more cleavage. "There, look at that. One little adjustment and you're on fire."

She's shifted the dress so low it's a miracle my breasts are defying gravity. "Definitely more aggressive. Do I need to start howling?"

"Kayla, no!"

"And hey, even if you don't get the guy in the corner, you can still do better than the old nerds who haven't stopped eye-fucking us ever since we walked in." She nods at a group of older men on the other side of the bar. "I don't even know who they are—dudes my dad works with, I think. Daddy paid for casino night, so of course a few of his buds are here too."

That explains the odd mix of people scattered around this boat.

"Just find yourself an *actual* seven. Please," she advises, pushing a fresh shot toward me.

Watching her drink is a little mesmerizing, the odd way she licks the salt and tosses the drink back like it's water. Her expression only changes when she sucks on the lime.

"Will do," I say sarcastically, snapping off a salute.

"Okay, sweet. I'm gonna play roulette. You interested?" She slides off her seat.

"Nah, you go on. I've got this." I motion to the next shot. She raises her eyebrows, rightly assuming there's no way I'll keep standing if I finish this next shot. But then she shrugs.

"Okay, Lemmykins. Enjoy yourself!"

Do I really look that miserable?

I glance back to catch the cute bartender's eye, but he's busy serving someone else. An old guy with creases in his neck below his ears.

It only takes a second to regret looking that way. Old Guy glances over at me, moving his head like a hungry bird.

Oof. I jerk my head away before he thinks I'm interested.

Right, I can do this.

So maybe this isn't how I planned to spend a sticky summer night off, but I'm here. I *can* make my own fun, whatever Kayla thinks.

I order a cocktail as I wait for the buzz to kick me in the face, scanning the large room. It's basically a giant bar with tables and corner booths flanking table games. Optimal for getting drunk and losing a metric ton of money.

Not my kind of fun. I wonder if I can find a man without spending a fortune—

"Hey, gorgeous." A loud, drunken voice interrupts my thoughts.

Oh, boy, here we go.

I turn around to find a guy in his forties sliding onto the stool beside me. There's a bead of liquid on his collar and I look at it, preferring not to pay too much attention to his greying hair or the way he flashes his gold watch. Three times, like I'm part magpie, drawn to shiny things.

He wields it like a secret swipe card that opens my legs.

Come on, dude.

"Hello," I say coldly.

"What's a pretty young thing like you doing at the bar like this?"

"Um." Is this what it's like to be chatted up? I already want to pass. "Drinking, I guess. Nothing like enjoying your own company."

I hope he takes the hint.

But he doesn't.

He laughs, throwing his large head back until he resembles a horse. His Adam's apple bobs and I try to catch the cute bartender's eye in case he's willing to rescue me, but he doesn't even see me.

All because Kayla's gone, probably.

"Are you here because you're a friend of what's her face? Kylie?" he asks. "The one from Old Mizzou? Surprised you ain't trying your luck with her. Good times for a college girl."

"Actually, I didn't go to college." And it's my turn to laugh as my drink—a toxic cocktail that's the same fading orange as the sunset—gets delivered. "I'm not here to gamble because I'm basically broke."

He cocks his head and stares. My liquid courage has gotten me this far, and now it's time to finish the job.

"My last three businesses almost bankrupted me. I *lost* money on a job walking a hyperactive rottweiler. The kids with lemonade stands have turned a better profit this summer than I will. I even tried to sell fresh-made Italian freezes. That went up in flames when the secondhand ice cream cart I bought off the internet started on fire. Literally, I mean. That was a bad day, but it's hardly the worst. Want to hear about them?"

"Hell no," he mutters, but his body language has changed. His shoulders hunch and he turns away.

Thank God. All this dude wanted was a young, fun college bimbo.

They're all the same and I'm so not his type.

"So are you married? Or just divorced?" I ask, playing it up as I nod at the white line on his finger where his wedding band usually sits, surrounding the tan.

"Enjoy the party, doll." Grumbling, he pushes himself up and staggers away.

He throws a look back like he's afraid I'll chase him.

Hey, at least we're having *fun.* Isn't that the whole point?

I take a triumphant sip from my cocktail and wait for my next victim.

* * *

SURPRISE, surprise.

It turns out being single at a floating casino bar attracts the grossest, most arrogant men on this side of the Mississippi. The adjustments Kayla made to my dress are only partly to blame.

Most of the guys who drop by offering free drinks don't bother hiding the fact that they're drooling at my cleavage.

Normally, I'd be happy I don't have to buy drinks.

The downside is Kayla has my drinks covered.

But the real losers here are the gobs of leering old bachelors and obvious cheaters looking to poach a girl half their age.

"Yep, I just turned eighteen! One more year of high school," I lie to the latest guy, who's nudged his chair close enough so his knee bumps mine.

I shuffle back again and giggle.

"No foolin'? You look mature for your age."

I almost flinch. Huge ick that my fake age just encourages the pig.

"I can look like a lot of things. But, um, aren't you a little old? No offense."

"Age is a hell of a number. Say, you've got pretty eyes." His hand drifts to my thigh and I swipe it away roughly. "Such long legs, too. Don't be a tease, little lady."

I shrug.

"Thanks. I grew them myself, but they also have an age limit. Sorry."

Undaunted, he licks his lips and leans closer.

Disgusting.

If I had to guess, he thinks he's a young stud here when he's probably in his late thirties. But I don't have to guess.

His strong cologne nearly knocks me out, and his dark hair is slicked back and tapered like a skunk.

"Quit fucking around. You're the hottest girl in this bar," he breathes, the beer heavy on his breath. No clue how many he's had, but it's five too many.

"I'm the only girl at this bar right now," I say. The only pathetically single one, anyway, judging by a couple older women with men in the corner. "But look, I'm not interested. Wanna take a hint?"

That wandering hand grips my arm, tightening.

"Sounds like you don't date much," he growls. "I'm paying your tab."

"Which is totally illegal. I'm underage."

"Bullshit. How old are you really?"

"Old enough to know a few drinks don't entitle your touchy ass to anything." I've had it. I try to shake him off, but he won't budge. "Seriously. Let go, dude."

I don't get worried until he laughs.

"Like hell. I can show you a good time, missy. I'm staying the night below deck."

Sweet Jesus.

If I hadn't finished my drink, it would be dripping off his face right now.

At least I'm wearing heels. I know from personal experience they can do some damage when they slam into a man's—

"Excuse me," a deep voice rumbles smoothly from the side.

I turn to see coppery-brown hair, sharp blue eyes, and a jawline worthy of the Himalayas. It's Mr. Twelve from earlier, and he's younger up close, maybe mid-twenties.

11

He's also standing close enough to touch, looking mighty pissed.

Then he *does* touch me, placing a hand on my shoulder and stroking his way down to my hand.

This is it.

My end.

I'm going to die right here on this riverboat by spontaneous combustion. Or maybe I'm already dead from too many drinks and this is a weird kind of afterlife.

Touchy-Feely narrows his eyes at Mr. Twelve.

"Who the hell are you?"

"Her fiancé—and you must be the clown asking stupid questions," Twelve lies—and so convincingly I believe him for a split second. "The question is, how long do I give you?"

"What? What the hell are you saying, man?" He fumbles for a second and finally releases me.

"That's what I thought." Twelve pulls me off the chair and into his arms. "You okay, baby?"

With you? I'm okay personified.

He's dreamy. Positively sinful up close, which rarely ever happens, and he has the shoulders of an angry god, tensed like steel as he holds me.

"I'll live," I whisper, a little too breathlessly.

"Get your legs working," he growls at Touchy-Feely, who tries to slam down the rest of his beer. Twelve grabs it out of his hand and *thunks* it on the counter. "I meant right now, genius. I'm giving you a very generous ten-second head start. If you're not gone by the end of my countdown, I'll see you in the river."

Holy. Crap.

The other man lets out a startled grunt, stares for two seconds, and then runs out of the room.

I turn back to my hero and smile.

And when he smiles back, clearly proud of thinking quick on his feet, it makes my knees wobble.

"Please tell me you're not actually eighteen," he says.

"Oh, jeez. You heard that?" I straighten my dress and step back. "Before you accuse me of underage drinking, I promise I'm twenty-one. Got my ID in here somewhere to prove it…"

He puts his hand gently on mine as I fumble for my purse. "Don't bother. I don't need it."

"Oh, um, okay."

"Just couldn't help noticing you were alone and stuck with that greasy fuck. Cruel of your friends to leave you marooned with these piranhas. You with Kayla?"

So he knows her. Not a shock, I guess.

He doesn't know my name, of course. I'm not sure we should even bother introducing ourselves, but maybe I can forge a new identity for tonight. He'll never know.

"Are you another piranha man?" I ask.

"Not tonight," he says with another smile that slays. "Just a handsome stranger."

"Did I say you were handsome?" I raise an eyebrow.

"Nah. I can hear your thoughts."

Oh my God, I'm laughing.

There's no way this guy doesn't know how freakishly gorgeous he is, but there's also no chance I'm about to play into his ego.

"Well, I suppose you're not bad," I say, following his lead as he strolls across the room. "Where are we going?"

"Roulette."

"Big gambler, huh?"

He glances down at me. "I feel lucky tonight."

We find space at a roulette table. I cling to his arm as he trades a wad of cash for dark-blue chips.

This is wildly out of my comfort zone. I feel like people

should be staring at me for being with someone like *him*, but for some reason no one questions it.

"What do you think?" he asks me. "Red or black? It's an easy choice."

"Red," I decide. "It matches my dress."

"Red it is. And what's your favorite number?"

"Why? You're already trying to steal my social?" Then I laugh, because there's nothing as absurd as a guy who looks this hot and rich being interested in my social security number. "My favorite number's eight, so go with that."

He nods at the guy in charge of the table, who spins the wheel once everyone's bets are in.

The tension thickens as the ball slowly loses momentum, tripping over the numbers until it settles on a red eight.

My heart lunges up my throat.

Mr. Twelve nods approvingly like he's not the least bit surprised.

"Knew there was a reason I felt lucky tonight, Lady Luck. Or should it be Lady Bug?" He nods at my dress.

I almost forgot it was peppered with small black dots.

"Thanks, dude. Is comparing me to a bug supposed to be flattering?"

"Ladybugs are good luck in some cultures. They're also damn cute," he says gruffly.

Despite everything, I blush. *Again.*

"So you think I'm cute? Very funny." My inner loser shakes her head violently in disbelief.

He lowers his head so it's right beside my ear. His breath brushes my hair, tickling the delicate skin.

"Show one man at this table who isn't staring," he whispers.

"Stop. Now you're just being ridiculous."

"Am I?" He raises his eyebrows at me and makes another bet.

Amazingly, he wins.

And wins.

And wins.

Doesn't matter if I make the bet or he does, it just keeps coming.

We win several rounds and leave a lot of jaws hanging on the floor, at least for the people who don't walk away in pure disgust. By the end of the game, he's got a whole stack of chips.

"This calls for a victory drink, Lady Bug." He takes my hand and pulls me back to the bar. "What's your poison?"

"Oh God, I don't know. I've had a lot of poison tonight, that's for sure." No joke. The world has devolved into random shapes and colors and him. "Whatever you're having."

He orders a neat whiskey that slips down as easily as melted butter, and before I can stop him, he's pulling me onto the dance floor.

Oh, I'm a hot mess.

Putty in his hands.

And those big, warm hands are on my back now. My chest is pressed against his, and I'm gazing up at him like those blue eyes are offering me the secrets of the universe.

"I'm not a lucky person so this is really weird," I whisper. "Like, it's bad. I'm a human black cat."

"You feel lucky to me." He slides a hand down to my ass and squeezes. "And I can feel you pretty well."

"Oh my God."

Did I say that out loud? No, I moaned it instead.

I am so, so screwed.

The crazy part is, I'm not even bothered by it.

"Too far?" He dips his head closer, his gaze firmly on my mouth. "Tell me and I'll stop right now."

I am going, going, *gone.*

Tomorrow, odds are I'll regret every second of this. Hell, I *definitely* feel pretty nuts right now. But it also feels good, and so does he.

"Lady Bug?" he urges.

"If you're going to kiss me, hurry up. Before I have second thoughts."

No need to ask twice. His mouth eclipses mine in a delicious rush that makes my nerves glow like string lights.

My blood ignites.

His tongue claims mine and takes us to cloud flipping nine.

* * *

I CAN BARELY REMEMBER the way to the guest cabin where Kayla said I could crash for the night.

He's still holding my hand, keeping me steady, following my confused turns until I find the right door and lead him inside.

As soon as the door shuts behind us, he detonates me again.

Another kiss.

Hard. Hungry. Rough.

Holy hell, I've never been kissed like this in my life.

My only serious boyfriend was a passive guy with awkward lips and a weak libido that had me leading everything. We never went past the make out stage, and I wasn't sorry about it.

Call it shallow, but he never made me feel wanted.

In a single instant, this man does what five months of dates never could.

And God, he probably knows how to do everything else, too.

I have no earthly idea what I'm doing in that department,

but judging by the confidence of his roaming hands, I don't need to worry.

All I need to do is be ready.

I shouldn't, I shouldn't, but I don't want to stop.

So, I don't.

Not when he unzips my dress and shoves it to my feet in a scarlet puddle.

Not when he picks me up and hauls me over to the plush bed.

Not when he unhooks my bra.

It's not fancy lingerie. It's supportive and comfortable, basic with no wire and wide straps. But he doesn't even care as he flings it aside and runs his tongue down my body.

"You're too goddamned beautiful to waste in the casino, playing arm candy," he rasps against my skin. "I want you all to myself."

"Liar." I grin, pushing at his chest.

I think he sees it as a challenge.

He laughs darkly and flicks his tongue against my nipple.

The sudden heat sends waves of pleasure bolting through me.

"Does this look like a lie?" he asks, motioning to the bulge in his pants.

Of course, he's huge.

The thick ridge pulsing his trousers honestly scares me a little.

"Oh, wow," I whisper. He slides a hand along my thigh and pulls off my panties, and my brain stutters. "Oh my *God*."

So, this is what I've been missing out on when I bowed out of the whole college hookup scene.

"You want this, Lady Bug? Tell me," he demands against my mouth.

He tastes like man mingled with a hint of whiskey. His

fingers draw circles at the top of my thighs, tickling the delicate skin, but never going where I truly need them.

If I were sober, I might worry about this as my first time.

Rationally, I know it's dumb and dangerous to be drunk and on the verge of having sex with a complete stranger.

I might consider the fact that I don't know his name and he doesn't know mine.

But I'm not sober or rational or cautious tonight.

I'm not boring old Salem Hopper.

For now, I'm Lady Bug, and the heat pooling in my core has more control over my mouth than my brain.

"Touch me. Wherever you want," I whisper.

He grins with devilish delight as he shoves my legs apart and slides a finger inside me.

A noise falls out of me that's so shrill I throw a hand over my mouth.

Oh my fuck.

He catches my wrist then, moving it away from my face as he slips another finger inside me, stretching me, short-circuiting my senses.

"Can you take it, good girl? Can you take all of me?"

I bite my lip until it hurts.

"Don't hold back," he growls. "Be as fucking loud as you like."

"What about…" I can't even string together a sentence as he strokes my inner wall. "W-won't people hear?"

"Do we care?"

For a second, we lock eyes.

And I fall into the heat, the humor, the dare twinkling in his gaze.

No, I decide. *No, we flipping don't.*

He reads my mind as I give myself over to his clever hands and wicked mouth.

Soon, I know I was right about one thing—I don't need to worry about my role.

He's in total control, and when he fingers me until I'm drenched and aching and so, so close, I think I'd give him my life.

When he pulls out, unzips his pants, and pushes into me, I tell myself I'm ready.

Wrong.

So wrong.

Nothing could ever prepare me for the world imploding into searing hot stars.

Everything condenses into fire with every thrust, slow and intense and soul-shaking.

Every breath becomes his.

Every moan becomes music.

And the only thing that remains is this bright, demanding pleasure he cuts through me with every slash of his hips.

It builds with every thrust, every gasping kiss.

His tongue mirrors the movement of his hips, claiming my mouth.

His hands tease my nipples, pushing me closer to the edge of no return.

"Fucking come for me, woman. Come like you never have in your life."

Like I even have an option.

When I shatter, he swallows my scream, grinding hot encouragement against my lips.

Muscles I didn't know I had tense as I go off.

Somewhere in the beautiful mess, his rhythm fractures, and his breathing deepens into growls.

He slams into me, his pubic bone stroking my clit.

I dig my nails into his back for dear life and hold on—*hold the hell on* while ecstasy consumes me.

Sex this good feels like flying, I think.

Because the aftermath is definitely falling.

When I'm able to breathe again, we're sticky and still sliding together as he pulls away with a rough curse.

"Shit. Guess my luck improved after leaving the casino tonight," he tells me, right before crashing down on his back beside me, staring at the ceiling. "Fuck me, that was good. I could go for a smoke and I don't even do cigarettes."

I giggle, slurring my laugh as I roll into his arms.

My cheek rests against his shoulder, which feels way too natural, too good at putting me to sleep.

Oh, this is bad.

But it's wonderful when he wraps an arm around me, and even though I want to savor this moment, the exhaustion takes me. I fall asleep to the steady beat of his heart while he runs his hand slowly through my hair.

When I wake up, I'm alone.

I already know I'll never see Mr. Twelve and his black magic moves again.

II: LUCKY DAY (PATTON)

Present

*C*all it my lucky fucking day.

I stare up at the tall, sleek high-rise we've named The Cardinal. Soon to be the city's finest hotel that's not technically a hotel.

There's no stopping the proud smile splitting my lips.

The tower looms over the distant Kansas City skyline like the elegant bird it's named after, a stark red logo lit like a flame at the top. It's not just the bird theme. We've borrowed a hint of style from the city's prominent World War I memorial and its eternal flame.

Even though I've seen this place hundreds of times during its renovation, it still makes me happy as hell.

This is it. So close to the big opening I can taste it.

The chance of a lifetime—one we've had our eye on since our last big deal with real estate mogul Forrest Haute went bad—and now that it's here, it feels sweeter because of the disaster that came before.

Well, *almost* sweeter.

Considering said disaster involved a big goddamned financial mess and a federal investigation, I think most people would rather get to the point without so much drama.

Except for Dexter, of course. Haute was the whole reason my brother met his now-wife and was hailed as a city hero for uncovering a sprawling crime ring mucking up the city.

Don't worry about Dex, *he's* doing great.

The rest of us had to stake our reputation on ordinary business—and that something is The Cardinal.

It's the height of modern luxury, the pinnacle of what our company, Higher Ends, specializes in. Sleek condo units with tasteful art and comfy furnishings galore. Rooftop pool bar. Full cleaning service, food, and deliveries on demand.

All the convenience of a luxury hotel without the stuffiness and plenty of privacy.

What's more, because I'm a master with delegating, it's a perfect fit for our internship meant for recruiting new talent, especially in management.

We'll have plenty of backups to help handle the daily affairs, plus any quirks that might come up.

Hopefully, our big opening stays quirk-free, considering this place is meant to run virtually on autopilot, but you never know. There's always *something.*

So far, the only downside is that I need to spend more time mentoring the new manager and making sure she's up to snuff.

Once, that might've been Dex's job with his workaholic lifestyle, but now that he's married and settled, it falls to Archer or me. And knowing Archer might scare the new blood away with his assholery, I stepped up.

Whatever. Let's get this over with.

I leave the gleaming exterior behind and climb the steps up to the building, finding my way to the common area near the information desk. It smells like a new build with that minty, freshly renovated smell.

That's one of the things I love about this job, being able to breathe your work.

Hell, if I wasn't born a Rory, I probably would've wound up in real estate anyway. There's nothing more satisfying than the smell of a new project coming alive, and because we're perfectionists, everything *is* perfect here.

The lobby seats are old-world leather. The drop-down widescreen TV looks futuristic, and there are silver trays with complimentary breakfast pastries from the Sugar Bowl. We'd never skimp on supporting my sister-in-law's bakery.

For a second, I stop and drink it all in.

Yeah, I'd stay here in a heartbeat.

Hell, I'd live here, if I wasn't already set up with a perfectly nice place. I just hope everybody else agrees and this place gets booked up to capacity before we can say—

A loud clatter to the left stops my brain.

I turn, just in time to see little hands reaching onto a table for one of the breakfast pastries I mentioned.

A kid. Stuffing his face like a greedy little chipmunk. And the second he locks eyes with me, he runs, heading for the sofa and spilling crumbs everywhere as the pastry falls apart.

There goes my leather sofa.

Fuck, what a way to start the morning. Who let a kid go wild in here before we have customers?

"Hey, get back over here!" I shout, holding in some other choice words that aren't child friendly.

He stops and looks at me with sharp blue eyes that remind me of my nephew, Colton. Except Colt is well-behaved and he *doesn't* wedge crumbs in every nook and cranny of a twenty-thousand-dollar sectional.

"I don't know you!" he says.

"Yeah, I know you don't. But you still need to get off the sofa, little man."

Wrong words, apparently.

He scowls at me like that pastry falling apart in his hands is suddenly made of mud. "I'm not little. I'm a big boy."

"Fine. Whatever. I hear big boys don't bomb other people's furniture with crumbs," I tell him, hoping it sinks in.

For a second, I think he'll smear what's left of that thing all over it just to piss me off. Then he just wrinkles his nose and starts making a half-assed attempt to wipe them off.

"There. All better, mister!"

"Not quite. Where's your mother?" I look around, but there's no sign of parents. Who lets their kid raise bedlam in a place like this? "You need to get down."

"No! My mommy says never go anywhere with a stranger."

"Of all the lessons he remembers…" I mutter. "What's your name, kid?"

"I'm not supposed to tell strangers. I'm not gonna tell you!"

"Just—please, get off the sofa. That's all I'm asking. I'll give you another pastry if you do." Bribery. That's one thing I've learned from watching Archer raise Colt practically alone. It works when you use it just right.

Unfortunately, I don't have my older brother's dad experience.

The boy folds his arms and glares at me. "I wanted hot cocoa but it tastes like crap."

Out of habit, I look at the coffee bar. It's been destroyed.

Coffee pools across the counter. A couple overturned paper cups and napkins are soaking up the mess as the rest drips on the floor.

24

That means the little hellraiser must've drank some coffee.

This morning just keeps getting better.

"Where *are* your parents?" I ask again, grabbing a gob of tissues and dipping them into the puddles of coffee, which instantly bleeds through to my hands.

Fuck.

Really, I should call someone, but by the time a cleaner shows up, I'll already have met the manager. The last thing I need is for them to see this chaos and panic, wondering what kind of clown show they've signed on to.

"My mom's here," the kid says, starting to bounce on the sofa again.

"Stop bouncing, for God's sake." I pinch the bridge of my nose. Damn, would it be so bad if I picked this munchkin up and restrained him?

I'm considering it until a woman starts yelling.

"Arlo!" She races across the floor, her heels clicking, young by the looks of it. Somehow, she seems weirdly familiar with her dark hair twisted up in a bun and hazel eyes shining with worry.

Soon, she grabs the boy's arm and helps him off the sofa.

"Oh my God, I can't believe this." With a ragged breath, she looks at me. "Sir, I'm so sorry for this. I have no words. Arlo, you apologize."

The kid—Arlo—shuffles his feet.

"Sorry, mister," he mumbles, watching me sourly.

"I'm really sorry for my son again," she says, looking back at me. There's a flicker of something in her eyes like she recognizes me too. Or maybe she's just about to die from shame because her tornado of a son just wrecked the brand-new common area. "I didn't mean for this to happen. I stepped away for *ten seconds* to get some printouts from the back. Holy shit, never again."

I give her son the stink eye.

"You're an employee, then. Unfortunately, we can't have children here, you understand?" I wait for her to nod. "We're just getting up and running. I have important business to attend to, I'm afraid, so I'm going to have to ask you to—"

"I know." Her cheeks are flaming.

My eyes drift down to the rest of her.

Neat figure. Supple hips. Curves that would tell any idiot why she has a kid.

She might be a flustered mom, but I have to admit she's rocking the MILF look.

"I didn't have a choice," she continues. "The babysitter skipped out at the last minute. Family emergency. I didn't have anywhere else for him to go, and I know how important it is to be here today. I'm sorry for the mess. Really. Here, let me clean that up." She grabs a wad of napkins and tries mopping up some of the coffee flood without much more success than I had. "Um, he's not usually like this, just so you know. He's a good kid, I promise."

"Sure." My veins ice over.

"Look, this won't be a regular occurrence. You don't need to worry about that."

Regular?

I sure as hell hope not.

If I see this kid demolishing the place again, I'll flip my lid. Also, she needs to quit apologizing before someone— probably me, admittedly—loses their cool.

First impressions are God. If the new manager from our mentor program walked in right now and saw this shit show...

Let's just say I doubt there'd be a second impression. And that would instantly be *my* fault with Dex and Archer breathing down my neck.

"Who are you, anyway? Are you cleaning or accounting? We're not supposed to have any other staff on duty today."

"Oh, right. Hi, I'm Salem. Salem Hopper?" She blinks at me like the name should mean something, offering me a hand while she keeps mopping coffee with more napkins. "Your new intern. Er, manager, I mean."

My manager.

My goddamned *manager*.

This day just charged into first place for historic disasters.

"Patton," I growl back, annoyed at myself for having the MILF thought a minute ago.

My brothers might think I'm an idiot when it comes to dating, but I don't dip my pen in the company ink. *Ever.*

Predictably, that realization only makes me notice her more. The way her blouse falls open at the top, just enough to—*fuck*.

Stop.

I have to turn away and stare at this gold abstract art piece mounted on the wall before I can look at her again.

"I'll call someone to deal with the mess. Let's get started, assuming you can find a way to keep your son entertained."

"Oh, yes. He has a coloring book and I won't let him out of my sight. I'll make sure he's set up before we begin Mr.— um, do you prefer Patton or Mr. Rory?" She tosses the sopping wet napkins in the trash and grabs Arlo's hand.

"Patton's fine," I clip, wondering who the hell recommended her—and how I managed to get myself mixed up in this shit.

This is the kind of comical mess Dexter normally steps in, like when he blabbed to Haute that he was engaged to the bakery girl when he really wasn't. His big fat mouth landed him a world of hurt.

27

Of course, since they're married now, maybe it wasn't all a colossal fuckup.

"You can call me Salem. Thank you so much for this opportunity. I couldn't believe it when I got the call," she says with a disarming smile. Again, I'm pissed at myself for hearing 'MILF' on repeat in my head.

She's legitimately pretty, though, if you can look past the beady-eyed little munchkin who looks like he's plotting to drown me in coffee next time.

"It's what we do," I say with a shrug. "Here at Higher Ends, we've decided we're better off building our management team from the ground floor rather than poaching talent elsewhere."

She nods enthusiastically.

The kid skips behind us until we reach the meeting room.

"I'll be right with you," she says with a polite smile.

I wait for her as they linger outside for a minute, whispering to each other.

I bite back a smile as the kid gets some 'mom talk.' How familiar.

The shit I pulled when I was knee-high almost put my poor mother into a coma.

I can't make out much, just a few harsh pleas for him to 'behave' and something about losing weekend pizza rights for the next ten years.

When she finally walks in with the boy sulking behind her, I show her inside and shut the door.

At least in here, Arlo can't cause too much destruction. Just in case, I hand him a Higher Ends notepad and a blue pen to go with the coloring book Salem pulls from her bag. While he scribbles away noisily, I gesture for her to sit next to me at the end of the long table.

"You came here with a glowing recommendation. Mr. Persephone himself, from the fashion brand. He knew my folks for years," I tell her, praying I won't have to make someone regret those words. "Your previous hotelier experience speaks for itself."

"I have a thick skin. Working at Copper Roof will do that." She gives me a strained smile.

Copper Roof? *That's* her experience?

The place is a frigging dive, just off the main highway leading into town from the Kansas state line. The place was never anything close to luxurious even in its heyday, when Elvis music and new veterans back from Korea were common there.

"Don't let it scare you. I knew this job wouldn't be easy and I love a challenge. After years working there, I can handle anything," she tells me proudly. "Trust me, I've dealt with roaches who had bigger egos than the nastiest guest."

That wins her a smirk, and I'm annoyed to admit she has a point.

"That's what I like to hear, Miss Hopper. I'll remind you that while I'm giving you a shot, your performance is what really matters in the end. The hours and sweat you put in with us are far more important than a few lines on a résumé."

I give her a quick rundown of her duties. How we've mapped out the daily operations, our system for dealing with complaints and improvements, the brand commitment to providing excellent service, and generally helping maintain the lofty standards set by our earlier successes.

To her credit, she takes quick notes in neat script that fits her vibe. With the blouse tucked into her navy pants, she fits the businesswoman profile perfectly.

Everything except the immaculate ass I shouldn't be staring at.

Minus the small child on the other side of the table, that is, who's looking at the pen like he's contemplating how to turn it into an ink cluster bomb.

I'm half convinced he damn well could.

But if he starts scribbling on walls or the furniture, I don't care who he is. I'll tackle him like a football.

"Patton?" Salem asks. "Mr. Rory? Sorry, did you want to say more?"

"Right." *Focus, focus.* There's a crease between her eyebrows. She probably thinks I'm an idiot. "Where was I?"

"You were talking about the perks..."

"Yes." I clear my throat. "There are several benefits associated with this job, as outlined in your contract. HR can answer any questions about your health insurance or the profit sharing. The most exclusive benefit we offer, however, is my personal mentorship."

"For sure," she whispers, leaning forward. A pendant around her neck swings with the movement, teasing my eyes to her neckline. "That's why I jumped at this job, actually. You guys, the Rory brothers, you're practically legends in business around here."

"I prefer notorious, but thanks." I snort. The latest hype has nothing to do with me or Archer or even our miraculous start-up success.

We're the toast of the town because everyone thinks Dex is a homegrown superhero.

"Unfortunately, my brother Dexter won't be helping out with this program," I tell her before any disappointment sets in.

"That's fine," she says with a smile that doesn't waver.

Damn. There's something naggingly familiar about the way her face catches the light, bringing out the gold flecks in her brown eyes.

Why do I feel like I've dealt with her before?

"There's a lot to be said for the company," she tells me cheerfully. "Your whole brand, really. I've done my homework."

"Have you?"

"Yeah! The way you forced your way into a crowded market, it's impressive. Your growth in the first five years is hardly matched by similar firms in much bigger markets. Plus, you've single-handedly reframed expectations around travel rentals. I mean, just look at the condos here." She waves a hand. "All the convenience of hotel living without the stuffiness and big crowds. The Cardinal *feels* exclusive."

I nod. "People with money like feeling independent without losing their creature comforts."

"And Higher Ends delivers." She's surprisingly passionate. There's no doubt she believes what she's saying when she looks at me like I can turn water into wine.

It's almost enough to forgive her little hurricane for tearing up my lobby.

"I'm glad you read up on us before you arrived. Now, if you'd like to come this way—"

"Look, Mommy!" Arlo skids into Salem's side, holding up a poorly drawn picture of a stick figure with a scowl so huge it's sliding off his chin. His eyebrows are angry Vs that take up a good proportion of his face. "I drew Mr. Grumpybutt."

Salem's face flames.

Wait. Is that supposed to be me? With *those* eyebrows?

"Arlo, go sit down," she hisses, pressing the back of her hand to her cheek.

"But Mom, you said—"

"Arlo! I'm so sorry, Mr. Rory. He's normally not like this, not in public. I swear." She glances around the meeting room desperately and whispers, "It must be all the excitement here."

Whatever.

I'm willing to bet my bank account it's partly the coffee he guzzled. Caffeine and children don't mix.

"It's fine," I say, trying to hide my irritation. Like it's

suddenly important that I'm not Mr. Grumpybutt, spoiler of everything fun beneath his twitchy villain eyebrows. "How about we get Arlo that hot chocolate—decaf, for sure—and have a look around?"

Arlo's ears must be fine-tuned for treats.

"Yeah! Hot choc-lit!" he shouts, throwing the notepad down.

With a firm frown, Salem takes his hand and admonishes him as they follow me back to the lobby, which has thankfully been cleaned.

"Coffee?" I ask, helping myself from the freshly refilled carafe. Our cleaning manager must've swept the area.

If there was ever a good morning for a strong cup, it's this one.

"Yes, please. Arlo, stand still." She bends and lowers her voice, though I can hear every word. "We want Mommy's new boss to like us, okay? Can you be a good boy?"

"Okay, Mom." Arlo doesn't sound like he's fully on board with this plan, but at least he stops wiggling like a rambunctious puppy until I can hand him his chocolate.

"Careful, little man. It's piping hot," I say before he can take a giant gulp.

He eyes me cautiously, but when Salem glares at him, he decides not to throw it back and scorch his tongue. With our drinks in hand, we head for the rooftop.

"The top floor is our *pièce de résistance*. One of the big draws of The Cardinal," I say in the elevator ride up. The coffee has already helped my mood, and Arlo seems more controlled, casually sipping his drink.

The doors open and we walk down the hall to the gold door that leads to the wide rooftop terrace.

This area was my idea.

Archer wanted something more subdued up here, but people don't want restrained when they're chasing luxury.

They want sheer, unadulterated opulence. Why half-ass it when you can feel like old money for a weekend?

Up here, we deliver.

Salem gasps and finally releases Arlo's hand. The kid rushes forward to explore the glass igloos.

"Holy crap, I never would've guessed," she says. "It's beautiful!"

"Especially at night," I tell her. "Here." I lead her to the glass walls so we can look out over the cityscape in the distance. Thankfully, the place is perfectly kidproof, so we don't have to worry about chasing her little wolverine. "There are fire pits for cool evenings and winter events, and soft lighting around the pool for summer. Though it's the view that sells it for ninety percent of the people who'll come here."

"It feels like I can reach out and pick up the city."

"Yes, that's how we're selling it. Close enough to admire the view with none of the noise."

"Are the igloos heated?" she asks, turning back to survey the area. The pool glitters in the lights draped above.

"Of course. They're aimed at our winter travelers. We spared no expense, courtesy of yours truly."

She wanders closer to one of the igloos and places her hand on it. The frosted glass doesn't reveal what's inside, and I nod at her to open the door.

"Go on. It's important you're familiar with everything."

She unhooks the door and swings it open, but just as she's about to duck inside, Arlo whips around the corner and crashes into me.

Lukewarm liquid splashes my chest.

Fuck.

"Arlo!" Salem yells as he rips away again, his empty hot chocolate cup rolling around on the ground between us. Sticky not-so-hot chocolate seeps into the fibers of a suit

that nearly cost me five figures. "Patton. Mr. Rory. I'm mortified."

Even the look on her face can't stop me from reaching my limit.

"Miss Hopper, are you sure you can control your son?" I grind out as she pulls me inside the igloo, perching her coffee on the walnut table and pulling tissues from her purse.

"I can. I will. This... this isn't how he behaves," she says miserably, dabbing at my shirt. "I'm beyond sorry. Forgive me."

"Maybe try fewer apologies and more lessons in manners next time. What if I was a guest?" I snarl.

Her hand pauses, just for a second, and she looks up at me.

Yes, I already know I fucked up.

"Maybe if *you* could try a little empathy, this wouldn't feel like the apocalypse," she snaps back. "I told you. I didn't *want* to bring him to a business meeting. I had no choice. It was bring Arlo or miss my first day at a new job."

"And your son's behavior is my fault now?"

Fury ignites her eyes.

"Mr. Rory, he's *five*."

"And? Even five-year-olds must have some idea how to act when they're raised right."

The second it's out, I feel like shit. Her wounded expression, those big hazel eyes, bore straight into me. Sadness and outrage live there.

"What *are* you saying? Try again. I told you, he's a good kid. He doesn't act up like this. He just isn't used to coming to work and he's bored out of his wits." She looks down at the tissues in her hands, which haven't helped the spill at all. Then she sighs. "God, what's the point? This obviously won't work."

She tosses the mess aside and grabs one of the folded

towels on the rack. Perfect for someone after a swim in the pool or, apparently, after swimming in cocoa.

She works on wiping the stain, biting her lip as she focuses.

This weirdest déjà vu pulls at me again, but why?

Where do I know those stormy brown eyes?

When has a woman like her ever touched me?

A second later, while she sucks her bottom lip in frustration, it clicks.

Shit.

Shit.

A thousand times, *shit.*

Lady Bug?

The most memorable one-night stand in my life, crackling with lightning chemistry, and here she is again, my manager and intern.

Fuck, I didn't know life could be so cruel.

The startled glance she shoots me still seems annoyed, but there's something different flashing in her eyes now.

I wonder if she's figured it out, too, even if I never gave her my name or phone number.

My skull feels like it's caving in.

"Enough." I reach out and take the towel from her. The stain is at the mercy of the dry cleaner now, no matter what we do. "Don't worry about it. I'll buy a new suit if I have to—and towel."

"If we got it early enough, it should come right out," she says. "If you just dab a little—"

"I don't need your help with my laundry, thank you." Harsh, but necessary. Otherwise, I might say something fantastically stupid. "Why don't you dip out early, considering the circumstances? You've had enough introduction for one day, and there's nothing here that can't wait for tomorrow."

For a second, her eyes narrow, like she wants to argue back. Then her expression goes slack.

"Okay. Maybe that would be best. I'm sorry again for the first impression. I really blew it."

I wish her hyper-caffeinated kid was still the reason why.

Only, the kid who doused me in lukewarm chocolate has nothing on a freak coincidence dredged up straight from hell.

"Next time, you'll make a better one," I growl. Lame as hell, sure, but I have to start un-fucking the damage somewhere. "I have another meeting to attend, so I'll see you soon."

I don't bother offering to show her out when she knows the way. And if she doesn't, she'll figure it out.

I need to clear my fucking head and figure out if there's a way to salvage this chaos without mauling my pride—or hers.

Because it's vastly bigger than me and the girl whose soul I rocked years ago.

I need to find out what this means for our company's crown jewel going forward.

The Cardinal is too big to fail, and I'll be damned if I let a clash of personalities bring it down.

III: ROLL THE DICE (SALEM)

*M*y one-night stand is my boss.

The biggest life-scorching mistake I've ever made is my boss.

The father of my child is my *boss*.

Inwardly, I'm screaming, and I can't show it.

Because the handsome stranger who turned my life upside down without ever knowing it is my flipping cocka-mamie boss, and there's nothing I can do about it.

This is the sort of Twilight Zone coincidence that's only supposed to happen in movies and *stay there*.

But this is real life and I'm hilariously screwed. I'm too paralyzed to even laugh.

I linger on the rooftop after he leaves, still holding the dirty towel in my hands like it's the only thing tethering me to reality.

It's definitely ruined, just like he said.

Just like this shiny new job after a morning that's been one long cataclysm after the next. Except now they all pale in comparison to finding out Grumpybutt is my unknown baby daddy.

"Mommy? Is everything okay?" Arlo asks, his eyes wide.

It's so not okay.

I'm pretty sure this day is the textbook definition of anti-okay.

He stares at me with those big blue eyes, just like Patton Rory's. Hopefully, that's something he didn't notice.

But I need to sit down before I throw up.

Wouldn't that be the rancid cherry on top of my crap-luck sundae? Arlo spills hot chocolate all over Patton Rory's suit, and I hurl all over his precious leather chairs.

"Everything's fine, baby," I whisper, bending to soak up more cocoa on the floor.

"Mr. Grumpybutt was mad."

Yes, he *was* mad.

And oh, does the Grumpybutt nickname fit him too well. Odd because that's not the man I remember.

Even through the casino haze of laughter and cocktails, I remember having fun. He was relaxed, kind, and actually decent to be around for a random evening of reckless gambling and sex with life-altering consequences.

But we were both younger and less burdened then.

Maybe grinding away at business for years ruins a person's sense of humor. I know it's all but obliterated mine.

"I think he's just busy, Arlo. Also, you did spill your drink all over him." I take his hand, leading him to the elevator. "Remember, you can't call him Mr. Grumpybutt anymore."

"But he *is* grumpy."

Sigh.

"Even if he is, we're polite to people, okay? *Be nice.*"

"Nice, yeah. Or you don't say anything at all." He recites it from memory.

It's a lesson I don't recall teaching him, but he's somehow internalized it, which is fine by me.

"That's right, big guy. Good job." I lead him back to the

meeting room and hand him a pen and more paper. Next time—if our lovely babysitter ducks out on us again—I'm bringing his tablet.

Screw the recommended screen time.

When I'm at work, I need to focus, and he needs something to do for entertainment besides drawing unflattering pictures of my boss.

The Grumpybutt portrait is still on the table, right where we left it.

Wincing, I give it a quick glance as I fish my laptop out of my bag. Today was supposed to be an introduction, but after this morning, I *need* to make a good impression.

Or, you know, try to paper over this disaster.

Ideally, without letting him know he's been a daily factor in my life for half a decade.

This string of horrendous luck has to end sometime, doesn't it?

Maybe I'm due for some good.

Maybe he'll come into work tomorrow and see what a fab job I've done and forget about today.

I am, apparently, a girl who daydreams miracles.

While Arlo scribbles—drawing more pictures of Patton Rory breathing fire, no doubt—I look over the operating fund. Even our quick, messy tour showed me this place specializes in personal touches.

The Cardinal aims to make people feel special, just like the smaller properties owned by Higher Ends.

With that in mind, I check the small part of our funds that hasn't been allocated to upkeep. There's just enough in the flex budget to add a few little odds and ends.

Complimentary beer, wine, and nonalcoholic beverages.

Fresh flowers in every room sourced from local florists.

In my experience, nothing makes people feel valued like flowers. Or maybe that's just because I never get them unless

Mrs. Gabbard chips in a few bucks to put Arlo up to it for Mother's Day.

"Mommy?" Arlo asks. "When's lunch? I'm hungry."

"Soon. We'll find someplace nice," I say, scanning my order list for other ideas like fine soaps or extra toiletries.

"I want more hot chocolate."

"Another one?" I frown at the screen.

My son loves chocolate more than life itself, like almost every kid.

"I didn't get to finish before it spilled!"

"You have a point. We'll get you some later," I promise.

That gives me an idea. A seasonal cocoa bar.

A warm drink and marshmallows for the fire in the lobby could add to the cozy atmosphere here, especially in winter. From what I've gathered, keeping up good traffic during the colder months is high on our priority list.

If the cocoa stand is well received, I'm sure we could come up with something similar and refreshing for summer. Fresh juice, smoothies, or iced teas.

Satisfied, I lean back in my chair and hash it all out in my head, looking out the window.

How they managed to get such prime land for this place when they're a smaller start-up, looking out over the Missouri River like that, I don't know.

Patton Rory might be a perfectionist asshole, but he's clearly doing something right. This venture is worth a few nightmares for his mentorship, I suppose.

If he continues to mentor me, that is.

There's no ignoring the fact that I'm one more disaster away from a pink slip, I'm sure.

"Come on, kiddo. Let's go exploring," I say to Arlo a little later, who looks like he's on the cusp of death by boredom again.

The Cardinal is good for a walk since it's absolutely huge.

Besides the rooftop pool with its fancy igloos, there's a basement gym and a bar. Everything is exquisitely presented, though some of the décor looks a little bland and too neutral. Almost like it's trying to appeal to everyone and doesn't stick with any style.

I make a mental note to study up on modern interior aesthetics when I get home. Art and design aren't my forte, but if a place ever looked like it could use more accents, it's The Cardinal.

I know I can't make that decision alone, but I can add weight on bringing in a good designer.

I buy Arlo a club sandwich and hot chocolate for lunch from the deli down the street, noting the many shopping opportunities right outside.

Location is everything and The Cardinal nailed it. The place has all the right Kansas City amenities with none of the bustle and noise of downtown.

By the time we're ready to go home, my life feels a little less daunting.

Not that I know what I'm doing.

I may be on knife's edge of getting fired, but at least I'm less likely to get lost, and that's an important first step in managing an entire freaking building.

"That was fun, Mommy," Arlo chirps happily from the back of my car as we head home to our apartment. "I wish I could come to work with you every day."

I give him a surprised look in the rearview mirror. Can he feel that pang in my heart?

He's like that sometimes, becoming the sweetest little angel when he knows I'm upset.

"Don't you like it at Mrs. Gabbard's house, sweetie?"

"She's nice," he says after some thought. His tone hints he's bending the truth for my sake. "But you're *way* nicer."

"I suppose I have to be. I'm your mom and you're stuck with me."

He giggles. "I had more fun this morning than I *ever* had with Mrs. Gabbard!"

Mrs. Gabbard, the sitter, lives in the apartment below us, and she's always been amazingly reliable—aside from today, when her daughter went into emergency surgery for a premature baby.

"I'm glad, Arlo, but it was just for today. Tomorrow, you're back to kindergarten."

"Aw, no. But Mom—"

"No, don't you 'Mom' me. I have to work if you ever want to see a new toy. Never mind keeping us fed with a roof over our heads. We don't make the rules of the game called life, honey, and sometimes you just need to play it." I pull up on the street outside the apartment and start to help him out of his car seat.

"This game isn't fun."

Well, no argument there.

I try not to laugh as he springs out the second he's free from his car seat and hurries ahead of me to the front door. "I don't wanna be stuck with Mrs. Gabbard, Mommy. I wanna go to work with you."

"But work gets boring, sweetie. You were getting tired drawing, cooped up in the room." I unlock the door and it clicks shut behind me. Like always, the small lobby is empty, and I usher Arlo to the elevator. We only live on the second floor, but I've taken him up and down too many staircases today.

"*I* thought it was fun," he insists matter-of-factly.

I boop his nose gently.

"A little too much fun, if you ask me. No more grabbing food and drinks without my permission. Definitely no more jumping around on furniture. Oh, and no more drawing people you know—unless you draw them the nice way."

"Hmph. Grumpybutt wasn't *nice*. And his hot chocolate was yucky." He's devastatingly honest in the way only kids can be.

"I don't know how you'd know," I say with a shake of the head, "seeing as you spilled it all over his shirt."

"The other hot chocolate, Mommy. It tastes like twigs and mud."

I laugh, wondering how old he'll be when he changes his mind on coffee.

The elevator dings and we walk over to our unit.

The apartment is dim as usual. At first glance, you might think it's okay.

It's spacious enough for a bare-bones one-bedroom, at least, and the silhouettes of furniture look nicer than they really are.

But the instant you switch on the lights, you'll see the ugly truth.

Everything I own is secondhand, beaten within an inch of its life.

"The other chocolate wasn't sweet enough either. It was so… bleh!" Arlo rattles on about cocoa as he takes a running leap at the sofa. It bulges under his weight. He sticks out his tongue for emphasis.

"You mean bitter?"

"Yeah! Bitter."

So was Mr. Rory, I think, shaking my head to dislodge the thought.

"Your tastes change as you grow up," I explain. Especially the rich clientele The Cardinal wants to be serving soon.

One more reason we need that cocoa bar. Surely, someone might appreciate a little whipped cream or cane

43

sugar to go with their exotically sourced ninety percent cocoa nibs.

"It was nice of him to get you a hot chocolate at all, even if you didn't like it much," I say, running out of adjectives.

There are only so many times I can say 'nice' when I'm describing Patton Rory without sounding like I'm mangling the word.

Arlo shakes his head until his dark hair falls across his face. He's about due for a haircut again.

"I dunno. You think *anyone* has fun with Mr. Grumpybutt around?" His bottom lip juts out.

Smiling, I sigh affectionately.

Then it's time to get to work on dinner.

I open the cupboard and scrounge around for some boxed pasta and a jar of marinara sauce.

Poor boy, I think while I cook. *He has no freaking clue he's talking about his father. But let's keep it that way.*

If he ever finds out Mr. Grumpybutt, a man who clearly doesn't like him, is his dad—

Nope. Can't do it.

I can't let that happen.

Go ahead and call it unethical or selfish or what the hell ever.

One night with Patton Rory blew my life to smithereens once. I'm not letting him do it a second time.

Also, this life was my mistake—not his—and I'm not dragging him back for money or involvement with a kid I'm sure he'd be allergic to.

At the end of the day, it's better for Arlo to think his father's a ghost than a man who wants nothing to do with him.

The sauce starts spitting out of the pot while I'm busy overthinking it and prepping some garlic bread to go in the oven. I almost burn my hand while I turn down the heat.

If I hadn't let myself go and had too much fun that one time—*one time!*—I wouldn't be in this epic mess right now.

Lesson learned.

No more fun.

No more randomness.

No more room for chaos.

It's work, money, and Arlo, just like it's always been.

That's been plenty over the last six years of my life, and it should be enough for the next six years too.

* * *

I CHEW my lip as I look at the artwork lining the corridors of The Cardinal.

It's perfectly nice, yes, if you like pastoral landscapes and nothing else.

They're all prints of famous paintings in the big galleries, mainly nineteenth century scenes of rural life, as I discovered last night when I looked them up. But that doesn't mean they'll be popular.

In fact, considering I didn't even *know* they were famous paintings until I did some research, they might not catch a second glance from a lot of our guests. And my research into the trends at other competitive, high-end modern hotels tells me they like color.

Daring. Bold. Bright.

Not bland and subdued.

I make notes of which paintings could be replaced with a splash of color. I imagine a real designer could make better choices, but if I can prove I've done my homework when I send these improvements to Mr. Rory, maybe it'll raise my abysmal standing in his eyes.

Maybe—and I might be shooting for the moon here—it'll

undo some of the bruising damage Arlo did to my reputation.

Mr. Rory didn't even show up this morning to the senior staff meeting.

Something else that sets me on edge.

Here I am, waiting breathlessly and dreading his arrival equally.

I want him to be impressed. I want this mentorship on my résumé more than anything, but ideally, I don't want to see him again beyond the necessary meetings, once I've got my bearings.

And no, I don't have a clue how to reconcile these two desires.

My phone buzzes and my heart jolts until I see the caller.

Not Mr. Rory calling to arrange another meeting—probably to fire me. It's Kayla.

I should ignore it. I *want* to ignore it.

Honestly, I'm supposed to be working, so the best thing to do is ignore.

But I can't, and we both know it.

Sighing, I swipe to accept the call. "Hey, Kay."

"Oh my *God*, you're alive! It's been forever, Lemmy." It's actually been about three days, but Kayla's attention span rivals a goldfish. "How's it going?"

"Um, it's fine."

"Just fine? I've heard The Cardinal is to *die* for. It's their big new thing, you know. The brothers' money-maker." She practically squeals with delight. I hold the screen away from my ear. "And now you're *working* there! How glad are you that I got you this gig?"

"*Super* glad," I gush, knowing she won't pick up the sarcasm.

My heart sinks into my stomach.

That's the real reason why I can't ignore the call—Kayla

put me here. And because it's Kayla, she acts like I should fall to my knees in gratitude for this *magnificent* act of charity.

"What's it like? Is it as lush as everyone says it is? Are the people nice?"

"It's gorgeous. We're just getting up and running, so no customers yet," I say, and for once it isn't a lie. "Especially the pool. They have these cute little igloos on their rooftop bar where you can sneak away. You'd love it. Very private."

"Ohhh, cool. Yeah, I know I would. I'm tempted to come stay to see what it's like." She giggles. "Maybe I could show it off on my Instagram. I'm sure the Rory bros would appreciate that if I tag them."

Oh, the things rich people do to get in each other's good graces.

I'm not sure if Patton Rory even *has* an Instagram, though. He doesn't strike me as the type to leave much time in his life for the rampant social media addiction that's swallowed Kayla whole.

"Sure," I say cheerfully. "Nobody as driven as them ever passes up free PR."

"Have you met them yet? The younger one, I mean—"

"Patton Rory?"

"Patton, yeah." I can practically hear her holding her breath. "Who else? There's no one else interesting there. I know Dexter Rory's married off now and the older one, he's like divorced or something. Woof."

Charming.

"Oh, okay. You know I don't keep up with the local gossip mill. Patton, I've met."

"Oh my God." This time she holds in a squeal, and I wince. "So what's he like? You need to tell me *everything*, Lemmy. He's pretty much the hottest goods in KC. Did you know I had him at a party years ago and I stupidly dipped out before I said hello? Daddy got on my case for being rude."

I keep walking, heading for the elevator, and press the button for the rooftop. Just to make sure everything's in place, I tell myself, but I know the real reason.

The view. I could use some serenity now.

"Um, well, let's see, he's tall."

"Duh! Nobody's jonesing over a guy if he fits in a cabinet. I know what he looks like, Lemmy. But what's he *like*? He's a walking thirst trap and I bet his personality—mmmm."

Holy hell, this hurts.

I want to tell her what a monumental prick he is, but honestly, she'd probably love the 'challenge' more.

"We just had a quick business meeting, Kay. There wasn't a lot of small talk," I tell her. "It was pretty down to brass tacks. He wore a suit and tie. We discussed The Cardinal. He tried to give me a rundown on my job."

Tried, yes. I don't elaborate. She doesn't need to know Arlo ruined said suit.

By the way, did I mention he's the father of my son?

"He wasn't shirtless?" She pauses dramatically before she bursts in my ear. "Kidding!"

Ha-ha.

I force a laugh so awkward my throat hurts.

"I mean, you *could* have discussed other stuff," she says. "You know, small talk. Smiled."

"He's my boss. It's my job. That's how this works."

I hate that I have to explain what it's like to work for a living. But honestly, I do when Kay's powerhouse father has pulled the strings for everything she's ever done.

"So you can introduce us?" She steamrolls right over me. "You've got an in now, lady. Help a girl out. I need to get serious. These good looks won't last forever."

I step out on the rooftop and stroll past the heated pool.

On the edge of the balcony, the breeze feels a touch chilly, but they've done a remarkable job of keeping this place warm.

"Look, Kay…" I stop to consider my next words.

Telling Kayla Persephone 'no' is not something that happens.

She takes it about as well as you'd expect. I'm pretty sure there are still royals in the world who can hear it without throwing a tantrum bigger than hers.

"I'm not trying to let you down, but this is my job. And it's new for me, y'know? I'm trying to keep things professional."

"Your job, yeah. Which I got you. You're welcome, Lemmy." Her voice is flat.

"Believe me, I know—and I appreciate it, Kay. This is such an amazing opportunity. But you know my dating life. I'm just not much of a matchmaker when I've been on the shelf for so long. Also, um, I don't want my boss to think I'm trying to hook him up with my friends."

"Oh, fine. Your job, your life, whatever. I get it." I can practically hear her rolling her eyes. "Still, not to trash the vibe, but you could be a teensy bit *grateful*."

My throat tightens.

It takes real effort to restrain the violent insults that want to claw their way up my throat.

"I *am* grateful. You helped me tremendously as a friend and I appreciate it," I clip.

"Well, yeah! Anytime. I mean, you're not *hooking us up*. You'd be introducing us. Where's the harm in that? Anything that happens later would be totally on me."

"Yes, but—"

She's animated again, acting like she can convince me to do her bidding through sheer guilt tripping force of will.

"You know he's hot stuff on the market. The most eligible dude in KC, some say," she tells me. "He's also a lot less accessible than he was before, I hear. Girls used to see him at bars and such, but ever since he got on this Cardinal thing, he's been scarce. The dude's a workaholic and he's *not* easy to flag down."

Right. Like that makes me feel better about setting her up with my boss, the man who legitimately rocked my world so hard it's never been the same.

"Sure," I say.

"You know what? All the brothers are hot, but he's the only one left who's really available. *Without* a kid, I mean." She pauses. "No offense."

"None taken," I lie. "But Kayla—"

"Salem. All my single friends would *kill* for an in like this, and you're holding the key."

So will Kayla, judging by her tone. She's already murdered her pride to go after Patton Rory like a cheetah chases down its prey.

"I get it," I tell her. "I really do. He's hot—I guess."

"Smokeshow."

"And you're no hag, of course. You'd make a lovely couple. But I wonder, maybe if you just walked in one day, would it be enough? I bet he'd notice you. Surely you can—"

"Oh, Lemmy, Lemmy. I can't believe this," she complains. "I've been *such* a good friend to you. I gave you this job and everything, and now you wanna dip on me when I ask for a teensy little favor?"

Yes.

Hell yes, you entitled frenemy brat.

If you were so desperate to snag Patton Rory, maybe you could've tried harder to hit on him at your *riverboat party years ago or gotten* yourself *this job.*

It's eating me alive, along with a hundred other things I can never say to her.

She'd never speak to me again if I did, and she'd absolutely find some new way to make my life a living hell.

Sometimes, I think I wouldn't mind the consequences, but I've been in her orbit too long to risk it.

Sadly, she *did* get me this gig and the mentorship, courtesy of her oh-so-important father, who made the recommendation to Dexter Rory personally. Even if it's becoming likely this was all a ruse to get her an *in* she wanted, there's no denying Kayla is the reason I'm here.

"Fine," I say firmly. "I'll see what I can do. But just so you know, he's not the smiley bachelor man you think he is. He's short-fused and grumpy and kind of a hardass, just between us. But Kay, I have to go."

I hang up before she can say anything else, barely resisting the urge to throw my phone off the building. I certainly can't afford to replace it.

As it is, I'm going to pay for sassing her by doing her bidding.

A man clears his throat from behind me and I whirl around.

Apparently, I'll pay for my sass right this second, because His Highness, King Grumpybutt himself, stands there in his full glory.

Today, he's decked out in a silvery grey suit that makes him look more imposing than ever.

He's a businessman through and through and he just heard me insult him on the *phone*. While I was supposed to be working.

Screw the phone. Can someone throw me off the roof instead?

There's an apology in me somewhere—*another* one, I mean—but I can't quite find the words. Nothing except a whispered, "I really hope—"

"I came by to let you know I've secured a company sitter for Arlo. A backup, if you need them."

"What?" I don't understand.

"So there won't be a repeat of yesterday," he explains, his face unwavering.

"Um, that's—wow." *Real coherent, Salem. Way to show him you're a consummate professional.* "Thanks, but there's really no need for that. He's back in kindergarten this week and our babysitter, Mrs. Gabbard, she's over her family emergency, so—"

"No." The word is hard, clipped. His gaze is steely ice, almost like the rest of him. "Parts of this position are on demand, Miss Hopper. Weekends, evenings. You knew that when you signed the contract."

"I knew that. You're right." I gulp and dip my head. *Pride doesn't work here*, I tell myself. *Just get over it and take the damn offer.* "Thank you. That's very kind. I'll call them if I need a backup plan for sure."

"She's available on call. Anyplace, anytime," he adds.

"Super generous."

There's a flash of suspicion in his blue eyes.

Obviously, he heard the conversation with Kay—and he knows I don't think he's kind or generous.

"We'll be touring the city tomorrow so you can see more of the properties in our portfolio," he tells me. "You won't be managing them directly, of course, but it's important for you to see the full scope of our operations. A broader view of the company might help you optimize things here."

I don't realize I'm pressing myself against the balcony until he steps back.

"Right," I say, trying not to sound breathy. "Thanks. Sounds wonderful."

"Don't be late, Miss Hopper."

I wasn't late today, was I, prick?

"No. I wouldn't dream of it," I agree, biting my tongue and ducking my head so he can't see the way my expression tightens. Hopefully, he thinks it's deference.

He nods and strides away like he can't get rid of me fast enough.

Joy to the world.

An entire day gallivanting around the city with a man who treats me like a human mosquito? Who doesn't have a clue he knocked me up? *Alone?*

Without even touching on our past?

I'm half-glad he shows no sign that he remembers that night.

The other half of me wants to confront him right now—at least about the hookup.

But even that feels impossible. It doesn't matter if it's a trillion times easier than telling Patton Rory he has a son who ruined his precious suit and tie.

There's only one way this goes down, and it's not well at all.

IV: CALL YOUR BLUFF (PATTON)

*I*f there's one thing anyone needs to know about my mother, Delly Rory, it's that she never takes no for an answer.

It's a trait we've picked up as her sons. While it's invaluable as hell in a business setting, it makes turning down dinner dates impossible.

No matter how much work I've got piled up, or how little I want to see everyone playing at happy family time, there's no skipping the dinners.

When I pull up to the huge, wide house with its massive porch behind the gate, my brothers' vehicles are already there.

"Sorry I'm late," I say when I get to the sitting room.

Mom leans against the fireplace, Colt sits with Archer on the sofa, and Dexter and Juniper are talking to someone else in the corner.

"That's all right, darlin'." Mom kisses me on the cheek. "Come say hello to Evelyn! She just flew in today and she'll be joining us for dinner."

The grey-haired lady Dexter was talking to turns, and I'm confronted with a familiar face.

Evelyn Hibbing has been Mom's best friend since they were schoolgirls, and she's come to see us over the years for extended visits. She's a small woman, almost owlish with her glasses, rounded shoulders, and a preference for wearing cardigans and sweaters in soft neutral colors.

"Patton," she beams, holding out her hands as she walks toward me. She's been part of the family for so long, it's like seeing your favorite aunt. "So good to see you again, dear. Have you been behaving? Are you engaged yet?"

"Hell no. And behaving, yeah. Just enough." I grin. "Hope you asked Dex the same question."

Dexter catches my eye and smiles, wiping his mouth with the back of his hand. Next to him, his wife elbows him in the side. She's decked out in a stunning green dress today.

"Don't even start," Junie mouths. "We're having a good time."

That man is *whipped.*

I hold in a laugh. It's honestly amusing to see my stick-up-the-ass brother so domesticated.

"Evelyn, how was your trip down? Surviving another winter back home? I hear it's nasty this year, even for Minnesota." I accept her kiss as she laughs. Right on the mouth—damn, no wonder Dexter pulled that face. "It's nice to see you. I didn't know you were visiting."

"Oh, you know I can't stay away for too long. There's no turning down good company and days that are a few degrees warmer." She looks around the room appreciatively. "Plus, your mom knows how to keep a house to die for."

"Well, perhaps I can keep a house, but if I so much as touch an indoor plant, it dies." Mom smiles and glances around fondly now that the party's here. She leads us into the dining room without even asking.

"Just wait until you try the cheesecake I made for dessert," Juniper whispers to me as we head to the table. "Get this— churro cinnamon, slathered in caramel. Dex will keel right over if a single crumb touches him."

That wins her a smile. My brother's nonexistent sweet tooth might've softened since he shacked up with her, but he'll always be a health freak at heart.

She's made him a better man, aside from the sweets. No question.

I'm also impressed with how easily she's made herself one of us, faster than I could've imagined. They've only been married a little over a year, but now I can barely remember a time when she wasn't at these dinners.

"Is that the secret to married life?" I ask. "Tormenting your spouse?"

"Only if your partner's worth tormenting," she throws back.

"Noted. I'll keep that in mind," I lie, knowing full well I'll be dead before I ever put a ring on any chick.

She slips her arm through mine and smiles. "Careful, Pat. Don't say something like that with your mom around, or she'll think you're wife hunting... So, are you?"

"Hunting? Do I need to mark myself with fake piss to lure in a mate?"

"Patton!" Her voice is scandalized, but I know it takes more than that to shock Juniper. There's laughter in her eyes.

"Charming my wife again, idiot?" Dexter asks, slapping my arm.

She slaps his harder.

"Don't take the bait," she whispers.

"When I'm so good at it? Let him live and learn," I say.

"Don't be a prick, Pat. It isn't always easy keeping the peace, and your mom's friend is here." Juniper doesn't miss a beat. That's why we like her.

56

"Is there any universe where you guys don't almost come to blows?" Archer glares at us.

I smirk back at him. "Not sure. Is it the universe where you're not an uptight bearwad made of—"

"Dinner!" Mom says brightly, her voice hard enough to cut through our shit-flinging. She glares at us, and unlike Archer's bullshit, which I get near daily, it's enough to make us shut our yaps and find our seats.

Evelyn beams at us like she's missed our dysfunctional little family.

"Isn't it so nice to see everyone here?" she asks as Mom brings out plates of steaming duck breast and fried biscuit gravy. "Promise me you'll never take it for granted."

"We wouldn't dream of it, Evie," Mom assures her. "This is always a special occasion, isn't it, boys?"

"We're here every week," Archer grumbles.

Colt pushes his glasses up his nose. They're a recent addition, making him look especially studious, and he seems hyperaware of them.

"Please don't tell me you guys are going to start fighting again," he says, in such a world-weary voice it sounds just like Archer.

"Hey, dude, we don't fight," I say. "We bicker. Big difference. You're lucky you don't have a brother."

"And I promise there'll be murder on the menu tonight if this bickering doesn't stop," Mom warns, stabbing her duck breast with her fork while she flashes a smile full of teeth. "What will it take to have one nice dinner together without so much ribbing?"

"A miracle?" I wait for her to laugh, but she doesn't.

That's what I get for being the single one, I guess. Flat jokes and a heap of fucking work waiting back at the office.

Dexter used to be the family workhorse, but ever since his wedding day, he decided Romeo time was more important and work should take a back seat to his personal life. Fine, but someone has to pick up the slack. And since Archer has Colt and it's a second job being a dad, now that workhorse is me.

"You must tell me more about the business." Evelyn fixes her shiny brown eyes on Archer. "Your expansions, your success, it's all very impressive. Especially for someone with an interest in real estate. I'm just fascinated."

She has an interest in property? That's news to me.

I glance at Mom, but she's discussing comics with Colt. Or rather, he's educating her about the comics he prefers and why. Mother looks lost when the kid starts talking about anime. I don't think she ever broadened her horizons past the household name superheroes and cartoons from the 1960s.

Thankfully, Archer steps up and gives Evelyn a few details about our current projects. I add a little about The Cardinal and what we're hoping to make it.

"Wow." She frowns like she's struggling to understand the concept, but that's nothing new. I've found that the older the person, the less comfortable they are with today's vacation rentals, even though the market keeps changing rapidly to embrace fresh concepts. "So you acquire properties you lease out as hotels?"

"You've heard of AirBnB and Vrbo?" Dexter asks. "We run on the same principle, but we specialize in high-end properties. Think hotels with great service, but exclusive. Many people don't want old-school hotels anymore—at least, not in the traditional way we think of them."

Evelyn nods. "I see. And you have properties in Omaha?"

I'm surprised she knows about our most recent acquisitions.

From the way Archer hesitates, I can tell he wasn't expecting this, either.

"That's right," he says. "It's a real work in progress and we won't have anything running until next year. For now, we're only operating in Missouri."

"Ah, that's sensible." Evelyn clears her throat. "You see, if you're expanding out of state… I just wondered if you ever might consider anything farther north? Like Minnesota?" She smiles at each of us. "I have a few proposals I think you'd love to hear."

Archer blinks.

Dexter glances at both of us to check we've heard her right.

It's hard to process what's happening.

Evelyn Hibbing, Mom's oldest friend, who only seconds ago could barely understand our company and never normally talks business at all, suddenly has a suggestion for expansion.

The silence goes on too long.

"I'd be happy to talk anytime, Evelyn. You'll have to buy me coffee, though," I tease. Mom smiles at me approvingly.

The surprise isn't lost on her. She probably knows I offered out of politeness, but that's more important to her than anything else.

Still, by stepping up here and being the model son in a business sense, I can stay in Mom's good graces. I'd like to think it helps make up for never being the big family man Dexter and Archer turned out to be.

And if I can keep Mom smiling with my head to the grindstone, maybe it'll keep her from forcing any match-making bullshit on me.

* * *

TRUE TO HER WORD, Salem isn't late.

I get to The Cardinal at nine o'clock sharp and find her

59

waiting by the front door in black pants and a pinkish blouse, her dark hair pulled back from her face. She climbs into my SUV quickly.

"Mr. Rory," she says stiffly as she settles in her seat.

"Again with the Mr. Rory shit? I said you could call me Patton."

"What if I prefer Mr. Rory?" Her gaze darts to me and away again.

I snort loudly.

Goddamn, I hate being *Mr. Rory*.

That was my dad's name, not mine. I've never felt big enough to fill his shoes just yet—but if that's what she wants to call me, I sure as hell can't force her to do otherwise.

Especially considering—well, fuck, *everything*.

"Coffee?" I ask, hoping to clear the awkward silence in the air. "I haven't had my morning cup yet."

"Sure."

My usual place, The Silver Swan, is just down the road. I pull up in the parking lot.

"Best brew in the city in my not-so-humble opinion. The dark chocolate mocha will keep you on your toes all day," I tell her as we walk inside.

"Right." She tenses when we step inside and she looks up at the menu.

It's the prices, I think. Her fingers go white as she grips her purse.

Damn. I never thought this place might be too expensive for her. She's a mom on a budget with a kid, and somehow, I get the impression there's no man in the picture.

"Don't worry about it, it's on me. Company perk," I growl, grabbing her little hand as she reaches into her purse and gently pushing it aside.

"...are you sure?" She blinks at me. "I can afford a basic cup of—"

"Screw basic. Nobody comes here for drip coffee unless they have a screw loose. Pick something off the real menu."

She stares at me like I've lost it.

Hell, maybe I have.

The girl behind the register greets us and I order my usual: double espresso mocha with plenty of dark chocolate.

Salem scans the menu and orders a latte that sounds like a splash of decaf in a glass of cream with honey.

Fuck everything about decaf.

I don't know how people drink the stuff and pretend they're doing anything to jump-start their day.

She glances at the drink in my hand and smiles while we head for the car.

"If I drank that, I'd be bouncing off the walls for days," she says.

"When you work as many hours as I do, you need rocket fuel. How do you function without caffeine?"

"Oh, I actually had a little coffee while I was waiting at The Cardinal. I didn't realize we were going to stop."

"Common courtesy," I lie, trying not to grit my teeth. "I thought you'd enjoy something from the best coffeehouse in Kansas City." It takes all my willpower not to point out that the cup she's holding now doesn't actually contain real coffee.

Still, it's nice to know she's not a caffeine-hating lunatic.

"Thanks. It's tasty enough," she says, though she doesn't sound like she means it. She glances at my cup as I put it in the cupholder between us. "Do you always like your drinks so sugary? You asked for extra chocolate."

"You sound like my brother Dexter," I tell her.

"The big hero?"

"Yeah. He likes to think he's wearing a cape or whatever after one fight with a mobster."

"I meant it as a compliment. You can't deny what he did was pretty brave."

"You compared me to a guy who took down a criminal enterprise."

"I still think it's a compliment." She shrugs and fastens her seat belt, taking a sip of that awful concoction masquerading as coffee.

"He's also a fun-hating health nut who melts on contact with sugar," I tell her. "He only learned to tolerate a pinch of the stuff for his wife's sake. She's a baker."

Salem bursts out laughing.

I hate how that sound sinks through me until I can feel it in my bones—and not in a bad way.

"Oh, wow. How'd that happen?"

"Long-ass story. Let's just say it was a fake relationship that turned real."

"Fake? You mean like the setup you see in rom-com movies?" She blinks at me.

"I don't watch rom-com, but probably. It was the dumbest move Dex ever made, yet somehow it paid off for him. Lucky idiot." Her face drops after I say 'lucky' as I put the car in drive. "For the record, I don't share his mission to purge the Earth of sugar. I just don't like too much cream. If I want coffee, I want its soul."

"You mean you like it bitter?" *Like you?* The implication in her voice is clear.

"I like to taste *coffee.* I'm sure you're aware that's not why we're here, though."

I take a deep breath.

Business, business.

She knows the real reason.

Now, let's see if we can get through one whole day together without someone being arrested for murder.

Our first stop is a small, but cozy rental home near the

edge of the city. Salem's face lights up and she gasps joyfully when we step inside.

It's far from the first time this place has triggered that reaction.

Nobody expects the tropical-looking interior, bright and airy with plenty of natural light, reclaimed wooden walls, and vibrant greens and pinks bursting on the walls behind impressive plants.

"Holy crap. It's like a trip to the Florida Keys without leaving Missouri," she whispers. "You worked on this design?"

"My older brother, Archer, he pushed for this look," I say, showing her around. She fingers the wicker furniture. "A taste of paradise, he calls it. He always loved my mother's old place down there, back when she had it. She used to spend a lot of time hopping around Florida and the Caribbean when she was young."

"Well, I love it. All this color, whoa." We step into the master bedroom. Even the colorful bedspread catches her eye—a brightly colored woven blanket—and she opens the wooden shutters to let the sun in. "Awesome light, even in here. Your brother must've had the windows modified."

"Arch insisted. He was proud of it in the end. It was one of our first acquisitions and it turned out a hell of a lot better than we imagined."

"So, are you guys always this hands-on with design?" She glances at me expectantly.

"Not exactly. When it's something as big as The Cardinal, or even our typical multi-unit place, we work off consensus and turn the rest over to designers. We do have a few smaller passion-projects that we handle ourselves, though."

"Interesting strategy. I love how this turned out; it's exotic and stunning. Archer Rory must have an eagle eye for detail." She can't stop smiling.

Why the hell does my blood heat?

Somehow, I get the feeling she wouldn't be showering it with so much praise if the idea was mine.

Later, I prove my point when we head to one of my projects. It's a modern, elegant home, and she wanders around in total silence.

"This is yours," she says without prompting.

I stare at her, resisting the sinking urge to ask how she knows.

"That's right," I say. "What do you think?"

"It reminds me a little of The Cardinal's look." She peers out of the floor-to-ceiling windows overlooking the peaceful backyard. "It's definitely nice and all."

"How generous," I bite off. "You called the other place *stunning.*"

"I did." She clears her throat. "I mean, look—Archer's house uses a lot of color. That stands out in a Midwestern city that loves its historic brick buildings and pretty basic neutrals for anything more modern."

"It's garish. Too whimsical for many," I snarl.

"I think you mean stylish."

"*This* is stylish."

Brutal pause.

Her eyes flare with challenge.

"This is expensive, Mr. Rory," she says firmly. "And it could really use some blinds. The sun must get blinding in the morning, and what about privacy?"

I look at the view, the fenced-in yard and old trees behind the house, and the fact that nobody could see into this room.

"Blinds would ruin the aesthetic. Clearly," I tell her.

"But just imagine walking around this place naked." She gestures at the almost wall-length window. "Imagine being *on show* like that if any neighbors looked through the fence."

Shit.

I blink away the thought of seeing her naked like I have sand in my eyes.

However annoying she is, she's got curves for miles, a body made to rock and fucking roll.

Otherworldly tits, and I should know because I—

No. Fuck you and your monkey brain, man.

We are not revisiting that night.

"This is an excellent neighborhood. I assure you no one goes creeping around here, peeping through windows, Miss Hopper," I say.

"It's not about that, though. You *feel* exposed here." She shivers and turns her back firmly on the window. "I don't like it, but maybe it's just me."

"You don't like it because it's mine." I immediately regret those words.

Something about dealing with this woman destroys every thread of professionalism I own. I'm sure it has everything to do with the fact that we've slept together.

"Anyway, look, it doesn't matter," I say, swiping my hand to regain composure. "If you're so desperate to strut around naked, we have a dozen other properties that would be a great fit for that. This house does solid revenue and we have no shortage of bookings."

A blush sweeps up her face.

"I mean, I don't—I don't *want* to walk around naked," she sputters.

Her delay amuses me. She's adorably awkward.

I give her a tight smile.

"Then there's nothing else to discuss here, is there? You raise an interesting point about the nudity factor. I'll mention it in our next senior leadership meeting."

"Oh my God, no. We weren't discussing *me* walking around naked. That was just a silly joke." She hurries to catch up with me as I lead her outside and lock up before she can rip more of my ego to shreds. "Dude, wait. Are you really going to be weird about me not liking your baby? You're the one who made this personal."

Slowly, I turn and look at her, hating that I love the defiance in her eyes.

"And you're the one who brought up parading around naked. What was I supposed to think?" *Anything except about her naked.*

I wonder if her nipples still look the same, large and round and suckable.

Does she still moan like molten caramel when they're trapped between a man's teeth?

Fuck.

She looks like she can read my filthy thoughts.

But she shuts her mouth, and I think I hear her molars grinding.

With the damage done, we head back to the SUV.

A tense silence hangs over us, as smothering as the ice-cold sleet that slicks the windshield.

"Look, Miss Hopper—Salem," I say as I pull away, desperately scraping my teeth over my tongue as I try to throw my imagination off teasing her nipples. "Why don't you choose the radio station before our next stop?"

"You want me to pick the music?" She glances at me, a hint of disbelief crossing her face.

"Usually, I listen to podcasts or audiobooks about business when I'm short on time to read them," I say through gritted teeth. "I thought maybe *you'd* like to listen to music. A simple courtesy."

"Oh. Okay." Her face softens.

I switch on the satellite radio and she flicks through stations, listening to a few seconds of each until settling on one she likes.

An eighties station.

Kill me now.

I've never been one of those people who needs to revisit the era he was born in. We get through half a song before I worry about the murder factor ruining this day after all.

That's when Salem starts *singing,* cupping her hands in front of her face like she's holding a microphone.

She croons out "Time After Time" in perfect sync to the music. Apparently, she knows this song word-for-word even though it had to be well before her time.

Murder is starting to look like the easy way out of this.

She sucks in a deep breath, ready to belt out another verse.

"I read your résumé last night," I say loudly, cutting off her next warbled line. "You've had a lot of business ventures in the past."

She drops her hands into her lap and finally—thank the fucking universe—stops singing.

"You really want to talk about my résumé?" she asks blankly.

Anything but the singing, yes.

"I was curious about your experience before you came here, aside from the three years at the motel."

"Say what you really mean. The *failed* ventures, you mean." Her tone hardens, and she turns down the music as she gives me her full attention. Somehow, that makes it worse. "That's what really caught your eye, isn't it?"

Shit. No. Maybe?

"I didn't mean—"

"Well, you're right. I have tried a lot of things and they haven't panned out," she whispers. "That's one of the reasons I went for this opportunity. So maybe I could learn enough to keep a real business alive."

I don't dare ask if she regrets it yet as much as I do.

"What inspired you to try entrepreneurship in the first place?"

She muses for a second, tapping her finger against her pants.

She has neat, trim nails. Not manicured, but well tended. Dangerously appealing when they're attached to nimble fingers that feel too good wrapped around my cock.

"I wanted to carve my own path," she says finally. "Everyone I knew was going off to college and doing whatever other people wanted. But I've always wanted to be my own boss and forge my own path, I guess. I didn't want to put a limit on how much money I could make, trading away my time and effort for a salary."

I nod firmly.

"That's the funny thing, though. I'd be making a lot more if I'd just settled with some company and climbed the corporate ladder. They don't tell you how many businesses go bust until you live it." She smiles sadly, staring out the windshield. "And if you put your chips on the wrong bet, you can work your face off and still wind up broke."

That gambling reference takes me back to the casino.

She looks away quickly. I wonder if some part of her remembers, too.

"Must've been hard, throwing yourself into new ventures with a kid." Especially a kid who was put on this planet to raise more hell than a nest of cobras.

"You know what's hard?" she snaps. "Everyone assuming I'm this fragile thing who never had a fighting chance because I'm a single mom."

"I never said—"

"Being a mom is hard, sure. Sometimes, the juggling act gets tricky. I'm sure you noticed the other day. But that doesn't mean I can't do it."

"That's not what I meant. Don't take it so personally. I

68

never said you couldn't do it. Obviously, you're still trying like hell, or we wouldn't be stuck in traffic, driving each other goddamned bonkers."

"Right." Like she finally figured out maybe she didn't need to fly off the handle at me, she takes a shaky breath. "Sorry. I didn't mean to go off on you. I guess I just—a lot of people make assumptions, you know? I thought you were ready to give me the same lecture. Anyway, for now, I've got my eye on real estate."

I do my best to nod politely.

"Actually, I've already cobbled together a few suggestions for enhancing The Cardinal's look, if you're interested."

"Suggestions?" This time I look at her, and she shrinks back in her seat.

Fine.

If her suggestions are anything like her instincts today, I'm not sure this will work.

"Don't you think you're getting a little ahead of yourself? This is still your first week on the job."

"Well, yeah, but—"

"You haven't developed a taste for the luxury market yet."

Her eyes narrow, but she folds her arms.

"I'm sorry I didn't like your place. It felt stuffy and cold."

"That's not the issue. You're new to this industry. You clearly have a talent for starting businesses"—and not finishing them, but that's not the point—"but this isn't something you can do on a whim. The shotgun approach doesn't work here. If you want to go places, you need to do what we did when we first stepped in—observe. Listen. *Think.*"

She grips her seat belt with white-knuckled fingers.

"Okay," she says quietly. "I get it. I'm sorry."

Goddamn.

I never meant to snap at her, much less hammer down her ego.

69

Too bad she's gotten on my last nerve.

Even so, I'm trying to help her. I'm acting like a mentor. I want her to understand this is a long game with tons of moving pieces, and one stumble early on in this industry can hurt you down the line.

Everyone has long memories here.

I should know.

I also can't stand the fact that she's been jumping around and flailing like many serial entrepreneurs. The scattershot approach usually ends in defeat, rather than stumbling on the next big thing.

I look across at her, at her set face and the hard line of her mouth under those big brown eyes.

What happened between us years ago hasn't stayed locked up in the past like I hoped. She may not remember me, but I think the energy is there. Call it subconscious or whatever the fuck.

It's here, right now, this ugly dynamic that has us bowing up at each other like alley cats.

That's why I'm snapping at her. Not that she's pissing me off. This shadow of a one-night stand I never imagined I'd relive.

Maybe we need to talk about it and drag this monster out in the open.

Goddammit, Pat, couldn't you have just kept it in your pants for one night on that boat?

I pull up outside the office. She throws her seat belt off like she can't get out of my sight fast enough.

"Salem, wait," I tell her.

She hesitates, and I hate every bit of this situation as she twists back around.

"What is it? What now?" she asks sharply.

It guts me how badly I messed up. I'm supposed to be the

professional mentor, the leader. Not the guy who's losing his shit at snide remarks every five seconds she's in the room.

"I need to ask you something," I say. "You won't like it, I'm not going to like it, but it needs to be done before this relationship—our professional relationship, obviously—goes any further."

Her face pulls tighter.

She faces me with wide eyes, glistening until the flecks of gold in them shine.

I hate that I notice her eyes so much.

I shouldn't notice fucking anything.

Sighing, I release the steering wheel with effort, trying to ignore the horror in her expression. According to her, I'm the bossman from hell.

And to make this better, first I have to make it worse.

"So here's my question," I tell her, locking eyes. "Were you ever on a riverboat casino?"

V: MISS UNLUCKY (SALEM)

ere you ever on a riverboat casino?

My heart stops ticking like a broken clock.

Patton Rory's words bounce around my head like a stray bullet, lodging between my ears.

Oh, here we go.

I wondered if he knew.

Right from the start when he gave me that strange, slowly dawning look of horror.

But I didn't think we'd do this now.

I didn't think we'd do this at all.

I thought he'd just pretend to forget, to convince himself it never happened, just like me.

Nope. Remember how I said I'm Miss Unlucky?

And of course Mr. Honesty chose the best time to have this little talk after kicking me to the curb for being an idiot, proving he doesn't have a single civil bone in his body.

Or is it some kind of twisted punishment? He's been annoyed with me all day.

So maybe that's partly my fault.

I'm sure I haven't been a perfect angel. Maybe I *have*

enjoyed the way he loses that mask of gruff professionalism, too.

God, there's no *maybe* about it, and now it's payback time.

He rests the edge of his hand against the steering wheel and turns to face me, a frown tugging his lips down.

"Salem?" he asks.

Shit.

I haven't said anything yet.

I'm just sitting here mute because I don't know what to say.

Panic and horror wrestle in my gut, threatening to turn me inside out.

What the hell do I do?

How does anyone respond to this?

"Yes," I say. "Yes." *Say something besides 'yes.'* "I think I was."

"Good." He sounds both relieved and annoyed.

"Yes," I say again, trying not to smack myself in the head.

"It was a long time ago now," he rumbles.

"Sure was," I say miserably.

Holy cringe.

"We were so young." He looks at me like he's reflecting on just how young *I* was back then. Barely twenty-one. Just a fresh-faced baby in the merciless world who didn't know better than to sleep with a man who was destined to become one of the most desirable men in the entire city.

I mean, from the way Kayla talks about him, he could be on the top one hundred hottest bachelors in America list.

"Young, yes," I echo. At least it's not just 'yes' this time.

Stupid.

He clears his throat like every word takes crushing effort. "Everyone in their twenties has bad hookups that might come back to haunt them. We all make mistakes."

Mistakes. Right-o.

At least it's taking him effort to get this out.

But is he really expecting me to answer? To throw my hands up and forget?

No chance.

Because his little 'mistake' changed my life forever and made everything ten times harder, even if I'd do it all again for Arlo infinity times.

Meanwhile, he's been grumping along, getting rich with his brothers, and slurping fancy coffees every morning that would make me bankrupt.

I'm stuck grinding with a kid—*his kid*—all alone in this city. Desperately trying to get off the ground before I'm thirty and figure out a stable life.

He looks at me like he's waiting for me to say something profound, to save us both from suffocating in the awkward silence.

Something better than one-word answers, which really are about the extent of my vocabulary right now.

My chest hurts like it's swarming with angry hornets.

The same ache I felt when I found out I was pregnant and alone.

It tastes like stress and fear and it promises to crush my organs if I can't make it stop. If I let it get the better of me, I'll forget how to breathe.

Don't cry, don't cry.

Not in front of Patton Rory. Jesus, don't do it.

If there's one thing I can't stand, it's letting him know what he's done to me.

I honestly can't fathom how he seems so unaffected beyond losing his words.

But I push at the ache, forcing every raw emotion into a condensed ball at the pit of my stomach, and let numbness replace feeling.

That's what helps me look back at him, feeling my face go safely blank.

If he wants a few pointless platitudes, fine.

"Sure. I wondered if you remembered," I say, my tone too flat. An expression crosses his face that I can't quite read. "You're right. Everyone makes mistakes."

"And I don't want ours getting in the way of our business relationship. That's why I'm dropping this on you—on us. Sorry if it makes you feel like shit."

Yikes.

Frustration reaches through the numbness and pulls at my heart.

I'm still in disbelief.

Because if he knew he had a hidden son, that would *definitely* get in the way of any relationship we'll ever have. I nod like a sagging puppet.

"It's fine. Really. It's whatever. It was a long time ago and we're clearly different people now."

"Salem—"

For a second, I close my eyes, willing myself to end this conversation without a full psychotic meltdown.

"No, no, I promise we're good, Mr. Rory. Just don't call me Lady Bug!"

Boom, there's my exit.

I fling the door open again and make my escape before my lungs seize up.

I've forgotten how to breathe and I'm drowning more by the second.

I just know I have to get away from the source of it right now.

The stark panic fades by the time I reach my car, a battered old Toyota. I unlock it with trembling fingers and shoot him one last glance.

He's still sitting right where he was, watching me in his rearview mirror with a startled look on his face.

I don't know what he expected.

I don't know what *I* expected.

Did I want him to apologize?

To fall on his sword for reading my mind and instantly knowing all the ways he's doomed me to life on hard mode?

To suggest we do it again?

God.

The very idea drives a painful giggle out of me—a desperate, breathy, hurt thing—as I throw myself behind the wheel and buckle up.

Yep, I'm blowing this.

Blowing it like a balloon animal specialist.

He won't want to work with me if I can't handle talking about a one-night stand we had *six years ago*. I don't know how I can even look him in the face after this.

If it weren't for Kayla recommending me through her dad, I'd be fired by now. No questions asked. Just a quiet letter asking me to leave before I ever really started.

I let my head clunk against the steering wheel, hoping it stops spinning at some point.

Angry emotions rise up again like old enemies you thought you'd never see again.

The nausea packs a punch, coiling in my stomach. Then more panic, lashing through my body like a current, straight to my fingertips.

Finally, the ache in my chest that attacks my tear ducts.

I squeeze my eyes shut, trying not to scream.

So much for Patton Rory calling me lucky.

I have the worst luck of anyone I know, and the bad stuff just keeps piling on. Keeps on smacking me in the face.

When my forehead hits the horn and makes me jump, I jerk back up.

He's gone now. Thank God.

Driving away in that enormous, sleek SUV that purrs rather than rattles every time you run the A/C.

What the hell ever.

Maybe he's right.

Sure, he could've said it nicer—or decided not to say it at all—but that doesn't mean he's wrong. Not even about the way I'm stumbling my way into an unknown career for the hundredth time.

Oh, I would *love* for him to be wrong just once.

But the truth is, I don't know much about this business.

I'm a guest in his world and I wish he was someone else.

Still, I have to make this work, never mind the instinct to call him and resign on the spot.

I've never succeeded at anything long enough to develop real expertise. Something else he's noticed and probably pities me for, if he doesn't outright despise me.

No one will ever take me seriously if they see a quitter.

Especially when you're moping around like this, a small voice says in the back of my head. *Get your crap together, Salem.*

Okay, nasty voice. Thanks for the pep talk.

I wipe my face and take a breath, wondering if this health plan from the company comes with good mental health coverage.

This whole job, plus dealing with my asshole baby-daddy boss, feels like trying to ram a square peg in a round hole.

Dammit, though, I'll try.

This will not be another Salem Hopper disaster.

No matter what it takes, I decide I can do this. If I can make it through a stint at Higher Ends, I can survive anything.

For now, I just have to keep going, one day at a time.

I slide the keys in the ignition and start the car.

The engine grumbles to life, and by the time I drive away, I'm done crying.

* * *

Before I get home that evening, I pick up Arlo from Mrs. Gabbard's, who's full of joy about her new granddaughter.

After spending a few minutes admiring photos of a baby that looks as red and wrinkled as a dried raisin, I escape up the stairs to our apartment.

"What do you think?" Arlo asks, holding up a drawing of what I *think* might be me. "Miss Peters told us to draw our heroes in class, so I drew you, Mommy."

That's a relief.

Last time they asked him to draw his hero in preschool, he drew Godzilla. That's what I get for letting the kiddo stay up with me to watch dumb monster movies.

"What a nice picture. You really brought out my eyes, big guy." I laugh at the oversized brown eyes as I unlock the door and usher him inside. "Where do you think we should put it?"

Our fridge has too many drawings to fit another masterpiece.

"Ummm… you could take it to work?"

"Oh." I do have an office at The Cardinal. Like everything else, it's larger and more luxurious than anything else I've worked in. There's plenty of room for pictures on the walls. "Sure, honey. That sounds great."

"I'm going to draw you so many, Mom. Gotta decorate your walls." He flings himself down at his little desk in the corner and sends all the crayons flying out of their box. "Oops! But I'm going to draw one for Mrs. Gabbard, too," he announces proudly. "Do you think she'll put it on her fridge?"

"She might." I grab a pack of meat from the fridge that's been defrosting. Stew it is. "Don't forget she has her own kids to show off, honey."

"Yeah, but they're *old*." He says it with so much scorn you might think they were in their fifties.

As far as I know, they're younger than I am, and way more successful.

"Maybe they still draw their mom pictures," I joke.

"No way! She never has pictures on her fridge. She has magnets." He holds up his hands. "Like so many magnets, Mommy. All from weird places."

"I think that's because she's traveled a lot, sweetie."

"Why don't we go lots of places?"

Oh, boy.

I stop, staring at the knife in my hand.

The answer is simple—I don't have the money or time.

It kills me that I've never been able to just grab my son and whisk him off to a beautiful national park or even to the ocean.

A little ironic, considering the grandparents he's never met live in California. But my parents were happy to send us into exile and I'm just as glad to stay the hell away.

"I wonder," I say with fake enthusiasm, "can you draw me a picture before I finish dinner?"

"Are you crazy? You bet I can!" He whoops and starts to scribble, head down and frowning at the paper. His tongue sticks out the side of his mouth and his chubby hands mash the crayon against the paper with unnecessary power.

It'll only buy me a few minutes of peace, but I savor them. I put on my favorite playlist on my phone and cut up the vegetables, adding them to the pan with the stock and potatoes.

Sometimes Arlo fusses over beef stew, but it's cheap, it fills you up, and it always leaves behind leftovers.

Tomorrow, I can come home and put my feet up without any worries about fixing dinner. Some TV time would be wonderful.

As I'm thinking about my evening off and enjoying the savory smells of dinner, my phone buzzes.

The name 'Grumpybutt' shows on the screen. I resist the urge to hurl it at the wall.

Why does he bring out the most violent urges?

And can't he leave me alone for *one dang evening*?

I hesitate longer than I should before I sigh and pick up.

"Hello?"

"Salem?"

Who else? "Yes."

"Mommy!" Arlo says, running up with a page fluttering in his hands. "I beat you!"

"Mommy's on the phone," I whisper under my breath, giving the drawing a thumbs-up even though I can't see what it is. "Hang on, sweetie."

"Sorry if this is a bad time," Patton growls, not sounding sorry at all.

"No, it's fine. It's not like I have a life." Too bitter? Oh well. "What's up?"

"Sorry for intruding," he says stiffly. "I know it's late."

It's half past seven, long after normal people call it a day, but apparently he doesn't know that.

But he's my boss. And after that trainwreck earlier, I can't refuse the call.

"I said it's fine."

"Okay, good." He takes a breath. It's just as awkward as I could've imagined, every single word we said before hanging between us like a wall.

Everybody makes mistakes.

Ugh, yeah. But not everybody winds up making them with their future boss.

"I'm just calling because I had an idea. I'd like you to throw together a survey," he says. "We want customer experiences from our other properties. Something broader than the automated survey that goes out after every stay. We'll take suggestions for improvements and look at integrating them into The Cardinal."

I narrow my eyes at the wall.

"I see," I say.

This feels like our conversation earlier, where my vocabulary topped out at two-word replies.

"Mommy! Look," Arlo whispers, holding up his picture and shaking it.

"Just a minute." I point at the phone. "Mommy's busy. Please keep it down."

"I won't ruin your evening by keeping you glued to the phone," Patton says. "I'm just curious what the data shows. You're right about one thing—there's always room for improvements in a space like ours. With the market being what it is, we can't afford to sleep on any opportunities, however small, to enhance The Cardinal's service and atmosphere."

Atmosphere, huh? So he is reconsidering those boring paintings?

He doesn't expand on that, but I know what he means. Highly competitive.

Higher Ends might be a scrappy rising star for now, but that doesn't mean they can't lose their edge in a tight market.

"Yes," I say, trying not to sound too smug. "I agree, and I'll pull something together."

Now can I go have dinner in peace without having my heart put through the shredder?

Not yet. He isn't done.

"You raised a good point today, Miss Hopper, but we really need suggestions sourced from the horses' mouths," he says sternly. Just in case I get too puffed up by being right— because of course he can't have *that*. "We need to ensure any changes are improvements our guests are truly asking for."

"Yeah, okay." I tap my nails against the counter.

"I also wanted to call and pass on Bekah's congratulations," he says begrudgingly. "You remember Bekah?"

"Yes. She works at the front desk." My tone is more snappish than I intend. I remember the name of the staff, I'm not a total idiot. I'm sure I've spent more time around them than him.

"She mentioned your cocoa bar."

"Oh, um, that's still a work in progress. I haven't started looking into the details about where we'd source it, or how much it would really cost." I brace myself, just waiting for him to tell me it's stupid.

"Bekah loved it so much she sent it over. I think it's solid, and I can already tell you the cost would be so incidental it's nothing our budget can't handle."

What?

My inner cynic wonders if this is his way of apologizing after giving me a sledgehammer to the face.

"That's great," I say carefully, trying to sound sincere. "I'm glad you're on board."

Awkward pause.

And I wonder if he's thinking back to our earlier conversation like I am, running over everything we said, replaying it in his mind and imagining a world where we never hooked up.

Unfortunately, we're stuck in this one, where we're living with the fallout of one messy night.

I could have played it off as being nothing—something weird and forgotten in the back of my mind.

I also could have told him about Arlo, gouged out my heart, and plopped it into his hands. I could've watched his face turn chalk white with the awful realization that he's a father, and he's entangled in my life far deeper than this mentorship he hates.

Honest to God, I could have done a thousand stupid things, but I didn't.

I just sat there and let him remind me how cruel fate can be—and I'm the one taking the brunt of it.

"I'm trying to apologize, in case you didn't notice," he says tightly. "Let's be real, I'm shit at it. But Salem, I like your idea, and it has nothing to do with me being a royal jackass earlier—"

Just then, Arlo bounces toward the hot stove and I rush over, pulling him away.

"Got it. I should go," I say, cutting him short. "I'm in the middle of dinner."

"Understood." He clears his throat.

Arlo tugs on my arm, demanding attention.

"*Moooom.* You didn't look at my picture," he tells me, shoving it toward my face, as high as he can reach.

"I'll start working on your survey tomorrow," I say back into the phone. "Hopefully, I'll have some results by the beginning of next week." Which means processing them over the weekend, but that's what I signed up for, right?

"Thanks, Salem," Patton says.

I end the call as fast as I can swipe.

If this is what it's like on the phone, I'm already dreading our next face-to-face meeting to go over the results.

Fingers crossed the 'mentoring' can wait a few days until things calm down.

Though I guess it's not a total disaster when he was trying to be nice. *I think.*

After telling Arlo how much I love his vibrant red picture of a brand-new animal unknown to science, I finish dinner and get it plated up before eight.

Success.

Arlo should be in bed by now, but it isn't happening.

I ignore the voice inside my head that tells me I'm a terrible mother.

"Did you have a nice day at school?" I ask. "How was story time?"

"Miss Peters read to us about a dragon who lost his socks," he tells me proudly.

He's a good kid, already on track to take school seriously. Let's hope it leads him somewhere better than the obstacle course I chose.

Also, I wonder who the hell plots children's books. Why would a dragon need socks?

"Big guy, when I was your age, we read classics like Inky the Penguin. But did your dragon find them?"

"Yeah! The sock wizard saved the day. Everybody thought he took them for a spell, but they were just under the washer."

"Yay for happy endings." I take a big bite of my pasta and sag into my chair. I should be more enthusiastic, but today has been A Day.

I'm exhausted.

And honestly, I'm a little jealous hearing about a dragon who has it so easy with his anticlimactic endings and all.

It's not every day when you're confronted by your old hookup-turned-boss and trying to mentally justify hiding his own son from him.

What is *wrong* with me?

But I saw how he reacted to Arlo once. That man and children can't coexist in the same room.

"Mommy?" Arlo's voice tells me he wants something.

"Yes, sweetie?"

"I want a button shirt."

Button shirt? I rack my brain, trying to decipher little boy speak.

"You mean a button-up shirt? And you do, huh?" I blink at him and put my spoon in my bowl. "Why's that?"

"Mr. Grumpybutt has one. It makes him look grown-up." He smiles mischievously. "I remember 'cause I spilled cocoa on it."

"You did, yes." I'm a little amazed he remembers the disaster when he can be so oblivious. I'm also stumped at kid logic. "But I thought you didn't like him?"

"I *don't*. I mean, only a little." Arlo looks at me like it's obvious. "But he owns a whole building, Mom. He's rich."

"Maybe so, but—"

"You gotta listen to him. That's not fair!"

I eye him carefully. Only five years old and he hates office politics. I have trained the boy well.

"That's how it works sometimes. It doesn't mean it's bad. You have to listen to me," I tell him. "That doesn't make me so special, does it?"

"No, but you're a grown-up!" He rolls his eyes so hard I laugh. "I'm just a kid."

"So?"

"So it's *cool* Mr. Grumpybutt gets to tell you what to do. He gets to boss around a lot of people."

Well, no argument there.

Arlo picks at his garlic bread crust.

"If I get a button shirt, I can be like him!"

Perfect.

Absolutely *peachy*.

My son, estranged from his unknown father, has decided after a *single meeting* to fixate on him. To flipping imitate him.

A man who would, undoubtedly, freak like his hair's on fire if he knew the kid who tore up his precious new property was really his own son.

A man who would absolutely go nuclear if he had to

contemplate giving up a shred of his seemingly perfect life-style to burn one hour as a dad.

Like I said, call me Miss Unlucky.

The gods of good fortune decided to forsake me forever after one random night on a casino boat, and I'll never be over it.

VI: QUIT WHILE YOU'RE AHEAD (PATTON)

*A*ll things considered, the next couple weeks go smoothly.

Aside from the fact that I can't get Salem's face out of my head.

The way she looked at me after I reassured her it was a simple mistake, and we don't have to dwell on it.

Like somehow, I'm the bad guy.

Like by saying that, I torched her feelings in a way I still don't understand.

Like I switched off some light inside her by calling it a *mistake*.

Why?

Clearly, that's all it was.

It's not like she has any lingering attraction to me. That's a one-way street, and I'm the clown who's been stripping her naked with every glance, even if I'd die before I act on it a second time.

Company ink and all.

Also, I've been with enough women to know when

they're turned on and when they want to throw me out the window.

I just hate that she's avoiding me.

Not totally, of course.

She's my employee and a manager here, which makes it impossible to ghost me completely, but she does her damnedest.

Conveniently, she misses my calls, sending back the world's shortest replies to my emails and texts. She tries like hell to pretend I don't exist during meetings.

"Do you have any suggestions?" I ask during the review of employee logistics—the first time we've seen each other face-to-face for more than an hour since the car incident.

She doesn't look me in the eye.

"I have a few," she says. *Quietly, damn her.*

"You mentioned the cleaning routine was disruptive to some of our guests."

"That's right." She launches into how we could handle the schedule better, given all amenities are open twenty-four seven.

I do my best to focus on what she's saying, and not the fiery-red lipstick she's wearing today.

Or the way the sadness seeped into her eyes when I asked if she was on that riverboat with me.

Or the brutal fact that I know what's under her neat blue blouse.

Or hell, the fact that long after that one-night stand, I could still smell her perfume on me and dreamed about the way she purred.

The way she laughed at the table games, before I found myself inside her, haunted me for months after that night.

She's not laughing now.

She looks like a woman who's forgotten how.

"Another thing, I think we should consider increasing

security. Maybe add one more person for the overnights," she says as I make myself pay attention to her again.

The ice in her eyes feels so frosty it makes the forty-degree day outside feel balmy.

"We already have two security guards patrolling overnight."

"I think we should make it three, enough to handle the rooftop bar and cover the floors every half hour." She pauses. "You wanted input. There it is."

She might be right. Bumping up our personnel also means better coverage for the cameras, without anyone skipping out on checking footage to finish long patrols.

"Why else?" I push back. "You must have another reason."

I'm leaning into this mentorship thing, wanting her to make her case as tight as she can.

For a second, I think she'll tear my throat out for hounding her, but she swallows hard.

Her throat tightens and I think she clasps hands under the table.

"This is a large building with balconies and several entrances. There are a lot of potential security risks here. Surely, our guests would feel safer with a little more security presence, and the guards wouldn't be stretched so thin. It will also save you from any bad PR out of the gates if it stops any incidents."

"Fair enough. And where would the money come from? This needs to work with our current budget. We're already near our limit for security costs."

"Well... if we streamline the cleaning schedule and make everything more efficient there, we wouldn't need to look further."

There's no point in fighting it when she's right—and we both know she is—but goddamn, I want to.

I stand up before she annoys me some more.

"Sounds like you have everything under control," I say, proud of myself for showing a little restraint. Dex and Archer, eat your fucking hearts out. "Well done, Salem."

"Miss Hopper," she says. "Please call me Miss Hopper, Mr. Rory."

My ghost of a smile dies.

What the fuck?

No matter how much she calls me Mr. Rory, I hate it.

But this is a professional environment. If she wants to keep this so rigid and stale we can hardly breathe, that's fine and goddamned dandy.

"Miss Hopper, I read you loud and clear." I nod at her and leave the room before I can say anything too *un*professional.

Then I spend the entire week licking my wounds. I search for something I can critique, not to reprimand her, but to teach her.

Yes, she's whacked my inner asshole over the head and it's hard to restrain him.

Still, there must be something she's doing wrong—something I can improve.

That's my role as mentor, right? To identify her weaknesses and help her obliterate them. To make her stronger, smarter, and better than anything she'd be without me.

But when I show up early in the morning, she's already there, splitting her time between her office and walking the halls when she's not at the front desk.

From discussing issues with Bekah to ensuring the rooftop pool and bar are ready to go by eight a.m., she's perfectly hands-on.

There's nothing I can fault her for with operations.

Not in good faith.

Not when she's so damn smiley with the guests, either, putting on this picturesque welcoming smile.

She's a human chameleon, I'm sure. Mostly because I've

never seen her make that face with me since that night on the boat.

Obviously, it's personal.

What else do I deserve for making it that way?

* * *

AFTER A FEW MORE DAYS MONITORING THE huge, streamlined beast that is The Cardinal, I head back to our office in Lee's Summit.

The Cardinal is our biggest new project, but that doesn't mean we don't have plenty more in the works. New deals to close, established properties to check, keeping up with the company's ever-growing portfolio.

"Hey, Archer? You in there?" I knock on his office door, which is slightly cracked open.

Weird. He's the kind of antisocial freak who loves to shut the world out—especially his annoying little brother.

"Hey, so I was thinking—"

The door falls open and I see Arch leaning against his desk, his sleeves rolled up, and Salem on the red sofa in front of him.

Laughing like he's the world's greatest funny man.

Shit, even Archer is making noise.

Archer—Mr. Uptight Frowny Fuck himself—might bust a seam if he keeps laughing.

I rub my eyes.

Is this real life?

She's known him for five seconds, and somehow, they're both giddy.

Honest to God, I can't remember the last time my brother smiled at anyone who isn't named Colt, Junie—and that one was a long time coming—or Mom.

Miracles never cease, they say.

I wish like hell this one would.

"Miss Hopper," I snap off. I check myself at the doorway because it feels like I've walked in on something scandalous. "I didn't expect to see you here."

"Mr. Rory." She looks at me, her laughter tapering off.

"Mr. Rory?" Archer raises an eyebrow. "Don't you know he prefers Pat?"

Goddamned great.

Now everybody in the office is picking up on our weird-ass dynamic because Salem can't just be *normal* and get over a naked mistake from years ago.

"Um, sure. I just figured we should keep it more professional since he's the mentor and all." She flushes.

"Doesn't matter what I prefer," I say stiffly. "I can come back later, if I'm interrupting."

"No, no, I was just leaving." Salem collects her bag as Archer looks between us with a frown. "I just came to meet the other masterminds behind the company."

"A pleasure," Archer tells her. "My door's open anytime."

Your door, Bro, is about to slam your face hard enough to bruise.

With pure stupid jealousy coursing through my veins, I hold the door for her. "I'll walk you down to reception. It's a big office."

"Not that big, thanks. I remember the way."

"Miss Hopper, I insist." I glower at Archer, annoyed with the curious gleam in his eye as he watches us.

"Don't go anywhere," I tell him. "I need to discuss a few things with you."

"Whatever, man. I'm not like you, jumping all over the city. I've got plenty of real work right here." He retreats behind his desk.

Dickwad.

Isn't that just like old Arch? Always slinging little comments that come back to bite you straight in the ass.

Usually, I'd lay into him—and remind him who pushed so hard for The Cardinal after we were up the creek when the Haute deal fell through—but not with Salem in the room, watching intently.

"Let's move," I growl, taking her hand and leading her back downstairs to the front desk.

She trails behind me, still clutching her purse. I don't even realize she's stuck to me until I feel her little nails daggering the meat of my palm.

"Ow. What the hell was that—"

"You're my boss, not my chaperone. Hands off," she snaps, shaking her head until her dark hair flops. I smell something like cinnamon drifting off her. "Are you that angry? That I went to see the nicer brother?"

The nicer brother?

The guy whose idea of a lively Friday night is watching CNBC and taking his kid bowling once in a blue moon?

Fuck!

No one who knows anything about Archer Rory considers *him* the nice one. He's the sensible one, the boring one, the restrained one. The petrified piece of wood you trot out when you want to intimidate someone like you're holding a club.

Shit, if there was a 'nice guy' competition, he'd lose the game by a mile.

My nostrils flare.

"I'm not angry," I lie. "I just didn't expect you to be here, that's all."

"Uh-huh. I figured if I was going to be a real part of this organization, I needed to know everyone I'll be working with. Not just my 'mentor.'"

The sharpness in her voice could poke a man's eye out.

"You won't be working with Archer much. Not directly," I bite off. "The Cardinal's launch and daily operations are my responsibility."

She glares at me with eyes that hold the same intrigue Archer's did, although her gaze is less friendly.

I guess a few days apart haven't stopped her from wishing I'd drop dead.

"You took me around to see your other properties my first week here," she says. "Doesn't it make sense I should meet your brothers, too?"

It does make sense, I'm sorry to say.

Usually, it wouldn't bother me, but Archer has never been the *nice* one. Not when I'm around.

Hell, even when I'm not.

"Look, you've got this wrong. I said I wasn't mad," I say through gritted teeth.

Amazing. I've only known her for a few weeks, but I seem to be talking through my teeth every time we're together. She's definitely winning at keeping her tongue in check.

Shit.

What happened to the fun, carefree girl I met what feels like a lifetime ago?

Has life ground her down that much?

"You say one thing, but your face says another." We finally reach the reception desk before she turns to face me. "I can find my way out from here, Mr. Rory."

"Salem, I expect you in this office nice and early tomorrow. Butt in the chair. We have some issues to discuss," I say, knowing she's been early every day this week, and just ordering her to be on time makes me a king-sized asshole.

There's derision in her face as she lifts her chin.

"Okay, bossman. Thanks for the advice. Ciao." Her voice drips sarcasm as she stalks away, her hair swinging behind her.

For God's sake, you prick.

Archer waits in his office when I return, glowering at his computer screen. Even though he doesn't say one word, I know exactly what he's thinking.

"Don't go there," I say, throwing myself into the seat.

"She's pretty." He looks at me.

"You were the one smiling at her like an idiot."

"Yeah, I've been keeping an eye on the situation and reading your reports." He brings up said reports with a single deafening click. I've been making them as I go, determined to do her justice as a capable manager while noting room for improvements.

It's never a surprise that Archer has been keeping track.

He always likes to feel like he's the one in charge while Dexter and I are just along for the ride, even when we all agreed I should be in charge.

"Nice to know you trust me to do a good job," I say sarcastically.

"She's gotten to you that much? Man, that's fucked." Now his eyebrows rise. "I didn't think having someone do their job would get under your skin."

"She hasn't gotten under my damn skin."

"Right." He leaves his papers to one side. "She's doing well from what I can see. Going above and beyond with her suggestions and the research summaries attached. That's the kind of attitude we should reward in management."

"I didn't come here to talk about Salem," I snarl.

"Salem, huh? Don't you mean Miss Hopper?"

"Goddammit, Arch, there's no need to be a face-slapping cock." That's the way we relate to each other, though, by pissing each other off to breaking point. Then sanity steps in when we need it. "I came by to talk about our expansion prospects. I need an update about the second quarter."

"You mean the ones I'm overseeing?"

I give him a pained smile. "Guess we're both in the same boat, huh?"

He sighs and leans back in his chair, though there's a gleam of appreciation in his eyes.

He knows how to be fair when it comes to this shit, I'll give him that much.

Accountability is always serious business in this company.

That's the Rory way, and we all play our part.

"Now that you've put your attitude away, let's talk like adults," he says.

* * *

I SPEND the rest of the week walled off in my office, only dropping by The Cardinal to make sure it's running smoothly.

It always is.

I'm annoyingly satisfied to see just how well Salem takes to this management role like a duck to water. It's even more undeniable now that we have real guests booking stays and bringing in revenue.

Throwing up distance doesn't evict her from my head any faster. Though I keep my cool when she's around, I'm dreaming of the distant day when I can move the fuck on without her dragging on my mind.

Especially without the memory of everything we did years ago, when we could share the same oxygen and not want to throw shit at each other.

For three entire days, I don't see her.

She doesn't intrude on my space, and when I drop into The Cardinal to see the latest progress, she's conveniently busy.

If she doesn't want my intrusion, fine. I'm happy to beat it back to Lee's Summit and work in my own office again.

My stomach churns at the horrid thought that I might be more bothered by that than her.

And I'm just thinking maybe we'll get through this mentorship sham without having to spend a ton of real time together when there's a knock on my door.

"Mr. Rory?" Salem pokes her head through.

The neat bun she's been sporting most mornings hangs loose now, sending dark curls dancing around her face. "I'm sorry to disturb you, if this is a bad time—"

"Come in."

Out of habit, I glance at the clock. It's past seven p.m. already.

What's she doing here so late?

Normal folks with lives and families are home and fed by now. I'm stunned she isn't with her son.

Then I see the little boy standing behind her with an evil gleam in his eyes like I'm the prick who's keeping them from dinner.

"Miss Hopper. Hopper Junior." I stand, hoping my disappointment doesn't show in my face. "What brings you by so late?"

"I just wanted to grab some marketing books Dexter recommended. I'm trying to get better at copywriting," she says. "He said you had them in here, like your own shared library. I guess I was surprised."

Yeah, that's what I get for having an office with custom shelves since my cheap-ass brothers skimped on furniture when we set up the place.

And what the hell? When did she meet my other lame brother? I thought I was the mentor?

Not that I've been doing much mentoring.

"I have a lot of books. I do know how to read," I grumble,

wondering why I didn't notice the winter draft seeping in through the walls until now. "Have a look and take whatever you want."

"Thanks!"

She darts past me, looking as tired as I'd expect after a full workweek with a kid who's—a fucking handful, that's for sure.

Probably like a handful of angry scorpions.

I lean against the desk and watch her. My eyes follow her as she scans the shelves, her little fingers running over the spines of the books as she takes in the titles.

Watch her hands, you idiot. Eyes off her ass.

Easier said than done.

Then little Arlo runs up and kicks me in the shin.

Not hard—he's a kid, thankfully—but it's jolting enough to shock me out of my stupor.

"Don't look at my mom like that!" he shouts.

"Like what?" I ask before I can help myself. *Bad question.*

"Like you wanna eat her. Like a shark!" He tries to kick me again, but Salem runs over and starts dragging him backward, her hair flying as she grabs him.

"Arlo! That's no way to behave. I know you've been reading your Animal World books," she tells him in a whisper, "but you can't go around calling people animals, all right? And you definitely can't kick people. Do it again, and you're grounded. Remember what Mr. Lee said in karate? Self-defense *only.*"

She signed this little punk up for martial arts? What the hell?

He sticks his bottom lip out and glowers at me again.

Right back at you, munchkin.

Shit, if he carries on like this in life, he may need all the self-defense lessons he can get. And where is the boy's father, anyway?

I hope he's not ghosting him, making the kid act out.

Nothing screams bigger chickenshit coward than a man who abandons his own son and lets him turn into a brat with a chip on his shoulder bigger than a redwood.

"I am so, so sorry, Mr. Rory. Arlo, he's still working on his discipline with practicing his karate moves. Not his strongest point," Salem says, straightening her back and looking at me. No, not quite at me—her gaze lands on the wall just past me, like she can't bear to look me in the face. "He's been taking lessons for a while. I guess he got a little overexcited. When we get home, we're going to work on talking about our feelings, rather than taking them out on strangers."

"Am I a stranger now?" I growl. "Is that why he kicked me?"

Her face heats. "Um… he thinks self-defense means defending other people, I think. He's really good for his age, so his teacher moved him up to yellow belt with some of the older kids. But I think sometimes the verbal lessons go over his head."

"Do not!" Arlo stamps his foot impetuously.

Christ, I hope he has a dad to steer him right. I'm so not the man who's programmed for situations like this.

"Arlo, enough." She looks at me. "I'll talk to him. I promise you I'm not the world's worst mom."

"Hardly. You're managing him as well as you can, I'd say." I glare at the kid as she turns her back. "Never mind karate, though. He needs anger management," I mutter under my breath.

"You could use a refresher, too," she whispers as I head back behind my desk—the farthest away from her demon imp as I can get.

I'll ignore that comment this time.

"Did you find your books?" I ask, hearing the ice in my

voice but not caring. "Take whatever you need. I want to lock up and get out of here sometime tonight."

"Don't you have staff for that?"

I raise my eyebrows. "My staff don't stay late just because I do. Only the owners pull insane hours."

I stand up and turn to the shelves, looking over our small marketing section.

"Here, this one's a banger. Dex and Archer will agree. We all read *The Millionaire Beast Within* a few months apart. Not long before we started cobbling together Higher Ends." I pass her the book.

She looks at the cover and eyeballs it skeptically.

"Thanks, but... I was kinda looking for something more serious on copywriting."

"I see two books on that in your hands." I nod at them. "Don't let the lambo on the cover scare you. The author, Denny Falco, he's a flashy dude who loves his fancy cars and gold. But he's giving you a master class in motivation and basic business theory." I pause, wondering if I should tell her why I really picked the book. "It helped me, Dex, and Archer. I think you'll find some value. Did you know he was a single dad with twins when he flipped his limo lead business for eight figures?"

Her face relaxes and she turns it over in her hands, skimming the backside.

"Okay, sold. I'll try not to judge it by the cover."

"Hell, if the cover matched the content, I never would've made it past the first chapter." I smile. "Give me your book report when you're done."

She laughs.

"Sure. Y'know, for a second I was amazed that you *do* read —and that you decided to be nice. Emphasis on past tense."

"Yeah, whatever." Arlo's loud yawn grabs my attention.

"Looks like you've got some reading to do yourself after someone's down for bed. Looks like he's ready."

"Am not." The kid yawns again, clapping his little hands over his mouth.

"Thanks, Patton. You're okay at this mentoring thing sometimes."

She shows herself out, flashing a quick smile over her shoulder.

Goddamn.

Every time I start to wonder how drunk I was to have ever had a hot night with this hellcat, she goes and reminds me why.

One more nuisance thought I don't need in my brain.

Just like the hard-on from Hades I have to sit down to hide.

VII: PLAYING CHICKEN (SALEM)

*A*ll things considered—and there's a lot to consider—this gig could be worse.

Good pay, good benefits, I'm handling the responsibility, and there's a lot of learning every week.

Of course, the downside hasn't changed, and it's a doozy.

It begins with Patton and ends with Rory.

One decent moment aside, I'm pretty sure working for him must be punishment for my sins from a past life. The job is perfectly rewarding—and although I don't want to admit it, the company sitter has come in handy a few times when Mrs. Gabbard wanted to spend time with her new grandbaby —but I just want to gag every time he texts me.

As the weeks drag on, he sends *so many.*

A few, I could cope with.

The odd request here and there, reasonable things like any normal bossman might ask. That's fine. I'd expect that from any job, especially one that comes with a solid mentorship attached.

Not that he does much mentoring besides giving me the Falco book. I have to admit, it's pretty good, an inspiring story about a driven man who worked his way up and carved his piece of the American dream.

It makes me wish I was doing something greater, rather than managing my way through the daily grind. But the book drives home the point that nobody ever gets anywhere without putting in the hours doing the boring crap no one else will.

And Patton Rory is very good at keeping me busy with drudgery.

One day, he wants me to round up data on what's being used in the rooms. He wants me to make sure housekeeping keeps trying out the imported Egyptian towels he insisted on furnishing in the rooms. He wants shiny new brochures, shoving our growing list of spa services in the guest's faces to boost profit margins.

Ugh.

There's barely even a break from it at home.

Half of what Arlo draws is his new favorite person, Grumpybutt the Great. I shouldn't, but I leave a few of his crayon sketches pinned next to my desk in the back office.

A few of the staff laugh whenever they come in, even though I don't come out and say it's our boss.

I guess the implication is clear in his mean blue eyes and scribbled eyebrows and that overly long tie. Always dark blue, just like his eyes. And sometimes my son goes the full mile, adding horns and a tail.

At least Patton Rory isn't as popular as he likes to think, and it has nothing to do with our personal history.

I switch on the sleek computer, listening to the whir of the guts, and fan my notes out across the desk.

That's how I like to work, making sense of the fragments in front of me.

It doesn't take long to get sucked in.

A lot of guests send the surveys back with the tablets

provided in the rooms. That data is easy to input, but others prefer old-school pen and paper. Particularly the older folks, who make up about a third of our current guests.

I figured that out fast the first week we opened and response rates climbed as soon as I started having physical survey cards left in each room.

I attack the physical copies first, making a pile of the completed questionnaires that grows quickly. I have my earbuds in and I'm humming to myself, jamming to my playlist and singing because I know it's late enough to be alone back here.

I barely notice when a shadow falls over me.

And I know it's him before I even turn.

He's just got that *aura*.

Some people might call it magnetic. I'd say it's more like he knows how to trigger my gag reflex without even being in my line of sight.

"What's up?" I ask, swinging my chair around and hoping I don't sound as instantly annoyed as I am.

Patton's lips tighten.

Was he smiling a second ago?

Ever since the incident in his office where Arlo—bless his little heart—decided to defend my honor from the monster man who's been plaguing me for weeks, Patton Rory has made a strange effort to be human.

Too bad I don't *want* human.

Human makes him harder to hate, and hating him is the simplest way I have to hash out my feelings about this whole crazy situation.

But that's another point entirely.

Humans also have parts.

And I've been doing my very best to not look at him too long, let alone remember how godly he looks naked.

That has no place here.

Especially not after Arlo gave him the metaphorical kick he needed to be an actual mentor.

"I just came by to check in. How are the surveys treating you?" he asks, like I should be grateful for the project.

"They're keeping me busy and I haven't lost any hair over them yet. So, yeah. We're good." I nod at the papers in front of me.

For a second, he looks at the questionnaires and frowns.

"We have that many people still using paper?"

"Some guests prefer it, believe it or not. It's an extra step where I have to add it to the spreadsheet manually, but no big deal." I offer him a tight smile. "I added the cards to the rooms, remember? Didn't think it was important enough to bother you with."

"Yeah. Good move."

"Don't worry about it muddying up our green commitment. It's all sourced sustainably from a local stationary company, and I personally make sure these get recycled again once I've recorded the responses."

There's surprise in his face as he looks at me, his eyes shining.

"Is there a problem, Mr. Rory?"

He hesitates before saying, "Yes. We have to get over this name shit. I know you don't like it, but will you please call me Patton like everyone else in this damn building?"

Oof. If only he didn't say 'please.'

It's weird, seeing him respond like a real person. Dangerous, too, for reasons I prefer not to dwell on.

Calling him Patton feels even weirder, but somehow, I don't quite know how to just shut it down.

He's technically right. Everyone else here *does* call him that.

There's an odd sort of chain of command with names and titles at Higher Ends.

For him, it's younger brother syndrome, I suppose. That's what our lead cleaning lady told me last week when I mentioned it.

"If you insist." I try not to smirk as I shake my head. "Patton it is."

Part of me thinks I should offer the same thing back and tell him to call me Salem. Not that he's needed permission lately. But it brings back memories of a night that never should've happened on a riverboat casino, and *asking* him adds a layer of intimacy.

"Thanks." He leans against the wall. "Mr. Rory's my old man's name and Archer's sometimes. I want nothing to do with it."

I'm surprised he sounds so harsh.

Huh.

I've also never heard anyone mention a Rory senior before.

There are the three brothers, and I've heard of a Mrs. Rory floating around town like a very rich social butterfly, but there's never been a patriarch figure making his presence known.

Bad blood, maybe? Or is his dad no longer around?

I hate how I want to know, and how he keeps humanizing himself without really trying.

"I get it," I say. "Miss Hopper feels like my mother sometimes. She's Mrs., of course, but you know what I mean."

He nods like he understands.

Must it always be so awkward?

But Patton Rory stands in my office and looks at me like he can read the thoughts in my head. Worse, like he doesn't *hate* what he sees.

Who are you and what have you done with my grumpybutt boss?

It almost makes me think of that night again and the easy

106

laughs we shared—until I remember my promise to never go there again.

"What else is on your mind lately?" he asks, leaning against the doorframe.

My eyes snag on his figure as he slouches.

God, even when he isn't trying, he slays.

He's a tall man with a runner's body, lean and built and powerful. Broad-chested and cut from pure sin from the abs on down.

Just looking at him makes me feel self-conscious. I wonder how he's only gotten *hotter* since our hookup.

Me, I bounce between twenty and thirty pounds over-weight. My skin has stretch marks that weren't there six years ago before a baby and a mountain of stress. I'm older and worse for the wear than when I was twenty-one, and I was never runway material.

"The Egyptian towels are a rave success. Don't let it go to your head," I say grudgingly. Anything to focus back on work. "They're harder to wash according to housekeeping, but I've had several guests say they're the comfiest towels they've ever felt. They even want to bring them home."

"Does it cut into the budget too much?"

"The one you approved? No, not much." I resist the urge to call him out more on the budget, but I can't fault him for not remembering every line item. "I also had another idea to ramp up the luxe feel. Handmade soaps."

The skeptical look on his face is priceless.

Egyptian towels—imported *from* Egypt—are clearly fine, but suggesting we try handmade soap from local sellers is outrageous.

"Handmade soaps," he repeats it like he's chewing a piece of lemon.

"Well, I heard from around town"—from Kayla, actually, but so far I've managed to keep her far away from here, thank God—"that your mom sponsors a lot of art groups. Is that right? This might be a cool way to give back to Kansas City, if she can hook us up with some local sellers who take bulk orders."

"You heard about my mother? Word does get around," he says flatly, but his frown seems more conflicted.

I wonder if I've messed up. Maybe it's weird hearing about his mom from me and getting so personal.

"Patton, I just meant—"

"It's not a bad thought."

I do a double take, blinking.

"It's not? Am I dreaming?" Yes, my mouth runs away with itself again.

His eyes brighten. Their glacial, soulless blue doesn't feel as arctic as usual.

"Don't get carried away," he says with a sly whisper of a smile. "I'll ask my mother for recommendations. If you can find enough room in the budget to get these soaps into every room, it's a deal."

"Of course I will!" I'm gushing confidence now. All because a man whose approval I'm not supposed to care about hasn't blown my idea out of the water.

If anything, he seems surprised, but in a good way.

Not like when Arlo kicked him in the shin.

"Before I ask, do you have any sellers in mind?"

"I can have a look around locally and see what matches our aesthetic. Otherwise, I'm happy to check out whatever you bring back."

"I'll get my mom on it. She never turns down a little sleuthing." He digs his hands in his pockets and shrugs. "She's the artistic one in the family, not counting my nephew. It skips a generation or some shit."

Whoa. Did he just admit there's something he's not good at?

"Honestly, I don't have much of an eye for art. But I'm trying."

"It's a good start, Miss Hopper."

"Salem," I say.

His blue eyes become glinting stars, brighter than ever.

Wow. When he's not scowling fit to ruin his face, when he looks *warm,* he brings me back to that night.

The transformation shocks me. He suddenly looks like a man whose company I might enjoy.

"Salem," he repeats, testing the word like he's tasting it in his mouth, savoring the flavor like melting chocolate.

Holy hell. It's more intimate than I expected, more than any time he's said it before.

"Anyway." *Back to work things.* "I should have the reports for you pretty soon."

"Cool. Looking forward to it." He gives the screen a quick glance. "Don't work yourself to death. I don't need them immediately. I also don't need you burning your evenings here and missing time with your son."

My throat tightens.

Yeah, this other Patton is definitely worse. I have no idea what to do when he's making himself so hard to hate.

"It's cool. I'd rather get this done."

"Only if you're pacing yourself." He pushes off the wall, ready to leave—and about time, too, seeing as this is the longest we've ever spent in each other's company without plotting mutual murder.

It does nothing for my state of mind, especially his eyes, so dangerously close to the looks he gave me when we—

No.

Then I hear him sigh and he stops, turns, and looks at me again.

"Listen, there's a group from out of town hanging out at the rooftop bar if you want to clock out early," he says. "You know, real estate agent types. I said I'd stop by and talk to them. The bar's open and comped if you want to finish up early and relax with a drink."

"Um, thanks. But I said I wanted to get this done before the weekend…"

The warmth leaves his face and his eyebrows pull down.

Ah, yes, Grumpybutt returns.

I'm a little relieved.

"Woman, it's Friday, and you're not scheduled to work weekends." There's a certain edge to his voice, suggesting he's back to talking through his teeth. "I'm not a total monster. If I say punch out early and your weekend starts now, act like it."

I purse my lips, annoyed that he's still on this nice guy thing even while he's bossing me around.

"I don't want to lose my place. Really and truly. I'd like to wrap this up so I don't have to think about it over the weekend."

For a second, I think he's about to march over and shut my computer off, then drag me up to the rooftop with him.

"Suit yourself. I tried." He turns to go before the drawings pinned up next to my desk catch his eye. "More of Arlo's talent, huh? He's a regular Picasso."

I snort.

The way he says *talent* sounds a little like he's accusing my son of a felony.

"He's prolific," I say. "I know I should watch out. I might have a kid bound for art school on my hands and I'll have to support him until he's thirty."

"As long as he doesn't flunk out and take over half of Europe." He pauses and puts his hands up. "Sorry. Bad joke. I know your boy wouldn't hurt a fly."

For a second, it looks like he might stop scowling after his very dumb history joke.

But then he notices the detail on the pages. The guy in the suit sporting dragon's horns and a tail, towering over several other frowny stick figures. Arlo even added a puff of fire coming out of his mouth.

That wouldn't be so bad if the stick figure closest to him wasn't labeled 'Mommy.'

Arlo definitely hasn't mastered subtlety yet.

Patton's face darkens.

Any hope for him stomping off disappears and so does my composure.

"That's not—um, I mean, I didn't put it up to poke fun. It's not meant to be offensive…"

God, I'm cooked.

I pin my lips together, lacing my hands at my waist, doing my utmost best not to burst into anxious laughter.

"Very unprofessional, Salem Hopper," he finally says.

And I lose it.

Not just a little bit, either.

Not the delicate lady-laughs I bet he's used to hearing from his colleagues and friends and even dates.

This is ugly donkey laughter that makes my face hurt.

Stop, stop.

Of all the things to laugh at, this is so not the one. But the mixed shock and horror curdling his face is too much to take without dying.

"Arlo's shameless when he gets stuck on something. I'm sorry he doesn't like you much," I manage, unremorsefully pinning the blame on my son, though I was the one who hung these pictures up.

"Don't apologize. The feeling's mutual," he growls.

I splutter to a halt.

Ouch.

I wasn't expecting that.

So, maybe Patton doesn't have to like his secret son—and

I get why he doesn't, just like I understand why Arlo has this weird love-hate thing going on with him—but knowing what I know makes it feel like an uppercut.

"He's just a kid." I stare at him, biting my lip.

"Yes, we've established that. Have you always let your son insult your bosses?" he asks, his tone clipped. Back to being asshole incarnate, I see. "I'm starting to see why your past ventures never got off the ground."

I flinch back in my seat.

Rude.

The silence crackles with heat, smothering us, but I can't think of anything to say.

I'm sure there's some way to play this off cool.

If there is, it eludes me. I'm too busy restraining myself from leaping up and slugging him in the face.

Then again, so what?

So what if he thinks I'm a serial failure? Anyone else would think the same thing after seeing my résumé. It's not the end of the world.

It's just one more low blow that reminds me why he's awful, and no truce will ever change that.

The irritation on his face fades as he studies me.

"Shit, what are we doing?" His eyes are the same arctic shade as before, but instead of a wall, I sense emotions there. I pick them out like colors in a rainbow.

Regret. Frustration. Anger.

Mostly aimed at himself, I think.

There's also something else I can't identify like the blurry line between indigo and violet.

"I'm sorry," he says. "Salem, I didn't mean it."

"But you did," I mutter quietly.

Maybe I should be so pissed, but there's no room for anger past the disbelief squeezing my lungs.

"I shouldn't have said that."

"For once, we agree."

He takes a step closer.

He could touch me now, if he wanted, but thankfully he doesn't. I'm not sure I could stop myself from throwing the small trash can next to me at his head if he did.

"Tell me what I can do to make it up to you," he says.

"Make it up to me?" I laugh harshly. "Like *how*? Taking me up to a rooftop bar and plying me with booze so I forget you insulted me to my face? That hurt, Patton." He looks away and I snort, the sound too bitter. "The last time we did that, we cursed ourselves. Just look where we are now, stuck together and ready to strangle each other."

It's in his eyes.

He flinches, even if his wall of a body doesn't quiver a bit.

"Go on, get it out. Tell me how shitty I am. Just know if you were anybody else on my staff—"

"So fire me!" I grip my pen like a knife, almost in disbelief at what I've just said. Here comes my next failure, I guess, served up piping hot. "Or if you won't, just—just let me work so I can get home at a decent hour without owing the babysitter overtime."

I keep my back straight, waiting for the inevitable moment where he knows we can't continue on like this. Where he pushes me out and brings in someone else to undo all of my hard work, erasing any mark I ever left on The Cardinal.

I'm sure he's just been waiting for an excuse, right?

But he flicks his gaze at the computer screen and the spreadsheets still displayed there.

"I want your report by Monday. Your own self-imposed deadline." That's all he says as he turns and storms out.

God.

I let my head thump on the desk, dislodging my neat cards and sending them cascading into a mess.

God.

This is it.

What is it about this ridiculous man that turns me into a pretzel of pure chaos?

How is it we can have an almost human conversation one minute yet it feels like pure torture the next?

I'm starting to see why your past ventures never got off the ground.

It's the kind of quippy thing I might say when I'm angry. Lashing out, claws extended, just like a cornered cat. Pure defense mechanism.

But he knows where it hurts, and with the disbelief fading, I'm left with the sting that resonates to my core.

"Blue-eyed prick," I mutter, picking up where I left off.

Why couldn't he have shown his evil side the night we met?

But if he had, I'd be trading Arlo for a different life, and I'd never do that in a billion years.

I just hate the fact that I'm stuck living this one, where he gets to be the biggest dick I've met, and I still have to thank him.

Without Patton Rory, though, my sweet son wouldn't exist.

That's a cruel, cold fact written in the stars.

The price is this creeping insanity, living another day where we're playing a game of chicken, and managing my feelings like I can somehow talk a volcano into staying calm.

VIII: SPIN AT THE WHEEL
(PATTON)

I never thought mentoring would break me after all my years in business.

I've organized deals and landed contracts that had the potential to bring the company to its knees in its infancy— and with the Forrest Haute case, it almost did.

I'll admit, that one was a blunder.

But even *that* stress hasn't rubbed me raw half as much as Salem Hopper.

Why is it so damn difficult?

She isn't the first intern I've ever had. The other property managers we have on payroll haven't caused me an inch of trouble.

It's a me thing, probably.

It fucking has to be.

It shouldn't bother me that she's still standoffish after my latest fuckup. She sent the survey reports to me as promised, finished her other work, and I sent back a handwritten note of thanks.

With anyone else, I would've made a call. Only, I know

she wouldn't take me growling in her ear as a sign of gratitude.

That goes double for the note, I guess.

When I went into her office for our weekly meeting, I saw it crumpled up at the top of her trash can.

What the hell ever.

I don't need her to *like* me.

Especially when I'm not particularly fond of her.

I just wish our relationship wasn't so goddamned frayed.

How hard is it to just shut our mouths and be civil?

It's our pre-work history, obviously. It's the only explanation.

I'm mulling it over with a scowl that's starting to hurt my face, staring at the massive floor-to-ceiling aquarium built into my home office.

Usually, it's my inner sanctum, the place where I can find a little peace from a world that never stops biting my ankles.

The colorful fish and rippling green plants never fail to take me a million miles away from my woes. When the octopus comes out, I imagine what it sees on the other side of the glass.

Is it a man living an easier life without tentacles, free to do whatever his heart desires? Or are we both just as trapped by circumstances beyond our control?

The octopus, countless miles from the sea.

Me, marooned in my world of work and bare-bones social existence, where the only woman I care to obsess over hates my damn guts.

Dark thoughts today.

It's not just the fact that I slept with her, but the undeniable truth that she represents a different time in my life. Another era when things were simpler, and I really felt *free.*

When I still had time to chase skirt without worrying about it backfiring on my business or the family name.

Shit, when did it all get so complicated?

When did I start to wonder if the fortune our effort brings in is even worth it?

Knock it off, fool. Before you start thinking like Dex.

Now there's a terrifying thought.

Snarling, I raid my bar and throw together an Old Fashioned—heavy on the bourbon—one of the drinks I know how to make reasonably well.

I try to relax as the tropical fish dart around. A couple seahorses blow by, fluttering like underwater hummingbirds.

The few times Dex brought Juniper over, she wanted to name them. Even the small cuttlefish that dart around the rocks, changing colors and signaling in their own secret, incomprehensible language.

Yes, my little saltwater menagerie is as mesmerizing as ever.

It's just not working today.

No matter how exotic, it can't pull me away from girl trouble with a woman I only fucked once years ago.

Can I get more pathetic?

I know why I've never named any of the creatures in my tank, though. I prefer the anonymity.

They have their lives, I have mine.

Sometimes they intersect, like God looking down on his free-will ant farm here. I can watch them from afar without intruding on their fate.

Naming them would change that, making it too personal.

You'd better believe I hate that shit.

Thinking of Junie reminds me of the family, too. Mom and Evelyn Hibbing. Her friend's been staying a while, trying to ride out the worst of her winter back home.

Damn, I promised her that talk about real estate, didn't I? Knowing it won't go anywhere.

Aside from having no interest in expanding that far

north, we're not about to make the mistake of partnering with outsiders again so soon.

Not after Haute. Not even for a family friend.

But I should hear her out as a courtesy. I can at least point her in the right direction, possibly help her find a better partner than Higher Ends if she's looking to sell.

I finish the last of my drink and push the glass across my desk.

Tomorrow. I'll talk to Evelyn and let her down easy to keep Mom pleased. Then I'll be back to brooding in front of my fish, wondering how grey this evil ladybug will make me with her soul-sucking hot and cold shit.

Salem.

My mind pings on something.

The meeting with Evelyn could be a good chance to demonstrate the art of negotiations—if we can stand inhabiting the same room and breathing the same air for that long.

Isn't that my job as a mentor? To man up and mentor her?

If I'm not careful, Dexter or Archer will get to her first.

Then I'll never hear the end of it. Her, talking about how wonderfully generous my jackass brothers are, and them ribbing me until the heat death of the universe about why I couldn't handle a young, energetic woman.

Fuck that entirely.

I pick up my phone and dial her contact.

It's late, and I idly wonder if she's out, taking advantage of the babysitter to have a night off. Does she ever get out for a date?

Or maybe she's passed out in bed because she doesn't have a workaholic problem that follows her home like yours truly.

"Hello?" Her voice is slightly breathy. "Can you just hang on one second?"

Oh, hell.

My blood heats.

What if I've interrupted her in the middle of something scandalous after all?

I hate that the thought of her having a normal sex life sends jealousy streaking through my blood.

It was six years ago, you deranged baboon.

Six. Years.

You have no right to her.

Yeah, but my dick doesn't know how to tell time, and neither does that little part of my monkey brain that thinks the only man she ought to have in bed is me.

She makes a raspy breath again.

The odds of this going well just plummeted to zero.

I'm half tempted to disconnect and text her instead when I hear her say, "Arlo, if you don't knock it off and get your pj's on in sixty seconds, I'll put them on for you. Don't be a baby."

I am the world's biggest idiot.

Of course, she's mothering the hellspawn.

I throw together a quick, simple martini from the bar, pouring vermouth while I wait.

When she comes back, she's just as breathy and apologetic as I've come to expect.

"Sorry about that. I usually have him in bed by now, but I got home late."

"It's after nine," I say, failing to hide the surprise in my voice.

"There was a lot to do at the office. All of those expenses and receipts you wanted me to get to accounting don't organize themselves."

My lip curls, knowing it could've waited for a few days.

So maybe I'm not the only one with a workaholic problem.

"I'm sorry for calling you this late, but a new learning opportunity came up and I'd like to bring you along."

"Learning opportunity?" she asks warily.

"Mentoring. I'm delivering some practical advice to an old family friend, and I thought you might want to sit in on the meeting to observe. It's a good chance to see how I work one-on-one with clients."

"Tomorrow?" She hesitates and I hear her whisper, "I'll say good night in a second, okay, big guy? Read your picture book." Then her voice gets stronger again. "Patton, I don't know if I can do Saturday. I promised Arlo we'd go sledding by the river while we still have enough snow from that last storm. You know it doesn't always last around here."

"It won't take all day. I can give you a ride, before and after. Or, if you prefer, the sitter could take him sledding while you're at the meeting."

"No. You don't owe me any special favors," she says sharply. "I know we have a history, but I'm over it. And I'm even more over obsessing about it..."

Like I'm not? Is that what she's implying?

"So am I," I bite off. *Goddamn.* "I don't ask any of my employees to work unnecessary weekends on short notice without making accommodations for them."

There's a silence.

I sip my martini, wishing I'd just poured straight vodka. A cocktail feels too lightweight for dealing with this impossible woman.

"Okay, fine," she says. "If there's something for Arlo to do during the meeting, I guess it could work. If you're willing, it would be great if you could pick us up and drop us off by the river later..."

If Mom has anything to do with it, there'll be plenty for him to do.

"I promise you he'll be entertained," I say. "My mom loves kids."

"Your mom?"

"The meeting's at her house. Like I said, a close friend of the family. That's what makes the stakes higher, and I want you to sit in and watch how I handle them. So, I'll pick you up around eleven. Hopefully that's a reasonable time?"

"Sure. Eleven's great."

Without giving her a chance to say anything more, I hang up.

Rude, maybe, but the less chance we have at leaping into another shitfight, the better.

I know we have a history, but I'm over it. And I'm even more over obsessing about it...

Her words float back to me, just like the way I lied to cut her off.

There's no reason this shouldn't be true. It was six years ago and there's no reason to cling to it.

But if it was all so easily said and done, this wouldn't be so difficult.

I wouldn't be jumping to conclusions about her sex life or fuming with unwarranted jealousy when she tells me she's over what happened.

As I settle in for a long night alone, the ugly truth stains my world, brighter than the yellow angelfish swarming by.

I'm still not over Lady Bug. Not by far.

And I'm deathly afraid I don't fucking know how to be.

* * *

I show up at her modest apartment at eleven on the dot to find Salem and Arlo waiting for me, bundled up in thick winter coats with hats and gloves.

The boy holds his large plastic sled by a rope. I grab it and

121

stow it in the trunk while she gets his car seat set up in the back before we set off.

Surprisingly, they're both pretty quiet.

Arlo keeps himself busy, looking at all the buttons on my dashboard from his place in the back. Besides a restrained smile and a few murmured words, Salem hasn't said boo.

The silent treatment works for me.

I switch on the radio, only to find it's on the same eighties station that had her caterwauling. Only, unlike before, when she did her damnedest to annoy me, she doesn't burst into song.

Oddly, I'd almost prefer it if she did.

It's ten minutes of awkward silence until we get to Mom's place.

Arlo makes a small noise as we pull through the gates. By the time we stop, he's in awe.

"Wowee," he says, his eyes like marbles. "This place is a castle! Are you like Batman?"

For a second, I pause.

"Yes. We went to school together, me and old Bats himself."

"Oh my God!" The little boy squeals and covers his mouth.

I glance at Salem, but for once she doesn't seem to find her son funny.

"Where's the harm in indulging him? A boy needs heroes," I whisper.

"You... Patton Rory? You really think you're cape material?"

I snort.

"So I'm a little more low-key than the guys in the comics. I'm retired from the whole crime fighting scene. My brother kind of stole the show with that one and he can have the limelight," I say as Salem steps out and wrangles her son.

I usher them both inside.

Predictably, Mom's waiting for us, draped in her usual vibrant red scarves and a wide smile.

"Miss Hopper," she says, giving Salem a kiss on the cheek. "Thank you so much for accompanying my son today. I know how precious your time is as a mom."

Salem's cheeks go pink. "Oh, um, thanks, Mrs. Rory. It's a pleasure. I've heard a lot about you, all good things with your art contributions."

She nods warmly. "Please, call me Delly. And this must be your son?"

"Arlo," he says shyly. "I'm going sledding after this boring meeting."

"How exciting! Young man, I wouldn't dream of leaving you bored while the adults talk. Come with me." Mom takes his hand.

After glancing back at Salem, who nods her consent, Arlo heads down the hall with her.

"Evelyn's in the library, Patton," Mom says over her shoulder. "She's very excited about her property. Please be gentle."

"I will."

Salem still doesn't say anything, staring after Arlo, her face tight.

All things considered, the introductions have gone about as well as I could hope—the kid hasn't kicked my mom in the knee, which is something—so I don't know why she's so uptight. Nerves, maybe?

"Can I get you anything? Water?" I ask. She looks at me like she forgot I was there.

"No, I'm fine," she rushes out. "Ready for the big meeting."

"Don't stress. Evelyn Hibbing's a perfectly pleasant woman and a longtime family friend," I assure her, putting a hand on her back to move her forward. When she moves against my palm, I can feel the heat in her blood.

"I'm sure she's great," Salem says, folding her arms. "I'm sorry, I just—I'm not normally in houses like this one. This place is spectacular."

One long look around shows me what she means.

When you grew up in this house, it's easy to forget.

My parents inherited this house from my grandparents, and Mom did everything in her power to retain its history and keep it fresh, which means the décor fuses the traditional —old-style gilded mirrors, heavy furniture, thick carpets— with modern touches. Paintings by local artists on the wall and geometric sculptures that look like a cross between five different animals. Healthy potted plants and touches of gold.

Light shines through the massive windows, highlighting the art like a proper museum.

"My mother's not a minimalist at heart," I say. An understatement.

"Wait." Salem stops next to a wall of photos. "Is that... Harry Truman?"

Of course, with all the extravagance displayed here, she'd find the one thing I don't want to talk about.

Family history.

If we're not careful, it always defines us Rorys.

It's too easy to become the local aristocrats, born with silver spoons in our mouths, rather than individuals who've lived and loved and suffered across generations.

"The one and only. Hell of a president, right?" I stop beside her. The same black-and-white photo has been replicated all over the place. Anyone who's lived in Kansas City has seen it on the walls of restaurants or hanging in schoolrooms.

For us, it's different.

Mom doesn't want to forget where we came from.

Archer's the same way, proud to a fault, and Dex—well, fuck if I know what Dex thinks about anything when he's so tight-lipped.

All I know is I hate it when our family gets looked at like an artifact. An extension of a distant president my great-grandfather helped up the political ladder with his old connections in the Kansas City political machine.

If people focus too much on our family's past, they don't appreciate the present.

They look at Higher Ends as a sure thing running off old money, and not the scrappy start-up that's had to fight with teeth and claws for every success.

What we're doing now has nothing to do with Truman or my grandparents.

"And your grandparents?" she guesses.

"Great-grandparents, yes. They were thick as thieves back in the day."

"Wow. It must be kinda nice, having so much history you can look back on. I'm sure it grounds you."

"Don't you?" I ask before I can help myself. "Have history, I mean."

"I mean, my family history isn't anything like yours... Your family left a mark. A huge one that'll always be there for the city," she says dryly, reaching out and touching the corner of the frame like it could transport her back to the 1930s when Truman was first elected senator.

"That's what it looks like, I guess. Still, we built Higher Ends from the ground up. None of us ever wanted to take the family name or the money for granted." I turn to face her, and this time she doesn't flinch. "My family history is insane. This house is insane. Hell, *my* house is pretty decent. But we're not *just* that, Salem. We're not bottom-feeders running off the past."

There's a flash of understanding in her eyes as she looks up at me.

"You're carving your own path. That means a lot to you, huh?"

"Damn right," I grind out. For the first time, I appreciate how good she looks with the coat and winter gear gone.

She's dressed casually in a textured sweater tucked into the waistband of jeans that hug the curve of her hips.

Shit, what hips.

I don't remember a lot from that night, but there's no forgetting her lush little ass.

I remember it in glorious detail, my knuckles turning white as I held on for dear life, railing her soul out from behind...

I shake my head until my brain rattles.

Bad idea, checking her out like this.

I *definitely* shouldn't wonder how much she's changed under those clothes now that she's had a kid, let alone whether she still has any fun that doesn't involve trips to toy stores and G-rated movies.

Whether she still makes the same noises as she did that night.

And shit, I absolutely should *not* wonder who the boy's father is, and why the hell he isn't in their life.

That's not my concern. Not my problem. Not my business.

Even if the thought of some sperm donor ghosting them pisses me off royally.

There's also a familiar stabbing in my gut.

Jealousy again, I realize, and I move back before it gets caught in my head.

Your one-night stand wasn't as special to her as it was to you.

Get over it already.

"Come on," I say. "We should get moving."

Evelyn's waiting in the library with tea, practically bouncing with excitement as we enter.

I'm almost glad to have Salem along, posing as my 'assistant.' It'll make this feel more like a real meeting and set the tone I need to let her down easy.

Hopefully, she won't be too disappointed.

"Hi, Evelyn," I say, accepting her kiss on my cheek this time. "This is Salem Hopper, my assistant with our flagship property, The Cardinal. Hope you don't mind her joining us today?"

"Not at all." Evelyn pours us both some tea, orange with rosehips, judging by the smell. "Here you go, dearie. Goodness! It's so nice to be here this time of year. It's positively balmy compared to Minnesota."

"That bad? Even with the last snowstorm?" Salem accepts the tea and sits.

"Bless your heart, no. That wasn't anything like back home. There, you can step outside and watch your breath freeze before you lose it in the blizzard." She laughs and sips her tea. "But where were we, anyway?"

"Wherever you'd like to start. Take us away," I urge, slurping my own tea.

We all gather our thoughts and drink for a moment. It's good to let the air settle first, and Salem clearly has the right idea. She's more composed than she has been all morning as she enjoys the tea.

"Now," Evelyn starts, her tone changing slightly, "coming here does help break up the winter. It's my third since Walt—my late husband, dearie—passed away."

"I'm sorry to hear it," Salem says.

Evelyn's eyes drift to the succulents in the corner.

"You are such a sweetheart. He was such an avid gardener. He spent his whole life running a chain of gardening stores. Why, I'd have to pry him away sometimes for a nice spring trip to Vegas. The miracles he worked in our home garden—we'd have vegetables all winter—oh, and the greenhouse! You should have seen it. All those bright flowers and fruits and herbs. I miss them dearly."

Salem's fingers tighten around her mug. "But I'm sure his memory lives on in the flowers."

"Oh, yes, it certainly does." She clears her throat and looks back at me. "But you're here for a reason, and I won't waste more of your time. The thing is—frankly, I read about Higher Ends taking off. I really admire what you boys have done, and in such a short time, too. It's a credit to the good head on your shoulders. Delly never gets tired of mentioning it, shameless brag that she is."

I smile.

"Thanks. We try," I say.

Honestly, the compliments aren't much different from the usual spiel I get with everyone else looking to work with us. Lofty praise first, then demands.

"I've wondered for some time—although you understand I've been very taken up since my sweet Walt passed away— if you could strike gold in the Minnesota market. Luxury rentals could make a *killing* on the lakes, especially in the summer. The property values are unbelievable. Just imagine, cabins with all the convenience of a hotel, but fully independent, leaving you free to entertain yourself as you wish. Boating and barbecuing and walking. You pick your poison."

"Yes, I'm sure you have to live it up while it's warm with the winters you've got," I tell her. "I'd guess everything shuts down in the colder months?"

"Ah, but winter is livelier than you'd think. You've heard about the ski towns up north? Lutsen and Grand Marais and such? God, they get buried every winter, but the young, adventurous types do love it. I know my skiers, Patton. They adore luxury and convenience without anything too fussy or crowded. They *want* what you could offer."

My gut twists, momentarily lost for words.

I have to admit, on paper, it doesn't sound terrible.

"Not to mention the fact that these towns are such tourist traps," she continues. "The market is *enormous* if you target the right areas. And as a native, I know precisely where you could focus your attention. When Walt was around, we used to spend so much of our offseason tromping around up there in small towns. Summers were too busy to do anything with the seasonal business, you see, so we lived like winter birds. The choice was bundle up and explore, or spend half the winter in casinos, losing our money."

Salem glances at me.

I know she's thinking the same thing I am—there's unexpected potential here.

But right now, it's *just* potential.

We can't get carried away.

"If this all sounds crazy, tell me this instant. You know I won't take offense," she rushes out. "But is it, Patton? Could you ever dream of committing to a new market far from home?"

"It's not as simple as purely committing," I say slowly. "There may be something here, but we have a process for market research. We need to cross-check competition, explore the history, the tourism traffic reports, for this sort of offering. Especially when it's, as you say, a little far flung from our home turf."

"Of course, of course." She nods her head briskly. "I wouldn't dare expect you to sign away your life at this little meeting. You're a businessman, after all, the same with all of you talented boys."

I try not to smile at the unintended patronizing note in her voice.

That's what happens when you're dealing with a woman who's known you since you were born.

"I'll speak to Dexter and Archer. If they're willing and the research looks promising, it might be worthwhile to pilot a single property or two. However, I can't make any definite promises today."

"Yes, I understand! Well, dearie, if that's even in the cards…" Evelyn lets her voice trail away and sets her mug down firmly. "Truth be told, my lovely Walt inherited several gorgeous lake properties I simply haven't had the heart to sell."

I stare at her. Several properties? I was expecting one, an old ramshackle cabin she'd like to unload for more money in retirement.

I don't follow Evelyn's life that closely, but I'm surprised.

"What condition are they in?"

She waves a hand. "Truthfully, they'll need some refurbishing. I won't lie to you. To bring them up to your immaculate standards, it would take some elbow grease. But with a little investment up front to pay the contractors, I'd be so happy to volunteer them as test cases for Higher Ends."

"I'll give it some consideration," I tell her slowly, wondering how I've shifted from a sure *no* to this. When did this little old lady turn into a master saleswoman? "We'll try to do our research promptly and get back to you." I glance at Salem and see she's taking notes.

Good.

I appreciate the fact that she still does it with an old-school pen and paper, which helps drive details into memory better than anything electronic.

"Thank you so much, Patton!" Evelyn spreads her arms and walks over. I submit to another crushing hug. Definitely not how these meetings normally end. "To even have this opportunity—oh, I appreciate this so much. You can't fathom how proud Walt would be."

"We'll do you both right, whatever we decide," I say.

"And you!" Evelyn turns to Salem. "You're so lucky to be working with one of Delly's boys. I hope you're learning your pretty head off."

Salem flushes again, the redness creeping up her neck to her cheeks. She doesn't meet my gaze.

"For sure," she says. "It's an amazing opportunity and a lot to take in. I'm super grateful."

Then the door bursts open and Arlo comes rushing in.

"Mommy!" he says excitedly. "Delly took me to the kitchen. We made cinnamon buns and cocoa."

Yeah, that's Mom, all right. I'm sure it took her five seconds to suss out the kid's favorite snacks.

"Did you now?" Salem plops him down on her knee where he can't do any damage.

"Is this your son?" Evelyn asks breathlessly, her face lighting up. "What a delightful little boy. And what's your name, pumpkin?"

"Arlo," he informs her.

The second Mom walks in, shutting the door behind her, Arlo grins at her.

Damn. At least he likes *someone* in this family.

"We had a lovely time, didn't we?" She takes a seat beside Evelyn. Salem stiffens. "I hope we're not intruding. Poor Arlo didn't want to be away from his mommy any longer."

"No, we were just wrapping up. And I'm sorry if he started getting restless, he's very attached," Salem says carefully. "Hopefully he behaved himself?"

"A *delight*," Mom gushes.

Of course, she'd say that. She's so desperate for more grandkids, she'll practically adopt someone else's munchkins. She loves Colt to death, but I think she'd like ten more just like him. Don't know how Junie and Dex show their faces around here and survive all the hints she keeps dropping.

The sooner they get around to making babies, the better for all of us.

Arlo looks at me with his beady little eyes.

"Your mommy makes good chocolate. Way better than yours," he says matter-of-factly. There's a dark smear around his mouth.

Salem notices it just as I do, wetting her thumb and rubbing it away.

"Arlo!" Salem hisses. "What have I told you about being nice? Mind your manners, big guy."

"But Mommy, he's not nice to you."

Aw, hell.

I wouldn't be the least bit surprised if Salem's face burst into flames. Mom and Evelyn both look at us like we're the center of attention.

Goddammit, here we go.

It would be so easy to say something about Salem giving *me* the cold shoulder, but that wouldn't get us anywhere.

"Kid, I'm learning. I'm thirty, not a hundred years old. That isn't too far gone to grow a little empathy, right?" I keep my tone light while Mom gives me an epic frown. Salem glances at me in surprise, then looks away. "Mom, don't look at me like that."

If we were alone, she'd be wagging a finger with some choice words.

I glare at Arlo, trying like hell not to let on how annoyed I am.

Way to go, little man. You think I got you into trouble with your mama, and now you're paying me back.

"But Mommy makes the *best* hot chocolate," Arlo says, throwing his sticky arms around her neck.

Thankfully, even a future Machiavelli still has the attention span of a bug when he's only five.

"Boys that age are such a handful," Mom says, giving Salem a smile that says she's seen it all before. "He said you were going sledding, yes? Give me a moment and I'll bring you a thermos for the road."

"Oh, you don't have to—"

"Nonsense. Everyone needs more cocoa. Even Patton." She eyes me with a look that says, *shut your mouth. Be nice. Drink up.*

"Thank you so much," Salem says.

"We'll meet you by the front door." I decide it's in our best interests to get out of here before Arlo has a chance to demolish my reputation more. "I'll give you that ride to the river I promised."

"That's so kind of you," Evelyn whispers. "You remind me of Walt. He was always so good with his employees, he never failed to treat everyone like family."

Salem blanches.

Her goodbye feels stilted as she practically runs from the room with Arlo bouncing along next to her.

I hold in a snort.

Real sweet, Lady Bug. Next time, let's make it more obvious how much you hate me.

"Take care, Evelyn. Always a pleasure," I say, giving her a quick hug.

"You don't know how much I appreciate you meeting me like this, and I adore the opportunity to work out a new venture." She beams at me. "Enjoy your sledding! And say, if she's single—"

"Not my type." I back away. "Sorry."

Shit, I need to *go.*

I don't bother telling her I have no intention of sledding

myself, and I join the others at the front door. Mom hands us a tall thermos and cups, and we head for the vehicle.

Salem straps Arlo in while I put everything in the front. The boy grins at me like he knows he's my personal inquisitor.

Yeah, fuck spending a second in the snow with them. I'm not trusting him anywhere near a sled and my balls.

I just need excuses to stay in the car.

Preferably before he has a chance to plow into me and put me in the hospital.

IX: BLIND BET (SALEM)

*O*kay, I'll admit it—I didn't think Patton Rory had it in him to be nice.

Like, not sincerely nice-nice.

Not can-I-get-you-anything nice.

Not let-me-reassure-you-about-the-deal nice.

I mean, don't get me wrong. He's still a walking iceman with the smarmiest glint in his eye. But today, he's been *decent.*

Maybe one of his nicer brothers crawled inside his skin suit and this Patton is an imposter, or he's had a personality transplant.

At this point, it's more believable than seeing Patton Rory behave like a normal human being.

Especially when his mom was so weirdly sweet, way more than I expected.

I basically imagined her to be an older version of him. Stuck up, optimized for inhuman good looks, and ready to mow you down in an instant with a nasty comment or two.

But she was genuinely kind. Friendly and generous.

Delly Rory made us feel at home even though I had no

right being in that big old house with a kid who can be a handful and a half.

It almost hurts to wonder if it's due to the natural bond, knowing she's his grandmother.

That still eats at me as I stand on top of the hill, watching as Arlo skids down to the bottom on his sled.

When he tumbles off it at the end and looks back at me for approval, I wave.

"Careful, dude! You have to hold on tight until it stops."

His face lights up as he runs back up to me, his boots sinking in the snow and the sled bouncing behind him as he pulls it by the rope.

Somewhere behind us, Patton waits in his car like the snow-allergic Scrooge he is. However nice he was earlier, he's gone back to being a turbo workaholic, if he isn't just avoiding us.

I seriously doubt he has emails to finish.

He's probably looking at his fat investment portfolio or streaming porn, waiting for us to hurry it up so he can drive us home. At this point, I'll be pleasantly surprised if he doesn't just call a cab.

Confusing.

At least when I hated him, I knew where we stood.

But I'm breathing too fast, I realize.

And I plaster on a smile as Arlo returns to my side. A few new flakes of snow drift down on us, settling on his coppery curls and the tip of his nose.

"That was so cool!" he yells.

"Glad to hear it. We don't get this kind of snow enough so late in the season."

"Your turn, Mommy."

"Hmmm." I hesitate. "Only if you come with me."

Beaming, he clambers on the sled. I send Patton a quick glance before I hunch down on the back of it.

He hasn't left the car once. He's just sitting behind the wheel, glued to his stupid phone.

Eh, maybe he really *is* working. He's that much of a control freak.

Sometime between our one-night stand and whatever this is now, the man lost any sense of work-life balance.

"Mommy!" Arlo sits between my legs and taps my knee. "Mommy, let's go!"

I squeeze my feet onto the sled and push off.

We rock gently for a moment before the sled dips and goes skidding down the hill.

Arlo screams happily, clutching at my leg for grip.

I'm caught off guard by how fast it is.

A second later, I'm squealing and losing my hat.

It flies off behind me before I can clamp it down on my head. But we're going too fast and there's nothing we can do now but hold on.

Soon, we veer off course and the ground levels out, slowing us down slightly before we plow into the piled snow at the bottom, laughing like crazy.

"Mommy, your hair's a mess!" Arlo pushes my mess of hair off my face and plants a huge kiss on my cheek.

"You know what?" I pull off his hat and ruffle his hair aggressively. "Now we match!"

He howls, grabbing for his hat and pulling it down over his ears.

These are the little moments every mother lives for, I think, leaning back on the sled and looking at the iron-grey clouds above, still sending small flakes spiraling down.

Sitting next to Arlo, I point up. "Check out that cloud. Looks like a polar bear, I think."

"Mom, that's a rabbit." He gives me a look of disdain only a five-year-old cloud expert can manage.

"Really? Then where are the ears?"

"Right there, Mommy. Look!" He jabs his mitten at the sky.

"Well, maybe if you squint really, really hard..."

He huffs impatiently.

My smile fades.

Now, every time I look at him, I just see Patton's dark-brown hair—coppery in the sunlight—and the same sharp blue eyes all the Rory brothers inherited.

Does Grumpybutt himself ever notice the resemblance?

I wonder.

If he has, I'm sure he's in denial.

Then again, it's almost worse if the idea never enters his head. What if he thinks I'm just some skank who sleeps around, and he was one more fling in a long line of blue-eyed boys that night on the boat?

You could always tell him, that nagging little voice in my head reminds me.

Yeah, I could.

That might fix the violent guilt that's eating me to the bone.

But I could also throw myself off a bridge into the freezing Missouri River, and it would probably be easier than dealing with Patton becoming my official *baby daddy.*

Ugh.

"I wanna go again!" Arlo announces, bouncing up. "And we gotta get your hat."

Retrieving my hat isn't as easy as it seems.

Somehow, it wound up stuck in a very big tree on one of its lower branches.

I stand on my tiptoes, but that doesn't do much good. Next, I try to pile up some snow and pack it down so I can reach for the tree's flimsy branches.

"Lemme! I'll get it," Arlo says, jumping excitedly.

"You stay, big guy. This one's a mommy job." One firm glance silences him.

I'm dead set on us having one nice day that doesn't end in tears or a broken arm.

Eventually, I snatch it off the branch and toss it at Arlo, who catches it and runs around in a circle like it's the big prize.

"It's got snow inside," he informs me when I make my way back down. "Watch out or it'll be wet."

I put it on my head anyway and shudder as his warning comes true.

"Well, it's back where it belongs now." I take his gloved hand and we walk back up to the top of the hill together.

For a second, it's like the world keeps shrinking.

Here, there's just Arlo and me, laughing and having fun with no worries beyond the winter chill. Like everything just clicked in place for one brief happy moment.

Then I glance up and see him.

Patton damn Rory.

He's left the car now and he's standing in his thick navy-blue trench coat, his arms folded, watching us like the real-life Grinch he is.

Talk about killing the vibes.

But as we get closer, I wave at him anyway, beckoning him over to join us.

Seriously, what *happened* to the carefree guy I hooked up with years ago? Did he ever exist?

Or was I so drunk I completely misread him that night at the casino?

I'm still wondering when Arlo flings himself at Patton the second he sees him approaching.

"Mr. Rory!" He remembers his manners today.

Good.

It's progress that he doesn't instantly go with *Grumpybutt*.

"Come sledding with us. Have fun."

"Sledding?" Patton's gaze flicks to me and I prepare myself for the inevitable dismissal. He's too busy, too important, too *boring* to relinquish his dignity for playing around in the snow.

"Yes." Arlo takes Patton's hand and tugs. "You go *so fast* and you get to do it over and over. Right, Mommy?"

"We've had a lot of fun, yes." Melted snow drips down the back of my neck from my hat and I shiver. "But don't bother him, honey."

"It's fine," Patton says, grabbing the sled from Arlo and positioning it at the top of the run. He puts one foot on it.

I have to rub my eyes as he looks at my son and asks, "So I do it like this, munchkin?"

What. Am. I. Seeing.

Patton, sprouting an actual sense of humor, partaking in something that isn't money driven?

"No!" Arlo giggles, his face flushed with excitement. "You gotta sit on it or you'll go snow surfing and then you'll fall on your face."

"Silly me. I thought it felt flimsier than the snowboards I remember when I was a kid." His eyes find mine.

I die a little right there, imagining him as a teenage punk with a snowboard tucked under one arm.

Maybe that's why he's doing this.

The nostalgia bug must've bit him.

"Like this, then?" Patton watches Arlo as he sits.

I guess it's my turn to feel the nostalgia bug's teeth. For a heartbeat, he looks just like the man I met that night my life changed, and it feels like six years haven't passed us by.

But I turn away before more incriminating thoughts eat me up—like how devilishly good he looks when he smiles with that obscene blue light in his eyes.

It's so much more lively and attractive than the brass tacks beast he is at the office.

"Hmm, I think I'm still missing something." Patton gently grabs Arlo, pulling him onto the front of the sled and wrapping an arm protectively around him.

He glances at me, a silent promise that he won't let anyone get hurt.

As soon as I nod, they're gone.

Crazy fast.

Faster than I went with Arlo, whipping down the hill like a rocket.

Maybe it's the extra weight, or maybe it's the way Patton leans forward, adjusting their center of balance with a wild grin etched on his face.

Either way, my chest tightens until my heart might break with mixed emotions.

Bittersweet confusion, a potent blend I don't know how to deal with, much less digest.

Why'd he have to go and pick today of all days to be a decent man? When Arlo's around, when he's with his *son*?

Also, the same day his son just spent the morning with his flipping grandmother.

It's like the universe schemed up a secret family day out, only no one knows it but me.

And that dagger of terrible knowledge in my heart plunges deeper.

My nose stings. Hot tears crowd my eyes that have nothing to do with my frozen cheeks.

As soon as the sled reaches the bottom and they stagger off it, Arlo scrambles to his feet and runs back up the hill to me, leaving Patton to haul the sled up to the top again.

"Mommy! Mommy!" Arlo gasps with the widest grin I've ever seen. "Did you see that? We went faster than a race car. *Vroom!*"

"Sure did, sweetie. Why don't you catch your breath?"

"He said he needed me to hang on and he'd hold me like a seat belt." He makes a face and reaches up on his tiptoes as I lean down to hear him. Even though Patton is far enough away, he couldn't hear even if he tried. "I didn't have to. He just didn't want you to worry."

My face heats.

Why on God's green Earth is Patton being so nice to me that even my little boy notices?

"Oh, yeah? And what would've happened if you'd fallen off, big guy?"

"I wasn't gonna!" he says dismissively.

"Sure." I glance up as Patton arrives. "Thanks for taking him down, Patton. He really enjoyed that."

"It's been a while," he says with a nod. "I used to come here a lot as a kid."

"Snowboarding?" I laugh before I can help myself. "I can't imagine your mom sledding down the hill."

"Nah, she stayed at home. I didn't hit the board until I was older. When I was little, my dad took us." There's a trace of sadness in his voice, but he hands Arlo the rope. "You ready to go again?"

"Yeah!" There's no lack of enthusiasm on Arlo's face. "We should have more sleds. Then you *and* Mommy could go."

"I'm okay, sweetie," I say, waving them on. "I don't mind watching. I'm having plenty of fun."

"Boring." Arlo wrinkles his nose.

"Why don't you go on ahead this next round," Patton says. "I'll keep your mom company."

You don't need to do that.

On the other hand, seeing him with Arlo a second time might be worse for my tangled bird's nest of a heart, currently wallowing in what-ifs and missed opportunities.

"Okay!" Arlo sits on the sled and Patton gives him a friendly push.

He screams his lungs out as he flies downhill, his small voice fading as he goes.

"I mean it," I say, folding my arms tighter against the cold. "Thank you again."

Patton sends me a wry, amused glance.

The glint in his eyes says he sees more than he should, more than I want him to. "Are you still the same manager who nearly threw me out of her office a few days ago?"

I'm thankful the hat and damp hair hanging around my face hides some of my blush. "Maybe if you weren't so rude then, I wouldn't have told you to get out."

"Touché." He looks back down the hill just as Arlo reaches the bottom. "I shouldn't have come at you so hard."

"No, you shouldn't have."

"For the record, I'm sorry." There's a strange softness to his voice I can't quite quantify.

Reluctance, maybe, for having to be in this position. Hesitation for having to apologize. Uncertainty over the fact that he's standing here in the cold watching my son.

Our son.

Oh, God, there goes my weepy brain again.

"It's fine." I look away before my face betrays how not fine it really is.

"Salem?"

Don't do this. Please.

"Honestly, Patton. Don't worry about whatever happened before…"

"I wasn't," he says. The sound of his voice makes me glance up at him.

Maybe the strangeness in his tone isn't regret after all, because now he looks like he's about to laugh.

Patton Rory, laughing, alive and carefree.

Today is a modern miracle.

"I'm starting to think you protest too much."

"Okay, Shakespeare." Smiling, I adjust my stance, moving my feet so they don't get too cold.

He chuckles. "That's the first time anyone ever called me Shakespeare."

"Which one of your brothers is better with words?"

He considers it before shaking his head. "I'm it. Wordsmith extraordinaire."

"Okay, boss. Whatever you say." I try not to hide my disbelief.

Patton grumbles and shoves his hands in his pockets.

That wins him a laugh.

"Something else Archer beats me at, huh?" he mutters. "What did you say to him, anyway?"

"What?"

"To make you both laugh like deranged hyenas."

I think back to the one time Archer and I met and he laughed—the time Patton walked in with a face like thunder, all Zeus glaring at me with brutal disapproval.

"Honestly, I can't remember. It wasn't that funny." My face grows hotter under the hat. It's so damp I've had enough, and I pull it from my head and shake my hair out. "Probably shouldn't have dropped my hat, it's soaking my hair."

"Salem—"

"Mommy, did you see? Did you see?" Arlo pants as he joins us again. He's losing his hat too so I tuck it back on over his ears. "I went so far this time!"

"I know, sweetie. I was watching. Do you think you can go faster again?"

"Yeah!" His movements are more sluggish as he clambers back on the sled.

I can tell he's getting tired, even though his determination outweighs any cry for rest from his little body. I give him a push and he whoops as he flies down again. We've made our own track in the snow, and his sled falls into its biggest grooves.

"You didn't answer the question," Patton says. "About Archer."

"Dude, it's not a big deal." Kind of a lie, but never mind.

"So why are you avoiding it?"

I sigh, folding my arms and facing him, knowing my hair's a rat's nest and I have a red nose worthy of Rudolph. Do we really have to ruin this?

Because if I tell him, I'll make a confession he'll despise me for. Again.

"You really want to know? Archer asked how we were getting along. I told him how Arlo drew you as Grumpybutt and you were pretty unhinged over it."

"Unhinged?" He glowers.

"Yeah, and your brother laughed. Because apparently the idea of me messing up so bad on my very first day was hilarious—and so was the thought of you getting pissy over a kid's drawing."

I half expect him to go off.

To explode at me again—to rake me over the coals for being unprofessional, which would be kind of deserved here—but he just blinks at me and inhales slowly.

"That would explain it. Arch never misses a chance to see me eat shit," he says.

"...so you're not mad?"

He glances at me and smiles.

"I'm over it, Salem. Let's just say we got off on the wrong foot and move on." He pulls off his glove then, offering me his hand.

Whoa.

I take it gingerly, ignoring that little pop of static between us.

Of course, it's a strong hand, thick and accustomed to doing harder labor than just working in an office.

Hands tell stories, but I don't know what his are keeping. Or what, as I pull off my glove, he can read in mine.

"Truce?" he asks, wrapping his fingers around mine. The tip of one finger reaches my inner wrist.

It shouldn't feel so intimate, but it does.

He's living proof that calloused hands can be sexier than they have any business being. Annoying.

"Truce," I echo, giving his hand two pumps before dropping it and fumbling for my glove.

At the bottom of the hill, Arlo makes the long climb back up, huffing and puffing like a little bear this time.

"I used to love coming here," Patton says with that wistful note in his voice again. "It was one of my favorite memories as a kid."

"That's why we're here today. I wanted to make some good memories for Arlo, and there won't be much winter left after this storm," I say before I can help myself. I'm telling him too much. "I also work too much to get out."

"Looks like he's having fun to me. Mission accomplished."

The observation makes my throat clench.

"Yeah," I say roughly before Patton can comment. "I think he is, and you're a big part of that today."

"That was awesome, Mommy. I went a hundred miles an hour!" Arlo puffs out when he reaches us. He looks between us before settling on Patton. "Sled with me again, Mr. Rory."

"Arlo, you've been at it for a while. And what's the magic word?"

"Please." He scowls but mumbles it.

"Okay, little man. One more round," Patton says. "Last one, though. My feet are turning into frozen meat."

Same here, but he's definitely taking the worst of it in those dress shoes since he didn't bring boots. And I wonder if he notices the way I'm shuffling around to make sure I can still get warm blood in my toes.

There's a lump in my throat as I watch Patton climb in behind Arlo and they take off.

They go blasting down the hill together, just like before.

Patton throws one hand up in the air like he's on a roller coaster.

Halfway down, they start losing their balance.

At first it's just a wobble. A twitch.

But after a few more feet, they're slamming into the snow.

For a second, I'm worried.

But then I hear Arlo laughing hysterically. Patton's deep chuckle fills the air along with him. He's holding my boy, narrowly preventing him from faceplanting into the snow.

Hello, core memory.

I'm sad that I'm the only one who knows just how special it really is.

And it's the proof I've been dreading. Patton Rory can handle a child, and that means he can be a dad.

You need to tell him.

Not right away, but sooner or later, he should know.

The thought makes me queasy.

Still, can't ignore it as they walk back up the hill toward me, Patton dragging the sled behind him. I can't unsee what I'm looking at now.

Father and son.

Together and happy.

Spending quality time together like it's normal for the first time in their lives.

Like they already know, at some basic instinctive level, which makes me feel like even more of a shitty villain.

My throat *hurts.*

"I think he's had enough. We should go warm up," Patton tells him when they reach the top of the hill. "You ready, little man?"

"*Moooom.*" Arlo tugs at my hand. "Do we have to?"

"If Patton says it's time to break, then yes, it's time." And I want to leave just as much as I want to stay. Talk about difficult.

"There's cocoa waiting in the car. The good stuff from my mother," Patton says, and Arlo sprints off at top speed.

His enthusiasm for the snow is only rivaled by his chocolate addiction.

I head back to the SUV stubbornly even though it feels like Patton wants to say something else. The steel wool lodged in my throat probably makes my face look weird, and I don't want him asking why.

Then there's no hiding the tears.

"Hey," Patton says, surprisingly gentle. "Are you feeling okay? You look a little frozen."

"Me?" My voice cracks. "Oh, no, I'm good. This wind just sucks, it makes my eyes water after a while. Totally the cold. Guess I'm more sensitive than I thought." Yes, I'm babbling, but I don't know how to stop. "It's nothing to worry about. Ask anyone and they'll tell you—"

When the world starts tilting, I don't have time to gasp.

My heel skids on an ice patch and I'm spinning.

There's just a second of panic, my arms windmilling, a squawking noise leaving my mouth.

Patton catches my arm right before I hit the ground and heaves me into him.

Into his arms.

I hold on before I can think what I'm doing, before my brain catches up.

Before I even realize I'm clutching Patton's strong shoulders and his hands are on my waist, holding me steady.

Holy hell.

This whole thing would be easier if he didn't feel so *solid* and warm under my fingers.

If his face wasn't so close.

If his eyes weren't so bright.

Our foaming breath swirls between us in the messiest moment of my adult life.

I'm hot and cold and winded.

So is he.

There's a red patch on his cheeks, probably from the scouring wind, which has really picked up in the last few minutes.

Yes, the wind, I decide. It must be.

That's the safest explanation. Because if it has anything to do with the fact that we're still holding each other tight, or the fact that I don't *want* to let go—

We are screwed.

These thoughts alone are beyond dangerous.

But his breath spirals against my lips and the only thing I can hear is my heart thudding as Patton stares at me. His tongue runs over his lips for a second.

Breathe, Salem.

Oh my God, breathe.

My breath catches.

For one glorious heartbeat I think he might do something crazy like kiss me until I melt through the snow.

It's been so long, but I remember how it felt. The heady desire, coming in waves, heat blooming through every nerve.

From the way his eyes ignite, like the sun catching summer waves in scintillating shimmers, he remembers too.

How do we even begin to deal with that?

"Mommy, what's for dinner?" Arlo cuts in, and Patton

releases me so fast I almost lose my balance for a second time.

"Oh." If I once had sane thoughts, I'm not sure where they went. "I don't know, sweetie. I'll look when we get home."

"Can we do pizza?"

"We'll see about that."

"Awwww." He pouts. "That means no."

"I know a great pizza place," Patton says. "I'd be happy to take you. My treat."

Good thing, too, because I know what sorts of places he likes if the coffee shop is any indication. High-end places that run a wine tab that costs more than my rent.

"I appreciate the offer," I say, trying to force a smile, "but Arlo's been spoiled enough for one day. Honestly, so have I."

"Aw, Mom!" Arlo juts out his bottom lip.

"Maybe next time," Patton says.

I don't meet his gaze again.

It's just easier.

"I'll have the notes from Evelyn back to you by Monday," I say. "Plus, more data from The Cardinal surveys. If you'd like, I can get a start on researching the northern Minnesota markets…"

"As long as it doesn't ruin your weekend." He nods, accepting the shift back to work. "I appreciate it, Salem."

"Mr. Rory?" Arlo says. "Can we have chocolate now?"

"Sure, kid." Patton gives Arlo a smile and opens the car door. A burst of glorious heat greets us. Like any decent newer vehicle, he was able to remote start the heater. "But we have to drink it outside, okay? Those seats hate sticky stuff."

I accept my cup gratefully after Patton pours one for each of us. I sip slowly as I listen to Patton and Arlo talking about superheroes.

Nice Patton came with his best game today.

If only I could decide if Nice Patton is really worse than Grumpybutt.

Patton catches my eye and smiles while Arlo continues a long lecture on the virtues of Spider-Man, who had it rough from the start because he was bitten by a spider.

Yep.

Nice Patton is definitely worse.

At least with boss Grumpybutt, I know where I stand, even if the view sucks and the service is rotten.

Nice Patton, he's infinitely scarier.

Dealing with him is a blind bet on the unknown.

Everything I've been running away from ever since the day little Arlo was born.

X: POKER FACE (PATTON)

*J*t takes me a full week to get Archer and Dexter together for a meeting about Evelyn's proposal.

She sent everything over in an email so we could scope out the precise location.

Even then, Dex is easily distracted, tapping away on his phone. What the hell has marriage *done* to my uptight ass of a brother?

I clap my hands in his face.

"Focus," I tell him. "I brought you guys in today so we could make a big decision. Evelyn deserves an answer sooner rather than later, whatever we decide."

Dexter gives me an annoyed grin. I barely recognize this man. It's like the work-obsessed demon that once possessed him has crawled into me instead.

"Okay, fine," he says, drumming his fingers on the table. At least that hasn't changed. "So she wants us to invest in one or two properties? The lakefront places?"

"Three cabins, technically. She needs funds to refurbish them, so she's effectively asking for us to shoulder the cost up front. She also wants a one-time use fee. Future payments will be split between her as retirement income and paying us back for the renovations."

"And you're okay with this?" Archer grumbles, pulling at his grey-shot beard. "That's a damn big investment up front on our part. Even for a family friend."

"The question is, do we think this market is worth it? I have a few answers." I bring up Salem's notes on my laptop, neatly typed and organized, scanning them again. "Preliminary research indicates there *is* a clear opportunity here. Traffic to the north shore is at all-time highs. Waterfront properties are booming, even for cabin purchases and such. There aren't enough rentals to go around, and high-end options are practically nonexistent outside Duluth."

I pull up the graphs Salem compiled showing Minnesota tourism and project it on the screen so they can see. I give them a minute to look it over.

"Can't see much downside, even if it will cost us a fair chunk of money to buy in," Dexter says. "We're also in a strong position. With The Cardinal off to a solid start, and first quarter revenues looking strong, where's the harm in expansion?"

"Exactly," I say.

"If we do things her way, there's limited commitment beyond the renovations," Archer says. "We can take the hit, yes—but it's still a risk. The question is, do we want to if things go sour?"

"Arch..." I roll my eyes. "Where would we be without a little risk?"

"Probably avoiding partnerships with men who could get us killed," he growls.

"Aw, shit. If you're talking about Haute again, you might as well—"

"Guys." Dexter holds up his hands. "I took the brunt of that mess, remember? Can we forget about it for ten

153

seconds? I swear, why does this shit always happen with you two?"

For a second, we turn our eyes down, trying to get back on track.

"I looked high and low for major risks in the research," I say, because I would never turn up to a meeting empty-handed, especially with Archer. "Look at the ten-year tourism trend for northern Minnesota. There's clearly a gap in the market that's exploitable. And if we use Evelyn's properties, we won't have to purchase them outright ourselves. If there's a black swan event and it doesn't work out, we haven't lost too much skin. We also won't have to worry about flipping underperforming properties."

"Losing is still losing. Even when it happens slowly." Archer wags a finger.

"Welcome to business, my man. Like it or not, you always have to take risks or you're not moving forward. There's also the potential for a huge reward."

I prop my chair up on its wheels triumphantly, leaning back, a dumb habit I just can't break.

"We have guaranteed rewards here in Kansas City," Archer says, but I can tell he's cracking.

The whole Haute incident scared him shitless. He never wanted to partner with anyone else, understandably, but this is Mom's oldest friend we're talking about. It's not like she'd ever crawl into bed with the mob.

This time, it's different. There's also less commitment here.

Plus, we'll be expanding our reach in a way that I *know* appeals to Archer once he's thought it through.

"I know our last partnership went way off track. But this is Evelyn Hibbing we're talking about. She's not going to call up a mafia hit man if she doesn't get her way. And haven't we been talking about moving north, even before Omaha came up?" I pause, letting it sink in before I continue. "We have the potential to get a foot deep into the market there, and if it works, think what else we could do."

Archer grunts. "We always said we'd make the decision to expand outstate *slowly.*"

"And this is us, making that decision now. Slowly." I stress the last word.

Dex glances at us. "When you're both done bickering, I think we should go for it."

"Of course you would." Archer's lips thin, knowing it's two-on-one.

"For fuck's sake, Arch, don't be like that. This isn't personal." Dexter flattens his hands in front of him. Now he means business. "The Cardinal is doing well. Spectacular, really, if the early bookings keep up into the spring. Think how we could capitalize on that."

"We can look into it," Archer grinds out. "I'd like to see more details on what repairs and renovations she really needs, and if we think it's worth the investment. If these places are falling down, it's a fucking veto from me. And if we agree, we'll get a contract drawn up and try to pilot *one* of these places for fourth quarter."

"Fair enough." I make a mental note. "If we get cooking and send up our own contractors with bonus pay, rather than looking for locals, we could possibly catch the late summer crowd."

"Sold." Dex puts his hands behind his head and stretches. "By the way, pass on our congratulations to your new manager, Pat. She's pulling her weight." He sends me a long, hard look. "You better be giving her the mentorship time she deserves and not fucking off."

"No half-assing it," Archer agrees, pointing a finger. "I know you."

"Since when have I ever half-assed anything with The

Cardinal?" I let my chair fall back on its legs and flip them off. "I could win business mentor of the year, you pricks."

Dex laughs bitterly.

"You're not winning squat with your personality. You and Salem don't exactly get along." Archer shrugs. "That's all I've got to say about it, though. This mentor gig is your responsibility. Don't let us find out you're shitting it up so bad we have to step in."

I glower at him.

"I recommended some of the books in your office," Dex tells me.

"I know. Guys, she's getting all the mentoring she needs, I promise." I huff loudly. "Hell, she came with me to meet Evelyn. I'm including her in all the major business activities, even beyond The Cardinal. I spent an hour sledding with her kid, and if you knew him, you'd give me a purple heart."

I grit my teeth.

The little monster wasn't half-bad, really, but they don't need to know that.

"Whatever you say, guru." Dexter gives me that grating skeptical look he specializes in.

"The fact is, she's got great instincts and she doesn't need much hand-holding. More like practical advice and more experience in the right situations." I lean my chair back again. "Hell, the cocoa bar alone will probably bring in repeat customers. She knows what she's doing. I'm just coaching her."

Archer raises his brows.

"So you're making excuses for sitting back and letting her do all the work. Typical Pat," he spits.

"I'm giving her *opportunities* to figure shit out," I throw back. "I'm even covering her babysitter for the long evenings when her usual nanny's out. What other job offers that?"

"Wait." Dexter frowns at me. "You spent *your own money* on a babysitter for her kid?"

"You?" Archer sounds just as incredulous. "Patton, I know you. You're a tight-fisted little shit who never learned how to spend money on anything that doesn't have fins and tentacles. What about this woman changed your mind?"

I don't answer.

I'm already in too fucking deep.

The last thing I need is either of these clowns adding to the confusion that's been churning up my blood wherever Salem Hopper is concerned.

"Make up your minds. Do you want me to be a good mentor or what? I'm not shortchanging her on anything, and that's the point."

"A mentor—not a sponsor," Archer says gruffly. "You sure you're feeling okay, Pat? You haven't gone and hit your head recently or been replaced by someone normal?"

A booming laugh falls out of him.

"Fuck you, man. I hope Colt brings home a rabid raccoon and turns it loose in your bed while you're asleep."

I know they're teasing, but knowing the weight of my history with Salem, this goofy conversation stings more than it should.

"Also, I don't have time to take your shit. I've got work to do."

"Patton—" Dexter calls from behind me, but I'm up and moving, and I slam the door behind me a second later.

Maybe pitching in to help cover her sitter expenses was a step too far, but what was I supposed to do? Tell them it was so her son couldn't come along and destroy The Cardinal's lobby again?

And where the hell is that kid's absentee father, anyway? I'd like to beat his face in.

Let them think whatever they want.

It's a practical decision.

And if we're taking on this Minnesota expansion, there's no more time for kicking back and gossiping like birds while we have a business to run.

* * *

I FIND Salem in her office, hunched over her keyboard with headphones on as she hums softly to the music.

I'm not surprised.

She runs around plenty, but she seems more at home tucked away here, in the back where she can organize and plan to her heart's content.

For a second, I stand in the doorway and watch her. It's always slightly cracked so the staff can approach her if they need to.

Like usual, her hair is piled up at the back of her head in a bun, the dark strands starkly rising against the pale skin of her neck.

She purses her lips as she works, turning them up to one side. I can see the reflection in the picture next to her, a photo of her with a younger Arlo from a couple years ago.

Shit, do not think about her lips.

Or the way they feel.

The way she had melted in my arms once, all buttery curves and gentle heat.

The way she looked at me right before she came on my cock.

It's like I was her entire world that night, and the sex meant more than a standard one-off fuck.

Damn.

I might hate her abrasiveness at times, but there's no denying she's still a knockout. Hazel eyes swirling with gold flakes, wide cheekbones, full lips made to torment my dick.

Six years ago was a brutal mistake, but now, even if I knew this would happen, I think I'd make it all over again.

Enough, man.

Screw your head back on.

I clear my throat, trying to banish the invasive thought as I knock on her open door.

"This a good time to talk?" I ask.

She glances up, but instead of the annoyed look I half expect, she just pushes a strand of unruly raven hair back from her face.

I bite back a smile.

No matter how neat her bun looks in the morning, there are always wisps that escape as the day wears on, curling around her cheekbones.

"Patton. Come in." She blinks at me. There's a strange awareness in her eyes and a flush creeping over her cheeks.

Maybe she hasn't forgotten the last time we saw each other and the civility isn't lost yet.

"Don't mean to disturb you," I say, closing the door behind me. Bad idea—I immediately open it again. "I just wanted to check in. You know, mentoring you like I should."

"No need to sound so reluctant," she says dryly. "I was just revamping the recommended 'winter eats' guide from the local restaurants for spring."

"Yeah?" I pull up a chair beside her and look at the screen. Instead of the usual high-end health nut options, she's added things like stews, pasta, barbecue, and— "Is that pizza?"

"Only the fancy stuff," she promises. "It's from the Italian place down the road with great reviews. The one with the woodfire ovens? They won some shout-out recently from a big national paper for their pies and gelato, and I thought we could use that."

"Our clientele tend to be very health-conscious."

"Oh, yes. I've been making note of the winter crowd, and

there's a trend toward younger guests. They're somewhat less inclined to eat like birds."

"Our current menu doesn't require *anyone* to eat like birds."

She swivels to face me.

"Think about it like this. You're young and active with money to burn. You've been out doing stuff all day, even in the winter. Sledding, walking, exploring the town in the cold and the snow, whatever. You come back here to one of the fanciest places in the whole of Kansas City, and you get a restaurant guide featuring salads and salmon dishes."

"It's hardly just—"

"Imagine if you knew where you could get good lasagna. Or pizza. Or barbecue ribs. All ready to grab just a few blocks away or order in. That's also way more authentic to Kansas City."

Truth be told, I've never gotten by on salads myself. Dexter's the health freak in our family, allergic to sugar and spice and everything nice until his wife started unfucking his palate.

I'll keep shamelessly loving a burger bursting with stringy cheese and grease.

"Fine," I say. "This is for the spring menu? It's coming up fast."

"I have a few more ideas. I'd like to try out the places in person first just to get a feel. You asked me not to change anything without data backing it up."

"So you're a food critic now?" I chuckle. "Any changes are supposed to be guest-led." And I suppose these are in a roundabout way. "Fine. But what about the restaurants we're abandoning?"

"I've thought about that. They don't care what dishes they provide as long as The Cardinal gets their business. Aside from the pizza—and I know that's a wild-card—we're still featuring a lot of food from the same places as before. Just for *different* food."

"For a similar price?"

She smiles. I try like hell not to notice the way one cheek dimples. It gives her a lopsided look that's irritatingly charming.

I must keep a leash on my dick.

"The restaurants won't be taking any losses, that's for sure," she says. "And it might help prevent food waste—some folks have been going out rather than eating at The Cardinal, which this new menu might help avoid."

I hold up my hands. "All right, I see your point. I told you to follow the data. If it says changing up the food works, then let's go for it."

"A vote of confidence? From you?"

Her dimple shows up again. I want to bite the back of my wrist.

"I'm not incapable of compliments, you know." I glance at her menu draft before leaning back in my chair, pushing it onto the back two legs. "I'll admit, you surprised me."

"You mean surprised you without letting my kid ruin another suit?"

I can't help smiling.

"It was a rocky start. It doesn't mean shit now." Understatement of the year.

"I thought you were going to fire me right there," she says wryly.

"I wanted to. But you came here with a recommendation that carries some weight. I had to give you a chance."

"And how much do you regret that now?"

My smile disappears.

She doesn't understand.

I don't regret it at all—and that thought makes me slam the chair back on all fours.

"You're doing well. Everything I'd expect in this role, plus churning out new ideas that matter," I tell her. "The Cardinal's better with your care and we're looking profitable. I'd be a damn fool to regret anything."

"I feel like there's a but coming…" Her gaze flicks away.

"No *but* this time. I'll even admit Arlo seems like a good kid—if he'd just rein in his sugar highs and cool it on the nicknames."

"Oh, like Grumpybutt? You're still mad?" She laughs. "I mean, it was bad of him, but you've got to admit it suited you."

"I don't have to admit *anything*." I shake my head. "You realize you're talking to the fun one out of my brothers, right?"

The guy who never gets taken seriously, I don't say.

"You?" She blinks at me.

"Who else? Archer's life has been about business before there *was* a business. He's too sensible and he has a lump of coal where his heart should be. Dex, he was the workaholic. Way more than me back in his bachelor days, if you can believe." I shrug because it's not true anymore. "I'm the little brother. The guy who has to work twice as hard if I want their punk asses to take me seriously."

"So, you're the one who knows how to relax? When there isn't something to prove, I mean?"

"Is that so hard to believe?" I'm incredulous.

She considers it, looking me up and down with a straight face.

"You kinda suck," she says, breaking into a smile that kills me. "But not all the time. I'll give you that."

Holy shit, stop the presses.

"Is that a compliment?"

She ducks her head as her cheeks burst pink, a few more

strands of hair falling from her bun. No surprise, really. Her hair looks so silky it's amazing it stays pinned up at all.

I wonder how she'd feel if I brushed them back behind her ears.

Would I be able to do it without giving in to the urge to fist her hair?

Shit, what would her skin feel like under my fingers? It's been so long and she was so soft, I've almost forgotten how—

No.

Dangerous, dangerous thoughts.

"Sorry for dumping the Minnesota research on your pile," I say. Back to work. Safe ground. "It's helping, though, and we're closing in on a decision soon. I can stick around and help you sort the latest stuff, if you'd like."

Her finger stills from tapping her desk idly. She sends me a compulsive glance.

"Help?"

"I've been doing the legwork with new ventures for a while. While it's all very tentative right now, we're looking at moving forward. We just need a little more time to ensure the big investment in these cabins will pay off."

"I never thought it wasn't serious," she says, but she doesn't start working again. She also doesn't look at me. The desk holds all her attention. "And I appreciate the offer, but I work on stuff like this better when I'm alone."

"You're like me, then."

"What? You're a spreadsheet loner, too?"

"Something like that. Not having to constantly communicate every last thought feels refreshing; it streamlines things. Even if teamwork is a necessity."

"Your brothers are that hard on you, huh?"

I glare.

"I wouldn't call that teamwork, more like obligation. Still, we get along well enough to keep growing. We can cooperate."

"It's funny. Before I came here, I never imagined there was so much internal friction with the articles written about Higher Ends. You're lucky the press hasn't picked up on it," she says, and I can't tell if she's teasing.

"We're mature enough to keep our shit-flinging private."

"Smart." She nods, tucking a lock of that dark hair behind her ear. "I actually had something I wanted to ask you, though..."

I stare at her, noting the way she *still* won't meet my gaze.

"Spit it out. I won't bite," I say, more dryly than intended.

"I just wanted to know if it was okay if I head out a little early today? Once I get my work done, I mean. Arlo has a karate lesson tonight and I can't be late."

"For sure," I say, wondering why she even needs to ask permission. Unless one of the staff—who seem to adore her —were to tell someone, I'd never know. "Your hours aren't as important as the deadlines. I've told you before. As long as you wrap up your work and sign everything off for our overnight guy, you can leave when you'd like."

"It won't be a regular thing," she assures me. "Just tonight."

"Was I complaining?" I stand reluctantly, hating that I wonder even more about her life. Why does she feel so small that she has to beg for time off just to be with her son? "Do you feel like you're handling the workload?"

"What do you mean?"

"Am I laying it on too thick?" Like the Minnesota project, which is outside her duties here. "I understand you need a life outside this place, Salem. You're a mom."

"Thanks. That's very considerate." She frowns, her brows knitting together.

Her surprise irritates me.

"I never like to overwork my employees. Like I've said before, that's for executives only."

"I'm not overworked, Patton." She turns back to her screen now. "As a matter of fact, I like it. And if I help contribute to your expansion, that's a great thing for my résumé."

For when she leaves.

Which is inevitable, sooner or later, because this job and a glorified mentorship isn't meant to be a long-term forever career. I'm sure she has dreams beyond the company, whether that's leveraging this experience for a new job or another business venture.

"Of course," I growl.

Understandable. All of it.

I just don't get why there's this anxious gnawing in my chest at the thought of her walking out of my life a second time, like a stranger in the night.

Goddamn, that isn't my place.

I shouldn't want to leave a permanent mark on her life.

Especially when her moving on is clearly what's best, the *only* thing that should happen in any sane world.

"Get out of here at a decent hour," I tell her.

When I turn around in the doorway and look back, she's barely nodding, already back to crushing her improvements like I was never here at all.

XI: LOSING STREAK (SALEM)

I get Arlo to his martial arts lesson just in time with a check in my hand for the instructor.

Another payment made.

Another activity he won't have to quit because I can't pay the tab.

Another round of messages from Kayla—*flipping Kayla* —ignored.

Patton doesn't need to find out I was only hired so I can be an unwilling matchmaker for my spoiled frenemy.

The heavy clouds hanging in the sky when I left the office have opened up. Thick white flakes stream down on the city, coating it in fresh snow.

I have to be careful driving. The plows are infamously bad at handling snap snowstorms with this sort of heavy, wet mush.

Any other day, I might be happy that it's my only problem.

Arlo loves the snow so much, just seeing it seems to make him calmer.

And my happiness comes from seeing his joy in the little things, enjoying how the world unfolds with a child's eyes.

I can handle a little cold and a couple achy feet tonight for his sake. There's no denying it's beautiful, too, even if it makes the roads dicey.

By the time his class finishes and we're walking across the parking lot, into the chaotic winter night, everything glitters with white fluff.

"Mommy!" He sprints across the slick parking lot ahead of me, his face still flushed from the junior karate moves. "Look, it's snowing."

He tries to catch a few puffy flakes on his tongue.

"And you need to tuck both arms back in your coat," I say with an affectionate sigh. "Come here, let me help you." I twist him around and push his arms back through the arm holes. "Now let's get you in the car before you catch a cold."

"Wait, wait! Mommy, you've gotta see this." He strikes a combat pose, holding one little fist up parallel with his shoulder and the other by his waist.

He looks so fierce I almost laugh.

"I saw it. I watched your whole class, sweetie, but very cool. Keep practicing. Your teacher will like that. Now, Mommy's getting cold, so can we practice more at home?"

"It's snowing!" he yells excitedly.

"And my fingers are falling off. I need new gloves." All of me is frozen, really. I've barely been outside for a minute and I can feel the wind snaking under my coat. "You can practice all you want once we get home, okay?"

"Promise you'll watch me?"

"Do pinkies ever lie?"

I bend down, hooking my cold little finger into his.

He laughs, shaking his head.

Then I herd him into the car without protest.

The thick snow feels like it's already an inch deep on the

sidewalk, and the melting slush under my shoes makes my feet number.

My fingers are a little clumsy as I strap Arlo into his kiddie seat.

"Can we go sledding again?" he asks.

"Maybe this weekend if it lasts. But don't count on it; we're getting to the point where this stuff turns to slush overnight."

"I wanna go now."

"Now? Oh, no. It's dark and I need to get you fed."

"That makes it more fun!"

More terrifying, he means.

"Arlo, no. We aren't going sledding at night in this mess. The roads could turn into solid ice if it drops a few more degrees," I say, voicing my biggest fear out loud.

"We can sled home on ice."

His innocence makes me smile.

"Maybe you can. I can't, big guy." I give a strap going over his shoulder one more tug. He folds his arms, but I just shut the door, ignoring his puppy dog eyes.

My breath smokes as I walk awkwardly to the driver's door.

Sure enough, there's a growing layer of snow on the car like icing, half melting as it lands on the warmer metal and trying to refreeze. I stop and scratch the ice off my side mirrors.

It's nights like this that make every Midwesterner wonder why they don't live in Florida.

This is too cold.

Bullshit cold.

The kind of breathy cold that spits across the city, frosting every living thing until you wonder if it will ever let up before trees buckle and power lines snap.

When I was little, I thought an ice dragon came down

blowing ice crystals, rather than fire. My mother used to laugh at how dumb it sounded, too practical to entertain childhood fantasies for a split second.

Now, I know better, but there's still the same sense of weird dread I used to get—especially when I look at the car's temperature and it says thirty degrees.

Right on the nose.

Just a degree or two away from unpredictable ice that will send this car skittering off the road if I'm not careful.

I start the engine and let the heater run, making sure the windshield fully defrosts before we start moving.

"It's like being in a spaceship tonight," Arlo says, imitating spaceship sounds that are way too fancy for this old car. "The snow looks like stars."

When I was young, I also used to pretend the swirling snowflakes illuminated in the headlights were some sort of time warp, too. But that was before I was the driver.

I hate driving in this crap.

At least the roads are pretty deserted, thanks to the weather. There aren't many cars out.

I ease us onto the next street, feeling the tires churn through accumulated mush.

Shit, don't give up on me now.

"Mommy," Arlo says quietly, sensing the tension. "What's for dinner?"

His favorite question, and the worst when I'm praying for the car.

"I don't know yet, honey. Please let me focus." I glance in the mirror and ease my foot on the gas.

I'm not a bad driver.

Not an amazing one, no, but not terrible. I have a lifetime of experience with how Kansas City streets get with spotty services and temperatures that can change on a fly.

But the first time I feel our wheels sliding with zero help from the brakes, I'm worried.

No, don't touch the brakes. Easy, easy!

"Mr. Spike said I was awesome today," Arlo says, his head still back in his karate class.

I nod because I don't want to scare him.

The stoplights glow red through the pelting snow. I swear it's picking up, coming down in soft pellets you can hear as they hit the hood.

I tap the brakes carefully.

The wheels skid and my hands clutch on the steering wheel.

I say another prayer—or maybe it's a curse this time—before the tires stick to the pavement and we stop.

Holy hell.

My heart pounds violently in my mouth, so hard I can taste it.

"Mommy?"

"Not now, sweetie. Hang on."

A big truck pulls up beside me, window down, puffs of smoke emanating from the cab. The guy glances at me with a cigarette dangling from his mouth and away again.

The light changes.

I put my foot on the gas and cross the intersection uneventfully.

Just a few more miles to home, but I can't unclench my hands.

Come on, come on. You've got this.

The snow hasn't lightened up at all, though. I'm pretty sure the temperature keeps changing by the second, bouncing up and down depending on the wind. Visibility sucks and we're not going fast. Still, I don't dare go a mile faster.

"Mommy?" Arlo asks again. "I'm starving."

I risk a glance back at him.

"I'll figure it out, Arlo. You're just going to have to wait for—"

A horn blares.

I whip my head around, just in time to see a car rocketing toward us, its too bright headlights swinging across the road like blinding knives.

He's sliding, knifing across the other side of the road.

Honest to God, time stops.

My pulse hammers like there's a giant hand squeezing me as I watch the car moving, the way it's going *to hit us* unless a miracle happens fast.

With a paralyzed calm, I tap the brakes and try to steer clear from the inevitable slide, but it's hopeless.

Jesus, not Arlo.

Anything but Arlo!

The horn screams louder.

Closer.

Closer.

I can see the driver now in the dark, his eyes panicked as he looks at me, his mouth twisted open.

Maybe he's screaming.

Maybe *I* should be screaming because I can't do anything else.

But I never get the chance before time unpauses.

The world swirls with color and my heart feels like it's trapped in a vise.

Now, I really am screaming, clutching the wheel helplessly.

I know the tires have lost their grip and I'm praying and begging and it's all happening too flipping fast as we swerve toward the car on solid ice, just as out of control as he is.

My eyes pinch shut.

There's a sickening *crunch!*

The car clips our side mirror clean off, sending us spinning onto the sidewalk. I open my eyes in time to see a snow-plastered stop sign turn red again as we ram into it.

The hood crumples. The seat belt cuts my chest.

Something rips at my neck like rope burn.

Then silence.

For two painful seconds, I regain my bearings, remembering how to breathe.

The thick snow falling over everything dampens any sound but my own breathing.

"Arlo!" I scream his name so fast my voice rips. I fumble with the belt, unclasping it so I can turn around. "Arlo, are you okay? Are you hurt?"

He's sitting exactly where I left him, his face unnaturally pale, his eyes wide.

He's in one piece, I'm sure, but shocked out of his little skin.

"M-m-mommy?" he whimpers.

"Oh, honey. Sweetheart." I'm breathing like mad but I don't know how to stop. "Are you okay? Does it hurt anywhere?"

He shakes his head slowly. "N-no. Dunno."

God, I should get him to a hospital anyway. But with this accident, we're not moving, and an ambulance—I can't afford an ambulance, can I? Not unless the kid's missing an arm.

I have no idea how the Higher Ends insurance plan even works; I haven't had time to look. And the car's definitely out of commission. Something hisses miserably under the hood.

"Can you move your hands?" I ask gently. "Your head? Be careful."

He holds his hands out and looks at them before he rotates his wrists. Then he moves his head from side to side.

"I'm okay." He looks out of the window. "The car hit us."

"Yes. Yes, it did." We could have *died* if we were going just a little faster. "Stay where you are, big guy. I'm just going to check to see if our car's hurt."

Though if that grating, steady noise is anything to go by, it doesn't sound healthy.

Outside, it's as cold as I thought and the damage looks worse.

The stop sign is bent, and the front of the car looks buckled like crumpled paper. Black liquid drips against the greyish snow slurry under my car.

I'm at a loss for words or what to do.

I definitely regret canceling my roadside assistance last year to save a few bucks.

Snow lands on my neck and melts, mingling with sweat, cold and unsettling.

Adrenaline vibrates in my fingers, insistent and screaming.

Do something. Move.

Oh, I know what I'd like to do.

I want to scream and cry and sleep. The seat belt burn on my neck stings.

I have crappy car insurance, of course, but I do have it. I just don't think it'll save me from disaster.

If the car isn't totaled, it's going to cost a fortune to fix. Buying another used car, that's more expensive.

First thing's first, though.

Climbing back in the car, I bask in the warmth for a second as I search for the nearest towing company and call.

The receptionist is polite and sympathetic, but there's been a slew of accidents tonight. They can't get to me for at least an hour and advise me to call 9-1-1 if it's a true emergency.

The next place tells me it'll be an hour and a half minimum.

The third place, way less polite, says it'll be well past midnight.

"Mommy?" Arlo asks cautiously as I rest my forehead on the steering wheel. "Can't we go home? I'm cold. Is the car broke?"

"The car's a little broke, honey, yeah."

"I'm still hungry, too."

Oh my God.

Don't cry. You're a strong woman.

You're alive and well and so is your son. Don't scare him.

"I know," I say roughly, swallowing the rock in my throat.

We need to get home before it gets much later, but that ship has sailed. It's already dark and freezing. Neither of us came prepared for weather like this, and I'm afraid if I grab the spare blanket from the trunk, we'll lose what little heat the car has left.

But it is cooling off in here way too fast.

We can't sit here for hours hoping help shows up.

I'm going to be sick.

Kayla *could* help us in a pinch, if she's sober tonight. Even if she's not, all she'd have to do is snap her fingers and someone would send a tow truck over, probably faster considering who her daddy is.

Landing me in moral debt for life.

But I never bothered replying to her latest message earlier, hounding me about when she can drop by for an intro to the magnificent Patton Rory.

It's the worst time for jealousy, but my brain doesn't care.

I hate her dating life.

Almost as much as I hate that I'm still in debt to her forever over this damn job.

Wait. This job.

Higher Ends has a commercial snow removal crew for clearing out their properties, doesn't it?

My stomach knots.

I hate asking anyone for special treatment, buuuut...

Surely, I'm allowed to use one company perk. And it wouldn't land me in a vicious cycle of obligation like asking Kayla would. I'm not sure she knows what friendship means if it isn't transactional.

I grab my phone and start typing.

Hey, it's Salem. We had an accident. We're a little stuck in the storm and the tow places are buried in work tonight. Any chance you could hook a girl up with one of the company guys? Just to dig us out and get a ride.

Sighing, I hit send on Patton's contact.

"We'll be fine," I tell Arlo cheerfully. "We'll be home soon."

"Good! I'm freezing. Brrrrrr!"

I don't dare switch on the engine again when something's leaking oil, so I just shrug off my coat and pass it back to him. "Keep that over your legs, Arlo. You'll be warmer."

While he babbles about the mysteries of airflow like only a child can, I hear another car squealing down the street, struggling with the ice.

Oh, what a night.

Then my phone lights up with an incoming call.

Patton.

No surprise, he probably wants more details.

"What do you mean you're stuck?" he growls, the second I answer, not even waiting for me to say hi. "What happened? Are you okay? Is Arlo with you?"

"We're... we're fine, yeah. It was a fender bender thing. Just knocked us off the street into a stop sign." It also scared the living crap out of me, but there are some things you don't say to your antihero boss. "We just need a ride home while I sort out a tow. We're kinda stranded."

"Where are you?" He's so gruff it sends a chill down my spine that has nothing to do with the cold.

I check my phone for the nearest point on the maps and rattle off a couple street names, an intersection with the stop sign we hit.

"Stay where you are. Keep inside the car if it's safe. It's fucking nasty out there. I'll be there soon."

"Wait, what? I just wanted one of the snow removal places. You don't have to—"

"Salem, I'm coming. Give me ten or fifteen." There's an edge in his voice I can't argue with.

Before I put up a fight or even think to thank him through the giddy tears blinding me, he ends the call, leaving me staring at my lap.

"Was that Mr. Rory?" Arlo asks excitedly.

I think we've moved on from Grumpybutt. I don't know if that's a relief or a pity. I just know there's a lead weight in my gut.

"That's him. He's coming to help us out tonight." My voice quivers a little.

I'm feeling things I don't even know how to describe.

"I knew it!" Arlo says it with a five-year-old smugness that gives me a shaky smile. "He knows so much about superheroes because he *is* one."

Kid logic.

He's also your father. But I keep that wild fact to myself.

I just try to calm my nerves and settle so I'm not a weepy, flustered mess by the time he gets here.

With Arlo still chattering away about debating comic book story arcs with Patton, I wrap my arms around my shoulders and try to stay warm.

* * *

IT TAKES PATTON TWENTY LONG, agonizing minutes to arrive.

I keep one eye on my phone for the time, fending off

Arlo's endless hangry questions. Eventually, a familiar black SUV pulls up alongside us.

Patton swings out, dressed in a thick winter coat and jeans. *Jeans.*

I must have disturbed him from unwinding at home. It's a relief to know he doesn't sleep in a suit, hardass that he is.

"You're a lifesaver," I say as I get out of the car. Outside, it's even colder than I remember, and I try to keep my teeth from chattering. "We really appreciate you coming out in this mess."

He sucks in a breath as he sees the damage to the front of my car.

"That's an ugly scrape. I called a guy I know to see if he can speed up a tow." He looks me up and down. "And where the hell is your coat?"

"The kiddo has it. And thanks, you didn't have to work any miracles..." My cheeks are on fire.

Rather than meet his gaze and see the concern flashing in his eyes, I work on getting Arlo out of the car.

He's wrapped up in my purple coat, absurdly large on him, now trailing halfway behind him in the snow.

"Mr. Rory!" Arlo says with genuine delight the minute they lock eyes. "I knew you'd come with the cool car."

Patton sends me a quick glance before switching his attention back to Arlo. I think my little boy keeps trying to find hidden James Bond guns and booby traps that pop out of secret compartments since he's convinced my boss has superpowers.

"Let me help you up to the escape pod, little man," Patton tells him.

"Wait, he needs his seat," I say, wrestling it out of the back seat and wishing it didn't look so beat up next to Mr. Everything New.

I get the seat in the vehicle while Arlo dances around in

the snow, seemingly oblivious to the temperature. Now that Patton's here, Arlo's chattering a mile a minute, full of stories about the snow and karate and the big crash and what he hopes to have for dinner.

At least someone's feeling better.

"Come on," I say to Arlo. "Let's get you in here." I brush off the snow and help him up, strapping him in securely. He squirms, making it difficult, and it's hard not to snap at him to sit still.

He's just a kid.

He doesn't know how stressful this situation truly is.

How close we both came to being hurt.

And without my knight in shining jeans charging to our rescue… tonight would easily be a bigger mishap than it is.

"There, all set," I tell Patton, shutting the door and brushing my slick hair back from my face. "I'm so sorry for putting you out again. The tow trucks were just tied up tonight and—"

"Jesus, Salem." He cuts me off, sounding irritated and worried. "You're freezing your face off and the kid needs a meal. Don't apologize."

"I'm fi—"

"You're not. Hold still."

I don't have time to finish lying before he slings his coat around my shoulders.

I'm instantly silenced.

It's insanely warm. I snuggle in before I can help myself.

There's also no escaping his scent, this woodsy aftershave that's so heavenly I'm able to forget the hell we're in for a second.

Who knew this would be the night I'd want to *breathe* Patton Rory? And right now, he smells like manly salvation.

When I look up, he's eyeing me curiously.

Maybe I should stop looking like I'm in a fabric softener commercial.

"What happened?" he asks.

"The roads were so slick. Another vehicle lost control and almost clipped us. I tried to swerve out of the way, but the ice was crazy, and I just—" I stop and shake my head. My hands are trembling. Shock, I guess, from how close we came to a bigger disaster. "We veered over and hit the sign instead."

"Are you okay? Both of you?" He gives me a sharp look.

"I'm sure we don't need an ER visit. It was a pretty slow impact, just scarier than it looked. We're good."

"You crashed. Your ride's banged up. You don't have to keep telling me you're fine." His anger feels sharp, lashing my feelings raw until they start climbing up my throat again.

I turn away so he doesn't see the way my mouth turns down. My nose stings.

Deep breaths, deep breaths.

Get a grip. You're overreacting. It was a minor accident, and he's worried about you. Arlo's fine. You're fine. Everything's fine.

Patton looks at the hood and sees the oil dripping on the snow, frowning the entire time.

"When the tow truck shows up, I'll have it sent to the shop I use. They do excellent body work. If it's salvageable, it shouldn't take more than a couple days."

"Honestly, dude. This is— You're going to have to tell me how much it costs. I'll call my insurance tomorrow."

I want to scream that he doesn't have to do this, but I know it'll slide off him like the melting snow. There's no changing this man's mind once it's made up.

"Screw the insurance. Don't worry about the damn cost until you're warm, fed, and you've gotten some sleep," he growls.

For a second, I squint, wondering who I'm seeing.

Thick snow dusts his hair and shoulders, and the wintry

shadows all around us bring out the blue witchfire of his eyes. It's a strange sight, seeing him in jeans that are so stark against the winter anti-wonderland.

This is wrong on every level. But I don't know how to begin to understand it.

Arlo bangs on the window, pressing his nose against the glass.

I jump.

"Listen to the boy, he wants to get moving," Patton says. "Your car will be fine, I promise. I work with good people."

What else can I do tonight but trust him?

So I happily throw myself into the warm leather seat of his car as he puts the heater on full blast. I hold my hands to the vent until the tips of my fingers burn delightfully.

"The weather forecast didn't call for anything this ugly," I say lamely, the guilt surging up from my stomach.

Fair warning or not, I should have been better prepared.

I should have reacted faster instead of panicking.

I should have taken us on the highway instead of these little side streets where holes in city services become pits that will swallow you up.

Arlo deserved better from me tonight, too, and I'm sad that I'm failing as a mom.

My nails dig into my palm.

"I don't think anyone saw this coming. Where to next?" Patton says. He sends me a quick glance.

"Back to my place would be great. Arlo's hungry and it's getting pretty late." I wince as I remember our other problem. Food.

"I want pizza for dinner!" Arlo pipes up from the back.

For once, I can't argue.

There's a pie shop just a couple blocks away where they can walk the delivery over to our place instead of risking their delivery cars. So yes, I'll order and we'll sit on the sofa and eat and for once I won't fuss about the cost.

"You can never go wrong with pizza. Choice of kings," Patton says firmly.

Arlo laughs. "Stay and eat pizza with us, Mr. Rory."

Patton side-eyes me, but I don't dare look at either of them. Instead, I stare dead ahead.

If I narrow my eyes enough, there's a chance I can bleed through into another dimension where my son *isn't* asking his unknown father to stay for dinner.

"Your mom's had a rough night, Arlo. Don't know if she wants company."

"Yeah, she does," Arlo announces with innocent confidence. "It's okay, isn't it, Mom?"

My lungs lock up for the hundredth time tonight.

This cannot be happening.

If I could snap my fingers and fall through the floor—to the center of the Earth, ideally—I would.

"It would be pretty terrible if I didn't say thank you," I say, well aware that Patton literally rescued us in time for a late dinner. "Patton, why don't you stick around for some pizza? If you don't have other plans, I mean…"

Those mundane words cut me from the inside out.

And he darts me a glance like he knows I'm mere seconds from having a nervous breakdown.

"You're sure you're up for that? Don't invite me on the boy's account."

"No, no, you didn't have to do any of this, but you did. I'm more than grateful." The words come out bitter and I bite my tongue. "I just mean I owe you one. Personally."

He navigates the icy roads with an expert hand and amazing tires that make the dicey conditions easy to manage.

"No special favors here. You might think it's a big deal,

but really it helps me," he explains. "The Cardinal's too damn new to lose a manager, even for a day. We can't afford any crappy reviews and we need you there for your shift."

"Business," I repeat. "Oh, yes. Of course."

It would be so easy to believe him, just going by what he says.

Except when he looks at me, his eyes say something else.

They shine like blue beacons, like I *matter*, and that scares me more than anything else that's happened tonight.

I can't start mattering to this man.

Not with our past.

Not with his son sitting in the back seat while nobody knows the truth but me. And if he has a deeper motive behind rushing to our rescue somewhere behind those unfathomable blue eyes—

I shut down.

I flipping have to or this won't end well.

Luckily, it doesn't take long to get to my place.

When he switches off the engine, the only sound is the soft patter of the snow in that familiar deep wintry silence.

"Thanks again," I say. "What sort of pizza do you like? I can order two if anchovies are your thing…"

Patton swallows like he's reconsidering this. Honestly, I wouldn't blame him one bit. We're on knife's edge, and if we're not careful, we'll destroy the delicate balance we've established that kinda-sorta works.

"Please, Mr. Rory," Arlo whines.

Patton smiles and glances at me again.

"I'm in the mood for a margherita style with extra garlic, if they have it," he says. "But I'll get the pizzas. My treat for you guys on a crappy night."

Oof.

I can't bring myself to protest.

God, now I'm letting this man treat us. I'm letting him in

my home, letting him look into my life, and somehow, I need to find a way to be okay with that.

Okay enough to share some simple pizza without freaking out.

"Ready when you are, boss." Smiling unevenly, I help Arlo out of his seat, and we hurry to the building.

Patton leads the way. I can tell by the way he walks that he's checking to make sure our path is salted and safe. I'm glad the maintenance folks are good about that here.

The cold nips at my face and seizes my lungs. I try to tell myself it's the only reason I'm struggling to breathe as we stumble over the last snowy patch inside.

All three of us.

Here we go, primed for our next disaster.

It's just pizza, idiot, I tell myself.

But I know it's not.

It's an existential threat to my world.

Whatever else happens, we can't have any relationship that crosses professional wires when it will bring him too close to the truth about Arlo.

And if my moral compass ever stops spinning—if I *choose* to tell him about his son—it has to be on *my* terms. Not because I'm falling apart and dumping everything in one long, chaotic panic attack after a rotten night.

As we take the elevator to my floor, I wonder what I'm really getting myself into with this pizza party.

Just how much damage can my heart take when I bring Patton Rory home?

XII: PEPPERONI PLAY (PATTON)

*I*n hindsight, I might have overreacted.

The problem is I don't regret it.

The logical thing to do was exactly what she asked—arranging a tow to take her home and get her shit sorted.

That's what any self-respecting boss looking out for an employee would do in my position.

Me? I had to freak the hell out and go in guns blazing the instant I knew they were stuck in the storm. The edge in her voice on the phone—fuck, I've never moved so fast in my life.

Now, here I am, tucked away in her small, warm apartment while Arlo talks himself up as reigning karate champ of the world. The kid makes it sound like he was born with black belt in his blood.

Must be from his mother's side since he sure as hell didn't get it from his ghost of a dad.

Salem watches us, sitting across from me in an armchair with fabric tape holding one ripped seam together.

I can't quite read the expression in her eyes.

Something haunted, wistful, a wariness I probably deserve.

It's probably not often grown men visit her place this late, especially with the boy around.

Knowing our past, barging in like I did was probably a dumb move, and she must regret it every second. But I'll sort out whatever the hell this is later, when I'm not in their apartment.

The doorbell rings and Salem jumps like a startled cat.

"Stay there, guys. I'll get the pizza."

"I loooove pizza!" Arlo tells me, pumping his fist like he's revealing some great secret. "It's my favorite but Mommy doesn't let us have it very often."

I suspect he thinks this is a character flaw.

"Your mommy wants you to eat healthy so you can grow up to kick some butt. Just like your heroes," Salem says, returning with two large boxes in her hands.

The little pizza shop up the street isn't one of those fancy places with all locally sourced ingredients and more cheese than sauce. Really, it's one step above pure take-out comfort trash, but when she lays the boxes down on the table and opens the lid and the warm, greasy scent curls out, I know he was right.

Tonight's perfect for junk food.

There's something comforting about the smell, and I close my eyes as I inhale.

To think, if I hadn't answered her call, I'd be scrambling eggs and spinach with a steak on the side at home. My go-to after a long day when it's reasonably healthy and it doesn't take long to throw together.

"Wash your hands, Arlo," Salem commands as he rushes toward her. "And make sure you use soap."

"Yes, ma'am," I say.

She glances up with a tiny smile.

Shit, I could stare at that smile all day. I'm glad she's getting over the storm rattling her.

Stop looking at her like that, a voice growls in the back of my mind.

"I'll plate us up," is all she says.

After we're all washed up and ready—and she inspects Arlo's hands to make sure he really *did* use soap—she hands out plates with one big slice for each of us.

We devour the grub eagerly in companionable silence.

Fuck me, this pizza is good.

It's just basic pepperoni, aside from my margherita pizza, but it's the perfect warmth, grease, cheese, and spice we need on a shit night.

"I don't care what anybody says. Best pizza in Kansas City," Salem tells me with an amused glance at Arlo, who's eating himself into a food coma. "I know a certain someone agrees."

"Who?" Arlo asks, chewing obliviously.

"He's not wrong. This is incredible."

"I'll let the owner know you think it's good. Strong endorsement, coming from a Rory."

"You know him?"

"His son lives in the building, just a few units down," she says with a shrug. "He's taken a liking to Arlo—or Arlo's taken a liking to him. I don't know how it happened, but they're friends now. He always stops to talk when he sees us in the hall."

I hate that I can see that. Arlo's a good kid, now that I've gotten to know him better. With his mom handling him alone, it's easy to appreciate how he's turning out.

What's harder is feeling jealousy flaring in my blood.

How old is this son, anyway?

How well do they really know each other?

The thought of some pizza slinging doofus on her home turf climbing through her window for a quickie after Arlo's asleep robs a little enjoyment from the cheesy goodness.

I swallow roughly.

I know, I'm being ridiculous.

But I can't get mad at Arlo for making friends with a guy who isn't true competition for a woman I'm not fucking after.

All around the apartment, you can see how simple his life is.

His small toy pile in the corner. A little desk with pencils and pens and crayons piled on top, mostly bundled together with rubber bands. A few photos of Salem and Arlo on the wall.

There's one propped up on the windowsill, showing him as a baby. A worn-looking Salem holds him with a tired smile on her face.

In that photo, she looks a lot like the girl I remembered.

Not as glamorous, maybe, but with the same reddish tint to her hair and the same youthful glow to her face.

"Sorry it's a mess here. If I knew you were coming, I would've straightened up," she says, bringing my attention back to her.

"Don't worry about it."

Even if I hadn't seen her photos, I'd remember better times, when we were younger and more carefree.

The way her hair, still half-damp from the snow, falls around her face probably has a lot to do with that now, making her glow. Plus, the way her cheeks look deliciously red.

Damn, the last time I saw her this flushed was—

No.

The intrusive thoughts about sexy times that can never happen again must end.

I can't believe I ever gave Dexter so much shit about his fake-engagement-turned-real when I'm this goddamn obsessed with a hookup from ancient history.

"Your place is charming," I say, remembering my manners before the silence stretches too long. "Homely and real."

"Um, thanks." Her eyebrow quirks. "You can spare me the compliments. I've been to your mom's house. That place is a palace compared to here."

"Yeah. Hasn't changed a beat since I was Arlo's age. I don't like it."

"Your mom's house? Come on."

"I'm not saying it isn't cozy. Just that the big Victorian mansion isn't my style with its size and suffocating history. If you ever visit my place, you'll see."

For fuck's sake, man. Stop encouraging more *visits from her outside the office.*

"Oh, I have a pretty good idea what you like." Her mouth presses together like she's suppressing a smile. "Minimalist. Modern. Black and white and grey."

"Is that so awful?"

"No, but this apartment isn't any of those. More like a cluttered box from the Great Depression."

"It's homey." I'm adamant.

"Yeah, okay. But thanks for not using more choice words where little ears can hear." She snorts.

I nod at Arlo's pictures and the photos on the wall. Everything is worn, just enough that it feels like they've lived here for a long time, settling into the very bones of the apartment.

"My mother's place isn't particularly homey anymore. I might've felt that way as a kid, once, but now that it's just her living there? The place is cavernous. Too extravagant and too huge for just her, even if she likes hosting her parties. We keep wondering when she'll downsize, but it's hard to get past the memories."

"Let her have them, Patton, if she can afford it. Your mom's a lovely person."

"Never said she wasn't."

Salem acknowledges that with a tilt of her head and glances at Arlo. He's basically nodding off over his plate after polishing off a second slice.

"It's been a long day," she says quietly. "Let me put him to bed. You can make yourself at home."

I stretch out on the sofa and help myself to more pizza. All the stress with the snow summoned a monster appetite. The rest of the pepperoni can stay—easy leftovers that will make the kid happy and hopefully save Salem from having to cook tomorrow.

Arlo's head lolls on Salem's shoulder as she carries him to bed. The tenderness in the gesture makes my stomach pinch.

It's sad as hell that she has to deal with this little guy on her own when clearly someone helped make him. My eyes flick back to her photos again, studying them closely.

There's no sign of a man in any, and oddly, no pictures with other relatives either. Where the hell are her parents?

It's a shit feeling, knowing the kid might not have a father or a grandfather at all. I can't wrap my head around it.

Having lost my old man, though, I know what it's like to be missing a dad.

Also, Salem deserves help.

After the day she's had, she shouldn't have to handle Arlo by herself, bouncing from one crisis to the next with dinner in between.

I have just enough time to polish off the remainder of my food before she reappears and joins me on the sofa, leaning back just like I am. Her thigh hovers about an inch from mine.

Don't notice her, you asshole.

Keep your eyes glued to the wall.

Does it matter? It's not like I'm going to do anything about it, never mind the raging heat in my veins urging me to reach out and touch her.

"Thank you," she says again with a sigh. "I know you keep saying it's cool and it's all for business, but you saved my skin tonight. If there's any way I can repay you, Patton, please speak up."

"I don't need repaying. I'm not a damn machine."

She raises her head as she looks at me, her hazel eyes glinting with gold curiosity.

"You say that now, but you came all the way out here, and you..." She raises her hand helplessly as her voice cracks. "I don't know. It just feels like a lot."

"I'm happy to help. Sincerely. Without sounding like an ass-kisser, I appreciate what you do for Higher Ends. The mentorship isn't much of a bonus, all things considered."

She snickers and mutters an apology.

"Sorry. But that sounds like you're being a *huge* kiss-ass."

"Well, I mean it." Somebody stop me before I say something else I regret.

But hell, she's here with her kid and a business she has no stake in. I don't know how she handles it.

"I suppose it's good to finally get a real compliment out of you," she says.

I swivel to face her. "Do I make you feel unappreciated?"

She hesitates.

"...it's more that you could just be nicer," she says slowly, but it's more of a yes than I want to admit. "I'm not saying you're the bad guy. I've messed up a few times and made everything harder than it needs to be."

"Everyone fucks up. That's life." I wave a hand. "Even me, if you can believe it."

Her eyes crinkle as she smiles.

Such a stark contrast from the way I first found her tonight, when her eyes were wide and dark with fear. Even after she was safe, she had that devastated look.

Now, in the safety of her own home, she's relaxed, and it's

smoothed away the tightness around her face that I've often seen around the office.

"You?" she teases. "I can't believe it."

"I know it's a lot to take in, but I'm far from perfect." I smile back at her. She blinks, like she wasn't expecting it.

Maybe we've both been too busy, shutting ourselves down, spinning this delicate dance where we're too fucking scared of offending each other to let us be real.

After tonight, I'm done playing.

"It must be a lot," I say carefully, looking around the room again. "Balancing all this and Arlo and your job at the same time."

Silence swarms us again.

She slowly loses her smile, stiffening and sitting up like I'm passing some sort of judgment.

"I didn't mean to pry. Just telling you what I see," I venture.

"It can be hard sometimes, I guess. But it's worth it."

She doesn't deny that she's doing this alone like I thought.

"I didn't mean to make you dwell on it. Or imply you're not doing a great job."

Her hands relax slightly.

"He's a lot sometimes. I love him to death, don't get me wrong."

"Isn't that every kid? If you hear my mom talk, we were little nightmares growing up. Ironically, Archer was the worst. First kid, you know. Big brother got real pissed when the rest of us were born and he was no longer the golden boy."

She gives me a bittersweet smile.

"I think Arlo would be the same way. Not that it'll ever happen." She tucks a stray lock of hair back behind her ear.

"Why's that? You're young. Plenty of time for more babies."

191

The hectic flush on her cheeks fades now, but that doesn't stop my imagination or my curiosity.

Usually, it's a blessing, helping me visualize fresh ideas. Now, though, it's a curse.

I'm too damn close to slipping up in ways I know I shouldn't. Not just poking my nose into her life where it doesn't belong, but letting my hands wander.

For the last time, get your brain out of your dick.

"I suppose I'd need a guy for that, and that means dating. Yuck." Her face screws up and she makes a disgusted sound.

I chuckle. That's one feeling we share, even if my reasons are very different from hers for keeping my bachelor card.

"Yeah, that's the hard part. A bigger family lightens the workload, though," I tell her. "Mom had Dad until I was small. He's gone now, but when we were kids, he'd take us out so we didn't destroy more of Mom's antique furniture."

"That must have been nice."

"I think Mom would've gone mad a long time ago if he hadn't." I'm not being even remotely subtle now, but fuck. I need to know for sure if this is it, all she has in her life. "Does anybody ever help you with Arlo when it's too much? Your parents?"

She looks down.

"I mean, there's Mrs. Gabbard, the babysitter from downstairs. She's been a huge help and she's a sweet lady. My parents are out of state." Salem folds her arms defensively. "And now that you got us the company sitter, I have a little more flexibility there."

That doesn't tell me shit.

Where *is* this girl's family? And the other half of the kid's DNA?

I guess that's the only answer my nosy ass gets tonight.

Safe to say, there's no man in the picture, at least.

It shouldn't feel like such a weird relief. I still can't believe some mystery meat would just knock her up and scram.

She deserves better, and so does Arlo.

And maybe it's the atmosphere speaking or maybe it's just my little head taking control, but I can't help feeling like life has dealt her a shitty, lonely hand.

"Do you want some wine?" she asks. "I have half a bottle open and it needs drinking. Nothing fancy, but it's not bargain stuff either."

It would be a mistake to say yes.

"Sounds great," I tell her.

She pours us both a glass in no time. When she sits back down, she's even closer to me on the sofa. Almost like she's trying to make holding on to what little self-control I have left a little harder.

"Sorry it's not the expensive stuff I'm sure you like," she says as I take a sip. "I probably shouldn't have bothered—I don't know what I'm doing."

"Hey. *Hey,* stop." I hold the glass up in a toast. "I'm not the snob you think I am. Wine's wine, it'll get you drunk just the same. I'm more of a cocktail man, but tonight, I don't give a damn. Drinking with you again has a certain charm. It takes me back to when we were younger and a whole lot luckier."

I can't help implying what else happened that night.

There are a lot of other things I could say about the memories my mind replays like a bad porno flick from the last time we drank together. But I'm pretty sure if I did, she'd throw that glass at me.

And I wouldn't blame her one bit.

"Was it really six years ago? Where does the time go?" I ask instead, as close as I can get without telling her how just being this close douses me in flames.

"Maybe for you." She swirls her glass, staring at the

burgundy liquid. "For me, it's been an eternity. Like another life. A lot's happened."

"Arlo?"

She looks up quickly and nods, sobered.

"You don't seem that different from the night at the casino. Older and wiser, maybe, but just the same in all the important ways."

A heavy second ticks by before she relaxes again. I think she's decided to sit here and dive into everything we thought we'd left behind.

"We were drunk, Patton. Basically strangers then," she tells me. "And you don't like me much now that I'm buried in baggage. I'm definitely not the same girl you met then, but it's kind of you to say it."

"Not true, Lady Bug."

Fuck. The name falls out of me before I can stop it.

She stares at me, horrified.

"...could you not call me that?" Her voice sharpens and she swallows hard, looking away like I'll turn her to stone. "I mean, do I really look like I turned out so lucky?"

I don't answer.

My muscle memory recalls bright lights and laughs and velvet on my dick. To me, she was Lady Luck made flesh once upon a fucked-up time, and the losing streak she's had doesn't change it.

All I can do now is hope she doesn't look down and see how hard I am, assuming she doesn't claw my face off first for stirring up bitter memories.

She looks down and her face heats, too soon to blame it on the wine.

When she looks at me intently, does she see how badly I want to kiss her?

Her tongue flashes out, moistening her lips.

Goddamn.

I've never wanted any woman this much in my life. It's absurd that it's *her*, the girl I've already had who's become as off-limits as buried treasure.

Normally, my relations are brief outside the bedroom. I bring few women back for seconds or thirds, much less fall into relationships that mean a damn.

But somewhere along the way, destiny stopped caring.

Years later, here I am, still wanting the same woman with a hunger so intense it strangles me.

"I'm sorry fate hasn't been kind to you. I can't tell you what you are and what you're not, but I can tell you this, Salem." I pause until I'm holding her gaze. "I never regretted meeting you. Not once. Not even when you showed up at The Cardinal to give me hell. I never wished it didn't happen."

"You didn't?" Heavy disbelief echoes in her voice.

"It was a good night. All of it. The gambling, the conver-sation." *And the hottest gravity defying sex of my life.* I don't dare say that, though. "Look, I'm not as stupid as I look. I know it's made things complicated now, but hell—I was young and stupid. You were everything I needed that night. After you, I didn't hook up that much, and when I did... well, fuck. It's like I was always chasing the same high I only found *once.*"

Her face blanks.

Yes, I'm spilling my spaghetti in messy piles now.

Baring my heart and the unspoken truths I haven't admitted even to myself. Because I *don't* regret the hottest time I've ever spent with a woman, just like I don't regret being here now on this disaster of a winter night with the dim lights that makes her eyes look dark and her lips delectable.

I want to be a stupid man tonight.

I want to kiss her into oblivion.

I want to own her.

I want her ruined until she's *mine again.*

And hell, kissing won't scratch this itch that's gone soul deep.

Not when I want to taste every part of her and press her into this worn sofa.

Not when I want her teeth in my hand, biting down as one ruthless thrust after the next rips an orgasm out of her.

Not when I could make her scream my name this time, when she never knew it before.

"Things were simpler back then, I'll give you that," she whispers, setting her glass down. I notice she's finished already. I didn't even notice her drinking much and I wonder if she just threw it back in a single gulp. "I miss it sometimes. Not that I'd trade Arlo for the past."

"Same," I confess. "Even six years ago, things were different for me. Less complicated."

"But you were always rich. You were successful, or close enough, right?" Her shoulders tense as she shifts to face me, tucking her legs under her. "Do you know how many times I *dreamed* about having your kind of success? Everything you've achieved, it's amazing."

"It came with a lot of sacrifice. There hasn't been much of a life outside work, but it's the life we chose, me and my brothers. My old man could've done something like this if he'd wanted, but he chose family instead. There are times when I wonder who was smarter."

Oddly, his death gave us the kick in the ass we needed to get serious about living and carving out our piece of the Kansas City pie that has the Rory name on it. Not just a piece of a long ancestral shadow we think we're entitled to by events almost a century ago.

"You talk like it's too late for you. You can throttle back on work, can't you?"

Salem's brows pull together as she searches my face.

I shrug, finishing my wine.

"Don't you want a family of your own someday?"

What a loaded fucking question.

"Someday," I repeat. I don't think it's a lie. "Up until recently, it was hard to imagine. Seeing Dexter and his wife so happy, and Archer with my nephew growing up—yeah, I wouldn't mind that, I think." Although the future feels murky as hell right now. I can't see what it might hold for me, or even if I want it to hold anything at all. "This can't be my life forever. For now, it's everything."

"You're smart for pacing yourself. That's where I go wrong." She unhooks a lock of hair from behind her ear and runs her fingers through it.

Yes, it's still my undoing.

Before any reasonable part of my brain tells me no, I'm moving, reaching out and tilting her face to mine.

I don't ask. Not with words. Not when her eyes widen, shining into mine.

Not even when she gasps.

I kiss her like a drowning man who needs to taste her just to keep breathing.

And she kisses me back, pushing a startled moan into my mouth that I drink greedily.

After a hot second, when my kiss is still a question, her answer sends fire through my blood.

Here, there's only Salem Hopper, with her honey-sweet mouth and her nimble little hands that slide through my hair, the curve of her hips and long legs made for sin.

Salem, with her tongue that meets mine with shared madness, fluttering with need.

Salem, who pulls me closer until our bodies tangle up in a memory and a moment that breaks time.

It's been years, but it's the same reckless wildfire.

She stokes the flames so good with every gasp, every touch from her wandering hands.

I grab her, haul her on my lap, and she settles there with a giggle.

Her lips curve under mine as she strokes my neck. Her fingers push under my sweater to find skin.

Fuck me, she feels divine.

I shift my hips and she wiggles across me, stealing a groan from my throat.

If there weren't so many layers between us, I'd already have her stripped bare.

I'd have my tongue on her clit.

I'd make her come for me like she did that night before we—

"Mommy?"

Fuck!

The panic is almost comical.

Salem leaps off me with an impressive agility and throws herself back on the sofa with a thump.

"Um, yes, big guy?" she asks, desperately finger combing her hair. The hair tie she used before is nowhere to be seen. Maybe I pulled it off and didn't notice.

Fuck, fuck, fuck.

"Can I have a glass of water?" Arlo asks from behind us, rubbing his eyes with one hand.

He's cuddling some oversized stuffed white penguin, chewing his thumb. He looks bleary and confused. I have no clue if he saw us.

Doesn't matter.

I should not have fucking crossed that line.

I shouldn't have complicated her life for a second time.

"I should go." My words trip over themselves. "Thanks for the pizza and the wine, Salem. Arlo, you take care."

She pauses in the kitchen and looks at me. Black pants,

grey sweater pulled over a pink blouse. She's a temptation and a curse, heaven-sent to make me sin.

"Sure," she says bluntly after a second. Her voice is torn, her lips too red.

You did that, idiot.

How will she ever face you again?

"See you at work," I tell her. Then I practically run from the apartment, slamming the door unintentionally hard on my way out. It's still snowing outside and my car is half-buried. The cold wind feels like a blade in my throat.

Still, I'd walk home through the bone-stripping night if I could turn back time one hour. If I could've hauled my ass up and left when she sent Arlo to bed.

I never should've let us wind up alone.

I failed the test like the gigantic dumbass I am.

"Clown," I mutter as I wipe the snow off the windshield and start the vehicle. "*Fuck you*, Patton Rory."

I'm sure she's saying the same thing right now a thousand different ways.

No wonder my brothers think I'm the hothead. The dumb one who never thinks anything through. The guy most likely to make bad decisions that blow us all up.

No fucking wonder.

Of all the mistakes I could've made, why did it have to be that trip down memory lane?

Why did I have to kiss Salem Hopper and make her life harder?

XIII: HEDGE YOUR BETS (SALEM)

*I*t's almost fitting.

I wake up to find my three alarms weren't set right for the morning, making me late for work.

Not only that, but because my phone did a system update in the middle of the night, it canceled all of my backup alarms.

I'm the reigning queen of bad luck.

My mom also used to tell me bad news comes in threes. I wonder if the same rule applies to the world's crappiest luck.

Today, with the way I'm sprinting around like a hen on fire and trying to get Arlo ready, that's strike one. I'll have to hope the other two only involve breaking a nail and winding up with an empty soap dispenser in the restroom.

"Mommy! We're gonna be late," Arlo calls as I run through the apartment in my robe, desperately trying to find clean underwear in the pile of laundry from a few days ago.

"I know!" I moderate my tone as I pick out clean clothes. "Go sit at the table, honey, and I'll get you a breakfast bar."

It's a grab-and-go breakfast day. Letting him eat unsupervised means he'll spill crumbs everywhere. I locate his school clothes and lay them out on the bed before getting dressed.

I'm going to be so late.

There won't be any coming back from this. And Patton—

Nope, we're not going there.

No point.

Before I crashed last night, I told myself I wouldn't think about it today.

As far as I'm concerned, the kiss from hell never happened.

Even if the thought of *not* thinking about it makes my stomach knot up about five different ways.

"Where are your shoes?" I ask Arlo as I grab my purse, simultaneously fumbling with my phone for an Uber. Maybe I'll have my car by the end of the day, if Patton's guys are really as good as he claimed.

Stop thinking about him.

"Mommy, I have a question."

I look up just to humor him.

"...why did you kiss Grumpybutt?"

Oh. My. God.

My blood freezes over.

"Honey, you can't call him that," I say absently as the question hits me full force.

I wince. A huge industrial brick sinks to the pit of my stomach.

Holy hell, where do I even start?

"Why'd you kiss Mr. Rory then?" Persistent little beast. I have to tell him *something*.

Anything but the truth.

"I didn't kiss anyone, big guy," I say, praying he'll believe me. "I bet you dreamed it. You were so sleepy last night, huh?"

"No! I saw you, Mommy. I got up for water." He frowns, one shoe in his hand.

Ugh, talk about bad choices—I can either gaslight my overly perceptive son or tell him I kissed my boss and I don't even know why.

"Arlo, last night was nuts. There are things I'm not sure whether I dreamed." My throat burns as I take the coward's way out, frantically ordering an Uber.

"But you—"

"Boy-o, let's get moving. We're going to be so late." I clap my hands. "Come on, shoes on. Or do you need help?"

Galvanized into action, he stops chattering, sits down, and slowly—*ouch, so slowly*—puts on his shoes. My phone pings me to say our ride is approaching.

I grab his little bag and miraculously, we leave the house before half past eight.

Hopefully, kindergarten won't mind that I'm late dropping him off. I don't think they will with half the city still digging out from the snowstorm.

Just like I hope no one else notices or cares that I'm late to The Cardinal. Surely, all the days I showed up early will count in my favor somewhere.

"Mrs. Gabbard will pick you up this afternoon since our car's still getting fixed." I give him a hurried kiss on the cheek. "Have a good day."

He waves and happily runs the short distance into the building, his bag bouncing on his back. I wave to a couple other moms, blissfully strolling along and clearly not late for work, before the driver takes off for The Cardinal.

To my relief, I make it in without incident.

Bekah gives me a wink as I hurry past, and I know my secret is safe with her. It's not that she doesn't like Patton— no one here dislikes him, I've come to realize—but staff look out for each other.

It's a nice atmosphere, really. One that I might appreciate a lot more if I hadn't climbed on my boss's lap and kissed him until my face hurt.

And not just a little bit.

A drunken peck or two, you can move past that without the world ending, but this—

This was infinitely more.

If I close my eyes, I can still feel the *way* he claimed my lips.

The rough brush of his stubble stinging my mouth, my skin, the thickness of his hair in my hands, the confidence of his touch.

Everything that hasn't changed over the years.

Everything, just like I remembered, and so much more, my body aching for him like a plant craves light.

Go ahead and laugh. I'm well aware this is the opposite of *not thinking about him*.

So much for that promise.

Work. I need to work, and most importantly, I can't be alone with these thoughts.

Sighing, I take a few seconds to touch up my makeup and ensure I don't look like I'm five seconds away from a mental breakdown. Then I invite Gwen, head of housekeeping, into the office for a check-in.

"You poor thing," she says as soon as she comes in, taking my hands and holding them tight. She's old enough to be my mom, and although I've only worked with her briefly, I'm pretty sure she thinks of herself as my office mom, even though I'm supposedly her boss.

"Patton told me what happened with the accident... No surprise, given the weather last night. You shouldn't have come in at all."

"Oh." Great. Patton told the *staff*? "I'm fine, honestly. It wasn't as bad as it sounds. I bet the auto shop will be done with my car today."

"Honey, you look pale."

"I'm fine," I snap again. "A little thing like that can't keep me from a day's work. After all, that's why he helped me out."

Her brown eyes twinkle, but she just says, "You've got a better head than me. I'd be off for half the week if that happened. Oh my, the stress from the repair bill alone..."

"Can't blame you," I agree.

"We have pretty generous leave here, you know. And sick pay. There are a lot of benefits. But that's not why you came to see me, is it?"

It feels a little like I'm in a dream. Or is it a nightmare, hosted by one of the nicest women I've ever met?

Either way, the world doesn't quite feel real anymore as we settle into a conversation about logistics, improvements, and supplies for each floor.

Nothing does since locking lips with the man who scrambles my soul.

And when I meet with several other supervisors to get their feedback, I'm just as disembodied. Maybe Gwen's right and I really should have called in today.

When I finally get a moment to myself, I look at Arlo's Grumpybutt art gallery pinned on my walls.

For a split second, I almost break down in tears, fighting the urge to stuff my palm against my mouth and *scream.*

Yep, I'm losing it.

I hate this entire situation so much.

My hands move ahead of my brain, and I'm in the middle of ripping the drawings down to shove in my drawer when there's an obnoxiously fast knock on the half-open door.

Here comes *strike two,* right on time.

I know it's Kayla before I turn around and smell her wall of heavy perfume.

She has a certain way of making an entrance.

Most people just knock once, maybe twice, sometimes three times. Then they wait to be invited in.

Not her.

She knocks away like a woodpecker, like she's tapping out a song, right before she barges in and flings the door at the wall.

Probably because she's so used to being invited everywhere. She can't imagine a situation where she's not treated like royalty deigning to grace us mortals with her presence.

"Lemmykins!" She throws her arms around me in an exaggerated hug and plants a perfumed kiss on my cheek, almost knocking me off my chair. "So this is your work lair. Niiice."

"Hey, Kay," I manage.

"Huh. It's kinda small, though, isn't it?" She wrinkles her nose as she looks around, probably wondering how normal people consider an office a luxury at all, before she forgets all about it. "Anyway, is he here right now?"

He?

It takes me a second to realize who. I just blink at her innocently.

"*Patton Rory*. Duh. I know you couldn't tell me much last night with the big storm and all. God, my Thai order was so *late* in that storm." She makes a disgusted face and looks around. Almost like she's just expecting to find him hanging out here even though I'm a humble operations manager and he's the flipping owner with a few dozen other properties to look after.

I try not to think about all the times he *has* been in my office, though. Or the fact that he saved my butt last night, only to ruin my life with that kiss like delicious poison.

Stop thinking about it, Salem.

"He's not here," I say lamely. "He's a busy man, you know. He's probably meeting clients or…" God, I don't even know. "Actually, I don't really know his schedule today."

"But you're his manager." The way she beams at me says everything—she expects him to burst in at any second and then drop down on one knee and propose to her at first sight. "You guys talk, right? About like business stuff?"

"Yeah. But that doesn't mean he'll just pop in here any second. Some days, I don't see him."

Especially not after last night. The way he went slinking off like a guilty cat after knocking over a flower vase.

He'll be avoiding me for sure.

Just as much as I'm avoiding him.

"You don't know that, Lemmy." Kayla sits in the other seat, the one Patton sat in that one time when we were actually being friendly—though not that friendly. "Besides, I've got time to kill. Let's just catch up and *see* what happens."

"You're just going to wait here?" I bite my tongue.

"Yeah?"

"But—"

"Um, how else do you expect me to meet him?"

I don't know. Another way. *Any* way that doesn't involve shredding what's left of my dignity.

Why can't she try one of the social events I'm sure they both attend? The ones I wouldn't be invited to in a thousand years.

Or, you know, at least not by waiting in my office like a tarantula in its little cave, biding her time until he arrives so she can pounce.

I have work, too, not that I'd expect Kayla to understand the concept.

"You could go shopping while you wait?" I suggest, knowing it's probably hopeless.

"Don't you want company? It must be so boring here." She pulls her phone out and flicks through her notifications.

"Do you know I posted three times on Instagram after tagging this place to congratulate my bestie? He didn't like *any* of them."

Ouch. If she's resorted to shout-outs for a complete nobody like me, she must be really desperate.

"He probably doesn't check his socials much."

"Yeah, but he follows me," she whines.

"So? That doesn't mean he's glued to Instagram." I try not to sound jealous.

She blinks at me like the idea of not spending half your life on social media is a foreign concept, right before she looks at her screen to deal with another twenty notifications.

Fine.

I find my headphones so I can drown her out. I'll just ignore her and work. It's not like she's taking up my space with her presence—though her perfume and the click of her nails as she sends another message is a little off-putting.

The minutes run by like molasses.

It's like time itself wants to amplify how awkward this situation feels. I don't get much done with her hovering around.

The torture lasts almost an hour.

By then, my eyes are glazed as I reread the same sentence for the fifth time.

Kayla jumps to her feet. She flicks her hair back and walks to the doorway.

I'm instantly filled with dread.

Patton's terse expression dissolves into annoyance as he sees her standing in front of him. If she had a tail, it would be wagging like crazy.

Worse, he looks just as illegally good as he did yesterday, though he's swapped the sweater for his usual steel-grey jacket and blue tie.

"Oh my God, hi! I've been waiting to meet you," Kayla

says, holding out her hand. "I'm Kayla—Winston Perse-phone's daughter?" She pauses, but when his confusion doesn't lift, she adds, "You know, from the fragrance line?"

"That's right." He forces a smile. "Nice to meet you, Kayla. What brings you by?"

She ignores the question.

I watch her lean in, flicking her gaze to his face, then down to his chest as she inhales sharply.

"I can smell our cologne right now. Great choice for a handsome businessman. Isn't it the best?" she croons, not moving away.

Shoot me now.

Actually, dump my body in the river to rot because I do *not* want to be here listening to this. Even if the flash of worry sweeping over his face feels mildly satisfying.

He glares at me like I'm somehow the reason he's stuck in this flirt trap, but I just shake my head and shrug.

Sorry, dude. Not my monkey and not my circus.

"It's a solid scent," he grinds out. "Is that why you're here? To discuss fragrances?"

"Oh, yeah! Kinda. Lemmy here, she's in charge of supplies and all... I thought your guests might enjoy a complimentary sample of our stuff for the rooms?" She grins like a shark. "We have options for the guys, too. Not just the Sand and Wind one you're wearing. Like so many options. I'm sure you'd love them all if you tried them out."

"Really?" He isn't remotely interested, his eyes going dark with disgust. "Thanks for the offer, but I'll leave you to discuss that with Lemmy. Or if you'd prefer, I'm sure I can find time for your father. Nice meeting you."

Oh my God.

Hearing him say that stupid nickname guts me in a new way.

Undaunted, Kayla gives him her signature smile and

purrs, "Aw, really? You're too busy to spare a few minutes? I'd love to get to know you—your needs better, I mean."

Nice, Kayla. Real subtle.

"I'm afraid my schedule's packed today." He puts a hand on the small of her back—which I'm pretty sure is almost enough to kill her—and escorts her out before she makes him punch her number into his phone.

I hear her saying something about how many Instagram followers she has through the door as he closes it.

I can't see her face, but I can picture it.

I try not to laugh.

She's fuming.

She wasted an hour with me, waiting for him, only to be shown the door in two minutes.

People don't do that to Kayla Persephone. *They just don't.*

But I'm pretty glad Patton just did.

"I'm sorry about that," I say as he reappears and—rips off his jacket? He grabs a water bottle and starts splashing it around his neckline, blotting it dry with tissues. "Um, what are you doing?"

"Remind me to never wear this goddamned brand again. It's ruined after meeting her," he mutters.

I giggle before I can help myself. Amazingly, everything almost feels normal again.

Almost.

Then I remember the hulking elephant in the room and my laughter fades.

Here it comes.

The apology, or maybe a grim, guilty-faced lecture about how it was oh-so-unprofessional even though *he* was the one who initiated the whole thing.

But he just tosses the used tissues into the trash.

"Is there a relative Arlo can stay with?" he asks.

Huh?

Definitely not a question I expected.

I hoped we'd just mutually agree to never speak about last night again, not entertain weird requests about my kid.

"There's a real estate conference coming up. This platinum circle event of big players in high-end vacation rentals specifically," he explains, talking into the void where I wonder if he can read my thoughts.

"Oh?"

"It runs through the weekend, I'm afraid. I know it's not convenient, but you'll be paid a travel bonus for your trouble."

…he's asking me to go?

Oof.

But more money. A perfect offer I'm hard-pressed to refuse. But at the same time, yikes.

"How long is it?"

"Four days. We'd leave this Thursday."

Four days away from Arlo.

Four days away from home with *Patton*.

"The venue's a beautiful resort in Utah. Highly rated and ultra-exclusive, one of the most decadent luxury spots in the country," he promises.

Oh, boy. My heart dips.

If I wasn't sitting, I'd need a chair right now.

Holy hell, this is a big ask.

A conference, which is big anyway, and a mini vacation, which I desperately need. When was the last time I had one *without* Arlo?

God.

"Salem?"

"…this is a lot," I say. "Could I ask around and maybe think about it?"

His gaze sharpens. The hot, conflicted look he gives me makes my stomach knot all over again, though I don't know what it means. It makes me think of last night, but incredibly, he hasn't even mentioned it.

I don't know if I want him to.

I don't get what's happening.

"Of course you can," he says, "but I hate to remind you this *is* a job requirement. It's also an excellent opportunity to broaden your horizons and learn from a crowd who can teach you more than I can. I'll have the company sitter on standby if your usual lady can't help, or I'll comp her myself if she can. This is very last minute and I won't be putting anybody out."

Yeah. So last minute, it feels like the roof is coming down on my head and I don't know where it'll leave me.

"Broaden my horizons… for the job, you mean?" I check.

"Obviously. It's business," he clips. I think he's avoiding the subject I desperately want him to talk about most.

"I see."

"I need you to join me, Salem," he says, and the sound of my name—the way it hovers on his tongue like he's tasting it —is enough to snap my gaze back to him.

"Okay. I'll see what I can do. Utah better be more than smelly salt flats and big rocks, though. I'm holding you to it when you said *luxury*."

"Do you still think I'd disappoint you, Miss Hopper?" His eyes narrow.

And there goes my heart, pattering away like it's broken.

I can't answer that, so I just shake my head.

For the first time today, his smile reaches his eyes.

* * *

THE MORE I think about it, the more excited I am, slowly coming to terms with a decision that feels less crazy by the hour.

By the time I finish work, I'm buzzing.

A vacation.

A real-life honest break from worrying myself sick about everything from money to what we're having for dinner.

Look, I love Arlo, but it'll be great to get away somewhere without him and just breathe for a few days.

I don't let myself think about Patton or that look in his eyes when he invited me on this trip. That's more complicated than the getaway I need.

Before heading home, I stop off at the Higher Ends office to drop off some paperwork—a thick stack of suggestions from the cleaning staff about process improvements for their jobs. Patton wants to work on employee retention strategies, especially with commercial grade cleaners in short supply around town.

The first time I walked into this sleek glassy building, I felt like an ant.

Now, I'm familiar enough to wave at the receptionist as I head inside. This time of day it's almost empty, and after leaving the cards in Patton's inbox like he requested, I make my way to the exit.

"Miss Hopper!"

I turn to see a familiar face hurrying toward me with a bunch of fresh flowers in her arms. Evelyn Hibbing?

"Mrs. Hibbing, hello. What brings you here?"

"Call me Evelyn, dearie, please. Everyone does." She pauses to look fondly at the flowers in her arms, cascading shades of reds and yellows. "Lovely, aren't they?"

"Totally. They smell like spring!"

She sighs proudly.

"One of my favorite things about flowers, you know. I came by with these to brighten up the place. Delly and I were at the market this afternoon and I thought the boys would enjoy a little color. So much better than the plastic wreaths they've kept up this whole dreary winter."

"That's so nice of you," I say.

"It's my pleasure, you know. Especially when they're taking time away from work to look into this little experiment I proposed in moose country." She smiles and pauses, pursing her lips. "I don't suppose you've heard anything?"

I hesitate.

"Uh, no. I don't sit in for executive strategy meetings or anything, unfortunately. Patton hasn't mentioned it much to me directly, though I'm sure it isn't far from his mind." I try to sound cheerful, knowing my market research tells me they're considering it.

But I can't stand to get her hopes up, if they decide it's a no-go.

"Oh, yes, yes, yes. I just thought—well, you and Patton have such delightful chemistry." She claps her hands together. "But that doesn't mean you have any unique insights into the business, I understand."

If I'd been drinking, I'd have sprayed it in her face.

Instead, I choke on my dry words. "We don't have—um, *chemistry*. I hope you didn't get the wrong impression about us?"

"No, perish the thought. But what do you girls call it these days, dearie? *Tension?*" Evelyn winks. "Don't worry, your secret's safe with me. I know how these things go, particularly with a little boy in the mix."

"There's no big secret, Evelyn. We're not dating," I insist, though every denial just sounds more like a lie.

What if she's right?

Ugh, I don't want to think about it.

"Here's a friendly tip—if you're looking to surprise him, Patton loves a good juicy cheeseburger. You'd think with all the money that family has, he'd prefer something more sophisticated, but you'd be surprised. He inherited his father's palate, I believe. Simple."

"I see," I manage numbly.

"Now, I'm not suggesting you take him to a drive-in or anything so obvious. But *if* you two kids go out for a business meeting and you just so happen to wind up at your favorite greasy spoon, put in a good word for old Evelyn, would you?" She sniffs the flowers in her arms and seems to sag, like the bones holding her up are collapsing. "I don't mean to burden you or complicate your life. I just haven't aged as gracefully as Delly, you see."

I have to admit Delly Rory has aged insanely well.

"You look fine. You're staying active. That's a win at your age, I'm sure."

"We lead very different lives as widows, Delly and me. I blame the cold back home. Oh, and the winter darkness... it's awful without Walt around to fly us to Nevada for a long weekend. Sin City was my very own light therapy back in the day." Evelyn laughs sadly. "Of course, I'm not saying I'm jealous of Delly. *Never.* She deserves every speck of happiness for all the wonderful things she does here. Kansas City has a lovely rustic charm, but Minnesota, that's my home. I can't wait to get back when things are greening up."

"I'm sure it's beautiful. You clearly have a way with plants." I eye the flowers again.

"Oh, yes, that was Walt's thing, and I suppose it had to rub off. I just love flowers, even when I had no hand in growing them. A few times, we even pitched supplying flower arrangements to the big casinos in Vegas, but alas, the distance just wasn't workable to keep them fresh in those days." She stuffs the bouquet into a large empty urn on the reception desk. "There. Don't they make this place pop?"

"They do," I agree, more enthusiastically than I feel.

At least we're on safer ground now. Talking about her

dead husband feels easier than whatever she suspects is going on between Patton and me, or the real estate deal I have no say in.

But why does she suspect anything at all?

Is the chemistry—*oh my God, that stupid word*—really so obvious to a family friend?

"I should get going," she says, picking up the entire urn, probably to put some water in it. "And don't worry, dearie, I'm on your side. We girls must stick together, especially when real estate moves like lightning. I'm sure a kind word or two will bring them around, right?" Her voice drops to a whisper. "And by the way, I think you'd make the sweetest couple!"

I watch her leave, speechless, as she shuffles away.

Wow. She's a little more aggressive than I guessed.

The audacity, thinking I have *any* say whatsoever over whether the Minnesota deal happens or not.

I can't decide if it's worse than her thinking there's anything cute about my awkward, self-destructive non-relationship with Patton Rory.

There's zero chance it evolves into anything good.

Zero.

Before this day can inflict more weird surprises, though, I hurry from the building. The last thing I need is to bump into Patton again somehow.

Actually, though, that's not quite right.

The *last* thing I need is a vacation with this man.

Save me now.

XIV: UP THE STAKES (PATTON)

*I*t's business.

    It's business, it's business, it's just goddamned business.

I've been repeating that mantra all day, ever since I picked her up outside her apartment early this morning.

It's what I've kept telling myself the whole time at the airport, with her fussing about Arlo and everything else she's reluctantly leaving behind for a few days.

And now, as she's sleeping in the seat beside me as our charter jet hums along, I have to repeat it again.

Because every mile closer to Utah makes it feel like a bigger lie.

Let's be real, these real estate 'conferences' are less about celebrating big ideas than they are glorified networking events. I've been to plenty in the past—alone.

No one ever questioned my solo appearances.

In fact, I fit right in with the sea of married or married-but-acting-single men. Once you know the jokes, the lingo, the backslapping, and the selfish, shitty attitudes from men who think they're miniature gods, it's easy to blend in.

Why, then, am I wanting to put on a show with Salem Hopper?

And why didn't I just fucking *tell* her my real motive for inviting her, besides leaning on the flimsy mentorship excuse?

It's not like I don't want to see her armed for success.

I do.

I want her to blind the whole world with how much she shines in this field, even more after seeing the way she forced a barbed smile for that clown of a woman.

Kayla Persephone.

Fucking pill.

I'm sick that she's the only reason Salem came to us, this done-up plastic doll who looks like she needs a day off her movie grade makeup and a brutal reality check.

Fuck me.

I hated seeing Salem, stranded and having to pretend she owes her life to this vapid woman. She shouldn't have to answer to anyone. Not when she has all the qualities to thrive.

Maybe that's when it turned personal for me.

This weekend of hobnobbing with the big fish in my world can't hurt, and neither can a little pampering. Maybe some downtime will give her ego the boost it needs to internalize her real worth.

She mumbles and twists in her seat, her head slipping down the inflatable pillow to my shoulder.

I freeze.

Shit.

This must be karma, right on time to meet my dumb ass for creating this predicament.

I've walked into this setup like a certified imbecile.

Now, here we are.

And here she is, all warm breath and dreaming flutters

against my neck, dead asleep and trusting and so killingly beautiful I can't look away.

I'm marooned in my seat, watching her like a kid looking through a toy shop window.

Control yourself, man.

Can I, though?

Or is it already too late?

You *knew* this would happen.

I thought separate rooms at the resort would help, knowing there'd be no opportunity to touch her then.

Trouble is, when she looked online and saw how expensive this place is at four figures per night, she demanded to know if my suite had a second room.

It did.

And that was enough for her to justify the savings.

So now we're sharing a suite and I'm going to have to sleep with her right up in my space, only one wall away.

How can a woman be so appealing when she *breathes*?

Maybe if I hadn't kissed her that snowy night, this wouldn't feel so lethal. But I know exactly what it's like, and I can't unknow it.

Hell, I know she wants me just as bad. If the kid hadn't barged in, I would've gotten drunk on her moans, shredding her clothes like a starving animal.

I keep still, ignoring the hard-on from hell, half hoping she'll roll back to her pillow. Hoping I can stand the weight of her head, the brush of her breath, the slight tickle of her stray hair without blowing a gasket.

I *can* do this, dammit.

I just have to forget every biological impulse chewing me to the bone.

No big deal.

Like now, I definitely don't want to take advantage of the

quiet, half-asleep morning flight to pin her against the seat and kiss her until she wakes up with a moan.

She stirs and sits up like she can hear the argument in my head, rubbing the grog from her eyes.

"Oh. Oh, crap," she whispers. "Sorry. You should have just pushed me off."

"I thought you could use the sleep after all that worrying this morning."

She gives me a sheepish smile and settles back on her pillow. "For me, this is a big deal. It's normal to stress a little."

"If I've told you once, I've told you a thousand times—you'll be fine. You've got passion and a damn good head on your shoulders—and if those fail you, you've got me."

She gives me a pained smile.

"Whatever. Tell that to my anxiety, Your Highness." Her eyelids flutter closed again and her breathing evens out as she turns away.

Fucking hell, this whole trip is going to be brutal.

But for her—for both of us—I'll try to be a good boy.

For Salem's sake, I'll try like hell to keep my hands to myself.

* * *

THE ZION PEAK RESORT is a gem tucked in beautiful desolation.

Nestled in the rugged desert landscape, its luxe gold and white stone stands out against the sandstone canyons and the late morning shadows spilling across the landscape like black silk.

It's the sort of otherworldly retreat that commands respect from everyone in this industry, including yours truly.

Salem looks around slowly as we pull up, predictably awestruck. I just hope she's still breathing while I check us in.

"Patton, wow. This place is *insane*," she repeats for the umpteenth time as we arrive in our suite. It's one of the larger units, half built into the hillside with its own private heated pool and a wide stone patio for lounging. "No wonder a night here costs more than a month's pay."

"It's pricey, yes. Another way this conference gatekeeps and makes sure it only pulls in the very best," I admit. "In this case, the admission price is worth it. Zion Peak is a desert miracle and a magnificent property."

"We have our own *pool*," she whispers, shaking her head. "Dang. I'm sorry I didn't bring any swimwear."

I blink away the image of her in a colorful bikini.

A man can only handle so much fire in his blood.

"Don't know that there'll be much time for swimming, truthfully. However, the resort has its own little mall in the main building. You're welcome to pick out something there, if you'd like."

"You mean if I could afford a designer swimsuit?" She scoffs.

I don't dare offer to buy it.

I'm already in too fucking deep. I'm a dead man walking if I have to deal with her prancing around half-naked.

"But this really is wild. Ludicrous. I may just sit and dip my feet in to warm up later. I know the desert gets chilly at night…" She trails off as we walk through the main room to the lone door across from a massive bathroom.

Wait, what? Shouldn't there be a *second* door to another bedroom down the hall?

She stops cold with the same question, staring at the large earth-toned bed pressed against the wall in a fully furnished bedroom while I stand behind her.

The *only* bed.

With my jaw clenched, I check the suite number on my

card again. I distinctly remember booking a two-bedroom suite.

Anything feels safer than watching Salem's mouth drop.

"So, uh… where's my room?"

It's almost laughable.

Here we are in paradise, this lovely room with its bamboo accent wall, soft colors, and crisp, white modern furnishings, feeling like we've just been gutted. A masterful room clearly designed for couples.

Hell, the place wouldn't be out of place for a honeymoon suite.

Dammit. I *knew* I should've gotten that second room.

"Somebody fucked us," I say tightly in the empty silence. "Sorry. This suite was supposed to have two bedrooms. I'll call reception right now and—"

"No, there's no need." She swallows before locking eyes with me again. "I mean, there's a sofa in the other room. And this bed, it's enormous. We could share it and be in different zip codes."

Does she even hear herself?

She's not wrong, though.

A person could starfish on the mattress two or three times over without touching anyone else on the other side.

Only, that doesn't change the fact that there's one bed.

One bed.

Only one bed for two awkwardly attracted people and a man fighting off his inner caveman like a feral monkey with a stick.

A single shared bed we're somehow expected to sleep in without turning into ravenous beasts tearing each other's clothes off.

"I'm calling them," I growl.

"Hold up. I know how much a room like this costs," she

continues, running her fingers along the silky bedspread. "I checked, remember?"

"I can afford another room, goddammit. I'm sure there's something available."

"And if there isn't?" She looks at me.

"Then *I'll* take the sofa, woman. We need *rest* if we want to make the most of this weekend."

"When you're the one flipping the bill? Um, no. And that's beside the point." She juts her chin out so defiantly I almost laugh. When a woman gives you that look, it means you've already lost. "You paid for this room. I agreed to it, and I also asked for one room. We'll be fine. I can survive a few nights in a place that makes my apartment look like a beat-up shed. One roommate, that's a luxury—and you won't even throw chicken nuggets around."

I snort, biting back a grin.

She's insufferable.

She also might think it'll be fine, but she hasn't met my self-control, or lack thereof.

Right now, it's hanging by its very last worn thread.

"Your choice," I bite off. "One room. One bed. Whatever."

"Okay. Now that we have that settled..." She sends me a nervous glance before stepping over to the floor-to-ceiling window and looking out at the mountains in the distance. There are more suites farther to our right, but the place does a remarkable job with positioning for maximum privacy.

It looks like there's nothing else around.

No one to hear if we—

Stop. Right the hell now.

But there's something else I need to ask her, and considering she's insisting on this death sentence of one shared bed, there's no time like the present.

"Salem?" Even saying her name feels weirdly intimate here—or maybe it's just the fact that I know what I'm about to say next. "I need to come clean. There's another reason I brought you here and you're going to hate it."

She stops halfway through smelling the fresh flowers on the small table by the window and flashes me a suspicious glance.

"Huh? You mean this isn't just a learning lesson in a gorgeous place I'm lucky to step foot in?"

"It is, but I also hoped you might help me out with a little problem." I clear my throat loudly. Her suspicious expression doesn't ease for one second. "I was hoping you might attend the conference tomorrow as more than an employee I'm mentoring."

Brutal pause. Her eyes sharpen.

"I'd like you to come as my girlfriend."

I wait to hear a pen drop in the grim silence, if she doesn't just pick up one of the large black ceramic coffee cups and hurl it at my head first.

She's so frozen I wonder if she heard me at all.

"Your *what?*" she croaks.

"I know it sounds insane. It's a big fucking ask." I hold up my hands before her gaze sets me on fire. "And yeah, it's breaching professional boundaries and breaking common sense... but a lot of these guys are married. Most of them, in fact."

"And you're not." She folds her arms, her lips twisted sourly. "But so what? Why does it matter?"

"Because these men have egos bigger than the moon. They're obsessed with optics. If they're not marching in with their wives, they're flaunting their weekend arm candy, whatever model mistress or exotic sugar baby they've hired to impress."

"Gross!" She inhales sharply. "And you—what? You want me to play that game? To be your accessory?"

I swallow.

"I want you to be taken seriously." I hold up my hands. "There are a lot of pigs who come to feed at these conferences, but that's not everyone. There's another class of professionals who shows up here. The classic power couple. Men with wives and girlfriends who have their heads in the game, usually sharper than their partners. They're some of the biggest movers and shakers around, and I've always had trouble connecting with the type when I'm a damn loner."

Her lips twist, mulling over my breathtaking stupidity.

"But if I walk in there with a brilliant woman on my arm, it could help us both connect with the real players. Have you thought about your future after Higher Ends, assuming you stay in real estate? There's no telling the doors these people could open."

"What, because they think I'm connected to you?" She huffs a breath. "How many connections do you think I'll make? Or really, how many connections would make this ruse worth it?"

"I'm not asking you to like it. Real opportunities never come easy in this biz."

"No, you're just ambushing me in this beautiful place in a slick room *you* paid for after you flew me in on a private jet. And I'll feel like a giant bitch if I don't agree just by being here."

Bam. Right between the eyes.

She's spelled out the asshole I am in two sentences.

Sighing roughly, I shake my head.

"You always have a choice, Salem. No gun to your head, I promise."

"So what happens if I say no?"

"Nothing." I shrug indifferently, like I'm not half hoping she does when I'd deserve every bit of it. "I'm asking for a favor. You turn me down, fine. We'll still go to the conference, work the crowds, and take in plenty of big speeches.

You'll walk away knowing ten times more than you did before you came here."

"A favor as my boss. Right."

"As a *friend.* I'm coming to you because there's no one else I could ask to put on a show like this."

There's no gold in her eyes now. They're so walnut dark I can't see any other color at all. They bring out the flush on her cheeks, though.

"As a friend," she repeats numbly.

"Remember how well we played it up at the casino years ago? I saved you with a play like this years ago. That was a hell of a night."

"*Hell* is right," she mutters under her breath.

I cock my head and stare at her.

"Dude, it's just... I didn't *need* you to save me," she flares, then stops, suddenly regretful. "I did appreciate it, though. I'll give you that."

"I don't need an answer right away. I just thought it might help us both to figure this out sooner."

The idea that any connection to me might help her career clearly upsets her.

I'm not expecting it when she holds out her hand.

"You know what? Fine. For this *conference* only, I'll be your girl. After this, we're even."

"Even Steven. Conference only. Deal." I shake her hand.

"No hanky-panky, obviously."

"Fuck no."

Liar.

"And you'll take me out for a nice dinner or two. I've never dreamed of eating at a Michelin star place before this weekend, but this place has one. I'd love to experience it just once."

"Done. Bring your appetite and a dictionary for the most

pretentiously named food in existence." I give her a mock bow.

She laughs, eyeing me suspiciously like she can read what's really on my mind, but then she nods and turns back to the window.

"Let's go exploring while we can," she says. "If we're going to be here, I might as well see what's out there."

The answer is a whole lot of nothing beyond the resort's landscaped gardens and flawless stone walking paths.

I've never been one for endless desert landscapes, but Salem doesn't seem to mind the alien desolation compared to our Missouri home. In fact, as we wander around the large complex, taking in the scenery, she gasps with new discoveries.

We're near the resort's giant infinity pool when she goes off again.

"This is humongous," she whispers, absently sliding a hand through my arm. "Look at the pool chairs, Patton."

They're nice, these freakishly ergonomic modern chairs, probably built to push your spine back into place without needing a chiro.

"I thought you'd like it here," I tell her.

"It's heaven." She kicks off her shoes and sprawls across a white lounger, tipping her head back into the evening sun. "Maybe I didn't bring a bikini, but nothing will stop me from a little sunbathing."

After the winter back home, the warmth really is pleasant, even if it's less than seventy degrees. I join her, lying back on the sun lounger and letting the heat trickle over my skin.

From here, the only thing I can hear is that empty, hollow sound of the desert valley between the mountains.

"This doesn't feel real," she says.

"The perks of hard work. Enjoy it."

"For you, maybe. I'm just riding your coattails. I could never afford this place without you."

"Maybe not now. In a few years, who knows? Find the right opportunity, serve the market, and the money comes faster than you think."

She sighs, shading her face with her hand as she looks at me. And maybe it's stupid to think, but lying here makes it feel like we're a lounging couple, not two people on a work trip.

"You put a lot of confidence in me. I'm not sure why."

"Why the hell shouldn't I?"

"Because I'm *me*, Patton. Like, even if I wind up with a stable gig, I'll never reach this level."

I snap my fingers loudly, pausing while she stares at me.

"What was that for?" she whispers.

"I'm done listening to you doubt yourself." I close my eyes. "Today, we're going to soak in our success and enjoy it without any worries about tomorrow."

I wish I only meant business.

"Is that an order?"

"Will you follow it?" I growl back.

She laughs. A heady, cheerful sound I haven't heard often enough.

"Okay, fine. I'll enjoy the evening and bring my game face tomorrow," she says.

There's still a smile in her voice. I can picture it without looking at her, the way her eyes crinkle and she bites her bottom lip when she's overthinking.

"Then it's decided," I say.

"Yeah." She pauses and there's a rustling sound as she sits up. I glance across at her, but she's watching the shimmering pool like she's imagining diving in. "Patton," she starts and pauses again. "Thanks for this."

"You're the one doing me a favor, honoring my jackass

request," I tell her. Her lips curl into another smile, and she looks away to hide it. "Just don't tell the guys I have eleven toes or an extra nipple or something."

This time, her laugh comes straight from her belly.

The warmth makes me laugh, too.

And our combined laughter echoes into the afternoon and melts under the silent, staring desert sun.

For the first time in ages, I remember how to relax.

* * *

DINNER GOES DOWN WITHOUT A DISASTER.

She's remarkably good at playing the glamorous girl-friend—Dexter, eat your fucking heart out—and it's a solid trial run even if it's just the two of us.

She's attentive and kind. I enjoy watching her reaction to the overpriced French-inspired modern cuisine more than I do the food itself.

In another life, I'd call it a perfect night.

Until now, crumpled up on a fine plush mattress that feels worse than a prison bed.

It's so dark I can barely see past my nose. The only light gleaming in comes from the distant stars on a moonless night. They all remind me I should be long asleep.

Instead, I'm here, flat on my back with Salem gently snoring away at the other edge of the bed, fighting a hard-on that could hit a home run.

Torture.

My brain sprints in a hundred directions, yet it always comes back to the same place, the same urge to take a great big bite of the forbidden fruit next to me.

If it wouldn't wake her, I'd get up and creep down to the gym, where I'd beat my muscles to exhaustion and pass out in the locker room.

But I'm trapped here, staring at the goddamned ceiling with ten thousand dirty thoughts stretched out for miles.

And damn, the girl can sleep.

I know she wants me—the kiss she gave back told no lies, dammit—but clearly the thought of sharing a bed isn't doing the same thing to her as it is to me.

Small relief. I think I'd be doubly screwed if Salem wanted it too, lying there wide awake next to me, but at the same time—

Fuck.

I try to wrench the oversized blankets from her, but sleeping beauty is apparently a lot stronger than any waking human.

She has them in a death grip, and yes, she hogs them all.

There's no getting them back.

What the hell ever.

I'll beam my frustration into the darkness, I decide, waiting for the sandman to show up and knock me out.

* * *

WHEN I WAKE UP NEXT, it's still dark and I'm warm.

Wait, why am I warm?

Velvety hair tickles my face. Not *my* hair.

I blow it away from my mouth so I can breathe. When I open my eyes and my brain finally catches up with what's happening, it's a miracle I don't yell.

Oh, no.

Oh, shit.

Salem Hopper.

She's what's happening.

Tucked up, invitingly warm, devilishly close Salem.

Maybe she's just a cuddler by nature whenever she shares a bed.

Either way, she's here now, up close and personal with her head on my chest and an arm slung over my stomach. She's even hooked her leg over mine and my skin bristles under her smoothness.

Kill me.

This close, it's impossible not to think of what could happen if either of us snapped right now.

It's impossible not to *smell* her.

My nostrils flare, tickled by that light citrusy cinnamon scent that's all Salem.

Before her, I never realized any woman could smell so good.

Everything about her feels like a formula patented to trigger every dormant bad habit I have.

Six years ago was long enough to start forgetting before she walked into The Cardinal.

But now—now, I'm stuck here and my dick knows what it wants to do about this.

About this proximity.

About us, with every inch of this disgustingly large bed to defile.

She shifts in her sleep, and I half hope she'll wake up.

Not because I want her to move, but because I don't know what will happen if she doesn't.

Don't think about that, you upside-down fuckhound.

Think unsexy thoughts.

IRS audits.

Dexter's kale lunch wraps.

Arlo putting his sticky little hands all over my aquarium, smudging up my precious view.

Then she turns her face closer to mine.

The night changes to dusk, just enough to make out her silhouette in detail. I can't tell if she's having a pleasant dream or a nightmare. All I know is that if her leg moves up any higher, she'll encounter something I can't plan for.

My cock jerks, anticipating her touch, her heat.

Then she whimpers something that sounds an awful lot like my name and the entire world stops.

Holy Mother of God.

This is it.

I'm dead.

Done.

If she's dreaming about *me…*

Of course, she could be dreaming about anything, but the way her voice sounded—well, I've heard her sound this way once before.

Six years ago.

I force myself to play like I'm as dead as I feel while she sleeps on beside me, every inch of me screaming to give in to a terrible mistake.

There's no chance I'm falling back asleep before my alarm goes off.

And I can't fathom how I'll survive three more nights of this sleepless tease, silently self-destructing next to the only woman I can't have.

XV: LUCKY NIGHT (SALEM)

*M*y head hasn't stopped spinning since we arrived at Zion Peak.

Everything about this place is dialed up to eleven and I haven't decided yet if that means I'm dreaming. The top of my arm might be bruised from how many times I've pinched it.

But that's only half of it.

The other half, that's entirely down to sleeping with Patton Rory but not actually *sleeping* with him.

"I can't *tell* you how excited I am to meet you," a man in a beige suit says with a grin too wide for his face. He takes my hand and kisses it like we're in some period drama. "Can't remember Pat ever bringing a lady around before."

Yeah, like it's any secret why.

I glance at Patton and the intent look in his eye. If I didn't know better, I'd almost think he's jealous.

Just looking at him feels dangerous considering how we woke up this morning.

Correction: how *I* woke up this morning—curled around him like a little monkey hugging a tree. He didn't know I was awake, of course, but being that close felt so good I couldn't help just lying there in the blissful confusion, somewhere between sleep and a very conscious what-is-happening panic.

My face whips away.

Yeah, looking at Patton right now is a bad idea.

I force my attention back to the stranger in front of me. He smells like pungent cigars and money.

There's a languid woman hanging by his side. Probably twenty years younger but still looking older than her true age.

"Charmed," she says. "You must be quite the woman to pair up with a workhorse. Please tell me you don't put in the long hours he does?"

"Oh, we find our balance. And it's wonderful to be here, truly," I tell them both. Patton sends me an approving smile. *That*, at least, isn't a lie. "I just can't believe he hasn't brought anyone else around before."

"He's a ladies' man, I've heard," the lady drawls. She's practically dripping real diamonds, and not the lab grown kind, I'm sure.

Patton slides an arm around my waist and I lean into him.

"Why didn't you tell me about your wicked reputation?" I tease.

I wonder why I don't feel more nervous.

I should be crawling out of my skin.

Instead, it feels scarily natural, falling into this weird role with him.

"A man always has one if he's any man at all. The nice part about reputations is they can be rewritten," he says, giving the lady a wink.

She throws her head back and laughs.

"And you?" the man probes. "What's yours, Miss Hopper?"

"A lady never tells—at least, not when she's keeping the lights on at the hottest place in Kansas City," I say.

They give back satisfied laughter.

They don't know it's a real miracle I'm pulling this off in the face of people so manicured and high profile they make Delly Rory look like a slob. A few of the Vegas developers alone here can buy off entire countries.

It makes me appreciate how real Delly seems. She keeps up a beautiful home and isn't frantically running from one plastic surgery appointment to the next, trying to cheat her mortality like everyone else here.

Wealth is a strange thing.

Sometimes when people work overtime to hide their flaws, it just reveals deeper ones—the kind that aren't fixed.

Patton drags me away for introductions with several other people, mostly the important power couples. They're a minority in the sea of older men.

Most of the guys come alone, and even the ones who wear wedding bands try to flirt like they don't.

I try to take it in stride, smiling and talking about The Cardinal. I laugh along with their lame jokes. Sometimes, Patton intervenes to help us escape—usually when the men start watching me like I'm tonight's dinner.

"That's enough, Grayson. I won't have you stealing her from under me," he says to a man in his mid-thirties who looks chiseled enough to cut rock.

Grayson looks at me with a grey-eyed sparkle that could be his namesake. "Isn't that for the lady to decide?"

"She has terrible taste. That's why she's with me," Patton jokes, and I laugh. There's an expression in his eyes I can't decipher, and it makes my stomach clench.

Smile. Play it cool.

It's all just a stage.

This is where I should grin and flirt back—either with

Patton or Grayson or both—but I've never been great at flirt-ing. That hasn't changed since I was twenty-one and clueless about how complicated life can get after one drunken night.

Patton offers me his arm.

"We should get going," he says to Grayson, who tips his drink to me.

It's a buffet brunch with a massive spread. Everything from eggs Benedict with Swiss chard and green olives to banana bread waffles and fresh fruit flown in from Califor-nia. Patton guides me through the chattering crowd and over to the food with surprising grace and poise.

"You're killing it. Keep it up," he says under his breath.

"Is everyone always so flirty?" My face screws up. "I thought that last guy was going to make a play for me right in front of you."

"When they see a beautiful woman, it's not unheard of. People with nine figures aren't used to taking 'no' for an answer."

My stomach leaps at the reminder of how just big the money here gets.

I almost miss his next introduction as a broad man steps in front of us. He's an elderly guy with a thick Texas accent and old-fashioned Southern charm. He's actually decent, though, grandfatherly in a way, and he makes me feel at ease for the first time all morning.

"You be careful lettin' this pretty one wander too far, Mr. Rory," he growls. "I hear she's saving your ass with that fancy hotel that ain't a hotel, huh?"

"Yeah. Beauty and brains. I'm the luckiest asshole here today and I know it," Patton tells him.

My heart somersaults as they laugh.

Pray for me.

Patton thinks I'm beautiful.

Or maybe he doesn't and he just said it for the ruse.

But I guess it worked either way. When we leave the breakfast room for a few light presentations, I feel better.

It's a half day of pep talks about earnings and rave successes with every speaker trying to one-up each other. By the time we're leaving just ahead of the small crowd, I'm less on edge.

"I didn't realize you brought me here so you could show me off like a new piece of jewelry," I tell him as we head back to our suite to change. "To be fair, I've never felt so shiny in my life."

"I'll take that as a compliment, Lady Bug. The women like you too, and you can trust their motives. You're not such a black cat after all and it's time you started believing me."

I want to argue back, but for once, he's not wrong.

Today, I *feel* lucky.

"Well, what now? I'm surprised they cut the first day short."

"We'll get into the real meat tomorrow, but remember, it's more about networking than anything else." He shrugs. "Next stop: Antelope Canyon. We have just enough daylight."

Back in our room, I change into capris and a cardigan. It's cool enough here, but a far cry from the winters back home.

"So, I know this might sound strange, but being hit on isn't the huge compliment you think it is."

His mouth curls into a smile. "I've never seen anyone fight so hard to run away from being the most interesting person in the room."

"...I don't know if you mean I'm interesting because of my appearance or because I'm with you. Neither of them are that appealing. I'd like to have a few more in-depth conversations if possible. I came here to learn, remember?"

"You will," he promises. His tone is good-natured, and when he flashes me another grin—not one of those awful forced smiles—I can't help smiling back.

That is, until I remember how it felt to wake up in his arms this morning.

God, I'm so confused.

This place may look like heaven, but surviving the rest of this long weekend promises pure hell. Especially at night.

How do I keep my distance when he's close enough to breathe? When I can't help accidentally rolling into his arms?

"So, Antelope Canyon? The couple who mentioned it this morning made it sound like a big deal."

"It's worth the drive," he says. "If you've ever wanted to visit another planet, this place is the closest thing."

"Sold. I don't get out enough. I can still count the national parks I've visited on one hand." My throat pinches.

I really don't want to explain why, how crappy my parents could be growing up, alternating between controlling tendencies and barely checking in on my life.

I also regret not bringing Arlo along for the ride. But that's why I came, isn't it? Not for sightseeing or to act out dumb roles with my boss, but so I can arm myself with a few more tools to give us a financial leg up.

Someday, when the money comes, I'll bring my son wherever I please. And if Patton Rory's knowledge and reputation helps me get closer to that, I can make peace with leaning on Lucifer later.

* * *

IT'S WEIRD.

Being in a car with him for the hour-plus drive somehow feels more intimate than sharing a bed. I know that makes no sense. Maybe it's because we're wide awake and we should be making conversation.

His rental car has all kinds of advanced cruise control

features, this hybrid SUV that drips expensive, and it lets him safely drive it down the highway with one hand.

His other hand sits between us the entire way, close enough to touch.

Close enough so I can see every detail.

Freckles, scars, blemishes.

The masculine bulge of his forearm, the path of his veins. I don't usually find veins interesting, but his are like a map I could study all day.

Ugh.

I've never felt this before.

I don't like it.

This man radiates an unsettling magnetism that flips my heart like a pancake. The way I could stare at every part of him and feel like I'm still finding something new every time...

Insane.

It defies all logic, and a twisted little part of me loves that it does.

The fact that he's calling me Lady Bug on top of everything else doesn't help, pulling me back to a time when life and love were endless possibilities.

We travel in near silence, and whenever I'm not consumed with his hand being so close to my thigh, I gaze out at the stunning scenery.

There's a wild allure to the high desert. The hills, the canyons, the way the sunlight and shadows dance across the landscape.

It's nice to roll down the windows and enjoy the fresh air. Sixty-four degrees, according to the car's screen. In the sun, it's warm enough to pull off my cardigan.

Soon, we're parking in a large lot and striding across the gravel to the ticket booth where Patton buys us both tickets. Then we join the guided tour, heading into the canyon. As soon as we're touring the wind-scoured rocks, I forget about the weather and basically everything else.

Antelope Canyon is flipping stunning.

Just not the way you'd call the sky or the sea or imposing mountains beautiful. This place is shock and awe in a serene, passive way.

This beauty feels like sunbathing as you take it in.

"Wow," I whisper almost breathlessly.

"Yeah." He presses a hand to my back, inviting me to lean into him. "A few thousand years of floods and erosion will do that. Give it enough time and even stone melts like butter. Pretty heavy stuff to think about."

"You've come here before?" I look at him.

"Three times. I always get out here whenever this conference comes up at Zion Peak. I like to think of it as Mother Nature showing off, reminding us how easy it is to leave a mark on the world if you throw enough raw power at it."

"A very Patton thought." I laugh. "Do you ever stop brooding? Just enough to stand back and admire the view?"

He nods slowly, turning his eyes to the gorgeously tinted walls. I never knew red could have a thousand shades.

I'm not sure if I believe in higher powers, but this place makes me feel small.

It's like peeking in on the universe itself, so vast and unyielding it steals my breath away.

The way he touches me isn't half-bad either.

Before I know it, I'm letting him run his hand down my back, leaving goosebumps on my skin.

Disaster imminent.

Yeah, this is definitely more intimate than sleeping in the same bed.

We're sharing a moment.

A lovely experience I wouldn't be having without him, and I wonder if he'd say the same.

With his money, he could come here anytime. But would he be looking at these rocks the same way?

Would he look at another woman the way he glances at me now with that sapphire glow in his eyes?

I wonder, and it scares me.

We take in the sights slowly, lingering behind the tour guide. I reach out and run my fingers along the stone.

Here, almost underground, the sun can't reach us and it feels cool. I stretch my arms out like I can borrow a few more precious seconds from this magical place.

The guide's voice drifts away into the distance, but that's okay.

For now, I'm taking this slice of reality and storing it away just for me.

"Salem?"

I open my eyes. I hadn't even realized I'd closed them.

We're practically alone in this maze of petrified waves with the rest of our small group moving on.

"What are you doing?" A frown touches his face. His fingers fall against mine, asking for my hand, urgent yet unsure if I'm crazy enough to give in.

Honestly, I don't know what I want to give him.

So I let my fingers decide—and they find a home tucked in his hand.

"I'm fine. I guess I just…" I shrug, embarrassed. "It's a vibe here. This place has been around forever. It's crazy to think about how long. But it's so peaceful. I wanted to absorb it a little, as weird as that sounds. The good energy, I guess."

"Good energy," he repeats skeptically. "Will you be breaking out the crystal healing wands next?"

"You never know." My voice drops. "I'm a walking disaster, Patton. Watch out."

Too honest.

But he doesn't flinch as he smiles.

"You don't need good energy, woman. You need a damn break. And you need more company than a hyperactive five-year-old who keeps you running ragged. You need me to—" He pauses as our tour guide rounds the corner, irritation written across his face after noticing we're missing.

"Guys, can you please try to keep up with the group?" He's polite but exasperated.

Patton pulls a face behind me. I struggle to keep my expression straight as the guide blusters and takes his place at the front while we rush up behind him to rejoin the group.

"Like I was *saying*," he starts pointedly, and Patton winks at me.

I dissolve into silent laughter.

I'm happily listening to the guide's lecture, but I'm not sorry we drifted off. Being here with Patton feels like the kind of luck and company that can't possibly be bad for me.

By the time we head out later, my hand still pressed in his, I've found my own energy.

I'm walking on sunshine.

* * *

WE GET BACK in plenty of time for another fancy dinner, this time with a group of large real estate investors from across the country.

The sun ripples, bloodred on the horizon as we change into our dinner clothes. Patton emerges in a crisp black suit.

I'm wearing the best frilly red cutout dress money can buy from a secondhand store.

Not that you'd ever be able to tell.

He stops and stares at me so hard I wonder if I've smeared my makeup.

"Um, what? Too much skin?" I ask nervously. "Just say the word and I'll change. I brought a few options."

"Too much *you*," he growls raggedly, striding forward until we're a breath apart. "Fuck, Salem, you make this too easy—and too damn hard to keep pretending. Can't decide which one's worse."

I shiver.

Because I know he's not just stroking my ego. There's no mistaking the molten look in his eyes, the raw hunger, the way he looks at the cutout around my waist.

If looks could tear my clothes off, I'm pretty sure I'd be naked right now.

"Don't change a thing," he rumbles. "And if anyone touches you or makes you uncomfortable, you tell me."

There's a violence in his voice that makes me shudder again.

"Um, okay. It's modern enough, though? No designer label, of course, but it was the best I could find on short notice. I'm honestly more worried what the ladies will think."

"You can stop. It isn't the dress at all. I promise you at least half of the women here would kill for your look. They shell out small fortunes trying to pretty themselves up the way you do naturally."

No words. I turn away, hopelessly trying to hide the redness creeping into my face.

That's serious praise I'm not sure I deserve. At least I'm grateful this getup fits flawlessly.

"I'm ready," I say, grabbing my black purse. "Let's go swim with the sharks."

Patton looks me up and down one more time, a strange expression etched on his face.

"Tonight," he says, "we're the goddamned sharks."

"Maybe you. Me, I'm bait," I say with a laugh.

"When we get back, woman, we're working on your self-esteem." And he offers me his arm as we step into the cool night to walk the short distance to the restaurant.

Although it was warm enough during the day, the evenings are still cold, and I wish I'd thought to bring a shawl or something.

"I'm nervous," I admit just before we head into the large well-lit entrance to the eatery. "I feel more like I should be serving these people at The Cardinal. Not pretending I'm their peer."

"You deserve to be here more than a lot of them. Trust me." He snorts. "Half these folks were born with money and venture capital coming out their ears. They built empires on easy mode without ever worrying about grit or debt."

"Well... I appreciate the fact that you're trying to make me feel better, Patton. But there's a hard limit to what I can make myself believe." I square my shoulders and flick him a glance as we stop near the door. "Shall we?"

"Tonight, I'm all yours," he says, and there's a midnight tone to his voice.

Holy Mother of God.

I don't dare think too hard about what that means as he whisks me inside, or that cryptic remark about my self-esteem.

The place is about what you'd expect, this time decked out for a large private dinner.

It's all the glitzy glamour worthy of a modern day Gatsby. Draped crystal chandeliers that almost touch the floor and gilded chairs. A white tablecloth and the fanciest forks known to man that require a degree in etiquette to use correctly.

Patton keeps a tight hold on my arm as we find our seats. His eyes scan over people, his smile equal parts invitation and warning.

"See that man there?" he whispers as we walk past a tan man with a creased face and a red tie. "That's Harry Goldblum —no relation to Jeff—and last year he bought a golf course in

Oklahoma that lost his company almost twenty million. His kids fucking hated him when he had to give up the private jet."

"What?"

"And the guy one seat over, beside you? He's been married five times, always to these supermodels from Belarus. All five girls left him before a year was up and went back to the motherland loaded." He nods at a middle-aged woman in a black dress with gold crosses a little farther down. "And her? She was the duchess of Chicago real estate once upon a time. Then she blew herself up with bad deals by marrying a football player with the IQ of a grubworm. She's been in and out of rehab for drinking more times than I can count."

"Oh my God. But why are you telling me this?" I hiss into his ear.

"So you'll understand they're not all winners here. You think you're out of place because you're not as rich and you've stumbled a few times?"

I blink at him, my lips forming a silent *O* as the realization sets in.

I appreciate the point he's trying to make.

But not as much as I'm gobsmacked by the warmth and sincerity, the way he's trying to *build me up.*

No one's ever done that before.

No one ever cared.

I'm choking back a lump in my throat as we sit. The serial supermodel lover introduces himself right away.

Life has taken its toll for sure with this one. His dyed black hair looks pretty odd on top of a face that sags. But it's more telling when he shifts so his knee brushes mine.

I rip my leg away and tilt closer to Patton.

No flipping thank you!

We make polite conversation and not even ten minutes in, I see Patton's point.

These people aren't geniuses or business gods or money magicians.

They're human. Conflicted people who, despite their enormous wealth and success, are just as flawed and corrupt as the rest of us.

And if they can stack up big money with their demons and a few connections, why can't I do the same with some elbow grease?

"Miss Hopper," Divorced Dude says again, leaning forward. I've already forgotten his name. Sweat gleams on his forehead and I look away. "I recommend the Hokkaido scallops. They're impeccable here. The sensation on the tongue—vanishingly few things can ever compare."

Yuck. And I don't mean the scallops.

Usually, I would give him a tight smile and ignore him the rest of the night. But tonight, it's different.

Tonight, I'm on the arm of Patton Rory, self-made hotshot from a family that rubbed shoulders with presidents. I don't need to shrink down and hide.

"Scallops, huh? Sounds a little boring with this menu. I had my eye on the coq au vin."

I toss my hair over my shoulder and look at him through my eyelashes for a few seconds too long. Just so he starts to sweat harder.

Then I smile until his face sags like a flattened tire.

Man, for such powerful men with mammoth egos, it sure feels easy to twist their balls.

"And what was your name again? I'm terrible with names. Sorry, I can't remember if we met this morning—or maybe I just met your date."

He clears his throat loudly.

"Joseph Richardson. No date. Not yet, anyway." His smile doesn't reach his eyes as he mutters, "You're Patton Rory's fling, I know that much. Didn't realize he liked them so mouthy."

Ohhhh.

It's hard to keep the plastic smile pinned on my face. Harder not to sidekick him square in the shin under the table.

So I just tap Patton's arm pointedly, pulling his attention away from another man on his opposite side.

"Babe, did you hear that?" My voice is artificially light—brittle, like it could shatter at a moment's touch. "Mr. Richardson called me your mouthy *fling*."

"Did he?" There's no mistaking the ice in Patton's voice—or the possessive way he leans over the back of my chair. "Why would he do that? Joe, are you drunk already? How many have you *had*? I haven't even seen a single gal here from east of London."

"My mistake." Joseph's face turns an unflattering shade of red as he huffs again, still too loud. "Fucking smart-ass."

"Sure was," Patton agrees and hands me my menu. "What are you feeling tonight, Lady Bug?"

I'm high as a kite on adrenaline.

This whole thing might be for show, but it doesn't matter.

We talk about the menu and I've almost decided on going French, but then he points out a local option I can't resist.

I pick the guajillo seared pork with roasted green chili. Patton opts for a wagyu filet mignon with a creamy lemon risotto. Then the lesson really begins.

It's a masterclass in the art of negotiation.

Patton shows me off without *seeming* to show me off. He talks up Higher Ends' success without boasting.

He advises and laughs, ingratiating himself with personal comments aimed at each of the people he's talking to.

Mostly, I listen, hating that I'm a little in awe.

"I hear your new venture is going well. You must be pleased," a man says as we order dessert.

I choose a slice of chocolate truffle layer cake.

Patton leans back in his chair. "The Cardinal? Yes, it is doing extremely well, but I can't take the credit. Salem here has taken it to the next level. Without her wading through the daily operations, we'd be treading water."

I flush for the hundredth time tonight.

"You must take some credit. You helped me get there. You *bought* it."

"And the single best decision I made was hiring you." There's that sincerity in his voice again. It completely brings me down. "Also," he announces to the table, "she's done everything with one hand tied behind her back ever since I met her. This lovely lady's achieved everything while being a single mother."

A few gasps ring out. A loud murmur passes around the table, and even the people who weren't listening before lean toward us, tuning in now.

"Bravo!" a big man yells, raising his glass.

A few seconds later, the whole table follows him.

"Holy crap, Patton." I press my fingers to my burning cheeks. Even the chocolate cake that's coming up won't help me recover anytime soon. "You... you didn't need to tell them that."

I'm dumbfounded he's staking his own reputation. What will they think of him dating a single mom?

"Proof of how hard you work? I think I did," he throws back.

And I die.

The lady I met before at brunch—the languid one, who seemed disinterested in me—claps her hands, her bangles jangling.

"Oh, dear! Most of the men here can't possibly under-

247

stand, but I do," she says, "That's a lot of life you're juggling. Raising a child all alone, that's a feat by itself. Never mind the rest of it. You simply *must* hold your head high."

Her eyes glisten like it's a familiar story.

I flash her an empathetic smile.

"Thank you," I mumble.

"She's a superhero," Patton says, and I think he means it. When he looks at me again, the pride in his eyes dances like stark blue starlight.

I'm wilting by the time dessert arrives, holding in a sigh.

Thank God.

Now I can turn my attention away and relax a little. Patton carries on, smoothly discussing his future plans without revealing any major details, all while he probes the others into revealing *their* plans.

It's no surprise they like to hold their cards close to their chest and require some coaxing.

Everyone, that is, except Harry Goldblum, who brags about his negotiations to take over another 'sure win' golf course in Miami.

I can't decide if he's stupidly determined or just plain stupid.

Dinner ends with a few people lingering for drinks, but we can leave the table.

A few men step outside into the night air to smoke. Patton leads me back to our room, one hand possessively resting on the small of my back, slowly burning me down.

"Wait," I say as we reach the room. "I know it's cold, but the stars are so beautiful tonight."

"Hardly the only thing."

I cough awkwardly.

"The evening's over, dude. I really appreciate everything you've done but... you don't need to keep up the act." Even though every single word he says reverberates in my chest, carving another mark on my heart.

Yes, this is pure insanity now.

Reckless and dumb and self-destructive.

But I don't stop him as he heads into the room and finds me on the patio a minute later, carrying a leafy green blanket that feels like a cloud.

"There," he says softly, passing it over and holding up a couple drinks he pulled from the mini fridge in our room. "No need to be cold. Or sober. Nice selection of local brews, if you'll join me."

No need for another drink. I had plenty of wine over dinner, and I can already feel it going to my head, but I accept it anyway.

We're already drowning, aren't we?

Why fuss when I can just admire the waves, even as they swallow us up?

"How'd you know I was a beer girl?" I ask, clinking the bottle against his. The loungers are soft, but I opt for the floor, leaning against the wall as I stare at the night sky. It's vast here. The near lack of moonlight makes the stars stand out like multicolored diamonds.

"Intuition, I guess."

"Did I ever tell you?"

"You told me a lot of things." He shrugs and sits beside me, popping open his can. "You're a dreamer, Lady Bug, always looking at the sky. That's the important part."

"I guess the sky's usually prettier than what's down below." I sigh. "Not counting the present view, I mean."

"Didn't say you were wrong."

I open my can and slurp beer.

My tongue tickles with delight and fizz.

It's not the cheap, watery stuff you can get everywhere—this stuff is locally brewed and there's real depth, an apple and toffee flavor that goes perfectly with this cool, fall-like evening.

"You outdid yourself tonight," Patton says after a moment, leaning his head against the wall. I pull the blanket up to cover my bare shoulders. "I know it's not easy mingling with that crowd of show-offs and blowhards."

I smile. "It wasn't so bad once I got the hang of it. You helped a ton."

"Helped you find your confidence? I hope so. I remember the first time I came to one of these things with Dex, years ago..." He rubs a hand across his face. "I felt like a minnow in a roaring ocean."

"And now all the big fish salute you and want a piece of your business."

"*Our* business," he corrects sharply. "I might be alone, but I'm representing my brothers, too."

"Didn't they want to come?"

"Dexter's too busy with married life these days, and Archer just *hates* this shit. Socializing, I mean. If it wasn't for Colt, I think he'd find the last cave in Kansas City and crawl into it forever."

I laugh at the ridiculous image.

I haven't seen much of Archer. Although he's pretty reserved, there wasn't anything obviously anti-social about him.

"So you're the social butterfly?" I nudge him in the side. "Or are you the bootlicker?"

He hesitates before he speaks.

"The sacrificial lamb. That's more accurate." His chuckle fades into the night. There's just the empty desert ahead and bright pinpricks of starlight beaming down.

Somehow, the silence accented by this landscape doesn't feel so suffocating now.

"I meant it, you know. What I said about you back there," he says quietly.

I don't know what to say.

But I am feeling things.

It meant a lot.

And where would I be without Patton Rory?

God, without the man who gave me my son?

New guilt rushes up like a man-eating wolf and bites me hard.

The night sky swirls with secrets, everything I want to say that's tearing my heart to pieces.

Without knowing what I'm doing, I lean closer.

First, my arm brushes against his, and his skin feels too warm, too inviting. I can't help leaning in.

With a surprised look, he tucks me against his side.

We share the blanket with our legs almost touching. And it's the *almost* that makes me turn my face up, staring with questions mirrored in the starlit night.

Every place we touch burns.

Every place we don't burns more.

Holy hell, the places I want him…

I swallow hard, praying he doesn't notice.

I'm not sure where my inhibitions went, but when his lips find mine, they're totally abandoned.

His kiss comes hot and wild like summer heat stolen from the distant white sands.

In the cool air, his mouth smolders, and he tastes like beer. My fingers tangle in his shirt, pulling him closer.

"Salem," he growls against my mouth.

I moan back.

His hand brushes my hair away so his hungry eyes can see my face, just waiting to be devoured. He pauses, and I freeze, wondering if he's going to turn me away after all this in a flash of reason.

But he shakes his head.

"You're so goddamned beautiful tonight," he tells me and kisses me again.

I can feel the electric current all the way to my toes.

I've never had any man kiss me like Patton.

It's not a whisper, not a question—it's a brute demand and God, I want to give in.

I want to give him everything.

When his tongue sweeps fully into my mouth, mine meets it.

When he pulls me into his lap, my legs straddling him, I whimper.

Gripping his shoulders, sliding my hands through his hair, trembling in his arms. Even when he's so clearly turned on, it's hard to let myself just *be.*

And when he picks me up, cradling me against his body like I'm weightless, I just wrap my arms around him and keep my mouth molded to his, savoring every spearing thrust as he claims my mouth.

His hand finds my breast, fingers stroking roughly through the fabric. It only takes a single bead of pressure from his thumb over my nipple.

I'm flipping melting.

Moans become hot gasps.

My legs part as his other hand roams my thigh, so deliciously greedy.

"Fuck," he rasps, breaking the kiss.

His eyes snap to mine, all blue witchfire.

There's no hesitation left in my brain.

None whatsoever as he hauls me up a second later and carries me inside.

I already know we're heading straight to the bed.

And I have exactly one panicked second before the déjà vu hits.

This feels so familiar as he lays me on the bed before him and eclipses me with his body.

Except this room is more luxurious, the bed larger, and I'm older and more certain and supposedly wiser.

Less drunk, at least.

I suck my bottom lip as his hands cover my breasts, picking up where he left off, teasing me with this rough pressure that leaves me shaking and soaked.

It's a struggle to hold my eyes open, and only then, so I can appreciate the rigid muscle of his torso as he leans back and pulls his shirt off.

I think he rips a button in his haste.

But he's bare for me, this broad-chested beast in all his wild, divine glory.

My hands slide down his abs—how are they even *harder* than I remember?—and then my mouth.

"Woman, go to town," he urges. "Fucking touch me wherever you please. I'm all yours tonight."

The edge in his voice gives me courage. So does the way he caresses my face. I kiss a trail down his neck to his belt-line, and soon those hot little kisses become licks.

He groans like thunder.

Wow. I never knew how much I missed that sound.

"I like this dress, it looks damn good on you," he says, right before he shears it open. The material splits, seams tearing loudly, and for once I'm not thinking about money. "But I like it better gone. Don't worry, I'll buy you a new one."

"Holy shit. Um, I've never had a man physically rip off my clothes before."

"You've never been with a man, then. Present company excluded."

I. Am. Dead.

No, I don't bother telling him my experience with men

has been stunted and hilariously nonexistent since my last encounter. I've spent my twenties in a sexual desert that rivals the remoteness outside.

Juggling a job *and* a kid as a single mom doesn't leave much time for dating, much less hooking up with guys who can cause you more trouble.

He throws what's left of my dress to one side and slides back off the bed, standing like an angry god as he looks me up and down.

Oh, I'm so tempted to cover myself in the face of perfection—the stretch marks on my belly, the fact that my boobs aren't half as perky as they were last time. But he shakes his head and swats my uneasy arm away from my chest.

"Don't."

I never thought a single word could be so loaded.

"But I'm not… I'm not as young or hot as you remember," I whisper.

"Bullshit, Lady Bug. I dreamed about you," he rumbles, moving back on the bed and pushing me down under him. "You know how many nights I thought about seeing you again? How many times I fucking came in my hand, remembering how we burned?"

Holy shit.

I tremble.

There's no faking the sincerity in his voice.

The feral glint in his eye would make any red-blooded woman weak, and I'm no exception. I'm so drenched I can barely think.

"I want you, Salem Hopper. From your eyelashes down to your toes, but mostly, I want to be buried in your tight little pussy."

My throat tightens. It's this weird, heady mix, being so aroused but so nervous, too.

"I hope I don't disappoint you." I definitely didn't wear

the right bra for this. And if he notices the stripes all over my hips, he'll re-evaluate his life choices.

I'm not anywhere near the same league as the Instagram perfect women he's been with.

He grabs my hands with a snarl.

"Look down. Look down right now," he tells me, and when I do, there's a massive bulge in his pants. "If that doesn't prove I'm into you, what will?"

"Another kiss, maybe. That might help," I whisper.

"Where?" His grin is so wicked it's lopsided.

Before I have time to breathe, he's hooked his fingers down the waistband of my panties and he pulls them down in one long jerk.

Then I'm open, a willing slave to his tongue.

He licks me.

Oh my God, he *licks me.* Hypnotic, teasing circles, leaving me so delirious the rest of the world goes silent.

When he finds my clit, there's nothing left to do but ride the storm.

So I close my eyes and arch my back, fisting my hands in the covers as his mouth takes me to the brink of insanity, sucking and licking until I'm completely gone.

When he stops, I almost faint.

With one hand, he slides a finger inside me.

Just one.

And it's enough.

My walls convulse and that fireball in my core goes off.

"Patton!" His name grinds out in this torn whisper as he wrings every last drop of sin from my skin.

Even with the whole world spinning, I force my eyes open, watching as he pushes my legs over his shoulders and devours me completely.

Watching the vicious pride in his eyes as he makes me ride his face to the bitter end.

Watching with my legs still shaking and his finger raised as he holds it up and sucks.

"Fucking decadent," he tells me, and then he's kissing me again.

He makes me taste myself on his lips.

It's frantic then, this feeling of falling, of not knowing where we'll land, of desperately trying to find every inch of pleasure together before we do.

When I have my wits again, I rip off his pants just as fast as he disposed of my dress. He fists my hair as I grind against him until he growls and shoves my legs open.

Just when I think he's about to take what's his—what's *always* been his alone—his weight shifts until he holds back, dragging his cock against my entrance.

"Tease!" I gasp. I'm breathless but I don't care. "Patton, please. I need you in me."

"Where's the fun in that if I can't make you suffer?" He licks the sensitive skin beside my ear.

He nibbles down my neck to my breasts.

"Say it again," he rasps. "Beg for me, Lady Bug."

There's something primal in his voice now. A dark thirst that pushes buttons I didn't know I had.

"I... I want you to fuck me, Patton..."

"Say please."

I'm moaning as he drags his cock against my clit, pulling back just enough to tap his swollen head on it.

"Please!" I'm almost screaming.

Finally, his gaze hardens with violent determination.

And his hips rear back as he bares his teeth, swallowing a curse as he pushes in. One relentless inch at a time until he's buried to the hilt.

Flipping electric.

It's obscene how much I *feel* him, every seething inch, turning me inside out.

It's so good I almost climax again in under a minute.

But I shift, encouraging him to run rampant, the better to take his punishing cock.

It's a primal thing, this need to be owned, just for tonight.

Tomorrow, we'll have all the time in the world for regrets.

For now, there's only this moment.

There's just Patton Rory, joined to my flesh, which is already begging to feel him come for a second time.

Call me insane—especially considering what happened before—but I only think about the missing condom for a split second.

I'm that ravenous, reduced to this depraved thing worshipping every thrust he gives.

"Salem, look at me," he growls, slowing his pumps and holding himself in me.

Gently at first, like he's testing my limits, then harder. *Faster.*

"I want your eyes on me while I fuck you."

Ohhh, shit.

My panting deepens. This is new and familiar and fierce.

He grips my thighs, pushing my legs back so he can look at me properly.

"Fuck," he grinds out. "Play with your clit before I come in you."

I happily oblige.

Without a second thought or fear or hesitation.

I'm so close to the brink I can't think.

There's just hot breath stalled in my lungs and the steady churning roar of my own heartbeat as I reach down.

I play with myself as he pounds into me, mimicking the movement of his tongue with my fingers, and my pussy tightens and throbs until I can't take it.

"Patton," I whisper. It's a warning, more messy breath than words. *"Patton!"*

"Fucking go," he orders. "Come on my cock. Come like you've wanted since the last time I fucked you."

He grips my thighs and raises my hips at the very last second.

Then I'm crashing over.

I shatter.

I drown in foaming pleasure.

I scream into his mouth when his teeth capture my bottom lip, drowning my ecstasy.

When he picks up speed and goes harder, deeper, I know he must be close, so I wrap my legs around him, digging my nails into his back.

A screwed-up part of me still hates this man for blowing up my life without even knowing it.

But a sicker part adores what he does to me.

No one else could ever splinter me like this or make me ache for his eruption like the desert craving rain.

And God, it's only the *second* time, but it already feels like a basic need I've been missing for far too long.

The sheer intensity, the way he fucks like he's just as conflicted, each stroke brimming with love and hate and unholy passion.

And I want him more than the air in my lungs when he bows up, tenses, and bruises me.

He slams his hips against mine with a guttural noise that might be my name—half curse and half prayer.

I never know.

Because another orgasm rips me in two as his cock swells, heaving in my depths, flooding me with magma.

Delirious.

I don't know I'm cradling him until I am as the rhythm dies in breathless rutting strokes, as my pussy milks him, as he empties his soul into me.

"Holy. Shit," I whisper, just as he collapses on top of me.

The smiling kiss he plants on my forehead feels oddly sweet as he rolls off, sprawling out and making the bed feel so much smaller.

Holy shit is right. What now, Lemmy?

What happens now that you've made the biggest mistake of your life a second time?

I don't know. He might be twisted up with the same horrible regret behind that smug mask.

Honestly, I can never seem to read all the different sides to Patton. He's absolute chaos, so multifaceted the light only reflects off of him and lets me see one edge at a time.

Right now, I'd give just about anything to read him, but I'm scared what I'll find if I dig too far.

Instead, I cuddle up with him in the vibrating silence, listening to our breathing and feeling the slow, steady hum of our hearts.

It feels wrong to speak.

But at least that familiar silence isn't scary. Not when it's so dangerously comforting.

And this time as I drift off to sleep, unlike on the riverboat, I know he'll still be there when I wake up.

XVI: BET THE FARM (PATTON)

*T*here's a black cat in my bed and she might be the luckiest little creature alive.

I am fucking blessed.

Soft morning light streams through the curtains and illuminates her sleeping face. I've been awake for a while now, staring at her in awe.

We're both still naked, though she's wrapped the blankets around herself in a snug nest.

Usually, this is the time to sneak away.

It's either a forgettable moment best left behind me or I have urgent business to get on with. But leaving, that's missing from my mind.

Shit, I'd *gladly* throw away an entire workweek if it means adding a few more hours to this morning, stretching out time like the gold sunrays spilling across her mahogany hair.

She's more relaxed in her sleep than I've ever seen. Her forehead lacks the lines that gather there so often, her mouth soft and her face worry free.

It's a crime this isn't her normal face.

I want her to feel peaceful.

Just about as much as I want to wake up beside her every morning without a care in the world—or a goddamned looming disaster.

Yes, I know. Everything about this is wrong.

The trouble is, it feels too right.

And she stirs, wiggling free from her cocoon of covers. When she opens her eyes and sees me lying beside her, panic flashes on her face.

Thankfully, brief. A startled second, a twitch of her lips before it fades behind the impassive wall she throws up.

"Morning," I say with a yawn. "Haven't slept that well in years."

"Um." She sits up, holding the covers up with one hand like a shield. With the other hand, she brushes her loose hair back from her face. "Patton, did we...?"

Oh, shit.

Not the words a man wants to hear from a woman after he's made her scream half the night.

"We did," I say carefully. "Let me guess, you regret it already?"

"No." She clears her throat. "No, but we should probably talk about what happened."

"What part?"

"The sex, Patton," she says flatly, finger combing her hair again. "I mean, the fact that you're my boss and we just slept together."

Yeah, I get the dilemma.

I just broke my cardinal rule, dipping my pen in the company ink and damn near breaking it off.

Every part of me aches to take her in my arms, but I don't move, staying propped up on my elbow as I look at her. "You regret it then?"

"I..." She stops, her eyes narrowed as she looks at me. "Do you?"

"Not for a second. I'd do it again in half a heartbeat." I give her a lazy smile. "In fact, when we're done talking, I'm game."

Her eyes flick to my lap, to the hard-on tenting the sheets before she looks away. She sucks her lip helplessly. "Shouldn't we figure this out first?"

"Figure out what, woman? The fact that we decided to stop bickering and fuck each other's brains out instead? Sounds like progress with this relationship." My jaw tightens on the last word.

Damn, this is bad when I'm casually throwing the r-word around.

I can downplay it to hell and back, but I think she knows this can't be brushed off as business this time.

I don't bother trying.

"No, it's not that," she admits, flushing. "I'm just thinking about the fallout, the consequences. What happens if someone else at Higher Ends finds out? What about your brothers?"

I snort loudly. "No one needs to know. Frankly, Dex and Archer are oblivious, and if by some miracle they're not, they'll keep their idiot mouths shut. We're adults, Salem. We're old enough to keep a secret. Hell, we're already pretending to be a couple for half this conference. If this is what we want—and I know I do—why is it anybody else's business?"

My voice burns my throat.

I can almost see the instant when she comes to the same conclusion, or maybe just finds the same twisted excuse for crossing lines that ought to be sacrosanct.

"Just for the weekend," she says quietly. "You're probably right. If we're careful, no one has to know…"

"As long as you're quiet. You think you can manage?" I pull her forward, kissing her until I growl in her mouth.

"I... I..." she stammers adorably as I sweep her hair back, closing my fist around a makeshift ponytail.

"I'm not going to make it easy for you," I promise.

"Challenge accepted."

The hot flicker in her hazel eyes cuts me in two.

This is how this woman brings me crashing to my knees.

The fact that she takes every challenge and inverts them, hounding *me* to be better in every way.

And as my free hand skims down to her ass, grabbing her until her moans taste like caramel, I can't say I mind *this* capacity one damn bit.

* * *

OUR ROUTINE CONTINUES through the rest of this surreal conference.

She's my woman for the giddy little real estate apes who now look at me with a newfound respect, especially the men who look on with boiling jealousy.

In bed, she's mine in the most primal ways. My very own atlas of sin and seduction I trace with my hands and mouth.

It's like I need her topography branded into my brain for life.

I can never bury myself in her tight little pussy enough.

I can never press her lips to mine close enough while I sink my greedy teeth into her tender flesh.

I can never leave her leaking enough of my come.

It's lunacy how well she's fallen into her role, warming my colleagues and my bed until I feel like I need a brick to the head to come back to Earth. Sometimes, I have to remind myself she's not mine.

Not for real.

And whatever this madness is, it won't continue.

Honestly, it shouldn't once we've left the bleached sands and canyons long behind.

But try telling my inner caveman that.

I've never been good at reasoning with that grunting, possessive fuck. When it comes to her, he has me in a chokehold.

The chemistry feels like a drug and it's just as addictive.

When we're not hobnobbing for business, we're finding quiet spots around us, places where I can fuck her against a wall or in the back of the car.

It's like we're back on that casino boat for an extended lucky stay, acting stupid and reckless and horny as hell.

God Almighty, I've never been so horny in my life.

I wake up wanting her when I've had her three times the night before, even when she's lying breathless in my arms after burying her head in a pillow so she stays quiet.

Insatiable.

That's the only word for a thirst this rampant.

We're at a quiet dinner alone when she taps her knee against mine.

I realize I've spaced out, staring and imagining how I'm going to remove that dress she's wearing tonight.

It's white and gold like the sun against white clouds.

Soon, it's going to be a ghost.

Or maybe I'll just bend her over the bed while she's still wearing it. Maybe I'll take her into the shower or out to the pool like last night and watch the stars dance in her eyes while I mount her and break her again and again, listening to her whimpers for mercy.

"Patton!" she hisses. "We're supposed to be enjoying this, aren't we?"

"I happen to be enjoying my dinner very much, thanks."

"Enjoying it *with me*."

"I am, Lady Bug."

She smacks my arm. "Can't you wait until we get back? This place is too expensive to be thinking about *that* all the time."

"On the contrary," I say, linking my fingers with hers over the table, "anyplace is suitable for what I'm thinking."

"You're crazy."

"I think you mean obsessed."

"You're shameless," she gasps.

I grin again.

Shit, I can't remember the last time I've smiled this much. Not since before I had the company, I'm sure.

This Mexican restaurant in Page, Arizona, is an intimate place without the resort's bed and whistles. We have a table in the corner to ourselves. No one from the conference is likely to show up here, we're mostly obscured from view, and the food is excellent.

Three good reasons to choose this particular spot.

"We can't right here," she says, but there's a look on her face that tells me she's considering it.

"There is a bathroom," I growl.

"Not sexy, Patton."

No, but it doesn't dampen my disappointment.

"I never said we should do anything besides eat here," I say.

As if on cue, a waiter appears carrying our food. A steaming pile of fajitas for Salem and carne asada for me.

"Thanks. This looks delicious!" Salem gives him a wide smile before she turns to me again. "Why are you glaring now?"

"Glaring? I'm not."

"If you're getting jealous over some college kid who just served me food—"

"Do you know how long it took you to smile at me like that?" I'm not jealous of that kid, no—not like the millionaire whales back at the resort who never learned to take no for an answer—but sometimes I hate the fact that it took her so long to warm up to me.

"You're my boss," she reminds me. "And when we reconnected, our history was pretty complicated."

"Still is," I say with a shrug, tucking into my food. "Six years. Almost a lifetime."

"For some people." She frowns at the table. Her phone, turned upside down beside her, vibrates and she glances at it. "Sorry. It's just the sitter, I bet."

"Arlo's?"

"Yeah, she's a rock star. They were supposed to go to this dinosaur art exhibit for kids over at the Nelson-Atkins."

"Don't turn him into an art nerd too soon. It hasn't helped humanize Dexter one bit," I say with a snort. "How's he holding up with you gone?"

She winces. "He misses me, I think. I've never left him alone this long."

"Ever? In five years?"

Her gaze hardens.

"You think I can afford a vacation *and* childcare? Cute." She sighs, her lips pulling into a sad smile. "I've lived a very different life from you, Patton Rory. Down here at ground level, people are scraping by."

Fair enough.

I forget that this lifestyle is new to her when she slides into it so seamlessly. It's easy to forget this is just a fleeting break from reality.

Not the way our lives will be from now on, even if there's no shortage of luxuries I suddenly have a mad urge to shower her with.

"You should call him," I urge. "It's still early enough. Say good night to your boy."

"Over dinner?" Her eyebrows sweep up.

"It'll be too late by the time we get back." I run my fingers along the rim of my wineglass. "Plus, I've got other plans for you back in our room."

She flushes and glances at her phone.

"Arlo would definitely interrupt *that*," she murmurs. "The kissing was bad enough. I almost died when he walked in. Do you think anyone here would mind?"

I nod at a rowdy bunch in a corner, clanking micheladas in tall beer glasses together.

From the looks of it, they're celebrating a birthday.

"Lady Bug, if they're in here bellowing like drunken rhinos, you can call your son."

"Come over here. We'll do a FaceTime," she says, beckoning me to her side. "He might as well see you too."

I shuffle over and after a few seconds, she video calls Mrs. Gabbard.

"Hello, hello!" a grey-haired lady says cheerfully. "I wasn't expecting you to call, dear. How are things?"

"Lovely, Mrs. Gabbard. I just wanted to see if Arlo wants to say hello, if he's still up?"

"Well, he's not in bed yet, that's for sure." The corners of her mouth pinch down as she walks through her apartment, carrying the phone. "Here he is, just wrapping up brushing his teeth. Look here, you rascal, someone wants to say hi."

The camera swivels to face Arlo, who's wearing Batman pajamas.

"Mommy?" He grabs the phone with a wide smile. "Mommy!"

"Hey, honey." Salem's smile is hardly any smaller. It's endearing how she looks at him. "How are you? Are you being good for Mrs. Gabbard?"

"Very good. I'm the best!" he proclaims. A suspicious claim if Mrs. Gabbard's heavy sigh is any indication. "I drew so much today, Mommy. I wanna show you."

"Wow, sure. But just a few, hon. It's late."

He takes the phone, nodding vigorously at Mrs. Gabbard's encouragement not to drop it, and leads us to the corner of the room and his little desk, stacked with fresh sketches.

"Look!" he commands, though his poor camera-ship means we can't see more than a few blurred lines. "I drew you, Mommy. You're driving your car."

"I do a lot of that. Great job," Salem gushes, though I know she can't see it any better than I can.

"Oh, and I drew Mr. Rory, too." Arlo holds up another sheet of paper that seems almost entirely white besides a few rolling lines. "He's a snowman."

Kid logic, you have to love it.

I'll admit my snowman likeness looks better than the other drawings he's come up with. Salem laughs and sends me a look that says she's thinking the same thing.

"How was the museum?" she asks.

"Awesome! They had a silver T-rex. I practiced shooting it till Mrs. Gabbard made me stop. Then we went out for food and it was so cold." He mimes his teeth chattering.

Kid's cute, even if he's a royal pain in the ass.

"I'll bet. We're lucky here, it's really warm," Salem says. "Isn't it, Patton?"

"Comfortably."

"There's no snow?" Arlo asks, a little awestruck.

"None," Salem says. "It's sunny. I wore my long sleeves outside today just to keep my arms safe from getting burned."

"Wow, like summer! In winter?" He loses interest in the weather and abruptly holds up a book. "I read this today."

"What is it, sweetie?"

"My Inky book! He went all the way to India and he even

met an elephant! I'm gonna write him a letter. You were right, Mom, he's the coolest penguin ever."

I can't resist smiling as I cut in. "You know, if you're lucky, sometimes Inky writes you back. I still have a letter from him floating around somewhere."

I don't tell them my mother framed said letter and I left it proudly hanging above my childhood bed until I moved out.

Of course, it's not really a magic penguin writing kids back and helping them make friends. Until recently, it was the author and creator, Clara Marshall. I read an article that says her nephew and his wife are doing great things for reviving the brand, ensuring the famous pen pal penguin lives on for kids like Arlo.

"Tell him where you'd love to go. I'm sure he'll write you back, Arlo," she says with a laugh. She shakes her head. "When we get home, you'll show me everything, okay?"

"'Kay. Karate too! I'll show you all my new moves." He drops the phone and scrabbles to pick it up again. "Don't tell Mrs. Gabbard," he whispers, so close to the mic the sound distorts.

I chuckle at his antics.

"We won't tell anyone," I say.

"Are you coming home soon, Mommy?" Arlo asks, a slight whine entering his voice. He's holding the phone so near his face all we can see are blue eyes. "I miss you."

"Miss you too, honey. I'll be back tomorrow."

"I hope so. Mrs. Gabbard wouldn't let me have ice cream and you *always* give me ice cream on weekends."

Salem glances at me helplessly, then back at Arlo. "Well, if Mrs. Gabbard says you're a good boy when we get back home, you'll get a little extra. Maybe we'll even go out for it."

"Yay!" He pumps his little fist.

"But now it's time for bed, okay, big guy? Can you do that for me?"

He bounces up and down, looking more like he's ready for a marathon. "I wanna stay up. Can I?"

"Do you want that ice cream when I get back?"

He considers it, his little eyes ticking like a clock.

His face falls as he comes to the inevitable conclusion. *"Yes."*

"So go get ready for bed. Mrs. Gabbard will tuck you in and read you more Inky. Give Mommy a kiss." She puckers her lips and he makes a kissing sound. "Okay, sweetie. I love you."

"Love you too."

"There we go," Mrs. Gabbard says, taking back the phone before it starts spinning again. "I'll see you tomorrow, Salem."

"See you then. Thanks so much for looking after him." She waves, and after exchanging a few more words, hangs up.

"He's a great kid," I say, and for once, it's not a total lie.

He's grown on me, about as much as any little hellraiser can.

For some reason, that makes her tense. I run a hand up and down her arm.

"Don't worry. I don't hate him anymore because he called me Grumpybutt and ruined my favorite tie."

"God, don't say it like that." She laughs awkwardly, but those lines in her forehead don't fade.

"It's fine." I kiss her on the temple. This time, she relaxes. "Should we head back? That pool is calling my name."

"Pool *and* beer," she decides. "It's our last night, after all."

The last night.

Shit.

That stirs my blood and brings up things better left unsaid. Right now, in the middle of a restaurant, definitely isn't the right time.

As soon as we're done eating, we head out. I'm still holding her hand when we break apart so we can climb in the vehicle and drive back to the resort.

Neither of us brought swimming stuff, but that doesn't matter now with a private pool.

My breath stalls when I see Salem pad out to the water naked.

I follow her in, doing nothing to hide my erection, and then we're in the warm water under an endless starry night.

"Last night," I growl, grabbing her waist and pulling her in. Her body fits against mine like it was designed for it. "How do you want to celebrate?"

"You mean besides beer?" She tosses her hair back and takes a sip.

"I meant *after* the beer."

"I blame the beer for this whole situation," she says, but there's the hint of a smile. I take a swig from the open bottle she brought out with her and kiss away her protests.

"Then I'll be forever grateful to the beer," I tell her. "And to you for listening."

She trails a finger down my front, skimming her way down my chest and abdomen. "I suppose you deserve some credit too, Mr. Rory..."

"So you do think I'm hot? About time you said it."

"I have my faults, but I'm not blind, Patton."

Grinning, I lean against the side of the pool and slide my hands down, cupping her ass. "What fucking faults, woman? Don't see any here."

She gasps wickedly.

"You're just looking from the wrong angle."

"What's the right one, then?" I lift her up so I can kiss her neck. Below, her nipple hardens, and I try not to take it in my mouth. "From here?"

"Patton—"

"Or maybe"—I hoist her up so she's balanced just above my cock, which is already hard, so ready to plunge in— "there's a better angle here. Surely."

She tightens her hands on my shoulders until her nails dig in.

"Not outside," she whispers. "Someone might hear."

"You'll just have to be quiet." Madness claims me. I tease the head of my cock against her slit, toying with the folds as she wraps her legs around me. Pool sex isn't necessarily the best idea, but there are two perfectly good sun loungers on the side.

If this truly is our final night together, I want to make it memorable.

With her legs wrapped around me and my hands gripping her ass, it's easy enough to carry her out of the water and haul her to the nearest chair. The cool air caresses our skin, but when she shifts her hips so I'm at her entrance, I don't notice the cold anymore.

Hell, right now, I don't think I'd notice if the whole resort exploded as long as I could still lay her down on this lounger and fuck her.

The ends of her hair are wet, looking almost black in this light, and her eyes are dark, all her thoughts shining like the stars above.

Lust.

Adrenaline.

Secrets.

There are so many things I still don't know.

Wounds she hasn't bared, whispers that singe the air before we sleep each night, but I don't care.

I just want *her*, secrets and all.

I'm not one for making love.

Usually, I like to pull a girl's hair as I fuck her from

behind or pin her hands above her head as I wring one orgasm out of her after the next.

Now, I don't want any of that.

I want her to know how much this last night means to me.

I want to try, hopelessly, to fuck her out of my system.

When I tumble her down on the bed, I take my sweet time, tracing the outline of her lips with my fingers.

I've already explored every inch of her skin, yet I slowly rediscover it tonight, letting my hands roam wild, hungry knuckles grazing her skin.

I squeeze her flesh like clay, wishing I could leave the imprints of my greed on it forever.

My tongue follows, mapping her with every moan, teasing and tormenting and leaving her dizzy.

"Patton—God!" she cries out real sweet for me.

Damn, when I finally reach between her legs, she's drenched and ready.

But before I can use my tongue there and bring her off, she grabs my hair and pulls.

"I want you in me," she whispers, wrapping her legs around me. "I want to feel you fill me now, Patton. Please."

If there's a man alive who can resist a plea like that, he's a god.

Me, I'm a mere mortal.

A fucking chump for a beautiful woman with a prettier soul begging me to turn her inside out.

Swallowing a growl, I grasp my cock, teasing it against her hot little cunt as long as I can stand.

She's so wet it's hard not to slide right in.

When she gasps louder, I press my free hand over her mouth.

"Quiet," I snarl. "Look at me, Salem. Tonight, you give me your eyes and your voice."

She nods, her eyes rolling back in her head as I push into her, one fierce inch at a time.

I clench my teeth.

I've never had my nerves fire like they do when I take her.

There are terrible seconds where I'm afraid I'll lose control and blow my wad like a virgin.

Thankfully, I'm not that wrecked. *Barely.*

She already knows to play with herself, the little minx.

She rubs her clit, using her other hand to pinch one nipple as she smiles up at me. She might as well be waving red at a raging bull.

My mouth pushes her hand away and I suck her warm nipple until she gasps through her teeth.

Music.

Goddamn music to my ears.

She's an entire feast for the senses.

Watching her, hearing her, feeling her pussy squeezing my cock—it's all one of the slowest, sexiest experiences I've ever had as a man. No model I've fucked with the money for endless salon treatments ever gave back this chemistry.

And hearing her frantic attempts to keep quiet as she nears her first orgasm is almost enough to push me over the edge repeatedly.

It's like I have to meditate while I work her body, find my zone so I can own her pleasure.

Breathing raggedly, I touch her face, stroking her cheekbone.

"That's right, Lady Bug," I tell her. "Don't you dare hold back. Show me fireworks. Come for me."

She bares her teeth, her eyelids flutter, and then—

Gone.

I feel it the instant her climax hits, the way she tightens around me like a vise. Holding my cock still while she pulses feels easier than wrestling a feral wolf.

Fuck, the way her breathing deepens and stalls before she moans loudly into my hand…

The way her pleasure vibrates through my skin, slipping out in messy cries from her open mouth, catches my very last thread of self-control holding back my inner beast.

I snap.

My hips go wild, pounding into her, crashing my way through one raging climax and pulling a second one out of her before the first ever ends.

I can't stand to silence her anymore.

My hand slips down, catching her by the throat, just enough to feel her pulse raging under my fingers while she comes like a painting, lively and red-faced and undone.

Her pussy clings to my cock, tightening, jerking me off while I thrust.

I'm too far gone to be ashamed that I can't last any goddamned longer.

My hips lunge, I bury myself balls deep, and erupt.

I finish inside her with a guttural noise that's more animal than man.

We both spill our souls into the night, screaming and roaring, waking whatever dead are long buried and forgotten in the desert hills.

The cool breeze nips my back against the mingled sweat and water from the pool, but our skin feels molten where it touches.

I've officially left the building—hell, the whole fucking planet—until I feel an angel's touch slowly stroking my face as I try to catch my breath.

"Hey." She runs her fingers across my face. "Hey, Patton?"

I open my eyes, falling into the hazel wonder of her gaze underneath me.

"Are you okay?" she whispers.

"No. Did you know you're the sexiest work of art to ever exist?" I grind out.

Do you have any fucking idea how impossible it'll be to let you go? Thank God I still have enough wits to not ask her that.

The smile that curves her mouth ignites her eyes to gold.

If I had a superpower, I'd hit pause. I'd freeze time so I never had to stop seeing her smile like this.

"It's been a pretty amazing weekend. I'll give you that," she says.

Reluctantly, I roll off her and hit the stone patio under us with a grunt. I lie there for a solid minute before I have the bones to grab a towel and help her clean up.

"You know what?" I tell her as we head back inside and flop down on the bed together. She snuggles right up to me like she was made to fit in the curve of my body. "There's no rule that says this *has* to stop once we climb on the jet home. Nothing besides the stupid little handshake agreement we made up."

"What do you mean?" She stares at me intently. "Patton Rory, are you second-guessing?"

"What do you think, Salem? I'm not second-guessing shit. I've made a decision. This thing we're doing now that's better than any high. The kissing, the sex, the pretend dating—it doesn't have to end. I don't want to put a pin in it. Yeah, I know you've got Arlo to think about and you'll be happy to get home, but I just—"

"It doesn't have to end," she echoes roughly.

It's my turn to stare while her eyes glow like gold discs.

"If you're cool with this evolving... so am I. But there's something you should really know first." She twists around to face me, suddenly twisting the covers around herself protectively, her eyes too wide and glistening.

All the peace and contentment that was there seconds ago has shattered. I don't understand.

"What is it, Lady Bug? What's wrong?"

"Arlo, that's what." She hesitates, clearing her throat. "He's —he's your son. Arlo's your son, Patton."

What. The. Fuck.

My heart damn near rips through my chest like an alien monster as she twists around to hide her face.

There's no way. It doesn't add up.

Salem Hopper, one-night stand from six years ago. And Arlo, he's her five-year-old kid with lightning blue eyes and dark hair and an endless appetite for shit-stirring.

Arlo, he's—

Oh, fuck.

He's mine.

XVII: DOUBLE OR NOTHING
(SALEM)

*H*ave you ever fallen down the stairs?

You know that awful moment when you're tripping.

Your foot skids off the edge or hits something that shouldn't be there, off by mere inches, destroying your balance.

You feel the ground shift and reach out desperately for something to grab on to.

You only have a split second before your vision starts spinning—just long enough to pray it's a short way down or for something soft to break your fall.

I'm falling in that killing slow motion right now, even though I'm perfectly still, turned to stone after I made myself look at him again.

Patton might be having a heart attack. Mouth open, eyes marbles, his healthy color turning ash-white like he's lost ten pints of blood.

Holy hell, this was stupid.

Holy shit, I never should've told him.

I never meant for it to come out like this—this sudden mess that feels like an ugly furball of guilt I just coughed up.

Before I dropped the atomic bomb, I never made up my mind about how to tell him at all, and now I've gone and done it.

I've given him the truth and there's no taking it back.

God help me.

Why couldn't I just keep my mouth shut and enjoy one more evening in paradise?

He rolls off the bed and stumbles back outside, toward the pool. I think he needs oxygen, and I can't blame him.

I follow timidly, half-afraid he'll walk right into the water and drown.

I shouldn't have let this long weekend go to my head.

Shouldn't have let him steal my heart a second time.

Shouldn't have flipping *told him.*

I'm breathless as he stops and whirls around to face me before he reaches the pool. In the darkness, I can't make out his features beyond the fact that he's pale, his eyes too dark.

"Arlo," he says hoarsely. "My son? *My son?*"

There's nothing good in his tone, just horror, heartbreak, fear.

You shouldn't have told him you stupid, stupid idiot!

"Patton... why don't you sit down?" I force out, taking his arm and trying to pull him to the lounger.

He doesn't flinch away, but he won't look at me either. It's like he's just waiting for an explanation I don't have.

"Salem," he rumbles, then stops.

He drops his head into his hands, pressing his long fingers against his face until the skin goes white.

"I just—I thought you might've wondered by now," I say quietly. "Did you ever?"

From his expression, clearly not.

"I know this is a lot. I'm sorry." I rub his back, wondering how it came to this, how I can possibly salvage this nightmare. "I never meant to tell you like this, it just kinda happened..."

"How *did* you mean to tell me? When did you mean to tell me?" he snaps.

His blue eyes flare, angry and different from the fire of our passion.

"I don't know." Maybe never. "I'm sorry."

"Why didn't you tell me before?" he demands again.

A fair question. Maybe the first one I'd ask, too.

The *how* is obvious, at least.

"Well, it's... it's complicated," I manage. Worst answer ever, I know.

I press my fingers into the lounger, feeling the luxe material give way under the pressure.

He inhales sharply, staring at me again, his eyes demanding answers.

"I didn't even know who you were until a couple months ago."

"When you started at Higher Ends," he finishes coldly.

"Yeah. That's when I realized exactly *who* I slept with all those years ago."

The tiniest hint of a smile curls his lips, then drops again.

His voice is strangled when he says, "I told you my name, didn't I?"

"...we were so drunk, Patton. I thought you were just some rich guy. Just some *guy* with a life to get back to where a baby wouldn't ever fit." And I never bothered looking for him because I didn't think he would care about the fact he'd had a son with me. "I didn't want that kind of friction, feeling like I'm forcing it, putting a burden on you. I didn't want my son growing up with a father who never wanted him."

Yep. I know I sound like the lamest human being on the planet.

But my worries are valid.

After all, I've orbited the high life just enough to know rich people don't like anything that comes back to haunt them. They definitely don't like human drama hand grenades chucked into their picture-perfect lives that turn their careers and dreams into twisted shrapnel.

"The pregnancy was a shock," I say into the silence. The dark desert beyond us feels bigger than ever. "A huge surprise, really. I had no clue one night could change my entire life so much."

"We had sex, Salem. We were goddamned drunk." Patton pinches his nose like he's holding himself together. "I should have worn protection—my mistake. But you never said you weren't on birth control."

"Dude. I wasn't expecting to get drunk and have a one-night stand with a stranger," I say, my voice perilously close to losing control. "Trust me, I've thought about that night a whole lot more than you."

He releases a breath through his nose. "So you didn't know who I was. You got knocked up and you never looked for me once?"

I stare down at the cold stone under my feet.

"Maybe I should've tried. Everyone wanted me to. My parents spent *hours* interrogating me about it. And Kayla, she was ready to send my dress to a forensics lab to have it scraped for DNA..." I can feel his eyes on me, burning, but I don't dare look at him and see the pity there. "But that's the thing. I was never going to let them find out I got pregnant from a random hookup."

"What did you tell them?" he asks, his voice softer.

"That the father was my deadbeat ex, this guy I dated briefly. They knew I kept my dating life pretty quiet, so it was believable. The irony is I never even slept with him, but they don't need to know that." I button my lips together before I reveal another truth I don't want Patton to know: that drunken night on that casino boat was my *first time.*

He doesn't need to know I was a virgin and the woman who kept his son a secret for years, all in the same freaking night.

"And Arlo? What the hell did you tell him?"

I swallow thickly.

"I haven't…" This time, it's my turn to put my hands over my face. "I always just told him his father was a man I met a long time ago and he went away. I always knew I'd have to come up with more than that someday. But he isn't old enough to understand yet, not really."

"Went away? That's it? Fuck." Patton cringes. I hate seeing it, but he asked for the truth. I can't give him any less now. "You make it sound like I *died.*"

That boulder in my throat just keeps getting bigger.

"For all I knew, you had. And making up lies about you—that was the least of my worries. My parents, they weren't the most understanding people…" I trail off again.

Huge understatement. My parents hated the fact that I derailed my life more than I did.

First, I hadn't gone to college, and then I'd gotten pregnant by some strange man and wasn't planning on marrying him.

I wouldn't even give them his *name.*

I can still remember the way my mom screamed at me, her eyes bulging. We didn't have anything like the Rory wealth, but my father was a doctor, and they were crazy social in a big city with a small-town feel where word gets around.

They couldn't stand their only daughter being a disgrace.

"My mom told me to get rid of him," I say quietly. "Not abortion—she didn't believe in that—but she wanted me to give Arlo up when he was born. But I couldn't, Patton. So they threw up their hands. They'd just retired, and they left for California. They wanted me to come with and start over, without my baby. I refused. I stayed here like an idiot."

"Alone." For the first time, he looks at me, his blue eyes agonized. "Yeah, fuck them."

"...what choice did I have?" My voice turns brittle, on the cusp of breaking. "No one would stick around for Arlo but me. I wasn't abandoning him."

"Shit, Salem." Patton runs his hands through his hair.

Shit's right.

I can't remember a time when it wasn't shit.

"You stuck around for him, yeah. You did the right thing, but who stuck around for you?" he growls. "I wasn't suggesting you should've abandoned him. I'm pissed knowing everybody else walked out on *you*, and I couldn't be there."

Oh, God.

I'm not going to cry over this.

I'm *not*.

Not even while my eyes are melting in their sockets and I can feel my soul bleeding out in the mess.

"It's not... it's not about what anyone wanted. It's not what I wanted for myself, I guess, but I wouldn't change anything."

No, I take that back.

I think.

I still don't know if I would take back telling him like this.

"I know now what I should've done. I should have told you sooner, as soon as I knew who you were," I whisper. "I just didn't want to pile more responsibility on you, especially when you clearly wanted nothing to do with us at first."

"Goddamn," he groans.

"And then things changed. You did want something to do

283

with me. I got scared. I thought if I told you, it would run you off and ruin whatever it was we had."

"You'd think that," he says, his voice heavy. "I gave you no good reason not to."

"I'm not blaming you," I rush out.

"No." His smile is a little too forced. "But it's true."

"Telling you something like this is a big deal. But then this weekend happened and today was so perfect, it just felt *right*."

"You've known all this time I'm Arlo's father," he says numbly. "Every single time we…"

"Yes."

"How could you stand to look at me?"

The softness in his voice makes my throat tighten.

"I don't hold it against you. You didn't know and that was my fault. And I didn't tell you because I'm expecting anything. If you don't want much to do with him now—or with me—I get it. I'm not holding you to anything."

"Salem," he growls roughly.

"Patton."

He bangs his fists against his thighs, shaking his head.

"I don't know what to say," he snarls. "I haven't had many girlfriends before, not serious ones, never mind a son. A family. *Shit*." He laughs, raking his other hand through his hair. I reach up and smooth it back down. "I'm not being articulate right now. I'm honking at you like a fucking mule."

"You just found out you have a little boy." I sniff, losing one hot tear down my cheek. "I think that's pretty understandable."

He huffs a breath and sighs.

"It's cold out here," he says, almost surprised. "Wait here, okay?"

I curl up in a ball as he disappears inside. For a brief, unreasonable instant, I worry he might flee. He might hot tail it back to Kansas City, back to the busy, prestigious life he had before I came and spat in his punch bowl.

Then he's back, handing me a white robe.

"Put it on, before you catch a cold," he growls. "Then come the fuck here."

Yeah, here come the tears.

"I need—" My voice breaks.

"Listen to me, you beautiful, dumb, marvelous girl." He presses a kiss to the side of my head. "This is a lot to take in, and I'll probably be freaking out about it all the way home. But if Arlo really is my son, I know what I want. I need to be in his life."

"Patton—"

"And yours," he continues. "If you'll have me. Fair warning, you won't keep me out easily, no matter how hard you try."

The avalanche begins.

I'm crying like a little girl.

All because he's just spoken words I never even dared of dreaming.

They're not gentle tears that streak silently down my face.

They're not soft and they're not a relief.

I'm bawling straight ugly tears with bone-shaking sobs. Even my legs quiver with the force of my crying.

"Salem." Patton pulls me closer, cradling me in his lap.

I'm small enough to rest against his chest, which feels like the entire world right now, this haven of him I never want to leave.

"Salem," he whispers again. My name has never sounded more intense on his lips. "It's okay. We'll be okay. I'm here."

I turn my face into his bare chest.

He smells like warmth and safety, like home, even though I've only been with him like this for a matter of days.

"You're not alone anymore. I promise," he tells me,

rocking me back and forth. His hand sweeps down my hair, smoothing it against my neck.

"I... I never thought this would happen." I hiccup embarrassingly loudly. God, I don't know where the tears keep coming from—no human being should cry this much.

But I'm not scared and ruined anymore.

I'm happy. This is far more than I could've ever hoped for.

Or maybe it's just sheer giddy relief. The sense that finally all this single mom responsibility isn't a lonely crushing weight piled on my shoulders that just keeps grinding me into the dirt year after year.

Arlo never had the life I wanted for him, there's no hiding that.

But now, if Patton steps up, my son might finally have dreams.

He could have a life he truly deserves.

And me, well... is it too much to think maybe I can have a fair shot at a fairy-tale?

It's almost too much, like you're holding a winning lottery ticket in your trembling little fingers.

"Talk to me," Patton urges. "Tell me what you're thinking."

I press the heels of my hands into my eyes until red streaks bloom against my eyelids. Then I shift, resting my head against his shoulder, my legs hooked over his knee.

Lying here like this, we feel like one person.

"It doesn't seem real," I whisper. "My parents left town when Arlo was only three months old. They gave me one more chance to give him up and join them. I told them to go to hell."

Patton's arms tighten around me.

"And I guess when you have to do something like that and the reality hits, it becomes all you know, right? Survival. So I learned to look after Arlo fast. I had to learn how to be a mother. And all the time, I watched as the world around me moved on. I was stuck with the label."

"Single mom?"

I sighed. "I told myself I was glad. I laughed about it some days. Better than having a dad who's only going to break Arlo's poor heart, right?"

Patton doesn't say anything, and I have to ask, even though I know it'll be a mistake.

"If… if you'd known it at the time, would you have really stuck around?"

Again, the only sound is his steady breathing, his chest rising and falling as he considers the question. His arms tighten around me.

"Honestly, I don't fucking know," he says eventually. "Back then, I wasn't the same person I am today. I'd like to think it would've shaken me awake."

"You were more fun, you mean?" I tease.

"A *lot* more fun. Or an irresponsible fuckwit punk, as Archer liked to say."

I laugh shakily through the tears.

It's almost a relief, knowing I did the right thing, even inadvertently, by not knowing who he was then and trying to track him down.

"I'm damn glad you told me tonight, though," he murmurs, his mouth grazing my ear. "Just like I'm glad you want me in your life, and Arlo's."

Yeah.

This weekend has taught me I don't know how *not* to want this man with every fiber of my being.

"I'm just amazed you want to *be* part of it. It's like being invited to swim around in a swamp."

"I'm addicted." It's a confession and seduction all at once. The only thing I can focus on is the way his breath feels so good against the shell of my ear. "I'm addicted to waking up beside you. I'm addicted to *this*."

This time, our kiss feels like coming home.

My feelings are too tangled to sort out and too overwhelming to understand. There's just this pulsing urge under my skin that speaks louder than any words.

I want him.

I need him.

I crave him, all mixed with the blinding knowledge that he's the father of my child.

He wants to be Arlo's father.

All those bittersweet moments, all the times when I thought we'd be a party of two forever—are those days really done?

"You're crying again." Patton breaks away and wipes my cheeks.

"I know, I know. Sorry." I scrub my face, still half laughing, half crying. "I am happy, I promise, despite all the evidence to the contrary."

"You haven't told me to fuck off or where to mail the child support check, so I believe you," he says with a wry smile. "Despite the evidence to the contrary."

"But we should talk more about it," I say. "About us, I mean. At home. We can hash out the practical stuff."

"Oh, so you *do* want me to mail that check?"

"Be serious!" I slap his chest.

"If you insist." His grin feels fragile, fading like a dimming lightbulb. "What do you want to ask me?"

"I just mean, if we're going to figure out a way to make this work, we need to organize it. You're still my boss and Arlo has no idea you exist."

"Wrong. He knows I exist," he counters. "The little man thinks I'm a fire-breathing monster in a suit."

"He did." I snort. "Now he thinks you bring supervillains to justice."

"Much better."

I sigh contentedly.

Just like before, the sky looks diamond studded, brighter and calmer over the desert. I can appreciate the majesty and the splash of the Milky Way reaching down like it wants us to know the universe approves of my confession.

"We won't tell anyone. Not at first. We'll figure it out," he says. "We can settle into normal life."

"But together?"

"As together as I can physically arrange."

I have other thoughts—other considerations—specifically about how we're going to handle spending time together as a couple without constantly sending Arlo to the babysitter, and what his family will say if we reveal we're dating.

"What about you?" he asks, toying with my hair. "Will we have to break the news to your folks?"

"Um, which part—that Arlo's father is fantastically rich or that we've reconnected? It's not a big concern. I still don't talk to my parents much." I wince. *Reconnected* sounds like we had more than a fling to begin with. But Patton doesn't seem to notice.

"Both?"

"You're not even going to protest my use of *fantastically rich*?"

"Call me egotistical, but that's not too far from the truth."

"That *does* sound egotistical."

He drops a kiss on the end of my nose. "Sounds like I need someone with their feet on the ground to call me out when I'm being an ass."

"An egotistical ass."

"See? Archer will love you."

I laugh and burrow into his arms. He wraps his robe around me, too, and I wish I could linger here all night.

"But in all seriousness, my family kinda imploded. We've never had a holiday or visit since they walked out of my life. Mom dances around trying to make amends, and so do I," I say, and although he doesn't move, I can feel the mood change. "That's the choice they made when they left."

"Probably better I don't know their names," he says sharply. "Otherwise, I might be tempted to pay them a little visit and talk some sense into them."

I wince.

"Er, yeah, let's not. Maybe stick to romantic gestures like flowers?" I wiggle around so I'm facing the hard look in his eyes. "I mean it, Patton. I'm okay without getting them involved. We'll cross that bridge if and when we ever need to."

"You're okay *now*," he agrees. "And not because of them."

"Flowers, Patton. Don't forget."

He releases the tension in his shoulders with a sigh. "Fine. But you've got to admit it's tempting."

"Almost as tempting as never seeing them again."

He gives me a reluctant smile and kisses me again.

"If you want a family, mine will be there in a heartbeat," he says. "They'll love you to death. And when we tell my mother—which doesn't have to be right away—she'll be stoked to have another grandkid. Dex will be pissed I got there before him."

I smile. "She must love your nephew. Archer's? Is there a wife too?"

"The mother left a long time ago now. That's a fucked up story for another time. I can't even remember her name some days." His nose wrinkles. "Besides, he's too old for her to play around with the same way. Arlo, he's perfect."

Just hearing Patton say that sends warmth shooting through my veins.

"We're going to have to ease him into this, you know," I say carefully.

"That's fine. It'll take me some adjusting too."

"And me three. But in a good way."

"Only good ways," he echoes.

I close my eyes and listen to the sound of his heart, which has slowed over the course of this conversation.

Can life really be this simple? Can I really escape the dark cloud that's always been hanging over me?

It doesn't feel real, knowing Patton Rory is accepting Arlo with open arms. Much less me as his—

Whatever.

Whatever we are.

I don't dare define it yet.

But maybe, in the future, if it ever gets that far, maybe we can be a family.

Maybe the day will come when I won't have to always temper my hopes and dread the next disaster.

And maybe I won't scare him off in the next five minutes by squealing with joy and kissing his face off.

XVIII: JOKERS ARE WILD
(PATTON)

*K*ansas City feels new and bewildering a week after our return.

My old routine, forever shattered.

Sure, Salem still lives at home with Arlo, who remains oblivious to the entire thing. I take them out on weekends and drop by often, even when she's not expecting me.

It's almost hard to process.

This need to see my woman, my son—fuck, *my son*—just to know they're alive and well and thriving.

What's harder is keeping a lid on my urge to march them out of that beat-up shoebox apartment and into my home that's ten times larger.

Too fast, I know.

This shit takes time.

The trouble is, time has fucked me over enough, thieving away years when I should've been in their lives.

Then there are the evenings when she's free, an hour or so before leaving the office, where I lock the door and throw her against the wall.

My hands, my mouth, they take.

They lay down the law.

My teeth catch her bottom lip while she moans delight into my mouth, my fingers working rough, brisk orgasms out of her clit.

I *need* to be inside her very soon.

Especially when it's goddamned impossible to keep my hands off her, though she stops short of letting me sweep everything off her desk and bend her over it. Always the same excuse.

"What if someone hears? The cleaners?" she whispers, like I couldn't snap my fingers and make them hold off on making the rounds with some contrived excuse.

Instead, we wait for the weekends, those rare slivers of time carved out between our busy lives when I can finally turn into a sheet-ripping animal.

Waiting for pussy this good is driving me mad.

I'm not used to anticipation.

Hell, I'm not used to any of this.

Usually, when I'm into a girl, I can bed her at will and I'm done in a matter of weeks, after I've worked it out of my system.

But Salem broke the old, familiar pattern.

She's broken *me.*

Yet the sex just keeps getting better as I learn her body and she explores mine.

Yesterday, before I could shove her panties aside and go to work, she dropped down and started opening my trousers.

I've never been more awestruck in my life, watching her hazel eyes flashing pure lust as her velvet lips engulfed my cock.

She has a few surprises, like taking me down her throat, so eager she gladly *choked* on my last round of thrusts.

And she still didn't stop, not until I exploded, fighting and failing to swallow my come before it poured out of her mouth, staining her collar.

This is the part where I make a fist and hit myself.

Instead, I rub my eyes, trying to focus on the mundane revenue projections in front of me.

It's only midday, too early to wonder if this is the day she'll leave this office leaking my come.

Any second now, Archer and Dex will show up for a meeting about the Minnesota expansion scheme. With any luck, Salem will come, too.

I dropped by The Cardinal this morning to suggest she attend.

Not because I'm hopelessly obsessed.

We agreed we weren't cut out for secrets. The sooner we fess up, the better, and there's no time like the present to assess what my brothers will really think of her being more than our star talent.

In a burst of madness, *I* suggested we figure out what this is soon, so we won't have to manage these secrets for long.

So now I'm due for another dinner where I'll watch Arlo, noticing all the little things I never caught before. He's inherited my hair and my eyes and my focus. Sure, it's all invested in drawing right now, but I used to be like him as a kid.

Razor-sharp. Always bouncing from one thing to the next. How the fuck did I miss it?

A handful, that's what Mom called me. And Arlo, he's growing up just like me despite the fact that I haven't raised him.

Genetics are crazy.

Mrs. Potter, our receptionist who's pushing sixty and also one of the most organized people I know, pops her head through the door.

"Archer called to say he'd be late," she tells me. "And Dexter should be here any second. I'm just heading out and thought I'd let you know since it's my half day."

I wave at her and check my phone just as it vibrates with a message from Salem.

Running late and traffic sucks but I'll be there.

I shuffle in my seat, trying not to fixate on her and failing for the dozenth time today, until Dexter finally shows up with a scowl.

"I figured I'd be late, coming from the bakery," he said. "One bad bout of freezing rain and every road in this city goes to shit."

"You are late, Dex, freezing rain aside."

"Whatever. I thought I'd be the last one in."

"Everyone else is flakier than you today, I guess," I say, watching as he sits down and checks the time on his phone like the OCD control freak he is.

Honestly, ever since he married Junie, his timekeeping has gotten worse—but at least he's also started apologizing like a real human.

Apparently, you *can* teach a grumpy old dog new tricks.

"Where's Archer?" I ask.

"Think he had to deal with some school thing for Colt," Dexter says.

My phone lights up with another message from Salem to let me know she's halfway here.

"Who's that? Someone special?" Dexter asks, nodding at the phone. "Have you finally met a girl who doesn't want to stab you with a pen after two days?"

"I meet a lot of girls, Dex. The benefits of not being strapped down with that prison badge." I nod at the wedding band on his hand, inwardly laughing at what a lying asshole I am.

I'm a father now, and by some insane twist of fate, I *want* to be strapped down more.

"Maybe so, you prick, but most of them don't make you look at your phone like that."

"Like what?" I shrug, feigning ignorance as my face heats.

"That *smile*. Trust me, I know the one."

Of course he does, the smarmy bastard.

"Junie pregnant yet?" I ask to deflect attention.

"We're not trying. I told you. Not yet."

"You're letting Mom down. She wants that second grandkid bad."

He snorts. "You'd better give her one, then."

My shit-eating grin disappears, and I say nothing. If only he knew how close to the truth he is.

Then the door flies open and Archer arrives in a boiling fury.

"Fucking. Traffic," he spits. "It's bad enough that Colt brought live fireworks to school and the principal called me in."

"Oh, shit. Don't tell me they suspended him?" I chuckle.

"No, thank God. He's a good kid, so they let him off with a warning. He's just oblivious. He thought he'd pull the gunpowder out of it for a rocket without talking to his science teacher first."

"*Collllt.*" I shake my head, trying not to laugh. This kid will either wind up as a crazy artist or a mad scientist. I can't guess which but it's sure to be interesting.

Flashes of my own future punch me in the face then. Everything a dad has to deal with the older their kid gets.

I'm so fucking unprepared it's laughable.

"Anyway, we're just waiting on Salem now," I say.

"Oh?" Dexter raises his eyebrows at Archer. "I didn't know we were expecting *Miss Hopper.*"

"You don't know everything, Dex. She's done a lot of research." I lean back in my chair, enjoying the feel of weightlessness. There's a certain balance you can find if you really try and it's always been oddly relaxing.

"Wait, you've had her working on this *and* The Cardinal?" Archer spits. "You'd better not be burning her out."

"You'll see when she gets here," I throw back.

Thankfully, we don't have to wait long.

Salem knocks cheerfully and walks in a minute or two later, her tan coat neatly tied around her waist and her hair pinned perfectly in place. I'm betting she stopped off in the bathroom to make sure she looked extra presentable instead of running right in.

That's professionalism. A few extra seconds spent on optics can make all the difference, and she knows it.

But all the professionalism in the world can't stop the fact that I know what she looks like *under* those clothes.

She narrows her eyes at me like she can read my filthy mind.

"Sorry I'm late, Patton," she says, taking a seat. "Hi, guys."

"Let's get started," I say. "I want to express a few concerns about the Minnesota properties. Salem?"

"So I looked into the properties we have our eyes on. Evelyn's financials finally came back," she says, passing out papers with her printed notes. "One has a hefty credit line out on it. I commissioned some photos from the inspection, which you can see here."

Dexter peers at the photos and his face turns white. "What the hell? She said they were fixer-uppers, yeah, but this looks *decrepit.*"

"Practically derelict," Archer agrees.

Dex throws the photos back on the table. "Christ. She suggested we'd need a few updates, not a complete overhaul."

"The renovations will be more extensive than Evelyn suggested," I say. "And it might be a full year or two before they're ready to be anything other than a money pit."

"So, what? You're on board with backing out?" Archer asks gruffly.

"Not so fast, I'm just talking facts." Although I'm torn over whether these properties are truly worth it. "There's something else, too. Mom mentioned that she gets the sense Evelyn is under some kind of stress—money trouble, probably."

"Shit. Not surprising if she's got these beasts pulling her down," Dexter grumbles. He looks at me and I know he's already figured out what Mom suggested. "She offered to help her, didn't she?"

"I told her no. This is purely business and she can't get in the middle of it."

Archer leans back thoughtfully, his eyes dark.

"Aw, hell. Normally, I wouldn't suggest mixing business and friendship, but... it's Evelyn." He sighs and rakes a hand through his hair—a familiar tell that he's about to make a concession. "Maybe we should *consider* giving her those upfront payments. The land alone is appreciating rapidly, even if the cabins will need some serious money."

"Maybe," Dexter says slowly. "Based on market projections, of course."

"Adjusted for inflation, Archer's right," Salem says. "But the market appears pretty volatile right now for vacation rentals in northern Minnesota. Conservative estimates might be smart."

Archer nods. "Right. We want to keep her afloat without tying up too much capital."

If you ask me, the photos scream money pit, even if they could still be profitable in the long run. But if Archer still wants to move ahead when he's normally the most risk averse, I won't be the guy who shoots it down.

Besides, Salem's market research looks impeccable as always. There's a gap for precisely what we're offering with the affluent folks who want to live a Scandinavian style lake life without leaving the continent—a niche we could easily fill.

"Agreed." I tap the table and let all four wheels of my chair hit the floor. "Fine. I'll work out a payment schedule and run it by you guys. Enough to help Evelyn and renovate at least one pilot property we'll target to launch before the year ends."

"Okay. And nice work, Salem," Dexter says. "Those market reports were flawless. Couldn't find any fault if I tried."

No doubt his number-crunching, money freak ass did try, too.

Dexter loves looking for errors almost as much as he loves studying nutrition labels.

"They were solid," Archer agrees. The tiniest jealousy bug bites the back of my neck when he smiles at her. "If you ever get sick of managing the day-to-day, we could use a full-time analyst here at headquarters."

Fucker.

I knew it.

Salem smiles, and just like with Arch, I know what's coming.

"Thanks," she says, "but I wouldn't make a good full-time number cruncher. I need to talk to people and move around to stay on my toes."

Yes, she does.

Salem Hopper has bigger and better dreams than being cooped up in our office.

I've seen her researching charter boats and marina businesses on the side lately. It has me wondering what the future will bring with her career plans, just like so much else.

Not yet, though. It's not my place to ask.

Not until we've figured out what we are—if we're meant to be anything at all.

Why ruin a good thing when it's barely begun?

* * *

FOR THE FIRST time since Utah, we have a date.

I race home early, meticulously cleaning up and agonizing over shirts in a way I haven't done since my teens.

You know it's catastrophic when a man puts this much energy into impressing a woman he's already fucked.

The plan is for dinner and a movie at my place—their first visit here—but it feels like more than that.

My son is coming home.

My son and his mother, walking into my house as a family.

It's strange as hell.

Stranger still that I'm a complete basket case over it.

I wipe the sweat off my brow, opening the door as they arrive, stuffing my phone back in my pocket after my security app alerted me they were coming.

Arlo stands on the front step wearing a dinosaur jacket, bouncing excitedly as he looks around.

"Wow!" he says, beaming up at me. "You really *are* Batman."

I guess it is a big place.

Salem used the word *obscene* when she first looked up my place.

Like Dex, I prefer the term 'quiet elegance.' I also think if someone gets this close to your house, they might as well know you're rich.

And Arlo hasn't even seen the pool out back yet.

"I don't think any hero has this much glass," Salem says as I usher them both inside.

The hall opens into a large open great room. Modern stairs lead up to the balcony on the second floor and the massive sofa curves around the glass table in the center.

The way she looks around and stops on me tells me she's noticed the fresh flowers I had delivered today, hoping to impress her.

Judging by that sly little smile, mission accomplished.

"Lemme see your bat cave," Arlo insists, but his eyes are wide as he takes everything in.

"No cave here, but I do have an impressive fish tank. Come see."

His eyes blow up to golf balls and he flies on ahead of us.

Why does my heart jerk?

He's sincerely excited over my big house. The cavernous house that, deep down, I'd love to have someone else living in.

No, not just someone. Salem and Arlo.

"Arlo, no running!" Salem calls with a giggle.

I thought she'd be more tense here, walking into my lair, but she seems more relaxed than ever in a cream sweater and jeans.

I lead the way to my study and the enormous aquarium that takes up the entire wall.

The subtle lights above and below illuminate the waters even when it's dark, mimicking a natural glow that won't disturb the creatures inside.

Sometimes I sit and watch my little creation at night, when my head aches too much to work and I'm in a mood to ponder these alien lives separated by glass, yet so intertwined with mine.

"What? It's like the zoo!" Arlo runs right up to the glass and smushes his nose against it. "This. Is. Awesome."

He isn't wrong.

The aquarium has won me admiration and a mountain of shit from my family ever since I had it installed. Especially when I had the octopus flown in from Seattle.

"I can't believe you called it a 'fish tank,'" Salem murmurs, sending me a smile when I glance at her. "Show Arlo the cuttlefish. He just read about them in his ocean book."

"Cuttlefish! Where?" Arlo's eyes bounce around excitedly.

"Up here, little man. Let me help you get a better look." I lift him up and settle him on my shoulders. "Can you see them now?"

"Yeah! That one's like a rainbow." His little finger points.

"And you see the way it shines in the light?"

"Yeah!" He grins.

"They do that to communicate. Almost like sign language, but they use colors instead."

I slow walk him along the glass so he can take it all in.

Salem trails behind us, happy to let me take the lead, almost as impressed with the show as her son.

Shit, my son.

My son is in my house.

My throat tightens ferociously and I swallow hard.

"More cuttlefish!" Arlo whispers excitedly, moving his finger around and counting them.

Colt used to do that a few years ago, even as an older kid. The animals are used to it, I think.

A bright-green fish floats closer to investigate, its mouth opening and closing, but Arlo's eyes never waver from the tentacled creatures.

"Why don't you tell us what you remember about cuttle-fish?" Salem asks him.

"They change color! Um… and they have beaks like an octopus. They shoot ink too."

Not half-bad for a five-year-old. I wonder about his memory, what else he can recall.

"I have an octopus, too," I tell him.

"What? No way!"

"Way," I whisper. "Let's see if he's out and not hiding."

We walk along the tank and I point out different fish along the way.

Sure enough, I find the octopus tucked behind a rock with only one tiny curl of leg visible, but the seahorses are swimming around near us, curious as usual.

Arlo looks astonished.

"You know what's interesting about seahorses?" I ask. "The males give birth. See there?" I point to a sac on the front of one seahorse. "That one's full of babies."

The boy's eyes are almost as round as the sac. "But I thought only girls can have babies."

"That's what makes seahorses special."

"I like the seahorse method. Way more fair," Salem adds, flashing me a mischievous grin.

I shake my head, biting back a grin. I can't imagine how this would be working out right now if our roles were switched.

"What about the other fish?" Arlo asks.

"Some lay eggs and some have live young, but the females work the hardest." I give Salem a quick, repentant glance.

She touches the small of my back.

A tiny gesture, but it's enough.

"You're a good teacher. I'm surprised," Salem says, "but don't you guys want to watch a movie? I was thinking *Spider-Man*."

The minute he hears that word, Arlo's interest shifts.

He starts wiggling until I'm forced to put him down and he runs out of the room, stopping just short of skidding across the wood floor.

"Be careful!" Salem shouts again. The blue lights wash out her face, making her look pale. "I'm so sorry. He's been giddy about this all day. He's a lot to handle when he gets into his hyper puppy mode."

"I know the feeling," I say, surprising myself. "It's nice as hell to spend time with him."

"You mean when he's not kicking you and ruining your clothes?" She laughs and leans up to offer a kiss.

I take her lips, parting them just enough to feel her breath as I slide a hand around her waist, then pull away before I can't control myself.

"We should head downstairs before he finds us. No need to repeat that incident." Before she starts moving, I lean in close to her ear. "Later, Salem. I'm going to break the bed with you tonight."

I love the way she shivers, the movement accenting her ass in those apple bottom jeans as she speeds away, throwing me a devilish smile.

Is it bad that a small part of me wanted the kid to walk in while we're kissing?

Then we could move past this.

Then he could understand, in his own little way, that I'm the guy with his mom and I'm not going anywhere.

For a second, I'm alone with the fish. The only light coming from the tank throws an eerie glow over my face.

So far, it's almost too perfect. Only, behind that glass, there's a stark reminder that chaos is always just a breath away, waiting to break through.

Sighing, I follow her downstairs.

They've already found my theater room with the huge

screen and large leather seats that can swallow a person for days. The dark space still manages to look cozy.

They're already perched on the longer sofa, sunk into the plush cushions.

"You have a lot of pillows for a single dude. So colorful too," Salem watches me toss the extras on the floor as I take the seat beside her with Arlo curled up between us.

"My mom gives me another accent pillow every Christmas. It's her thing," I mutter. "Guess she thinks if she buries me alive, it'll summon a wife from nowhere."

Salem laughs loudly.

God, I love that sound.

I also wonder if my mother's black magic worked, considering they're here and we're about to have our first family movie night.

The next look she gives me is lidded, more thoughtful, but I don't let myself dwell on it as I start the movie. Arlo bounces up in his seat, impatiently tapping his thighs.

His excitement is short-lived, though.

We're less than half an hour in when the exhaustion hits, and his eyelids start drooping. His little head drops against my side and he's out cold.

That's where he stays until after the credits roll and Salem's fingers tighten in mine.

We share a silent, knowing smile.

I never knew how warm and suggestive a human hand could be until I held hers for the last hour.

I'm not sure how I haven't combusted into bits.

In the flickering light from the screen and Arlo's soft snore, it all feels half like a fever dream. So surreal I'm half worried I'll blink and wake up in my boring old life.

Am I really here with my son sleeping away, holding the hand of the woman who gave birth to him?

Yes.

Fucking *yes.*

And it doesn't make a lick of sense why a joker like me should be this lucky.

That beat in my chest gets stronger, though, like my heart wants to break through my ribs and escape.

"I hope he isn't drooling on you," Salem says as she stretches, gently easing Arlo away from me. "I'd better get this little boy to bed."

"Let me." I scoop him up, catching his head against my shoulder, using a softness I never knew I had not to wake him.

He stirs and mumbles—something about an octopus, I think—and we pad upstairs slowly. I'm walking him toward the guest room with a big enough bed for the boy and his mother, a perfect place for them to—

I catch myself mid-thought.

No, shit.

This is too new, too delicate for assumptions.

Still, it feels right as I carry him into the room. Salem sets his little backpack down in the corner.

That might be a good sign.

When I decided which room they should have, I picked this one deliberately.

Right now, it's decorated in earthy browns and off-white. Modern and cozy without being too bright or intimidating.

If I close my eyes, I can see into the future, the walls plastered with movie posters. The bathroom is right next door, and he could have a bunk bed against the wall.

The next room over, a small walk down the hall, that's my master bedroom.

Danger.

It's scary, having thoughts like this when we haven't even made the decision to be a family yet, but I can't fucking help it.

They crowd my head more by the second.

Arlo stirs as I lay him on the bed. His eyelids flutter, but he just rubs his cheek on a chubby hand and goes back to sleep.

"Thanks, but I'll take it from here," Salem whispers.

I half want to argue that if he's my son, I should be more involved.

Then again, she's put him to bed for five years. It's her domain and I'd be a jackass idiot to challenge that, wouldn't I?

One day, maybe.

Tonight, I'll prove I have a functioning brain.

"Okay. I'll wait for you outside," I tell her, holding back a balmy smile.

I still can't believe he's *my son*.

Two little words for a pint-sized human with world-shattering significance.

"All the excitement tuckered him out," she says as she closes the door gently behind her. "Thanks for carrying him up."

I pull her into me and she collides with my chest, breathless and smiling, even though she tries to pin the smile away.

"He's a good kid," I tell her. "Truth be told, today meant a lot to me."

"Yeah? You mean it?" She inhales sharply.

"You know I do."

"Patton, you have no idea how happy I am to hear it." She rests her hand against my chest, flexing her fingers as she glances down at the contact. "This evening has been so special."

I kiss her then, my animal hunger taking over, deeply enough so she comes back up for air with a messy whisper of, "We need to be quiet."

Luckily for us, my bedroom is only a heartbeat away. The

NICOLE SNOW

walls are thick enough to avoid too many worries about sound, considering what I paid for this place. Before we head out, she leaves an old baby monitor on the nightstand next to Arlo.

A minute later, she's all *mine*.

I'm growling, taking her to the bathroom, stripping off her clothes before our feet even touch the tile.

I don't give her time to admire the walk-in shower with its heated bench or the double rainfall heads ready to amplify the steam that's already so thick around us. She can do that later, preferably when I'm buried in her.

I barely switch the shower on before she's against the wall.

Fuck yes, she's ready.

I know she's soaked before my fingers even open her pussy.

They don't play long before my greedy cock demands attention.

We're two strumming hearts and all friction under the hot spray, and again in the bed.

We make our own violent music from instruments of need denied for far too long.

I fuck her with a raging fury that rips me in two.

Soon, she's exploding on my cock, grinding my name into the pillow and then my hand, hounding me to come inside her.

No hesitation.

No choice.

There's just this rough, bone-shaking, guttural thrust as I drive into her womb and unload, filling her like I want to breed her again.

I know it sounds like lunacy.

I don't fucking care.

Something about having one surprise kid with her makes

me feral, dredging up this wild possessive instinct from the depths of my soul.

"This feels like turning a page," she murmurs later, curled against my chest. "…tell me it's not just me, Patton."

The words lodge in my chest, carving out a home.

It's a dream and a promise all at once.

I wrap an arm over the dip of her waist and pull her against me.

"It's not just you. And we should tell him, Salem. I know it's early, but it's killing me to spend time like this without him knowing."

Like I said.

Lunacy.

She tenses.

"I know, I get how you feel, but…" She hesitates. I know her answer before she gives it. "It's just so soon."

"You said you wanted to wait until we were sure." I push my forehead to hers, kissing her, pulling back only to lock eyes. "In case you couldn't tell, I've made up my damn mind."

"I know, and I—well, I did, too. But I think we should wait, Patton. Just a little while longer to be safe."

Bitter disappointment churns in my throat, but I keep my voice level as I say, "Okay. I get it."

"Please just give it time. It's not like I don't want to."

"I will. You're right, Lady Bug." There's nothing to do now but agree with the voice of reason.

She has ten thousand times more experience raising this boy than I do.

Also, it's a big adjustment. So mammoth it could crush the poor kid if it isn't done right.

She kisses me again, tracing her fingers along my jaw. "It means a lot that you want to step up," she murmurs. "I just want to help you do this right."

I smile into her teasing touch, everything tempting my mouth to want to blow her to pieces again.

"I know. We can't rush into this."

"You're just impatient," she teases, flashing her tongue.

"He's my son, Salem, and he doesn't know it. He doesn't recognize me." I take a breath before I can tell her the dream I've had damn near every night since Utah.

It's the one where Arlo sits at my breakfast bar, drawing one of his masterpieces. He's busy scribbling and he calls me *"Dad."*

"I hope this is enough for now," she whispers, kissing the corner of my mouth, then the tip of my nose. "This right here. You and me. This is good."

It is, and it should be the world.

Just having her safe in my arms like this is one dream come true.

But I'm an impatient creature.

I'm not stick-up-the-ass Dexter or boring levelheaded Archer.

I know Arlo's mine. I can see myself mirrored in everything he does now. His love for pizza, the way he's into superheroes, how he throws himself into new experiences so fearlessly.

His life.

His eyes.

Fuck.

Before, life was all about making money and trying not to shit things up like the spoiled brat most people think I am. Whether that was thanks to Higher Ends or the Navy or just growing up in a house where money and wealth were piled on my shoulders from day one.

Until now, I didn't have a clear idea of what the future should look like.

It was always vague, caped in fog like the early mornings

this time of year. But the sun has risen and I see what's nearly in my grasp.

All mine for the taking, if I'm man enough to reach out.

And I *want* to.

I want to know what life will look like with Salem Hopper, when I can step up to be a dad and her man.

This time, I want forever.

XIX: ONE BIG WIN (SALEM)

*A*s the weeks trickle by and winter thaws, we start living part-time at Patton's place.

Entire weekends plus half the evenings during the week.

At first, I was worried Arlo would question it, but he's taken the big change in stride.

After all, what kid wouldn't want to spend more time in the 'Pat Cave'? I can't stop laughing at the goofy nickname Patton came up with for his place.

Pretty ironic when the place isn't that cavernous when people are there.

It's modern and warm and infinitely more than anything I deserve. The place would make my parents eat their materialistic hearts out.

But it's not the house that has me spinning.

It's the plain, cold fact that I can't get enough of Patton Rory.

The craving feels like a force of nature, this weird emotional magnetism that only gets stronger with every visit. The more I get used to being around him, the more time I want to spend with him.

The fewer nights I want to sleep alone.

The best mornings are the ones where I wake up in his arms.

Well, sort of.

My butt always seems to be magically glued to his dick every time. It only takes a few minutes to feel him go *other* places.

It's no surprise, then, to wake up with my head halfway off the pillow, his arm draped over my waist, and my legs twined in his.

I sleepily regain consciousness before shifting until my back presses against his bare chest.

God, how is he always so warm?

It feels too good on these late winter mornings.

His heat soaks into me. I bite my lip when I feel his hard-on. The movement makes him stir and his embrace tightens.

"Patton?" I whisper. I grind against him, this time deliberately, feeling him harden to his full glory.

My eyes flick to the charger clock on his nightstand.

Oof. We won't have long before Arlo wakes—if we have any time at all—and there's a little something I'd like to finish before then.

"It's morning. Wakey-wakey," I whisper.

"I'm up." His hand creeps up my shirt and cups my breast before I can say another word. "You really think I'd miss my favorite wake-up call?"

"Would you? I'm not wearing panties."

I feel his chest swell as he inhales.

"Goddammit. Have I ever told you how hot you are?" He reaches around me, trailing warm fingers along my stomach and dipping down, skating across my thighs and drawing circles on my hips.

My legs open, encouraging his fingers to find their way home.

"So eager." He chuckles, the sound low and dark in my ear. "You're going to spoil my fun."

"Oh, the things I have in mind won't spoil anything."

Finally, he reaches the sweet spot between my legs.

I gasp at the contact when his thumb grazes my clit.

"Not so loud." I swear I can feel his smile as he nips my ear.

As he slides his fingers through my slickness, I arch my back and twist my hips, just enough so his cock nudges my entrance.

The hand on my breast hesitates for a second as I roll and wiggle myself onto him.

Oh, just the tip.

I need to feel him.

It barely lasts before he sucks my throat, adding his teeth.

"You tease," he groans, taking my hips and sliding me the rest of the way down.

Heaven.

He fills me, stretching my walls in the best way.

The eye-rolling moan that slips out of me tastes like pure melted honey.

We've fucked so many ways by now, but this is one of my favorites.

Softly.

Quietly.

Nothing between our slick, steaming flesh except the want boiling the air.

It's a claiming, tender and intense, yet so different from the drunken excitement of our first time or the heated wildness of other romps. Here, in the moment, joined by our bodies, we're one.

He nips my neck again—not hard enough to draw blood, but with just enough evil intensity. Shock mingles with the pleasure building in my core.

"Never forget you're mine," he rumbles, coiling my hair in his fist.

I think it's a substitute for the three little words neither of us are ready to say.

"Yours," I whisper, hearing his breath go ragged as his thrusts quicken.

"Say it again."

For a hot minute, I can't.

Especially when he does that thing where his thrusts jackhammer, quickening abruptly as he brings me so *close.*

"Yours, yours." My breath hitches. "Patton, please."

"Good girl," he rasps.

Then his palm crashes against my ass and I'm gone.

Coming!

He pulls me in, just in time to stifle the messy hitched noises pouring out of me as my pussy convulses around his punishing cock.

He makes me come so hard I'm thrown back to Zion Peak, to our very first night, where my eyes glowed with so many stars.

And he just plunges deeper, harder, bringing rough strokes that break reality.

He finishes with a gritty curse as he fills me with come.

My whole mind whites out, pleasure arcing through my nerves like live wires until I short-circuit and slowly drift down from the high.

That's the awe of having sex like this.

We flipping own each other.

You can call me ignorant and inexperienced when I'm definitely both. But I never saw it that way before—sex was just a physical act to satisfy a need, like scratching an itch.

And yes, sex like that is fine.

But this is different, swirling with emotions that tug my heart. Every time he touches me, I'm lost in the moment.

Happily lost with him.

And when I twist around to meet his gaze, dark with desire and that heady purple mark he's left on my neck that I know I'll need to cover up, I know he sees the same thing mirrored back.

Right now, nothing exists but us.

And he's still not done. The man is part machine.

His fingers tighten on my hips. His other hand works my clit, rubbing, slowly tracing circles meant to rile me up for another round.

"Again? So soon?"

"Woman, I'm still hard as a brick. I could stay in bed with you all day," he growls. Another half confession.

Seems like that's how we speak these days.

These careful, half-formed thoughts and near confessions and little hints that come out loudest when we're most unfiltered. What we don't say is that this insanity is more than we ever could've dreamed.

That our red thread of fate already feels like a knot—and pulling it apart would mean brutally slashing the cord, dropping us on our heads.

It's a terrifying thought, but so is how hard and fast I've fallen.

"Arlo will be up soon," I whisper.

"Humor a man."

Smiling, I close my eyes and lean back into him, enjoying the feeling of his hand splayed across my belly. "Good morning to you, too."

"The best," he agrees, reluctantly moving his hand away.

We lay together until the morning sun streams through the blinds. It's getting brighter and earlier with spring closing in.

A second later, a not-so-distant *thud* tells me Arlo's awake.

Patton's arm falls away as I sit up quickly, trying to ignore the heavy sense of doubt about what's ahead.

"What's wrong, Lady Bug?"

"...are you sure today's a good idea? I mean, are you *certain*?"

"Why would I not be sure?" He blinks as I look back at him, watching as the laziness fades from his face.

"Because it's your mom and your family and I'm..." I hesitate. We've never given it a name even though it's pretty clear. "I'm with you," I finish lamely.

"Dexter already knows. If Archer's brain wasn't mixed up with a moose at birth, he'll know it too."

I slap his shoulder, laughing, but he's right.

Dexter Rory *has* been dropping hints lately.

Dropping by The Cardinal to compliment me on the way things are going. Just *happening* to arrive at the same time Patton does and annoying his little brother to death.

The comments, too.

Sly remarks about how well we work together and how much we seem to enjoy each other's company. Last time he was around, he even invited me to a dinner with him and his wife. That's *definitely* not something you do for a random employee.

"They won't be angry, I promise. What has you so worried?" Patton sits up and brushes my hair back from my face.

"Archer might be..."

"Then Archer will realize he's an idiot for not seeing what's happening right under his nose."

"And your mother?" I swallow thickly. That's the part that really scares me.

I burned my bridges with my family ages ago, and Arlo never knew them.

Until now, the thought of adopting more relatives

through Patton never occurred to me. And what will they really think when they figure out Arlo's a Rory and I've kept him hidden for five years?

If they don't approve of me—

Yeah, I'm cooked.

"Stop it. Mom already loves you. You know that. Nothing that's happened will change her mind one bit," Patton says, folding an arm around my waist. Maybe it's weakness, but I lean into him. "She's only going to love you more."

I so wish I shared his confidence.

"She likes me just fine as your employee, you mean. But not as your—" I stop cold.

I don't want to say the word.

"My girlfriend?" he says firmly.

I watch his eyes flash, so bright and confident it scares me.

"Is that what we are, Patton? Boyfriend-girlfriend?"

"Why wouldn't we be?" His grip tightens, holding me in place, though I know if I tried to move, he'd release me. That's what's so addictive about this man. He wants me enough to hold me close, but he respects me enough to let go.

"You saying you don't want to be?" he demands when I don't answer.

"We just never talked about it."

"This is us talking. Now."

He sounds so serious it makes me laugh, loving the moody scowl on his face.

"Thanks, Captain Obvious. Where would I be without you spelling out the conversation?"

I twist to face him completely and put my hands on his face.

Slowly, he takes my hand and raises it to his lips.

It's incredible how the rake of his morning scruff and his lips take me apart.

"You'd still be mine," he answers.

"Yours," I echo, trying not to tear up.

And he kisses me after he kisses my hand, a dangerous edge to his mouth as he claims mine.

"It's decided. We'll go with girlfriend," he says, sending butterflies swarming my belly again. "That enough for you to quit fussing? I'm sure about this, Salem."

"You're not even a little worried about how they're going to react? With Arlo, I mean?"

He rests his forehead on mine.

"You don't really know my mother yet. She'll be thrilled out of her gourd. I'll probably need to tie her down to keep her from taking off. But that won't even be today."

I smile. "Even if she knows I kept him a secret?"

"Salem, Salem," he growls. "Why, after everything, is your self-esteem trailing miles behind your success? *Enough bullshit.*"

"I just…" I don't know how to articulate it, this annoying uncertainty weighing me down. "I'm your employee."

"What do you want me to do? Fire you first?"

"Dude, it's a conflict of interest."

"We weren't employees when we hooked up and made a kid. Plus, I'm pretty sure my brothers would rather keep you at The Cardinal than risk having you step back and let someone less competent take over." He rubs his nose against mine. "Also, us *not* dating isn't an option. Firing you is, in theory," he murmurs.

"What about Arlo?"

"What about him? We do this one bite at a time. Introducing you as my girlfriend now will be a whole lot easier than digesting the whole truth at once. Trust me."

The anxious knot in my belly tries to climb up and spout more silly questions, but I choke it back down.

This is Patton's family. He knows them better than I do, no argument.

"Okay," I say.

"Remember when you told me about Arlo? We'll ease into it."

"I know, I know. I trust you."

And I do.

He kisses me one last time for good measure, then slides past me off the bed.

"Speaking of Arlo, we better see what he's up to," he says, glancing back at me with a hint of that wicked smile he saves just for me. "Damn, woman. From the way you're acting, I might think you've never met a man's folks before."

Deep breath.

"I haven't."

He stops midway through finding a shirt from his huge walk-in closet.

"Ah." The material slips through his fingers as he turns back to me. "Ever?"

"I never had a serious boyfriend before you came along. Then with a newborn it was impossible, and after he got older, I was focused on my career, so yeah." I shrug, hating the crawling, itchy shame that comes with this confession. "This is it. My first time."

"God, Salem. I didn't mean—"

"You didn't think?" I quirk an eyebrow, daring him to smile. "My dating history isn't very long. Or complicated."

There's another loud *thud*.

Arlo!

I swing into action, throwing on a robe over the t-shirt I wore to bed.

"I'd better go see what he's up to," I say ruefully. "Just in case he's out of his room, destroying your house."

"It's a big place. He'd have a hard time ruining it."

"Don't say that to his face. He loves a challenge."

Patton smiles, but it partly fades as he walks with me. "Hey, Salem? Thanks for trusting me."

He could be a morning god, standing there in a shirt open at the collar, his hair still mussed from sleep. His eyes have that sleepy, sharp look he specializes in.

I don't know how it happened, but I've placed all my trust in this man.

A smile curls my lips.

An answering smile lights in his eyes.

Thankfully, there's no disaster waiting down the hall, just Arlo dumping his backpack out, trying to find his tablet.

We're not expected at the Rory estate until dinner, so we spend the day together.

Patton takes us to the zoo and Arlo gets to scream with excitement at seeing all the animals from his nature books in the flesh and fur.

After we come back, Patton takes Arlo off to his study with the aquarium to talk about fish while I get ready.

Soon, I'm staring at my reflection in the mirror.

Mom used to call me pretty girl before I failed at life. When I was little, she'd brush my hair for half an hour sometimes. Now I know that's because she wanted me to go to college, get an education I don't need, and marry a man my parents low-key picked.

Yeah, that was never in the cards.

About the time I passed on college, she never complimented my looks again. Maybe that's when I stopped believing I could be pretty, too.

When Patton calls me beautiful, it doesn't quite compute. I search my face for signs he isn't crazy.

Hazel eyes shot with gold.

Dark mocha-brown hair that ripples down my back when I let it.

A pointed Cupid's bow on my upper lip.

A dark mole on my jaw, too low to be a beauty spot.

Eyebrows that need professional help to curve right.

Dimples that dip my cheeks even when I'm not smiling. They'll sink when I get old, sucked into my skin with all the other wrinkles and lines of old age, and probably sooner than I think.

Will he still call me beautiful then if we're together?

I brush the skin around my eyes. No deep lines there yet, except when I smile, but they'll be coming soon enough.

Snorting, I drop my hand and reach for my makeup.

Thirty feels like it's coming fast, but it's not a death sentence.

If I haven't made it yet, that's not a crime.

I haven't failed.

I have my crap together and I have a wonderful son.

Except, there's still this burning need inside me for *more*. Patton fulfills that need beyond my wildest dreams, but I don't just want to be a rich man's arm candy, assuming he's crazy enough to stick around.

At least the makeup brightens my face.

I brush my eyebrows into shape, cover the mole, then apply eyeshadow that brings out the gold in my eyes.

There.

Now I feel prettier with my flaws smoothed out. I curl my hair and leave it hanging loose over my shoulders, wishing I could leave my brain hanging too.

It's just his family.

Just his filthy rich mother and two driven brothers who eat ambition for lunch.

But you've met them before.

Yes. As his employee.

Sweet Jesus, I hate my inner dialogue.

I tighten my fingers around the mascara wand as my phone buzzes on the table beside me. I wrinkle my nose.

Kayla.

Of course it's her calling right now. Of *course* she'd interrupt this moment with some invented crisis or a new demand that's all about her.

For a hot second, I consider declining the call.

She'd message later, though, furious to know what I'm doing that makes me too busy to talk to her. My best friend. My *only* friend.

She has a real knack for rubbing salt in the wounds and making it feel like a kindness.

It's also not worth the hassle, so I grab the phone and answer, hoping to keep this brief.

"Hey, Kayla. What's up?"

"You don't sound excited to hear from me, Lemmy." I can almost hear her pouting. "If you didn't want to take the call, you didn't *have* to."

"Sorry, Kay. I'm just doing my makeup. You know how it is."

"Oh? You're wearing *makeup?*" Her tone changes like she can smell a juicy secret.

"It happens every once in a while."

"What for? Have you got an event?" She pauses. "Oh my God, is it a date?"

"Nothing important," I lie. "How was Hawaii?"

It's the only thing that's kept her away all this time—a long trip island hopping around the Pacific to distract her from the fact that Patton Rory hasn't asked about her once.

"Amazing!" she gushes. "Did you see the photos I put on Insta? It was beautiful. So warm and relaxing. The surf was amazing and the turtles were cool. We even did a turtle tour with this lady who had like a cheetah cat. Can you believe that? She barked at me to put down my camera a few times and not to get too close, but still. It slapped."

I roll my eyes and scrunch my hair, encouraging my curls to stay curled. Maybe I need more hairspray.

"Turtles, huh? Aren't they a protected species?"

"Ugh, yeah. I wouldn't have even hurt him with a little pat on the head. But they got all up my ass about how it's a law there and shit. Crazy, right? They wouldn't even let people surf by their little roped off beach area."

My eyes roll right out of my head.

"I thought you didn't surf?"

"No, but the guys do, and *that* was fun."

Guys, plural. Okay. Hopefully that means Patton is already old news in her squirrel brain.

"And how did they hold up?"

"Oh, one guy was definitely a nine, and you know I never say that lightly. He's Japanese and his dad owns a robot company back in Yokohama. He was so formal. Dude showed up for dinner with *flowers.*" She giggles.

Thank God. Maybe she's finally moving on after all.

"Did you guys hook up?"

"Duh." She snorts. "But he's not as amazing in bed as you'd think. Some guys think dick and money is all it takes. They've got no game. I fell asleep every time he talked about his AI crap and crypto money."

Well, damn. How disappointing.

"So you're not seeing him again?"

"Why would I? I told you, he's from Japan. Talk about long distance." She uses the same tone she would scolding a child. "Besides, he's no Patton Rory. I'm saving myself for the best, thank you very much."

"Kay... you literally just hooked up with another guy."

"Three guys. You didn't think I'd spend a month in Hawaii flying solo, did you?"

Yikes.

"What if Patton found out?"

"What if? Okay, look, I know you're not familiar with this sort of stuff, that's cool, but guys like Patton, they get who they want, when they want. Like on demand. I bet he hooks up with girls all the time."

Not true.

I know it isn't, but the thought that he could makes my skin crawl. I roll my shoulders to shake off that imminent spider feeling.

Patton may have been like that once—we've barely spoken about his body count or old habits and at this point I don't want to—but he's not like that now.

"If that's the case, what makes you think he'll be interested in you?"

"Um, hello? Because I'm on his level. Come on, Lemmy, keep up. I'm the caviar and the rest are all bread girls." She sighs. "Anyway, what are you doing with makeup? Are you seeing someone?"

Help me.

It's burning the tip of my tongue, the truth about the only girl Patton Rory is seeing.

But if I do that, she'll freak.

She'll probably work overtime, grinding me into dust, especially if she thinks I 'stole him' right under her nose.

Not to my face, of course. She'd be sickly sweet and absolutely murderous behind my back.

First, she'll tell everyone who's anyone in this town that I'm just another 'bread girl' who slept with him to get ahead. I don't have much of a social life and even fewer opportunities, and what little I do have revolves around Kayla and her favors.

Or if I confess to dating Patton, her grudges.

I don't need her rumor mill spinning in overdrive and frankly, neither does Patton.

Also, if she finds out, she'll tell my parents for sure. We haven't spoken in years, but the second they get wind of it, they'll be all over me.

Total circus.

I don't even know if I'm ready to have them back in my life. Not without a real heartfelt apology, certainly.

"Yeah. It's a date, I guess." My shoulders sag. Truth and lies all wrapped up in one nice unit, so close you can't tell where one ends and another begins. "He's in real estate."

Truth, but lie, because my intention is to deceive—and Kayla slurps it right up.

"So exciting!" she squeals. "Tell me where he's at this instant. Out of ten?"

"Easy ten."

"Oh, okay. But how would *I* rate him?"

I can't bite back my smile. "You'd probably give him a ten, too, Kayla. He's hot. Like Arizona heatwave."

"Shut up!" She gasps. "I can't *wait* to meet him. After you get Patton on board with me, we'll do a double date."

Hell no, we won't.

Patton knocks and enters the room with Arlo in tow. He frowns at me, and I mouth Kayla's name.

"Honestly, Kay, I can't really do anything for you," I say. "You guys have met several times. You'll have to close the deal, right?"

She huffs a breath. "That's a little selfish, Lemmykins. I bet if you arranged another few meetups, I could hit the zone. He's probably just intimidated, but once I show him how down-to-earth I am, he'll be smitten."

Holy hell.

Her gross image of Patton is so different from the real deal it's like calling a cartoon scribble a Picasso painting.

"I'll see what I can do. No promises."

"You're the best, bestie," she says, happy again. "I'll pop on over soon. Say hi to Patton for me when you next see him. See ya!" The call, thankfully, ends.

I drop the phone back on the table with a groan. "Sometimes I hate that girl."

Arlo clambers onto the big bed and starts bouncing before I stop him with a glare.

"Queen Bee Kayla is icky," he informs me.

"Arlo! Whatever you do, keep that to yourself." I want to tell him that isn't nice, but the nickname rubbed off yours truly.

I never said I was perfect, okay?

"The boy's right," Patton cuts in. His voice is tight, and when I look at him, his eyes glitter with that sharp, suppressed anger. "And you're damn lucky you hung up when you did, or I'd have been tempted to tell her what I think."

"Patton, no—"

"It wouldn't happen with her in a thousand years, even if I was single and dry as the Sahara." He strides forward and kneels beside me. The sight of him kneeling by my chair is enough to make my heart flutter. "Never, Salem."

I stroke my hands through his hair.

I'm not oblivious to the little eyes watching us.

We haven't told Arlo everything, but after weeks together at Patton's house, he's pretty much figured out we're dating. Kids deserve more credit than they get.

Thankfully, he just told me I'm cool for dating Patman, and that was the end of it.

A little anticlimactic after everything.

Still, Arlo retches at the sight of us kissing.

"I prefer flowers," I remind him.

"And that's why I let you finish the conversation. But you already know I've found my woman, right? She's sitting right in front of me." His voice softens. "And she looks like a knockout tonight."

This time, I don't let myself question it. I just press my lips to his while his hand finds my waist, nudging me closer.

"Ewwww, you guys!" Arlo screeches. "Gross! Mommy, stop. He can't kiss you unless he beat a bad guy."

His movie logic makes me break away with a laugh. I beam Patton one more quick smile.

The warmth in my chest unfurls as I replay his words.

You already know I've found my woman, right?

We haven't spoken about forever, but at times like this, it doesn't feel like an impossible dream.

Not today, maybe, but in a matter of months or years...

"Don't bother with Kayla what's-her-face anymore," he says, standing. "I know you think she's your friend and you owe her for this job, but all she does is trample you."

"She doesn't mean to. I guess."

"Doesn't she?" He lets the question hang in the air. "Salem, she knows exactly what she's doing. The more you feel like you're not good enough, the more you rely on her to *make you* good enough. It's toxic as hell."

I want to tell him he's wrong, but he isn't.

Truth be told, Kayla Persephone shouldn't scare me.

It's all in my head, and it has been for so long, this feeling I'm just not good enough.

As Patton picks up a squealing Arlo and carries him from the room, I find my bag. I just wish I wasn't feeling down going into the family dinner.

How will a broke single mom look like she's remotely good enough for him?

I hold in a massive sigh.

The trouble is, I want to give Arlo and Patton everything they deserve. If I could reach up and catch the moon with my bare hands and offer it to them so they know how much I care, I'd do it in an instant.

But everything good takes time, and good things come to those who wait.

In the meantime, let's meet the fam and knock their socks off.

XX: WILD CARD (PATTON)

*A*pparently, despite being a member of this family for three damn decades, I had no idea just how much shit my brothers are capable of hurling at me.

Just showing up with Salem on my arm opens the floodgates.

"I never thought you'd be into the secretary type." Archer shrugs and laughs, popping open another beer as he leans against the front step. The porch leads into the backyard, where a pristine lawn and garden meets a swimming pool in the nicer weather. Right now, it's still covered for winter and the grass is brown.

"Yeah, man, I would've thought you'd give Miss Willis a chance." Dexter grins. "She's been hitting on you for years."

"I'm not into secretaries. For fuck's sake," I growl, leaning against the aged wood and taking a deep breath. "You guys can knock it off. It just happened."

Inside, somewhere, I hope Salem's holding her own. Not fending off a similar assault of teasing questions from my mother, though she wouldn't be half as bad as these piranhas.

Mom has a moral backbone and she isn't nearly so

obnoxious. That's more than I can say for the two leering ass-vampires in front of me.

"Sex doesn't just happen, Pat," Dexter says. "First you gotta take off her clothes."

"Or *she* does," Archer interjects. "Let's not assume little brother knows everything just yet."

"His first big boy relationship. How sweet."

"Get fucked. Both of you. With a rusty screwdriver," I mutter.

"Yeah, and how fucked is she to be with you? What did you *do* to her, Pat?" Dexter asks. He hasn't stopped beaming his smarmy grin ever since we walked through the door, arm in arm. "I always thought she was nice and levelheaded. But I guess some chicks have a few hidden buttons, if the right screwball comes around and pushes them just right—"

"Enough," I snarl.

"Dex is right, I just can't see it. Salem's smart, organized, and easy on the eyes, and she's with you?" Archer squints at me. "Did you pay her?"

"Boys!" Juniper's nose wrinkles as she steps out on the porch. "You're talking this much crap before dinner? Can we be civilized for one evening?"

"He deserves it," Dexter says, receiving a smack across the head for his trouble.

Thankfully, Junie isn't pulling any punches tonight.

I owe her.

"While I don't doubt Patton's been a royal pain in the ass in the past," she says, giving me a narrow-eyed look I definitely deserve, "he's bringing a girl around *for the first time*. So be nice."

"You don't need to whisper," I say. "I'm right here."

"Oh, I know. I need someone around who can enjoy a dessert that's not eighty percent cocoa." Smiling, Junie holds out a tray of her usual delectable cupcakes. "The two on the end are for Dex. They have about as much sweetness as he does, which is absolutely none right now. The rest are for the fam and our guests." She holds up a finger. "*If* you guys can play nice."

"Aw, Junie." Archer grabs the fattest cupcake on the end, stuffing it into his mouth. "We always play nice. Stick around and learn."

"Well, I'm just glad Patton found someone who likes him," she continues.

Ouch.

I nab a cupcake, happy for the distraction. "I'm *still* right here, you know."

"Yes, you are," Junie says, leveling a finger at me. "And you listen to me, Mr. Patton. If you even *consider* breaking that poor girl's heart, I will cut off your balls and put them in a cake."

That's weirdly violent for her.

I blink dumbly.

"She means it, too," Dexter says flatly.

"Of course I do. She's a nice girl, Pat. Behave yourself." Junie wags her finger again.

"Goddamn. What's a guy gotta do around here to convince you I'm serious about her?"

"We know you're serious. She's here, isn't she?" Dexter slides an arm around his wife's waist, pulling her close. She smiles like he hung the damn stars. "You've never brought a girl home before. Not since high school."

"I didn't bring Vanessa over for a date," I say. "Not to meet Mom, anyway."

"No, you brought her over to fuck in your room—only Mom came home too soon." Archer doesn't laugh much, but tonight he makes an exception.

Junie clucks her tongue with disapproval, but her lips quirk up.

"Are you boys going back to being crude before I even leave?"

"Sweetheart, we have to start early," Dexter says with his married man shit-eating grin. She slaps his shoulder and makes her way back inside, leaving the cupcakes with us on a small metal end table.

Sometimes I don't know how he ever poached a girl who can meet him head-on *and* cook. I used to think it wasn't fair.

Now, with Salem in the mix, I'm not begrudging my own luck.

Archer leans over and flicks me between the eyes.

I swing at him and barely miss.

"What the hell was that for?"

"Stop thinking about her. You get the wolfiest look on your face," Archer says, rolling his eyes. He's the only one of us left still fanatically single.

For the first time, Dexter doesn't join in beyond chortling.

Probably because he's also guilty of having stupid looks on his face whenever he thinks about Junie.

I take an angry bite of my cupcake—strawberry and chocolate today—grateful for the burst of flavor to drown out their bullshit.

It's almost obscenely sweet, and that's how I like it.

"I should check on Mom," I growl, taking Junie's exit as an escape opportunity.

My brothers shrug and go back to talking about new real estate prospects around town as I head inside.

All shit flinging aside, I think I got lucky.

When I showed up with Salem and Arlo in tow, Mom could've made this hard.

In fact, I expected her to say something—or at least have me introduce Salem as my girlfriend—but Mom just pulled her into a big, silent hug and that was that.

Maybe it was the dress.

It's nice enough for the occasion, but it still accents my woman so well I can't wait to rip it right off her. Especially after that ridiculous call with her so-called friend, but we were pressed for time and Arlo was already bouncing off the walls.

I hear voices and head through to the sunroom at the end of the house.

Outside, it's still so cool this place feels drafty, but Mom doesn't believe in practicality. She worships *atmosphere.*

For a second, I linger in the doorway, just watching them.

My family.

Even the thought makes my throat tighten.

There's little Arlo, playing with an old set of army men and military vehicles I used to own when I was a kid. He rams a plastic tank through a group of blue soldiers and dammit, I can't help but smile.

Have you ever felt like you're seeing a memory made flesh?

That's me right now, awestruck at how much Rory blood is really in the kid's veins. He's just missing an older asshole brother or two to come screaming in at the last second with their plastic jets firing spring-loaded missiles.

Junie and Salem are on the sofa together. Like any good woman willing to shack up with Dexter, she took Salem under her wing immediately.

Evelyn Hibbing sits with Mom on the other sofa, sipping a negroni and chatting away. She'll likely hang around for a few more weeks while Minnesota thaws enough for her liking.

If that isn't picturesque enough, Mom strung up fairy lights. The place glows with this cozy lantern orange that shines off Salem's hair.

Honest to God, I could stare at her forever.

"Patton?" Mom says, and I blink, dragging my gaze off Salem's slow smile to Mom's knowing grin. "Don't just stand there gawking. Come join us."

"Mr. Patman! Come play." Arlo leaps up and takes my hand, dragging me over to his miniature battlefield. "You can be the tanks," he tells me, grabbing a big artillery piece a couple feet away.

"So you think the name fits, huh?"

Arlo laughs, too oblivious for the history lesson I'm hinting at. When he's older, I think he'll learn to appreciate George S. Patton like my old man taught me.

Another family quirk. My namesake comes from a great uncle who served as one of the general's right-hand officers in Europe, but that's a story for another day.

Putting on my game face, I try to live up to the name, steering the tanks into a tactical position, only for Arlo to stop me and move them back into the open.

"I can't see them when they're back there! How're they gonna shoot bad guys?" he asks. Infallible logic.

"They'll attack when the enemy gets closer. Tanks need better range and a good line of sight to hurt the enemy. Trust me. Did you know I was named after a famous general?" I ask as Arlo makes explosion noises, standing over the blue soldiers lined up against us.

I think I lose a tank and fire back.

The boy knocks over a mess of soldiers, clapping his hands in delight.

"Have you learned about World War II yet, Arlo?" And what do I know about age-appropriate history?

"World War II? Yeah, the movies."

"You know how big it was and how many men fought, then," I tell him. I smile and crouch down next to him. "Lots of folks had relatives in the war. Even you—*probably.*"

I add the last word as an afterthought, despite knowing he's too young to guess any hidden meanings.

Hell, it's right at the tip of my tongue, aching to tell him the truth about his family. About his father. About *me.*

But he purses his lips and stops making battle noises as he looks at me. I'm not sure he understands.

For the hundredth time, I'm dumbstruck by how close his eyes are to mine—and how stupid it is that I didn't notice before.

Then again, no one else here has mentioned it yet.

Or maybe they're afraid to contemplate a world where I'm insta-dad.

"What about you?" he asks. "Were you in the war?"

I chuckle and ruffle his hair.

"Nah, the great big world wars were before my time. I'm not *that* old. And not a soldier, kid. I had a brief stint in the Navy instead. I like to think it helped straighten me out and built a little character." I point at his ships a little farther away, mostly old battleships modeled on the type from the First World War.

As a kid, I thought all ships were still like that. I was disappointed when I enlisted and found out battleships were long obsolete, and the average aircraft carrier mainly serves as a floating airbase for distant missions in combat a sailor never sees firsthand.

"You were on ships?"

"Yeah. A destroyer escort. We sailed around with a big group of ships to help protect the carrier, where the jets take off."

"Wow, cool! You should be the ships." He waves me over to the toy ships. I pick up the battleship and smile, fond memories rushing back. "Was it fun?" he asks.

"The Navy? If you like waking up at six a.m. and busting

your butt past sunset, it was a blast. Makes the rest of life seem easier, though."

"Did you go on sailing ships?"

"Not often, but I trained on them briefly." I try to hide the melancholy in my tone.

It was an odd time in my life, finishing growing up alone with no father. My older brothers had already moved out.

Whether I knew it or not, I was quietly reeling from Dad's death. I thought sailing around the world might hold some answers, but the constant training and the isolation from family didn't help much with loneliness.

It just kept me out of trouble and molded me into the playboy idiot I became when I came home. But a playboy idiot with an ironclad work ethic.

"But you're not a sailor now," Arlo says curiously. "You're a boss. Mommy told me."

"Your mommy knows a lot of things. Listen to her."

"Okay!" He turns back to his blue soldiers again, slowly reforming them in a neat line.

While he's distracted, I head over to the sofa beside Salem, but Evelyn catches my eye first and gestures me over to a cabinet where Mom keeps the good booze. There's a half-empty wine bottle sitting on top of it.

What I want more than anything is to sit down next to my frigging girlfriend, but apparently that's too much to ask.

A quick drink never hurt anyone, though, so I meet her beside the bottle and pour us both a glass. She's dressed up tonight, wearing large gold earrings.

"Patton, darling." She accepts the glass with a clink of bracelets. "Don't you look handsome? It's so wonderful to see you boys together again."

"Thanks, Evelyn." I submit to her perfumed kiss.

"Oh, and I wondered when you might introduce her.

Doesn't it feel better to come out in the open and leave all the games behind you?"

I smile.

Technically, I never got the chance to make much introduction.

Mom started treating Salem like family the second she was through the door. Even now, I can see from the set of Salem's shoulders that if she's not quite relaxed, she's not feeling the near-panic she was before we showed up.

"It's new to us. Didn't want to rush anything," I say, sipping my wine. Compared to the beer I finished outside, it's fruity and sweet.

"Of course, of course. But anyone with eyes can see you both have real affection for each other. It's charming, just like with my dear Walt back in better times..." She sighs. Her eyes glisten as she shakes her head. "But that's enough of that. I hoped I could catch you alone, Patton."

I cock my head.

"Sure, what's up?"

"I meant—oh, dear, I meant somewhere a tad more private, if it's not too much trouble? Do you have a minute?"

What now?

I glance back at Salem, who's listening to Mom talk about her recipe arsenal like they've known each other forever. I'm sure she can handle herself for a few more minutes.

"All right. Why don't we head into the office?"

"Perfect idea!" She leads the way, slipping away from the room so quietly it's entirely possible no one sees us leaving.

Arlo stays engrossed in his army men. I notice the ships started winning since I left the game and hold back a smile.

The office is a small room that's really more of a backup for any kind of work. Really, when there's any real work or reading to do, we always preferred the library with its overstuffed chairs, massive antique desk, and potent smell of old books. Mom sometimes uses this room to send a quick email, but besides that, the computer would be collecting dust if my mother wasn't such a clean freak.

"I'm really sorry to pull you away like this," Evelyn says as soon as the door's closed. She smooths down her dress. "The thing is, well... I've been talking to Archer and he's great, but I wanted to speak with you about the property."

My blood drops a few degrees.

Is she going to back out? That would be surprising, knowing how much she wants this to go ahead, but in business you can't take anything for granted.

"Of course. What's on your mind?"

She hesitates, her eyes flicking away from me to the window.

"Oh, it's all so embarrassing, but the offer—the payment schedule, I mean—it's all so generous." She gives me a pained smile.

"I'm sensing there's another but coming, so let's hear it," I urge.

"Yes, well... I'm afraid it just isn't going to cut it, even with the incredibly kind renovation investment you've offered. See, that would do it for the pilot property, but for me?" She sighs and then clears her throat loudly, clasping her hands tightly. "Please don't think ill of me—though I won't blame you if you do. I have debts, Patton. Little things I thought I could manage that just kept snowballing hungry monsters. Walt's medical bills, they put me in a bad place, and—" She clears her throat, wincing. "Lord knows I've tried to make it work. I've tried a thousand times, but the numbers just don't add up and there's never enough money."

Oh, shit.

I guess I should've seen this coming.

I nod firmly, keeping my face neutral.

She grabs my hands then, digging her fingers into the meat of my palms.

"Please don't tell Delly, dear? If she ever found out, I'd die."

"No, Evelyn. Your secret's safe with me," I say, wondering how it came to this. Yes, I'm the brother who agreed to hear her out and who got the ball rolling, but we make decisions about the company as a team.

If she's coming to me because I seem like the softer one, she's right.

Archer wouldn't agree to commit another dollar to this experiment.

In fact, I'm surprised he agreed to the upfront investments at all. Any big profits we make off this will be far down the line, if they materialize at all.

"Forgive me. I know this is awkward," she whispers, her voice shrinking with every word. "And I'm dreadfully sorry for springing this on you tonight. The thing is, now Delly's greenhouse is almost ready for spring, and I need to get back home soon."

"Sure, I figured you would."

She sighs, her eyes glassy and distant.

"Truth be told, I can't say I'm looking forward to going back—it's so cold there, you know. It'll be a couple more months before I can start doing anything outside. But it's time to go home. Your mom has been so wonderful for letting me crash here so long."

"She doesn't mind. She loves the company. I'm sure she'd keep you if she could."

Evelyn laughs, shrill and sudden, wiping at one eye.

"I'm so glad to hear that. And I know you're right. It just helps to have reassurance." Her smile hangs on her face. Sad, almost broken.

Damn.

I'm not the touchy-feely type or the kind who'd win any awards in empathy, but I hold out a hand as she gets up to leave.

I know what she's asking, even if she's too ashamed to come out and say it.

"Look, I can't commit company money," I tell her sternly. "That's not something I could do on my own, no matter how much I might want to. However, what I can offer is a personal loan. Purely between you and me. Whatever you need to get your life back on track beyond the deal with Higher Ends. Once you're in better shape, we can take it out of your cut from the cabin fees, if you'd like to do it that way. Once they're up and running, of course."

"Oh! Oh, really?" She blinks rapidly, breaking into the strangest smile. "Patton Rory, you wonderful man—that's too kind!"

She flings herself forward, smothering my cheeks in old lady kisses.

Chuckling, I push away as she laughs along with me.

But her smile fades a second later.

"I must ask again, you wouldn't mind keeping this between us, would you? The others, I'm not sure they'd understand. And poor Delly, you know how she is! She'll start giving away your inheritance if she thinks I'm in trouble."

"Already done," I say. "How much do you need?"

"Oh, not too much, I hope. Although…" She hesitates, wincing again, sucking her thin cheek into her mouth awkwardly. Her skin seems so slack it makes a flapping sound.

"Evelyn, come on. I deal with big figures all the time. Don't be afraid."

"Yes, I know it's just a few—well—"

341

"Is twenty thousand enough?" I pull out my wallet and my checkbook. She stares at me. "Forty?"

Again, that pained smile.

I try not to sigh, unsure if I'm feeling bad for her or legitimately surprised she needs so much for living expenses.

"Could we round up a touch? An even six digits will do."

A hundred thousand dollars?

Whatever.

I hide my surprise as I pull out a pen and my checkbook, quickly scribbling out the amount.

"Here you are. Let me know if you need more."

Her hand shakes as she takes the check I hold out.

"You're so generous, young man. So human." I'm a little concerned she's about to start ugly crying, so I pat her on the back and motion to leave.

"I should probably get back to Salem and help her with Arlo before someone trips on his army men."

"Of course, of course! You're a natural with the little boy, by the way. I can't wait for the wedding, Pat." She scurries to her feet with a wink and throws open the door for me like I'm some sort of king.

It's a little disturbing, honestly, the way she needs to grovel like I'm her very own guardian angel. I've handed out business loans and attended my share of charity events, but this feels more personal.

I'm relieved when I find Salem just up the hall. Her face clears when she sees us coming, and Evelyn hurries forward, her hand outstretched.

"I never did tell you, dearie," she says as Salem gives her a hand—and me a confused look. "You make such a perfect match with Patton, and your little boy looks cute enough to eat right up!"

"Thank you," Salem says, flashing me an amused look.

Evelyn pats her cheek and continues on with a spring in her step. Salem looks up at me. "What was that all about?"

"Oh, she just wanted to ask for a favor."

"What favor? The Minnesota deal again?" She frowns, the corners of her mouth pulling down.

"Don't worry about it. It's under control," I say with a smile.

To my surprise, Salem doesn't smile back.

She just tugs at her wrap, pulling it down her arms to cover them. For the first time, I wonder why she left the others.

"Care for a walk?" I ask, offering her my arm. "It's pretty mild outside."

Her gaze flicks to my face and away again. "You don't have to do this. It's supposed to be a family dinner."

"If Mom wants to complain, there's plenty of that to go around with her *other* two sons. Hell, we'll probably find them out there too."

After another second of hesitation—just long enough for me to wonder if she's really okay—she slides her hand through my arm and follows me down the hall to the side door leading into the backyard.

The stars are underwhelming tonight. The Utah desert will always put Kansas City's clouds and light pollution to shame, but Salem still tips her head back and inhales the evening air with a smile.

"Want to tell me what's wrong?" I ask. "If you like, we can walk over to that bench first."

For the first time, a smile touches her lips, and she nods at the bench.

"It's my dad's old spot," I explain as we get closer. "He used to love sitting here. He was big into poetry and history books when he wasn't busy with numbers. He'd waste away whole evenings with a book in his hand, always somewhere else."

"You should read more like your dad," she says, hesitating next to the bench. "But do you really want to sit—"

"Yes. Come sit, Salem." I pull her down on the cool metal next to me. Dew glimmers everywhere in the evening, coating the faint outlines of budding trees.

Normally, I don't linger around Dad's old brooding spot much.

I have to admit, there's something calming about being outside tonight—or maybe it's just her. The air isn't fragrant yet like it'll be come summer, but it cools my skin and gives me space, a distance I appreciate from the enormous house I grew up in.

"I don't know how to explain it," Salem says quietly, tracing the floral patterns on her dress. Goosebumps dot her arms, but she doesn't move like she's cold.

Instead, she spreads her fingers, inviting the air in to cool her skin.

"Has someone made you feel like you don't belong? Is it Archer?"

"No, nothing like that. Everyone's been so nice. Too nice, maybe. But I guess that's the issue..." She looks at me slowly. "You have such a lovely family. For me, that's pretty alien."

With my gaze smoldering, I take her hand.

"Don't be afraid. Whatever happened with your folks, it won't happen again. We don't send family packing into exile."

I shake my head, holding back the curses her parents deserve. How could they do that shit to their own daughter?

And all because she wouldn't give up a kid they felt was a wrench being tossed into their little lives?

People are strange fucking birds sometimes.

They can also change, and not always for the better.

Thankfully, it hasn't happened much in my own family. I can see how foreign that might be to Salem.

Look at Dex, the ultimate workaholic human android before Junie.

Archer, he's so reserved he'd make a fridge magnet look outgoing.

Me, I'm the risk-taker. Shallow and self-centered, or so everyone says.

Mom, she's the glue holding us together, but not because we need it.

"What was so bad about it all? The unfamiliarity?" I ask gently.

"Nothing. Nothing *bad*, I just…" She looks at me, her eyes wide with dark feelings pooling in this light. "I was talking about the future and your mom started showing me some antique jewelry after I talked about looking up inspiration for art and décor at future properties."

"And?"

She hesitates, sighing loudly.

"Don't you get it, Patton? We're bound to disappoint them, disappoint her, once the truth comes out. We're basking in all these smiles and glitzy stuff and it's all going to come crashing down."

I don't understand the tension in her voice.

"Why? Because my mother showed you some old jewelry and you talked about the future?"

"Because good things don't last! Not for me. Not for a black cat."

"Lady Bug, fuck." I take her icy hands in mine.

All of her feels cold, really, but she's too stubborn to admit it and let me warm her.

"Good things do happen," I tell her, trying to be gentle but I'm growling anyway. That's what she needs right now, a gentle touch, even if it's frustrating as hell to have to convince her she deserves better than she's gotten before.

"I wish I had your confidence." She sighs again.

"Salem, look up." I wait for her eyes to meet mine before I say, "The good things are coming. We're living them right now. You deserve them."

She presses my hands to her lips, a kiss like spring rain.

"Yeah, you're right. I know you are even if I don't want to believe it," she whispers. "Thank you."

"You're being ridiculous, you know. All everybody talks about is how great we look together. My brothers can't believe I scored a woman like you."

She laughs harshly.

Let her wonder. If they weren't being real, they wouldn't have ripped the shit out of me over it.

"Now stop brooding and put this on." I shrug off my jacket and drape it over her shoulders. "It's been a good night. My mom loves you. She loves Arlo. You've made friends with Junie, and you know what would make it better?"

"What?" Her hot tears shock me when I feel their heat, clinging to her face like rain glazing the trees.

"If we told Arlo. End our night on a high note."

"Hmm... yeah." She swallows and looks away, considering it. "It would be a big finish."

I wait, but she doesn't say yes.

Fuck.

Look, I get that I'm throwing one more big wild card her way when she's in an environment where she's second-guessing everything.

I'm also one impatient prick.

"I take it that's a no," I say flatly, keeping the irritation out of my voice.

"I'm sorry, Patton. It just feels too soon. I promise we'll do it soon, when we can figure it out."

"When it isn't soon at all, you mean." Like I said. *Prick.*

I resist the urge to curse and stare at the house. I know I'm throwing a fucking tantrum and I hate myself for it.

But hell, if we told everyone about Arlo—if we told *Arlo* about me—we could go that extra step, starting a new chapter.

We could be something greater than the lonely, doubtful creatures we've been for too long.

My ass hurts. It's like my dad's old bench wants to add insult to injury, a rough spot in the weathered metal rubbing on my hip.

Salem slides an arm around my neck and presses her body against mine.

Usually, that's enough to soften me up—or harden me, if I'm being honest—but now I'm not in the mood, even with her in that airy dress.

"I'm sorry. I don't want to disappoint you," she murmurs, kissing my cheek. "I know you want him to know, and he will. He's just at an age where we have to be careful."

"He's brighter than you think," I snap. My shoulders slump a second later. "Sorry. I don't mean to be harsh. I just hate the years I've wasted without my son, and we need to make up for lost time."

"We will." She kisses me again. At least her lips are getting warmer now. "I'm the problem, Patton. I admit it. It's not just his reaction I'm worried about. It's losing this—losing you—when it's all so new. Can we please just have a little time? Just so I can be sure."

With a hand on her waist, I ease her back.

"I understand. This shit will shake up our lives permanently, no question. But I love the little man. And I want him to have a family. A real proper family beyond his mother,

Salem, with everybody in this house knowing there's a new little Rory to spoil."

Her eyes twinkle as she pulls away.

"You love Arlo, huh?"

I blink at her.

"He's my *son*, Salem. Of course I do." The other words— the same ones for her—stop dead on my tongue.

Shit, maybe it really is too soon.

Now isn't the moment. I can feel it in my skin.

And maybe I'm more like her than I think, holding back for the perfect opportunity, even if it's hard to imagine.

Regardless, that perfect moment, that massive declaration, it isn't happening tonight. That doesn't make us bad people. It just makes me conflicted.

"I'm going back inside to talk to Mom," I say. "Stay out here as long as you like. Keep the jacket."

"Patton—"

"Think about what you want," I tell her. "Because I already know."

When I reach the door, I look back to see her huddled into my coat, too large over her slim shoulders.

She's staring at the sky again with a look that's way too much like I remember my old man wearing as the clouds move in, covering the tinsel stars.

Yeah, it's hardly just Salem being ridiculous tonight.

I snort at my own stupidity and close the door.

XXI: DOWN AND OUT (SALEM)

*I*t feels strange waking up in my own bed alone again.

My place has never felt smaller and it's always been mouse worthy.

I take a minute to stretch, my fingers brushing the wall and my toes scraping the end of the bed. There are a few shirts strung up by the heater to air dry and a suitcase on the floor I haven't put away yet.

Arlo isn't awake yet, and it's quiet as a tomb without Patton around.

Of course, he's never stayed over here.

My choice, mostly—I didn't want him hanging out in my crappy apartment when we could slum it in his mansion in style. But I also wanted a safe environment for Arlo, just in case things go sideways.

It always comes down to Arlo when my own selfish feelings aren't in the driver's seat.

He deserves better, but he also shouldn't get too used to nice things when it could all come crashing out under us.

But if Patton walks out on me, he won't abandon his son.

Whether I like it or not, the Rory wealth is part of Arlo's life now, and it could easily sideswipe his future. I don't know if that's good or bad.

Ugh, why is this so hard?

I drop my head in my hands, jamming my fingers into my eyes until I see stars.

I'm doing what I do best.

Worrying.

The great family dinner, our big relationship reveal, it was all just a few days ago. How does it already feel like half a lifetime ago?

His whole family knows we're a thing and I haven't seen him since he took us home.

My fault. Partly.

But after the way he left me outside, I decided we needed some time apart, and he didn't argue. Probably because he was frustrated I turned him down again.

Probably because I was a little thrilled he said he loves Arlo—and a lot let down that he wouldn't say the word to me.

Also, we need boundaries.

Space. Borders. Walls.

Time in our own homes where we aren't changing too much, too soon, and I don't have to freak out about how it's influencing my son. It's just crazy unsatisfying.

I roll over angrily, jerking my phone from its charging cord.

He still hasn't texted.

Fine, whatever.

I wasn't expecting him to and he has no obligation. But every morning since that night, I've wanted to wake up to a message.

In a single frenzied month with barely any time alone and

so much mind-blowing sex, Patton Rory has changed me into the unthinkable.

Spoiled.

That's what I am.

He's submerged me in kindness and stability I don't know what to do with. I'm inexperienced, acting like a lovestruck teen when I should be handling an adult relationship.

One where we don't talk for days at a time because we're busy.

And I know better than anyone how busy Patton is.

His job is his life and right now, even on a Sunday, he's probably working. Or getting coffee from that fancy place down the road.

Never mind the fact that he sometimes gets *me* some coffee.

Groaning, I toss the phone aside and try to muster up the energy to climb out of bed.

It's better that Arlo spends some time in his old home and old life. Patton's fairy-tale palace is a dream, not a reality for us.

Don't get me wrong. I want Arlo to have the world, but that's not the world—that's a parallel universe no five-year-old should have to digest.

He's awake when I get up, though, sitting at the kitchen table with an overflowing bowl of cereal I left out last night.

"I did it, Mommy!" he tells me proudly as he digs in. There's milk splattered around his bowl.

"Have you got enough there, big guy?" I ask, grabbing a dishrag. It's still so early the sun has barely risen, though that just means it's around seven this time of year. "I was going to make you pancakes."

"Pancakes?" In his excitement, he hits the spoon and cereal flies everywhere.

I stare at the milk slowly dripping on the floor, trying to shoot him a scolding look before I break down and laugh.

If we were at Patton's, in his gleaming modern kitchen, he'd just chuckle and wipe it away with a damp cloth and a joke. Here, on my own, it feels more like I'm on trial.

Another chore.

Another mom dilemma where I have to pretend I'm a shining example of a human being and not an immature gremlin.

Another cute, stinging moment *alone.*

What else is new? Rinse and repeat.

"I love pancakes," Arlo tells me, like I'm not well aware. They're at the top of the list for bribing him to start a good day, up there with pizza and ice cream. "Are you gonna make them now, Mommy? Can we have banana and choc-lit chip?"

"First, I need to clean up the mess you've made. Then we'll see."

He has the grace to look a little ashamed, but he perks up quickly. "That won't take you long."

No, it won't, but it sure as heck would go faster with another person here to ease the burden.

I hate these thoughts.

I hate my brain for having them.

Just like I hate the way I'm constantly comparing my past mistakes to Patton's life on a gold pedestal.

Deep down, I don't think I'm worthy.

And I also have the awareness to know I'm not because *I'm* the only one thinking it. The Rorys were incredibly nice to me, or else money taught them to hide their mean streak way better than my parents ever did.

Still.

It feels like it can't last.

Someone or something has to come along the minute I'm

settled in and burst the bubble—and there's a good possibility that something is *me*.

It's not like I'm new to self-sabotage.

"Where's my tablet? I can't find it!" Arlo asks loudly as I wipe down the chair leg and catch the last milk splattering the floor.

"I don't know, sweetie."

"Help find it, Mommy. Please?" The *please* is tacked on as a question, but at least it's there. That took long enough to get him to memorize.

"I can't do both right now. I only have two hands," I tell him. "Have you checked under your bed?"

While Arlo pops up and zooms around the house, searching high and low, I get started on the pancakes. I really hope the tablet turns up. He'll be sad and bored out of his wits for days if it doesn't.

If Patton was here, he'd help with the cooking or the tablet hunt, I'm sure.

Instead, I'm tripping over my son and his zoomies while I crack eggs into a bowl.

"We'll look again later, hon," I say after he's given up. His bottom lip juts out, endearing and frustrating at the same time. "So do you think Patman's your favorite superhero?"

"He can't climb buildings and he doesn't have laser eyes... but he's still cool."

I smile. "What's so cool about him?"

"He's rich! He sails around the world and fights bad guys. He's named after a famous general." He strikes a karate pose and chops the air. "His car's pretty cool too."

I'm not sure what he means by fighting bad guys. But there's no denying the rest is true, and it pours out of my little boy in a hero-worship rush.

God.

"Some great heroes have sad stories, you know," I say,

smoothing the batter. "Like Batman. His parents died when he was young, didn't they?"

"Yeah." Arlo shrugs, unbothered.

I need to be more blunt, so I set the bowl down and ask, "Arlo, do you ever wish you had a daddy?"

His face snaps up to look at me and he frowns.

"Oh. Uh." He chews on the question for a second, watching me with ferocious intent.

Holy hell, he looks just like Patton when he's focused.

Then he smiles up at me, but he still doesn't answer.

"Arlo?"

"Don't worry, Mommy. You're better than ten dads. I don't care."

Yeah, I think that spilled milk from earlier has nothing on my heart exploding.

"I love you, kiddo." I give him an impulsive hug he doesn't try to wiggle out of for once. "But it's okay to want a dad, too. I know the other boys at school have them."

"But I don't *need* a dad, Mom. It's okay if he's gone. I dunno." He's so calm, his voice light and easy. Unlike his mother, who's having a nervous breakdown over starting this conversation. "Are the pancakes almost done? The banana smell's making me hungry."

He sniffs the air like a starving raccoon.

Laughing, I try not to let my vision blur and heat the pan to start cooking. With all the emotional distractions, I added too many chocolate chips. But they're going to be good. My stomach growls right along with his.

I cook silently while Arlo hums to himself, drawing on his notepad. The instant they're done, he runs over and grabs the sprinkles from next to the stove.

"Thanks, Mommy!"

"Hey, hey, not too many! This is already like having dessert for breakfast." I wag a finger at him.

He laughs at me mischievously. "What if it's both?"

"You need breakfast before anything else. No arguments, young man," I say, cutting a banana into discs to throw on top.

In response, he shakes a whole pile of sprinkles on top of my handiwork once he has the plate.

"There's banana right there on top. It's healthy!" he proclaims through a mouthful of pancake.

Oof.

What if he inherited Patton's sweet tooth and his fighter logic?

"I have a question before you stuff your face," I say, abandoning any hope of being subtle. "What if your dad came back one day? How would you feel?"

Arlo shrugs, more interested in his food than adding another parent to his life.

"What if? We're friends with Grumpybutt." Knowing he's said something he shouldn't, he sends me a wicked glance. "No one's cooler than him. If we're gonna have a guy around, he should be the dude."

The dude.

Yeah, I'm dead.

If there ever was a flashing neon sign from the universe, this is it. I'm not sure whether to laugh or cry hysterically, so I settle for scooping him up and kissing his face, which is already covered in chocolate and sprinkles.

"Mom!" He squeals and this time really does try to wiggle free, smacking the back of his head into my jaw as he goes. But he's laughing, and so am I, because it's like a weight I never knew existed has been lifted away.

I'm free.

We're free.

And I need to tell Patton that I'm sure the big confession won't be a disaster.

355

This could fix everything if I just screw my head on and do it.

He always wanted me to tell Arlo from the beginning. I just kept looking for reasons why it could shatter everything.

Peering into darkened corners and unspoken words and the gaping distance between Patton's lofty life and mine. But maybe what I actually needed was trust all along.

My phone buzzes from the other room and I head back through to grab it. Maybe it's Patton calling to offer me the coffee I know he's almost certainly gone out to buy.

Only, it's not his name on my screen.

Unknown number.

I chew my lip, staring at the phone as it buzzes in my hand again before I swipe and hold it to my ear. "Hello?"

"Salem?"

"Yes?" The voice is familiar, but I can't quite place it.

"It's Delly, Delly Rory. Sorry to bother you so early, but it turns out a certain little someone forgot his new toys and his tablet when you were over. I wondered if you'd like some brunch with me?"

Now isn't the best time to point out Arlo just wolfed down three mini pancakes. If there's one thing I know about little boys, though, it's that they have a bottomless stomach for being spoiled.

"Sure, that sounds lovely," I say, doing a victory dance around the room. "When would you like us over?"

* * *

THIS TIME when I approach Delly Rory's enormous house, I don't feel like it's going to swallow me whole.

Patton wasn't invited to this little meetup. It feels more than ever like I've been accepted into a secret little club.

Girls' club. Mothers' club. The Rory women club, maybe.

After our near-fight a few days ago before dinner, I didn't think meeting up with Patton's mom could create this sort of champagne-bubbly feeling in my belly, but here we are.

A brunch invite with Delly.

"Remember, big guy, you've got to be on your best behavior," I remind Arlo as we walk up to the huge castle-like door, hand in hand. "Be polite, like last time."

"I like Delly. She's pretty nice." He also looks like he's fizzing with excitement.

"She's a nice lady," I agree.

The door flies open and Delly, with her immaculate white pantsuit and pink scarf, beckons us in. The woman has a knack for always looking runway stylish and regal, and today is no exception.

"So glad to see you again!" she gushes. Unlike when I'm talking to Kayla, it doesn't sound forced. "Hi, Arlo. I bet you were missing your tablet, huh?"

"Yeah! I couldn't find it *anywhere*." He launches into telling her about his hunt with a dramatic style that could rival Indiana Jones. Delly gives me a pat on the arm as she leads me to her dining room.

Evelyn is there, too, clasping a mug of coffee in her hands as she nods at us warmly. She's a little more casual than Delly, but there's no doubt some of her best friend's charm rubbed off, or she's just a natural at looking poised and stylish too.

There's never any doubt she makes a good impression, anyway. It's the way she holds herself, I think.

But is she always like that or is it just the added pressure to blend into this fine house for her extended stay?

Not that I'd blame her one bit.

Just breathing the air here makes me obsess with the infinite ways I don't fit in. Not that it stops either woman from acting like I'm an honored guest.

I give Evelyn a wide smile as I sit. We're in the same boat, her and I—outsiders to the Rory court, even if she's so much closer to being a regular than I am. Still, we should stick together.

"Salem," Evelyn says, sipping her coffee. She smiles over the rim, just enough to show a flash of teeth and a soft crinkle of her eyes. "So lovely to see you again. You must have some of that orange cake. We just whipped it up yesterday with a little help from Junie. Delly, could you grab me another piece?"

Sure enough, there's fresh cake on the small coffee table that smells like citrus heaven as Delly starts carving slices.

Arlo grabs his plate like a hungry little ghoul and devours his piece before plugging in his headphones and watching one of his favorite animal YouTube channels on his tablet.

"It's a huge relief to have it back," I say, nodding at the boy. "He would've been so disappointed if it hadn't shown up. It's like the nicest thing we own."

No exaggeration.

I had to pull long hours flipping secondhand junk online just to scrape together enough for that Christmas present, an iPad with a durable case that can handle his abuse.

"Ah, I wish I had one of those. I could use it for the airport today." Evelyn's smile deepens. "He's a good boy. I'm sure there was someone watching over him and his little toys."

She sets a tall glass of orange juice in front of him.

He looks up, offering her a smile and a mumbled, "Thanks."

Better than nothing, I guess.

"Boys," Delly says fondly, glancing over at him and his tiny, puckered frown of concentration as a man on the screen lets a nasty-looking centipede crawl up his arm in some tropical environment. "I imagine he was a little nightmare this morning."

"Only a little." I laugh. "Honestly, I think he was sure I took it and misplaced it."

The cake is downright decadent—Juniper's expert baker touch for sure—and I eat my slice in about three big bites despite my best intentions to seem ladylike.

"Patton was a Tasmanian devil as a child," Delly says, glancing at Evelyn with a conspiratorial smile. There's something so pleasant about them, two old friends. I can't wait to have her as Arlo's grandma, and maybe Evelyn as a great aunt of sorts. "Remember that time we visited you in Minnesota, Evie?"

"How could I forget?" Evelyn laughs cheerfully. "Right in the middle of summer, the sticky dog days. You were staying in one of the lakeside cabins."

I wonder if she means one of the cabins Higher Ends is looking at refurbishing. I lean forward, elbows on my knees, wondering if I'll learn anything useful from a business standpoint I can recommend to Patton and his brothers.

There's value in knowing a property's history, the lives and laughs that have happened there over time.

Also, though I hate to admit it, I'm curious about any and all stories of young Patton. There's so much of his life I still don't know.

So much about *him* that's a mystery, and I want to learn every little detail.

"He must've been about seven on that trip," Delly says with a faraway look in her eyes. Her gold bangles clink dully as she links her fingers across her knee. "He was just learning to swim properly, and it was a hot summer. Terribly hot."

"Those were the days, out in the sticks. Back then, the cabins didn't have good air-conditioning, so we spent all our time by the lake, hoping to catch a breeze," Evelyn explains.

I think I know where this is going, but there's something compelling about hearing them feed it in little bites.

"He was a brave boy, always wanting to swim. I told him not to go in too deep, but he wasn't the kind of boy to listen to his mom. Or his dad. Or his older brothers. Or even *me*." Evelyn smiles. "So, when we weren't looking, guess where he swam. I think Lake Mesabi must be around eighty feet deep. The little beast didn't even bring his lifejacket..."

Evelyn moistens her lips, looking at Arlo. My heart tightens, knowing she's probably imagining what might happen if Arlo swam out that far. They were a similar age—it must feel like looking back in time.

Has she noticed their similarity yet?

But then she glances back at me with a flat stare.

"He disappeared," Delly says. "We were beside ourselves. My husband and Evelyn's, they threw themselves in the water, swimming after him."

"Poor Archer wanted to go in, too," Evelyn reminds her. "But you told him to stay on the shore."

"He was too young and that lake was deep. I wouldn't dare risk another son. But between them, they got Patton out. His little lungs coughed up so much water." Delly's face looks white as she remembers it.

Evelyn nods glumly. "A tragic reminder of how fragile life can be."

I glance at Arlo, but he's oblivious to the scary story, chewing his lip as he remains glued to his animals.

My heart won't stop racing and I wasn't even there.

To me, my son doesn't seem so fragile, but that's because I've seen him jump down stairs and patched up countless scraped knees.

But really, he's small.

His hands, clutching the tablet, are tiny. If something were to happen—

No, not today.

Not ever.

I'm being ridiculous.

Nothing's going to happen because we're not by a lake, and after that story, I'm not sure I want to take him to one until he's in middle school.

"You know," Delly says, leaning forward and placing her hand on my arm, grabbing my attention. "It's been great getting to know you. These old stories aren't half as interesting without any new ears."

I smile.

"It's been nice, Delly. So is bringing Arlo around for company. He could use the practice with his social skills. School just doesn't cover every situation."

"Of course. He's a lovely boy, isn't he, Evelyn?"

"To die for," Evelyn agrees.

"But I appreciate your honesty, Salem," Delly continues. "Patton hasn't brought any girls home since high school. It's a hard thing being sincere and authentic."

"I mean, I can't be anything else," I say.

An eyebrow quirks as she smiles. "You'd be surprised how many others try. I'm a little protective of my sons—not that they need it when they're grown men. Until Dexter got engaged, I feared they'd stay allergic to dating forever. And Archer? You don't even want to know."

That actually piques my curiosity, but I laugh along with them.

"Some women get funny ideas. They see this big old house and think they know what we want to see and what my boys expect." She laughs and the tension drains from her shoulders. "They aren't great at it when they try to go through me, always playing up their looks and eggshell personalities. Patton, though, he knew how to pick them when he was younger, or so I thought. Then the truth would come falling out, whether he screwed things up or not."

I take a long pull of coffee, hiding the way my stomach pinches at the thought that I'm being compared to his old dates, even if it's favorable. And how fast will that change when they figure out the truth about Arlo?

"Well, I'm an open book. What you see is what you get, like it or lump it."

Well, mostly.

Delly's face splits in a grin.

"We already knew that, honey," she says, that hint of Southern drawl she has making its way into her words. But all that does is make me feel guilty.

Soon, soon.

The whole truth and nothing but.

After I've told Arlo first.

But it feels like that moment is coming too soon, bearing down on me like a bison stampede, wild and inescapable.

Part of me wishes she'd take a good long look at Arlo and figure it out right now. I can't wait for all the lies and deception and half-truths to end.

Once everything is finally out in the open, we can move forward, whatever that looks like.

Is this how Patton's been feeling ever since he found out? It's pretty rotten, like insects crawling under your skin.

Enough.

Today's the day, I decide, standing abruptly. I need to tell Arlo and show Patton I'll do what it takes to make this work.

"Come to think of it, I should see Patton," I say. "I just remembered there's something important I need to tell him."

Delly trades an indulgent smile with Evelyn. "We understand. Say no more, dear."

"Absolutely," Evelyn says eagerly, clasping her hands. "Young love makes me jealous."

I'm grateful they're so kind.

One step at a time. Let's not get too carried away.

"Come on, Arlo. You can watch more later," I say. Delly picks up his empty glass, and he reluctantly pauses his video. "Say goodbye for now."

He submits to a happy hug from Delly and a pat on the cheek from Evelyn, and finally I make my escape. I'm hoping it doesn't look rude to run away so fast, but the sooner I do this, the better everything will be.

"Mommy…" I'm a little distracted as I throw on my coat.

Where are you? Are you free this evening? I text Patton on our way out the door.

"Mommy," Arlo says, tugging on my arm. "My lips feel funny."

"Funny how?" I ask absently.

"Itchy."

I look at him and smile.

"It's all that orange juice, I bet, on top of the cake. Do you know it had pieces of real candied oranges in it?" A little reaction around his lips to a citrus overload wouldn't be new.

"Why are we rushing?"

"I'd like to see Patton this evening," I explain.

Arlo doesn't protest as I strap him into his car seat and we set off, only to be stuck in late morning traffic five minutes later. I lean on the steering wheel, tapping against it impatiently.

"Mommy," Arlo says from the back. "Mommy, I don't feel good."

I barely have time to turn around to see before orange spray bursts from his mouth, covering him in a complete mess. He lurches, more cake coming out, almost undigested.

Holy shit!

I look for a way off the road, but there isn't one.

We're stuck.

God.

"Hang on, sweetheart." I keep my voice calm, unshaken, though panic sweeps through me.

I might have to put the big reveal on hold if he's getting violently sick. He's only had a few stomach bugs over the years, and they always hit hard and fast.

I'll be lucky if I don't get it. Last time, I spent two days hunched over a toilet, regretting everything I'd ever eaten for the last year.

The traffic inches along. I swing into a parking lot for a gas station, knowing I can start cleaning him up there.

"Stay calm, big guy." My fingers are too tight on the steering wheel. "It'll be okay. I'll just get out, find the wipes, and get you all cleaned—"

I stop cold as I look at him again.

He doesn't say anything.

His eyes are half-closed.

His lips are too pale and his eyes are drooping and glassy.

Is he breathing?

Panic.

My own breathing becomes a deafening roar in my ears as I fling my door open and run to his side. There's too much sick everywhere, and the only time he moves is when he keeps convulsing, heaving himself dry.

Oh my God, no.

I start using my fingers to clear his airway, holding his head, trying not to shake.

All I can smell is rancid orange.

"Arlo?" I shake his shoulders, but his head lolls loosely. "Arlo!"

He's still breathing, yes, but he's not responding.

He barely seems conscious as he groans.

My hands shake like leaves, fluttering around his face. I'm

probably supposed to do something to help right now, but all I can think of is the fact that he's *not freaking there*.

He's dying in front of me!

"Arlo, Arlo," I beg, my voice choked. *"Arlo. Please."*

By the time I have the wits to grab my phone and hit emergency, I'm screaming into it.

Soon, he isn't moving at all.

XXII: BAIT AND SWITCH
(PATTON)

$\mathcal{T}$he weathered brick building looks uninspiring from the outside.

There's a balcony on the third floor with twisted iron railings that have seen better days. I let myself inside with the key and frown, taking it in.

The plan is to convert the place into a luxurious house with rustic charm, but right now, it's a tumbledown three-story house. The hall shows off the tall ceilings, at least, with stairs leading up to the second and third floors, and the kitchen is straight ahead. I check that out first.

Dexter was the one who suggested we look at this property, and after Archer took a second look, he agreed. This is my first time here, and I bring up the floor plan on my tablet, making notes.

The kitchen seems roomy enough with plenty of counter space, but we'll be gutting it and overhauling everything with high-end finishes and appliances.

As I move through the house, I can see why it caught their eye. The bones are good.

The place is also a steal at its current price, and although there's a lot to do cosmetically, the structural issues are minor for a building this old.

A basic gut and renovate job.

About as good as it gets in this business.

The only thing left to decide is the décor and style, which our usual experts can help with.

The location is a unicorn. It's a nice neighborhood, close but not too close to the city center, which means the interior should feel inviting.

My instinct pings on soft white with Japandi style finishes. Or maybe old-world black frames and hardware with a rubbed oil look. Salem might have a point about my natural tastes.

Wood, then. Archer will agree in a heartbeat.

A nice pale wood like beech or white oak or pine.

Yes, pine.

That will lend a light homey feel and pair with the modern bright lights and ceramic lamps that feel like natural additions.

Another home away from home in the making.

This isn't the extravagant escape some of our other properties are. It's a roomy, practical place for a couple or an entire family looking to enjoy a few nights away in affordable luxury without being right downtown. A hidden sanctuary oozing history from its pores.

I make a few more notes on my tablet and step onto the balcony. The back of the property opens up to a park, and in the late morning light, the city looks especially vivid.

Salem would like it here.

Fuck, I can't stop thinking about her.

Even at work.

Especially at work when it's painfully inconvenient.

Double fuck.

I haven't replied to her latest texts from a few minutes ago, hating that they're already burning a hole in my pocket.

When the hell did I get so soft?

Then my phone rings and my heart does this annoying leap when I see it's her.

I've been avoiding her, yeah. Deliberately, ever since that moment at Mom's.

Not because I don't want to talk to her, but because I don't know what the hell to say.

What else *can* I say to convince her to let me be Arlo's dad? Obviously, I can't go behind her back to tell him. Even if I understand it abstractly, it still hurts like an iceball to the face.

So what if I've been spending the last few days at home, missing her and drinking too much and hating the fact that her absence makes me self-medicate, brooding in front of my fish?

Stupid.

Messy.

Dumb.

Pure jackass, and yet I'm doing it anyway.

I inhale sharply and accept my fate as my finger swipes the call.

"Hey, Salem. I've been meaning to call—"

"Patton." My name feels like a gunshot, the word sharp, panicked. My grip on my phone tightens as it rips through me. "Something's wrong. Arlo, he just—he won't wake up." A sob rattles her voice.

What. The. Fuck.

It's a gut punch, so swift my lungs deflate.

I have to lean on the old railing to stay upright.

"What happened? What do you mean he won't wake up?" I try to keep calm, my voice clipped like I haven't heard since my Navy days. She needs strength right now, not this roaring frustration surging up that threatens to blow me into a thousand pieces and scatter me to the winds.

"I don't—I don't know. I was just driving. He started vomiting everywhere. I called an ambulance as soon as I could pull over."

There's no siren wailing in the background. They must've already reached the hospital, I hope.

"Where are you? The university hospital?"

"Y-yes," she strangles out, choking on the words. "He's with the doctors now. They took him straight in."

"Okay. Salem, sweetheart, I need you to breathe." I can't think straight enough to give her better advice. I'm just barreling through this damn house until I'm back outside, fumbling with the keys to lock the door. "I'm on my way. Is anyone else with you?"

"No, no, it's just me."

Of course it is, you idiot, I tell myself bitterly.

She has no family here. The closest thing she has to a friend is a vapid Instagram girl who cares more about her looks than human decency.

I close my eyes for a furious second before getting in my SUV and starting the engine.

"I'll be there soon," I promise. "Stay put and wait for me. It's going to be okay."

I hope like hell I'm not wrong.

Nothing about this makes sense.

I hate that I can't make any big promises and she knows it as well as I do.

But Arlo should be fine. Kids don't just up and die for no reason, do they?

Then again, if he's out like she's saying, if he *won't wake up*—

My throat burns, the same acid feeling clawing at my eyes.

Goddammit, my son is hurt.

I don't understand what's happening.

Still, I can't fall down that abyss or I'll wind up paralyzed.

The boy might be my son and a damn good kid, but I've only known him for a whisper. Barely a couple months. Such a tiny portion of my life for a little human who's become a bigger piece of my world than the sky.

No fucking crying now.

No rough words.

No freaking out and flying fists.

You need to be there for her.

You need to be *there*.

The traffic is god-awful thanks to some big concert downtown, plus the usual stream of latecomers running their errands.

Arlo must be okay.

For me, for Salem, for our family.

My mind reels, wondering if we'll have to tell my mother that Arlo was my kid and that she never had a chance to know him.

What if he never finds out I'm his dad?

My hands tighten on the steering wheel until I think I'll tear it right off.

When I finally arrive at the hospital, parking is atrocious. I slam my way into an empty space, not bothering to make sure I parked straight, and sprint for the entrance through the vast garage.

Upstairs, the receptionist directs me to the waiting room. I take the stairs three at a time, leaping through the last corridor until finally I see her.

Salem.

She's tucked away in the corner of the waiting room, her legs crooked under her. She's just staring at the wall.

It's like someone picked her up and poured her soul out.

"Salem," I call, and her head jerks up. Some of the emptiness drains from her face, replaced by relief, and she uncurls herself, holding out a hand.

Then her face crumples.

"Salem," I growl again, pulling her into my arms.

Awkwardness forgotten—everything but this, the painful knowledge that our son is seriously sick and there's nothing either of us can do.

She wraps her arms around me and buries her head in my shoulder. I cradle her closer, wishing I could whisk her away. There's nothing more depressing than a waiting room filled with worried souls, just like the woman in my arms.

This is where people go to wait for miracles. Waiting and hoping because no one can guarantee life, not even if they have an MD behind their name. What else is there to do in a hospital waiting room but quietly scream at God and the universe?

Salem's hand pulls me closer, just for a second, before she shrinks back.

I slide a hand through her hair and smooth it down her cheek, though she isn't crying. Her red eyes say there's been too much of that already.

"I'm so glad you're here. I missed you," she whispers, one hand gripping my wrist like she's scared I'll disappear into thin air if she stops.

Fuck.

It's so easy for her to say that, and it unlocks something in my chest.

"Missed you, too, Lady Bug. I wouldn't be anywhere else. How are you? How's Arlo?"

The question I need to ask and almost don't want to know.

It feels like Schrodinger's cat. If I don't ask, he might be fine. He might be recovering. The ugly truth doesn't have to exist if I don't call for it.

But dammit, I need to know.

She doesn't cry, but her chest heaves. For a second, I wonder if she'll have the breath to tell me.

Her hair falls limply around her face. She takes a strand and pulls it roughly, twisting it around her delicate fingers.

"Salem?" I tilt her face up so I can read it properly, searching in her eyes for answers the way astrologers watch the stars.

She releases a shuddering breath.

"I... I don't know," she says, still twisting her hair around. "It just doesn't make sense. We were out and it was a normal day, Patton."

Fear grips my chest and I inhale deeply, all I can do to keep my voice level.

"Look at me," I tell her, and finally she focuses, two pinpricks of awareness gleaming through the shock. "What did the doctor tell you? What *happened*?"

She presses her lips together so tightly I can't see them.

I grit my teeth with effort.

It's not that I want to rage at her—hell, I want to wipe the sadness from her eyes and make sure she never feels it again —but there's this jagged vibration in my chest that needs to come out.

She inhales and wipes her dry, red eyes.

"It was a normal morning," she says quietly. A whisper, really. I pull her closer so I can hear her. "I swear he didn't eat anything awful. He didn't have anything I didn't."

"So they think it's food poisoning?"

"No, it's..." She swallows so hard I see her throat dip. "More like regular poisoning."

"What the fuck?" I barely remember to keep my voice

down as other people look at us. "What do you mean, regular poisoning?"

"I don't know. I don't *know!* One minute, he was fine. The next, he's throwing up everywhere and I couldn't—" She tears at her hair. I catch her wrists to hold them still, pressing them gently to my chest. "I should have known something like this was bound to happen," she says, more quietly this time.

"Salem—"

"We know I'm bad luck. It follows me everywhere. I just thought it would hurt us, not Arlo. I didn't think it would ever come after him."

I resist the urge to shake her.

"Salem," I say gently. "That's crazy talk, all right?"

"Is it?" Her eyes are damp and she shakes her head. "Then how did this *happen*? Tell me."

Not because of some crazy bad voodoo curse bullshit, that's for sure.

But she's upset.

I'm upset.

The last thing we need is to give in and make this whole situation worse.

What I need to do is find out what the hell happened before I go insane.

Before anything else happens to Arlo.

"It's not bad luck, so stop saying that," I tell her again. "You're not bad luck. You're the best damn thing that ever happened to me. We just need to find out how the hell he wound up poisoned."

"I can't leave him, Patton. I can't—"

"I know. I'm not asking you to. Let me do it." I will rip the world apart piece by piece to get to the bottom of this. "I'll call my mom. She'll—"

Salem grabs my arm and pushes it away from my pocket.

"No." Her voice is tight. "Don't call her."

Huh? I'm officially going to lose my shit.

"Sweetheart," I say, freeing myself from her grip. "She needs to know. She can be here with you while I figure out what happened."

"We were over there for brunch."

My heart stalls.

"You were?" My eyes narrow. "But so what?"

"I just don't want your mom worrying about it or thinking *she* had anything to do with this. That's impossible."

"It's her grandkid, Salem. Even if she doesn't know it." Even if Arlo doesn't know, either. "Please. I need to tell her."

Salem paces away from me, her shoulders hunched, and I grab my phone. Then she turns, her mouth hard. "So you're going to call her anyway?"

"I don't have a choice," I bite out. "Hell, if anything, that's where I need to go. What if he got into something at her house?"

"But *what*? He was with us the whole time!" she hisses.

"I don't fucking know. A plant, a chemical, something." I'm no expert on poisons, that's for sure.

But there must be something.

"He wasn't anywhere near any plants. He was with us in the room the whole time and he had the same cake we ate!" Her voice is so urgent and she wraps her fingers around my arm as she pleads. "Please don't. You can't tell her."

"Why? Because she doesn't know Arlo's mine?" I shake her off. Now isn't the time and place to argue about that, but I can't just sit here and wait. "This is bullshit, Salem, and you know it. You need support, and I need answers."

This is the worst time in my existence to start an argument, but if I stay here, I'm going to go insane. "Listen, I can't just sit around and do nothing."

"Staying with me isn't nothing." She takes my hand, her fingers so tight. "Please, Patton. Stay."

God fucking damn.

If they were with Mom, that means there's something at the house. Whatever happened wasn't deliberate, I'm sure, but the sooner we figure it out, the faster we can fix this.

If something nasty jumps out and I can just tell the doctors—

Hell, maybe there's an antidote or something if I can just find out what caused this.

"I need to go," I say, "and I need you to understand."

"I *don't* understand. He didn't go near anything poisonous."

Clearly, he did if he was poisoned. My jaw tightens as I hold in a hundred stinging emotions I can't release. Not without making this worse.

She stares at me, her long eyelashes clumped and her mouth quivering. I don't know what any of this means for our relationship if I walk out right now.

But I can't stay while my son's life is on the line and we're fighting in the dark.

I hate that she doesn't want me to find out what happened.

"Call me," I say, turning on my heel.

She doesn't say anything at all after that, and though I'm glad she's not trying to stand in my way, it feels like she's giving up.

The darkest day of my life dims a little more and it's not even evening yet.

So I just climb back in my vehicle, which is miraculously still where I left it without a ticket on the windshield, and set off for Mom's.

* * *

MOM LOOKS JUST as shell shocked as I thought she'd be.

"What do you mean, *poisoned*?"

"I mean poisoned-poisoned, Mom." I rifle through the cupboards in the kitchen, tossing everything on the counter in frantic handfuls. "He's in the hospital now."

"But I don't understand." Her hands flutter helplessly and she loosens the scarf around her neck. "What could he have eaten?"

"Don't know, Mom. But it must've happened here."

Unless it was at her apartment, but a poison this violent would probably be too fast-acting for that. They were here for a while. The ones that hit your system and make you vomit up your lungs generally aren't slow and creeping.

I hope.

Fuck, I don't know what I'm doing. I'm desperate.

"What did he eat?" I ask, pulling out the glass container with the cake inside for a look. "Did you make this?"

"Yes. Just yesterday with Evelyn and Juniper."

"And you all had a slice?"

"Yes, Patton," Mom says, her voice wilting. But her eyes are wide and flashing with concern. "I swear, we all had a slice from the very same cake. We all ate it off the same clean plates and as far as I know, the rest of us are fine. We had coffee and little Arlo had orange juice."

Damn. Just like I feared, that doesn't tell me much.

I need to hear from another witness, just in case there's something Mom overlooked.

"Where is she?" I growl.

"Evelyn? Oh my, probably at the airport by now. Archer took her after Salem left."

Wretched timing.

She won't be around to ask, though we'd probably know by now if she suddenly became deathly sick before her flight.

"What else did he drink? Water?" I demand.

"Just the orange juice. I'm sure of it. The same brand I had for breakfast, that fresh-squeezed stuff they sell down at the river market, and I'm *fine*." She breathes roughly, her eyes closing as she shakes her head. "I just don't get this. I need a moment, Patton. I just need some air, I need…"

She trails off. We both know she doesn't have to say it.

She needs the same thing we all do—for Arlo to be okay.

For the millionth time, I hate this shit.

The front door slams hard enough to rattle the house then. I look up.

Footsteps come thumping down the hall. There's only one person I know with that angry elephant walk.

Archer. He has this way of stomping around like he wants his feelings to reach the center of the earth.

"Goddamn," he grumbles when he sees me in the kitchen. I open the fridge to find the orange juice, almost empty now. "Been a real bastard of a day. First Colt stayed up too late playing his Xbox after I told him *twice* to get the hell to bed. Then the traffic, taking Evelyn to the airport—Christ. I was stuck listening to her sob story for almost an hour."

I'm barely listening, too busy sniffing the open juice carton.

Smells like orange. Everything seems normal.

But a second later, as I turn to him, his words sink in.

"What sob story, Arch?"

"Nothing, man. Don't worry about it." He folds his arms, deflecting like he shouldn't have said anything.

My eyebrows snap up.

"Goddammit, Arch, this isn't the time to play stupid." I slam the carton on the counter so hard juice sprays out. My heart shouldn't beat like this when it's probably nothing. "What sob story?"

"I told her I wouldn't say anything," he grumbles.

"Funny," I say, my voice heavy, "because I told *her* the

same thing."

He stops scowling and studies my face. "What? What are you talking—"

"Archer, what *story*?" The harshness in my voice surprises even me.

Then he sighs.

He tells me the same thing Evelyn told me—she's neck-deep in debt and she can't make the deal we offered her work —so he offered her a private loan. A hundred and fifty thousand in his case, softie that he is.

"Shit." My gut clenches. A brutal possibility hits me like a brick. "She played us, Arch."

"Evelyn Hibbing? Hell no. There's no way she'd ever—" He stops, his face souring. He prides himself on being the kind of guy who doesn't get played, especially not by a little old lady who's been around for our whole lives.

I don't wait for his response. I'm already texting Dex, asking if she told him the same thing.

Yeah. How'd you know? he replies a minute later. *She pulled me aside when I came to pick up Junie, after they baked a cake.*

My head's about to pop right the fuck off.

I still don't understand how it could be related to what's happening to Arlo, but I know it reeks.

I dive into the trash can, pawing through it like a demented rat, the dread in my gut turning to solid lead.

Something isn't right here.

"Hi, Archer," Mom says as she comes back in. She attempts a weak smile. "Did Evelyn make her flight okay?"

I swing around to face her. "We need to do a sweep."

"If there's any poison in this house, it won't be in the kitchen," Mom says, frowning. Archer glances between us.

"Poison? What are you guys talking about?"

"Doesn't matter," I snap. "I don't mean obvious poison,

378

Mom. We need to look for what's missing. Is there anything out of place around here?"

Archer catches on immediately, but instead of agreeing, he frowns. "Do we need to call the cops?"

Mom stares between us, bewildered.

"Please, Mom. Trust me, just have a look around," I urge.

"What are you boys not telling me?" she demands.

If I tell her now, it'll bowl her right over.

Evelyn Hibbing is her oldest friend.

Her oldest fucking friend who just played us like a fiddle.

"I promise there's a reason," I say. "Please, hurry."

She nods and heads out of the room. Then Archer rounds on me.

"You want to tell me why the hell you're upsetting Mom like that? So Evelyn squeezed us for some money before she heads to Miami—so what? And what's this about poison? It's frustrating, yeah"—his jaw clenches until his temples pop— "but it's not like we can't afford it. We can settle this bullshit later."

The lead in my gut turns to ice now.

"Miami? What the fuck? She told me she was going home."

"Nope, she was definitely headed to Miami. I dropped her off at the airport. She joked about sprinting off to the Bahamas after catching some sun. I guess she took a long trip there with her husband, back when they were young."

I think back to my last conversation with Evelyn, about how she wasn't looking forward to heading home because it would be a couple more months before Minnesota would defrost enough to do much in the garden.

My vision starts swimming.

It's almost my turn to be sick.

Something is gravely fucked up here, and we need to unravel it ASAP.

XXIII: COUNT YOUR LOSSES (SALEM)

*T*he hospital bed looks like a huge white ocean holding my tiny sleeping boy.

Arlo's eyes are closed now. His eyelids flutter against his cheeks, a sign that he's dreaming.

God, he's so pale he's almost fading into the bedsheets.

Only his hair—the same rich coppery dark brown shade as Patton's—stands out.

I gently sweep it away from his face. There's a tube running up his nose and a bandage across the back of his hand where another tube was placed.

According to the doctors, he's stable.

But stable doesn't mean okay.

It just means he's not about to drop dead. Who knows if that could change.

I just need to keep watching him. Keep assuring myself he's okay.

The seconds crawl by, torture in every passing beat.

His shallow, soft breathing doesn't change.

They assured me he isn't in a coma and sleeping like this

is natural with the meds he's on, but nothing about it *feels* normal.

"I love you, big guy," I whisper over the distant murmurs of the hospital.

Foxglove poisoning.

That's what the tests say, according to the doctor who found me hours after they finished pumping his stomach.

We were lucky, he said, because we got Arlo in fast, when he could still get help. If we'd waited—

I don't want to think about it.

Not everyone gets so lucky. The doctor made that clear.

I shudder at the thought of what could've been. The way he said it so matter-of-factly with only a flicker of worry behind his round spectacles.

So professional, as if kids dying from weird plants is an everyday occurrence. As if *my Arlo* becoming one more statistic would just be a bad day.

He didn't mean anything by it, though. I know that.

Too much tragedy hardens anyone involved with medicine and human health.

He also can't answer the most damning question of all—*how?*

"Arlo," I whisper, stroking his hair, but he doesn't hear me. I press my lips to his forehead, hoping that somewhere deep in his dreams, he knows his mom loves him.

"Hey," Patton says, pulling up the seat next to me. "How is he today?"

I close my eyes until my voice steadies so I can answer him.

We've sent a few texts since he left to go on his wild goose chase, but I don't know if I can forgive him for walking away from me so easily.

It's our son. *Our* son and Patton left me at the hospital alone.

Even if he had the best intentions, it's hard to forgive and forget.

"Salem." Patton's voice is so rough, reaching to take my hands in his. "I know you don't get why I had to go, but—"

"It's foxglove. The poison," I say, cutting him off.

Apologies can wait.

Maybe by then I'll be in a mood to listen.

Right now, all I want to do is scream at him, but they'll haul me out of this hospital if I do that. And I can't leave Arlo. I can't.

Patton's forehead lines with worry, mirroring his frown. "What do you mean? What else did they tell you?"

"He… he had a near-lethal dose. And no, he didn't *eat* a foxglove. I'd have noticed that. It's also not the sort of thing kids his age just pick up and pop in their mouths. He's stable now, but…" I can't finish.

"Shit." His gaze hardens and he glances at Arlo, his frown deepening as he studies our shattered boy, cradled in a pit of off-white bedsheets with tubes running in him.

It's my child lying there.

My boy who almost *died*.

The shock won't stop gripping my throat.

I should be stronger, more functional. But it's a stumbling block, tripping me up every time I try to send my thoughts in a new direction, away from the nightmare fact that *Arlo was flipping poisoned and he almost died.*

Patton runs his hands up my arms, his palms warming me where I'm cold. When did I turn into a human ice sculpture?

"You should come home," he urges gently. "Take a break. At least go down to the cafeteria with me and eat something. Rest."

"And who's going to look after Arlo then?"

"My mom's on her way."

"But—"

"Lady Bug, I know this is hard for you." He uses the endearment like a weapon—or is it a plea? "I know you want to be here with him, but we need to talk. You also need sleep."

"I can't leave him now," I say, my voice no more than a whisper. "What if I leave and he wakes up and I'm not here? What if he stops—stops breathing?"

Patton flinches, a movement so small I almost don't see it.

"He won't," he growls firmly.

"You don't know that."

"You said he's stable, right? When do they think he'll wake up?"

"...I don't know. Not before morning, I'm sure."

"And they're checking him. Constantly. Plus, my mom will call us the second anything changes. I'm sure of it."

Nothing's guaranteed, but he takes my hands and links his fingers with mine.

"Will you trust me? I'm trying to help," he whispers, his blue eyes fixed on my face. The same cutting midnight-blue eyes Arlo inherited. "And you need to be well for him."

If I speak again, I'm definitely going to cry, so I just nod and let him guide me up to my feet.

One hand remains around my waist, steadying me like he knows I might keel over if he stops holding me up.

Warmth blooms under his touch despite my resistance.

He's too good at making me feel less alone.

Ugh, I need to get my feelings in order.

I'm still annoyed at him for leaving me. And I'm doubly annoyed at him for taking me away from Arlo, even though common sense tells me I should at least eat with my stomach growling like a wolf.

One tiny break can't hurt, can it?

I can feel my heart ripping as we walk away from Arlo.

Delly meets us down the hallway, her usually bright smile dim and twisted.

"Oh, my darling!" She hugs me quickly, holding me tighter than her small frame should. "I'm so sorry. I have no earthly idea what happened to that poor little boy."

"It's okay. I don't blame you at all," I say.

"I do. He ate *something* at my house." Her face crumples.

"That's not your fault, Mom," Patton says quietly.

"How do you know?" Delly turns to him, and for the first time I notice the way her mascara isn't picture perfect beneath her eyes. It's been running, the same with the foundation on her cheeks where tears must've cut a recent trail.

"We'll have answers soon," Patton promises, though his expression doesn't ease. "Look, we need to go, Mom. She needs dinner and Arlo needs someone with him. Can you do that?"

"Gladly." Delly gives Patton a perfumed kiss on the cheek, and then it's my turn. "I'll call you the instant anything changes."

"Thank you." Patton reaches for my hand again.

Soon, we find out the cafeteria just closed, so we leave the hospital holding hands. The cold wind beating me in the face is another shock, and he throws his heavier coat over my shoulders.

My chest aches. Anger and resentment and affection battle, turning my guts into knots, and I don't know which one will win.

To my surprise, he doesn't take me to his house.

He brings me to my apartment. A brutal lump in my throat makes it hard to breathe the second I look around.

Arlo's toys are scattered across the floor. The bowl from pancakes this morning is still in the sink.

Oh, if only I'd taken a rain check and had that brunch with Delly another time.

It all feels so long ago.

I don't think I can hold it together.

Patton slides an arm around my back, and for the second time since hearing the news, I'm in his arms. He holds me tight, almost until I can't breathe, and that's a good thing.

But I can't relax into him with all the unsaid things between us.

He pulls away like he senses it, leaving one hand lingering by my hip.

"You should eat first. Then we'll talk," he says.

"I want to talk now."

His eyes are dark pools at night, almost pained with shadows, but he nods.

"Okay. But at least let me make you food."

My kitchen is a mess, but he doesn't seem to mind as he finds a knife and a cutting board. A companionable silence falls over us with his rhythmic chopping.

I sit on the sofa where we first kissed.

This cramped, beat-up apartment feels dizzy with memories.

"I'm sorry for leaving," he says eventually. "I know how bad you wanted me to stay."

I rub my eyes. If there was any makeup smudged there, it's long gone. "I didn't want to be alone, Patton."

"I know."

"And you left."

"I had to. I couldn't sit back and do nothing. I'm sorry," he growls, sighing heavily. "I think my efforts paid off. I know who did it, and I couldn't tell you in front of Mom."

Huh?

My head whips up. I stare at his back and the bunched muscles moving under his shirt as he chops vegetables. The world feels almost too enormous as I reach down inside and pull up a single word.

"Who?"

"Evelyn Hibbing. Goddamn her." His voice is pure violence.

"Wait, what?" I sit up straighter. "No way, you—you can't be serious. She's just a harmless old lady. She's just—" I stop cold.

She's Evelyn. Sweet old grandmotherly Evelyn with her flowers and bittersweet Minnesota memories, missing her husband dearly.

Evelyn, who's told us time and time again how wonderful we are together.

"I know it sounds batshit," Patton says, his voice heavy. "That's how we all felt when we figured it out. Arch and Dex, they're thinking it, too. I'm not crazy."

"I just don't—how? *Why?*"

"It wasn't just the poisoning, Salem." He comes and sits next to me, taking my hands.

And he explains her schemes with the personal loans, the nearly half a million she collected from all three brothers, stealing their money and cashing the checks after baiting them with the same sob story.

Lying to them, using their pity and their generosity against them.

"I don't understand." I shake my head, even though I think I do. It's just too horrible to contemplate. "But why poison him? Why would she want to hurt Arlo?"

"She needed a distraction. The cops called the banks and the money's already been sent to some overseas account," Patton growls, finding taco shells in the cupboard and opening the bag. "She landed in Miami hours ago and we've been trying to get in touch, but we haven't been able to get through. Odds are she's already left the country."

"Jesus Christ. Holy shit. I don't understand," I repeat,

kneading my forehead until my skin burns. "I mean, she's that greedy? She's that cruel for *money*?"

"Human nature." Patton shrugs. "It's an ugly fucking thing if a person's priorities are screwed up. I know mine will never be right again as long as she's free. If I ever track her down, she's dead."

My heart drops.

"Patton, no. Leave it to the police. You seemed so calm about this…"

"I'm not," he snarls. "That lady was my mom's oldest friend and she deceived us all. She *lied* to us. She almost killed our son." His throat works as he stands, rushing back to the pasta meal simmering on the stove. "Don't worry. As much as I'd like to go after her and strangle her with my bare hands, that's not what'll help us the most right now. I know that."

And I know what he's saying without saying it. He's here, helping me because that's what will make the biggest difference.

He's also right, but it drains the good will I had. I thought he was here because he *wanted* to be, not because he felt like this was the place where he could do the most good. Not because he's obligated to be a messenger for bad news.

I can't bear to sit anymore, and I stand up, pacing around, carefully avoiding Arlo's toys. I don't even look at them.

This was partly my fault. I'm his mother. I'm supposed to be in charge, and somehow this money-grubbing witch *poisoned* him right in front of me.

The smell of seasoned ground beef simmering suddenly turns my stomach.

"Arlo will be fine," he tells me, but this time I wonder if he believes it.

"How did she do it?" I pinch the skin on my elbows until it hurts. "And how come nobody noticed?"

"She clearly planned it in advance. We were blindsided."

"That doesn't change the fact that I missed it. She was trying to hurt him and I didn't notice." Did she put it in his cake? Surely, she couldn't have if we all ate it. "He's only five! I should have been more aware. If I hadn't been so self-absorbed—"

"Salem, stop." He turns and grabs my arms, holding me in place. "Listen to me, this isn't your fault."

I want to believe him so desperately I'm shaking, but I'm his *mom*.

I'm supposed to protect my little boy and I couldn't.

"I don't know. What if he just got into something when I wasn't looking? Foxgloves, they could be anywhere," I say absently.

"You know that's not true, especially this time of year," he rumbles.

Yes, I know for a fact that's a weak little lie.

I know I'm falling apart.

"Dammit, woman. Stop beating yourself up and look reality in the face," he growls. "The whole world isn't out to get Salem Hopper."

"Easy for you to say," I flare. "This sort of stuff always follows me. And now my rotten flipping luck rubbed off on my kid."

"This has *nothing* to do with you, and everything to do with a greedy fucking snake. One sick, backstabbing monster who wasn't what she seems."

"But she chose me," I whisper. "Out of everyone she could hurt, she picked us. She picked Arlo."

He strides back into the kitchenette and starts dishing out dinner, this one pot pasta concoction with meat and tons of garlic, judging by the smell.

Slowly, deliberately.

If he's pissed, I can't blame him. Not with how I've melted down.

I can see it in every line of his shoulders and the tense, careful movements—but he's trying to keep it together. For my sake, he's trying to be kind.

"I don't believe it was personal," he says. "You were just there. She's an opportunist, using Arlo to make her escape the same way she used fifty years of friendship with Mom to fuck us over."

"Does that make it any better?" My mouth twists bitterly.

He looks at me slowly and nods.

"No," he admits. "But it proves it's not about you."

I accept the meal he's made for me in a bowl, grateful for the thick dusting of parmesan on top. It's simple, just jarred sauce and a few spices, but right now I'm hungry for anything.

I still have to make myself take small bites, wishing I could digest the latest news as easily as the food.

Arlo nearly died.

If Patton's right, Evelyn Hibbing poisoned him. Apparently for no reason besides the fact he was there and she needed a diversion.

And I was too oblivious to notice.

"Eat," he commands, sitting on the sofa with me after he grabs his own bowl.

We eat together in my tiny apartment where Arlo should be, forcing down a meal neither of us really wants.

Once I've eaten it, though, I start feeling better. It's amazing what stable blood sugar can do for your energy.

"She hasn't called," I say, checking my phone for the fiftieth time since we left the hospital.

"That means there's nothing new."

"Yeah, I guess." I rest the cold screen against my forehead. "I don't know what I'm going to do, Patton."

He touches my arm. Featherlight, almost like he's afraid to commit to touching me fully, worried it'll break me.

"You're going to rest. Then you're going back to that hospital to be there when Arlo wakes up. The first thing he'll want to see is his mama."

Tears nip my eyes.

"And you?" I let my lips part with my next breath.

"Me, I'm going to figure this shit out before it drives me crazy. Exactly what happened, blow by blow, every scrap of evidence I can get." He folds his arms, but then he forces a smile for my benefit. "Maybe someday, we'll laugh this off like Mom does after I nearly drowned that summer."

I can't do this. Mentioning his mother brings back all the memories of being in her house. Being *welcomed* into his family like I deserve to be a part of them.

Honestly, I don't even deserve this rock of a man sitting here who made me food, much less the people he loves.

I don't deserve him.

All my previous resentment dissolves into a hollow ache in my chest that promises to drown me in numbness if I just push hard enough.

"I'm going to tell Arlo you're his dad. You'll always be in his life," I blurt out. "Whatever happens. I wanted to tell you that earlier, before everything blew up with him getting sick."

Patton frowns, switching his attention from his empty bowl to my face. "What do you mean *whatever happens*? What's about to happen, Salem?"

I look down.

I never meant to do this, but the words are boiling up, scalding my throat. I sigh.

"I know you don't believe me when I say I'm bad luck. But look at us. Look at this. Look where I *live*. None of this would've happened if you'd just stayed away from me."

"Don't start that shit again."

"I'm no good for you—no good for your family."

"And you think that's your decision?" he asks coldly.

"Isn't it?" I fire back. "Your family is super *kind*, Patton. I... I've never had that. Probably for a reason."

"Bull. Shit," he spits both syllables. "You don't get to make that call."

"But it's my choice. If I think it's better we go our separate ways, well..." It's so hard to swallow around the sadness lodged in my throat.

"Like hell." He glares at me, burning away the warmth that usually sparks in his eyes when he looks at me. "Where the fuck are you right now, Salem Hopper? Where is this coming from? You can't let one brutal mishap blow everything apart."

"I'm thinking about the boating thing in the Ozarks," I say. "I'd like to start over if... if Arlo seems well enough, that is."

Patton freezes. Hurt sweeps across his face, wilting the anger so fast I almost miss it.

Big mistake.

I shouldn't have spilled my guts like this. Not in the middle of an argument while my son is sick, especially when I'm not really sure about anything.

But my brain and my heart are scrambled eggs.

"This isn't really about Arlo, is it?" His voice stabs me with an accusation I can't deny.

I close my eyes.

"Is it, Salem?"

"I don't know," I whisper. "You're just—look who you are, Patton. And I'm *me*."

"For fuck's sake." He pushes up from the sofa, daggers in his eyes.

And I can't be mad when I pushed him to this.

"Wait." I reach for his arm, jumping up to follow him to

the door. "Patton, wait."

"For what? For you to realize I love you?"

Those three little words rip me in two.

Then he gives me a pained laugh that chills my soul.

"What's the point of waiting for someone who's so damn scared she won't stop running from the past? To believe me when I tell her she isn't cursed?" He pauses, shaking his head. "Let me go. I need to comb Mom's house for that fucking plant, right down to every carpet fiber if I have to."

"Patton. *Patton*!" The strength of my yell rips at my throat and I grab his arm, only for him to shake me off. "I didn't mean it. I didn't—" Except I did and he knows it.

It's been on my mind for weeks, this half-baked backup plan forged from my own deepest fears. All because everything was too good to believe it could last.

He doesn't slam the door.

He just turns, looks at me one last time, and gently shuts it in my face.

But I fly after him, wrenching it open again.

"Wait, come back!" My voice bounces off the empty stairway as he runs down two steps at a time. My legs are shaking too much to chase after him. "Patton, please. Not like this…"

But it's too late and it's my own stupid fault.

My knees finally give out as the killing truth sinks in.

I fall on the steps, shoulders shaking as I cry, every bitter emotion I'd been suppressing flooding the surface as the sound of Patton's footsteps slowly fade into a biting wind.

XXIV: ALL BETS ARE OFF
(PATTON)

J waste about an hour, mindlessly driving around Kansas City in a windstorm before I'm calm enough to go back to Mom's.

I should have fucking known she'd self-destruct.

A few weeks in paradise can't overcome a lifetime of trauma at the hands of her asshole parents.

I'm strong, but I can't keep her together.

Not when she doesn't trust me enough to let me.

Not when she doesn't believe in herself like I do.

Not when I dropped those haunting words—*I love you*—and she couldn't goddamn say it back.

Whatever happens with Arlo, she's signaling it's over.

The worst part is, I want to hate her and I can't.

Hate would be so much easier than whatever this stewing emotional chaos is.

Anger, yes. But also a hurt I didn't think I'd ever feel—the kind that tears out organs.

All because she's a prisoner to this bullshit idea that she's Miss Unlucky.

I chew on my thoughts so hard I accidentally bite my inner cheek.

The blood is just the icing on this rancid cake tonight.

The city is deserted with the chilly wind and it's approaching midnight. A couple lonely, determined joggers sprint down dark streets.

Once, I might've joined them on a night like this that's made for soul-eating thoughts.

Not now.

Not while my son is in the hospital.

You'll always be in his life.

Her cruel promise drifts back to me and there's so much to unpack there. I don't have the brains or the balls to go back and hash it out with her.

How will co-parenting work when she's on a fucking boat somewhere?

It's clear she doesn't expect me to be there by her side.

Does she want me to just hang around and wait until it's convenient for her to come back for the odd weekend when I can see my son? Will I need a lawyer, hounding her for visitation rights?

Will Arlo be a tennis ball, slapped around like every couple who splits and can't agree to anything?

Fuck, I hope not.

It can't come to that.

But I can't rip them apart, either. Whatever else she might be, Salem's a great mom, and she has a good relationship with the boy.

I swing into a gas station lot and let my head thunk back against the seat. All this shit feels like a conversation for another time, when Arlo isn't stuck in the hospital and I'm not rattled from her breaking things off the way she did.

Or did I break them off, too?

But what was I supposed to do when she told me she was leaving to chase a new dream that doesn't include me?

This has clearly been on her brain for a while.

I have an ugly feeling this boat shit has been in the cards for weeks, even if it wasn't spelled out until Arlo got sick. She's just been waiting for the right time to bail because she just can't handle the fact that I could make her happy.

That life might stop spitting in her face and let her have an honest to God *family*.

I don't know if I hate her or I love her or it's somewhere in between, this disgusting no man's land haunted by her betrayal and Arlo's poisoning.

All I know is, no matter how pissed I am right now, I won't go hurting her.

My phone buzzes.

I'm sorry, Patton. I'm sorry a hundred times.

I'm back with Arlo. If you don't want to talk right now, I get it. I'll keep you updated and make sure you're authorized to hear from the doctor.

Guess she's just as hurt and confused as I am.

This lunacy hurts, partly because it's familiar. About as much as finding out my dad died when I was too young to even comprehend it.

At least then, I didn't really know what it meant.

That was an accident, too, Dad and his stupid damn plane.

Terrible, yes. Life-shifting.

Yet we'd pulled together as a family because of it. We came together for Mom and three lost boys figured out how to grow up faster.

Years later, Archer came up with the concept for what became Higher Ends. We each did our time in the military and experienced the world before coming home to the only place that ever mattered.

Why is this so hard?

Why can't I make Salem see?

A tragedy is only a fucking end if you run.

I grit my teeth and toss my phone aside.

There's no chance I'm speaking to her again until this situation gets sorted. Once I have evidence to nail Evelyn with maximum criminal penalties and Arlo has recovered, *then* we can talk.

The winds keep howling as I drive back to Mom's house. Even though it's late—morning now, technically—all the lights are blazing in the house, and two other cars are parked in the driveway.

Archer and Dexter. Of course they'd be here. They've probably gotten a head start on tearing through walls, looking for a single scrap of that poison plant.

Juniper greets me in the hall, an apron around her waist and her red hair scraped back in a bun. Her eyes are shadowed as she pulls me into a hug.

"Oh my God, Patton. I'm so sorry," she murmurs.

"For what?"

"Arlo. I can't imagine how I'd feel if my—" She stops and bites her lip like she knows she just said too much.

"What?" I stop myself. The way she's looking at me says everything. "How did you know?"

"I have eyes, you know. Unlike the rest of them." She snorts. "But don't worry, Dex doesn't know. I thought you'd spill the truth when you're good and ready."

"Why didn't you say anything?" I shake my head.

"Because if you wanted us to know so bad, you'd tell us." Her eyes are steady, though I know from experience she's got a temper to rival Dexter's worst bad day.

It's firmly tucked away now. She's not angry at all.

"We're family," she says, putting a hand on my arm. "And Salem—now she's family too."

Gut punch.

But she'll have to be, like it or not, if Arlo's going to be a proper Rory, and he will be. Still, hearing Junie say that scrapes every nerve raw.

"Patton? What's wrong?" Her hand tightens as she looks at me, searching.

"Nothing. It doesn't matter."

"Pat, you done stealing my wife yet?" From the other end of the hall, Dexter leans against the wall. His smile is forced and humorless.

Usually, I'd throw back some shit about being the charming one, but my joke well is dry today. I can't even smile.

"Everyone's in the living room," Junie says quietly. "Your mom, too. She got back a little while ago. I'm sure she'll be glad you're here."

That makes one of us, I suppose.

I wonder if they've told her the news yet.

Mom isn't stupid and she'll figure it out soon enough.

Junie, Dexter, and I enter the sitting room together. By now, Mom is usually upstairs, reading until she falls asleep. But tonight, she's slumped along the sofa, her eyes red and swollen. If she had any makeup on before, she's cried it off.

The ice lodged in my chest grows colder. Evelyn fucking did this, even if Mom remains blissfully ignorant.

"Pat." Archer holds out a hand, then drops it. "Good to have you back. How's the kid?"

"He'll survive."

"Salem?"

I shrug, and Junie frowns at me.

But Mom finally registers my presence and turns her big eyes on me.

"Patton," she says brightly. I've never seen her this anxious. Not since Dad's funeral, probably.

The last of my beating heart ices over.

"What did I miss?" I ask harshly.

"Patton!" Junie tugs on my arm, but I shake her off. If they wanted gentle, they came to the wrong place. I used up my softness on Salem and now I'm dry.

"That's not an answer," I say. I stride to the mantel because I can't sit down. Not again. Sitting feels like *waiting* and the last thing I want to do right now is waste time. "Will you guys tell me what happened while I was gone?"

Dexter and Archer glance at each other.

"It's Mom's jewelry," Dex says, and Mom starts crying into her hands. Junie's eyes glisten as she wraps an arm around Mom's shoulders, fumbling in her pocket for a packet of tissues.

I feel nothing. I'm too hollowed out.

"She stole it," I guess flatly.

"All the expensive stuff," Archer says. "The antiques, the one-of-a-kind pieces..."

In other words, all the shit Mom owns that's actually worth something. Not just money, but memories, some stretching back longer than we've been alive.

She had a few of her grandma's old pieces appraised a while back and it came back north of a million.

Fucking hell.

I feel something now.

The kind of slow, killing rage that torches every good thing inside me.

And it *feels* good to be this angry at someone besides myself, besides Salem, because that anger's incomplete and muddled.

This is different.

This is a death vow.

With Evelyn, I want to tear her grinning, lying face off.

"I'm still in disbelief. I just can't believe she could do this.

I feel so violated," Mom strangles out, wiping her eyes as Junie hands her a tissue. "My oldest friend, and for no reason..."

"Shhh, Delly," Junie says. "She must have had a reason, even if it was a terrible one." She looks pleadingly at Dexter, but for once he has nothing to add. No quip, no wisecrack, no assurances.

He's usually good at reassurances, but I guess that's one more thing Evelyn stole away.

"I invited her into my home. I thought she valued my *friendship*. She watched you boys grow up." Mom moans into her hand, biting her knuckle as she looks at me. "Was it always all a lie?"

I don't know.

Her husband certainly fished me out of the lake before I drowned. I don't remember much about that day, but I know he saved my life.

Evelyn, she just stood around in a panic. Was it in her head somewhere then?

Did she see us as easy pickings if she ever needed a lifeline? Was there already a heartless vulture inside her, waiting for a fresh carcass?

Or did it change when her husband, Walt, died? When grief ate her soul like that hungry crocodile in Egyptian mythology?

"It's not your fault," Archer says, his voice low and angry, gunning every word. "She lied to us. All of us."

"But *why?*" Mom wails. "Why, Archer?"

"Because she could, Mom." My voice is a sword. Everyone in the room looks at me. Maybe I shouldn't state the obvious. "You showed her the jewelry years ago, didn't you? You two shared everything. Did she know about the appraisal?"

Weeping, Mom pinches her eyes shut and nods painfully.

"Yeah. She knew we had money and she needed it. That's enough. That's the entire fucking reason."

"Language, Patton," she snaps. "Your father raised us better. We can't panic and go to pieces now."

"Dad's dead," I tell her, striding past them all into the sunroom. It's quiet and dark here and I don't bother flicking on the lights.

She's redecorated plenty since I lived here, but I still know my way around.

Evelyn sat here with Mom and Salem and Arlo not long ago. Evelyn pretended to care while she hatched an atrocity.

The wind howls against the huge glass windows.

Every part of me feels just as cold as I burst through the French doors, walking to the small shelf near the door leading into the backyard. The world holds its breath, silent even though the light from the sitting room soaks across the potted greenery inside.

They're plants they must've picked up from somewhere recently, lined up in a neat row. Mostly flowers by the look of them, perched inside here for another week or two until it's warm enough to put them outside.

"Patton." Dexter calls my name. "I don't know what you're planning, but it's a bad idea."

"Slow down and think. We looked high and low. We couldn't find anything related to that plant," Archer says. They've always been on a different wavelength from me, my brothers, and it's never been such a stark contrast.

I suck in a cooling breath of night air. "I'm going to find that backstabbing bitch."

"Sure." Archer's voice is skeptical. "But we need hard evidence to make sure she's nailed down."

Dexter puts a hand on my shoulder that I shake off.

"Cool down before you do something stupid," he warns.

My jaw is so tight it might snap. I'd welcome the pain.

"Something stupid? You mean like going after Evelyn myself?"

"What, you think you're a bounty hunter now? The police are—"

"The police are useless in a case that's international," I snap. "Look, I'm not about to leave this shit to a police report and some FBI case file that moves like a sloth. She could've killed my son."

Shit.

Archer staggers backward and Dexter freezes.

So many questions hang in the air as I storm away from them.

Salem, I could handle being calm around, but not my brothers. They know me too well.

And fuck, it all went down here in this house.

Evelyn was in this *house* and she tried to poison Arlo. How? There must be something left, some loose end she forgot.

"Son?" Archer asks eventually. "What do you mean, your son?"

"What do you think I mean?" Hiding won't get me anywhere. The whole charade is fucking pointless. I'm done pretending and I decide to own it. "Arlo's my son, Arch."

Dexter stares at me like I'm a stranger.

"Salem's kid," he says. "Her son, he's yours? Are you sure?"

"But you've only been with her for…" Archer's voice fades away as it finally hits him. "Shit. You guys were together before?"

"Barely. We hooked up once years ago." I shrug. The draft blowing in isn't enough to calm my temper. "She had Arlo. I never knew until we reconnected at The Cardinal."

"Holy shit. You, a fucking *dad*." Archer laughs dryly, rubbing his eyes.

"You beat me to it," Dexter says miserably. "Cheating prick."

"And now my son's in the hospital. Because of her." I shake my fists before I punch something. "I missed out on years of his life and Evelyn did her best to make sure I'd miss his future."

"Patton—" Dexter starts.

"No. I don't give a fuck whether you think it's a bad idea or not," I tell them, shoving my way outside. I need to breathe. It's so cold my breath clouds in front of my face. "If she'd just stolen money or jewelry from us, whatever. I'd let the police handle it. But not this. This is too personal."

Archer nods, the only other person who gets it when he's a father himself.

"Okay, what's your plan? You must have something in mind after we turned this place upside down to make sure we didn't miss anything. Go."

He doesn't have to tell me twice.

* * *

I'M at the hospital by visiting hours the next morning, fueled by coffee and distilled rage.

It's not as overwhelming as it was last night, which gives me time to think over everything.

Archer would be fucking proud.

As I approach Arlo's bed, I flag down a nurse and ask her what the situation is. She looks tired as hell. Really, everyone in this hospital looks like they've been pulling sixteen-hour shifts—the staff shortages in medicine are real—but she gives me a warm, faded smile.

"He's doing better," she says. "The doctor wants to keep him over the next few days for observation, but after that, he should be free to head home."

I don't bother hiding my relief, the way my lungs heave with the weight of the world coming out.

He'll be okay.

My son will come out of this, alive and well without any serious damage.

That also clears the way for me to track Evelyn Hibbing to the ends of the Earth and drag her into handcuffs.

As I head into the room, just like I did yesterday before everything came to a head, I find Arlo and Salem asleep. She's curled up on one of those uncomfortable chairs, one leg tucked under her and the other wrapped around the chair leg.

In her sleep, she doesn't look angry or bitter or afraid.

She looks more worn than the nurses and almost as pale as poor little Arlo. Her mouth is parted and it makes her look almost obscenely vulnerable.

Even though everything we said to each other echoes in the space around us like a stray bullet, I want to hold her. I want to banish the hurt on her face, lingering in her long eyelashes and the dark arches under her eyes.

You don't have to run anymore, Salem.

Goddammit, trust me.

But I don't say anything out loud.

I'm quiet so I don't wake her, pulling up another chair by Arlo's side. By the time I turn my attention to him, I notice he's awake, his eyes half-open as he looks at me. The tube in his nose must itch like mad. He tries to scratch.

"Easy, buddy," I whisper, leaning forward to take his hand. It's small and chubby, and I'm grateful it still feels healthy enough, too. "How are you doing?"

"Patman... what happened?" He groans, glancing at his mother and back to me. "Where am I? I feel funny."

"You'll get better soon. I spoke to the doctor and he's really impressed. You're a strong kid and you'll be out of here soon." I lean forward, gently squeezing his fingers. "You had a little mishap with some food, but that's over now. Your mom brought you in so you could get some help. I came to tell you about your superpower."

"Superpower?" His eyes light up.

"Yeah. You're braver than ten men combined. Basically a little lion. You just woke up and you're not afraid of anything." I smile hopefully.

His smile turns into a grin. "Brave like you? Like General Patton?"

I wince a little inside, but he's too damn cute and groggy to correct.

"Exactly like that. Guys who drive tanks for a living don't have half your courage."

"Wow!" He nods, satisfied, resting his head back on the pillow. "I miss my tablet," he mumbles.

I try not to laugh.

Kids are all the same, and there are times when they put adults to shame. Maybe because they haven't been buried by other people's crap yet.

It makes me smile as I smooth back the hair from his forehead. "You gave us all a scare though, you know."

"Didn't mean to." His eyes fly open. "Oh, no. Mommy's car. I didn't mean to barf everywhere—"

"Hey, hey, shhhh. You were amazing, okay? I promise she's not mad. Everyone's so proud of you, little man." I squeeze his hand. Salem hasn't stirred, lost in her sleep over the whispers.

Fine.

I don't want her to see me just yet.

I could use a little of his courage myself when I don't want to face up to whatever our last conversation means.

"I don't like the hospital." Arlo wrinkles his nose. "It smells funny. Like before a bath with too much soap."

"Yeah, these places are rough."

"The bed feels hard too."

"You'll be back in your own bed soon," I promise. "And once you're better, I'll take you somewhere warm and sunny, okay?"

His eyes light up, making him the most animated I've seen him so far today. "Like the beach? Do you think there will be dino shells?"

"Dino shells?"

"Like from dinosaurs."

"Oh, you mean fossils?" I used to love dinosaurs when I was his age. Knowing Arlo loves them too makes me smile wider. "Sure. In fact, I bet I can bring you a dino shell soon. I can find you some real seashells too. How does that sound?"

"Awesome." He yawns heavily.

This isn't the time or place to tell Arlo I'm his dad, even though he's still holding my hand like it's the most natural thing in the world. I've held Colt's hand a few times over the years, mostly when he was younger, but this feels different.

The kind of right that only comes from your own flesh and blood.

Shit, I need to leave before I lose it, and before I change my mind about leaving at all.

Salem can take it from here as soon as she wakes up. I'm certain she'll do a better job of looking after Arlo than I can. She's been there for so many years.

"Maybe we can put them in my aquarium, huh?" I say. "I think the fish would like a fossil or two."

"And the seahorses!" he whispers.

"Yeah, those guys too. But right now, I need you to do something for me, okay? I need you to focus on getting better and being good for your mom. You keep her company, Arlo."

He frowns. "Where are you going?"

"Florida. Just for a few days," I tell him, but he doesn't look like he registers what I've said. His eyelids droop shut again, and he lets out another cat-like yawn. "I'll be back real soon, okay?"

He doesn't answer since he's already out.

I give Salem one last glance and get up, beginning to walk away.

Only, I turn and retrace a few steps.

Gingerly, I rest my hands on her shoulders, kissing her on top of the head. She only stirs slightly without waking.

"Hold on, Lady Bug. I'm going to make sure no one ever tries to hurt Arlo again, and then I'll come home and we'll sort this out."

XXV: DOWN TO THE WIRE
(SALEM)

*I*ncredibly, it only takes a couple days for Arlo to recover.

Two days of sitting by his side at the hospital in that endless bustle of muffled noises and claustrophobic disinfectant before he turns back into his normal chatty little self with puppy energy.

Two days of running through every single thing I could've done differently.

Two days of agonizing over Patton.

Every time I close my eyes, I see his face. The way he looked at me when I told him about my plans to strike out on my own—a plan that isn't even a plan. A plan that I've slowly been researching as a parachute escape from all things Rory related.

A just-in-case backup I have little confidence I can actually make a reality.

God.

I didn't think it was possible to screw up this bad, but I've done it. Maybe it's not rotten luck that's following me after all.

More like karma grabbing me by the throat and throwing me through the wall.

Delly Rory takes us back to her house from the hospital the day Arlo gets discharged.

"I insist, dear," she says as I strap Arlo's kid seat into her expensive white SUV. "I know how difficult these past few days have been for you."

"Thank you so much for the food." I stifle a yawn. "I don't know how I'd have gotten by without it."

"You're welcome. And you should thank Junie, too. She's the one who's been cooking up a storm in our kitchen with a little help from her lovely grandmother."

I drag my fingers over my eyes.

Junie. Another near-stranger whose kindness I don't deserve. Clearly, none of them know about my fallout with Patton, even if I haven't heard from him in days.

"I appreciate it. More than you'll ever know," I say as I climb into her passenger seat.

She tells stories about Patton as a kid all the way home, thinking they'll entertain me.

And yeah, I'm amused when she tells me about the time four-year-old Patton ate crayons after Dexter convinced him they were candy. But she doesn't know story time slowly carves more chunks out of my heart.

There's something different about Delly today that makes me wonder.

She's dimmer, more subdued.

Evelyn's betrayal, probably. It's wilting her like a bright flower under a merciless heat lamp. The warm, easy smile that's been there ever since we met seems more forced now, a mask she wears for appearances only.

It makes my heart hurt.

This lovely woman shouldn't have to fade like this.

Not when she glitters like Kansas City itself on a long summer night.

"I've got a spare room you can use," she says, changing subjects so fast I almost get whiplash. "I made them up for you. You don't have to stay, of course. But Arlo can, if you'd like, while your parents are visiting."

My jaw pops from being clenched.

I don't know what possessed them to call, really.

But that's a lie. *I do.*

In my panic after Arlo was rushed to the hospital, I stress-dialed my mother. She didn't answer, of course, but I'm sure she heard me crying on the voicemail, desperate for comfort from a source I can't trust.

The damage was done, even after I texted and told them it was a false alarm.

She called me yesterday and insisted they were flying in on a charter jet from some pharma guy Dad met at the golf course. They're due very soon and I don't know what I'm going to say to them.

I don't know what I *want* to say—if there's anything to say at all.

After so long apart, effectively estranged, we barely know each other.

Motherhood has changed me a lot, obviously. I'm guessing they haven't changed one bit.

I chew on a hangnail anxiously.

It's a real relief to have Delly helping with Arlo so I'm free to meet them *without* him—they don't deserve to see him right away after what they've pulled over the years—but the uncertainty makes me break out in hives.

I don't know if I even want him meeting his absentee grandparents, the same people who wanted me to give him up the minute he was born.

I also hate that Patton won't return my messages.

He's opened my texts, leaving them on Read. That's worse than not knowing if he ever saw them at all.

I almost crack and ask Delly where he is, but I'm not sure I want to know.

I was worried for him after he made noise about going off on his own to find Evelyn Hibbing. How dangerous could she be?

And what prayer would I have of stopping him?

We arrive at Delly's house soon, just before sunset. It's blazing with light against the pink stained sky when we go inside.

Arlo's stay has left him sleeping, and he dozes on my shoulder. Dexter and Juniper are there in the great room, along with Archer and his son, Colt.

"Good to see you," Juniper whispers, giving me a brisk hug. "Need some help putting him to bed?"

"Just show me the way."

We leave Delly to settle in with her family. I follow Junie upstairs to the spare room Delly made up for us. This house must be about a hundred years old, yet the guest room is still bigger than my apartment.

And although Junie hasn't been part of the family for that long, she seems completely at home in this enormous space.

"Don't feel obligated to stay up and chitchat if you'd like to catch up on sleep. You've been through a lot," she says, catching me looking at her.

Unlike Delly, whose sense of style is immaculate, Juniper looks more comfortable in jeans and an old tee than high fashion. And although she's beautiful in her own way—could she be anything else to wind up hitched to Dexter Rory?—there's a sweet simplicity to her, too.

I'm a little in awe of the way she seems so confident here when she must be around my age. Does that all come from Dexter or from running the best bakery in town?

If I had a successful venture under my belt like her, I might flit around glowing too.

"You look like you manage pretty effortlessly," I say. Arlo stirs as I lay him across the big plush bed and pull off his shoes. "How do you manage it?"

She laughs. "Delly, that's how! The brothers, they take a bit to get used to—Archer especially was slow warming up to me—but Delly? She's always treated me like the daughter she never had. Not bad for a boring baker girl, huh?"

"If you mean an awesome one, you're right. I'm going to come in and try some cupcakes soon. Arlo could use a little spoiling after this scare."

She smiles. "That'd be cool. We certainly try to make everything yummy at the Sugar Bowl. But this family, I thought they'd be more stuck up. Giant sticks up their asses, just like I thought about Dex at first." She winces. "But they're not like that at all. I was so wrong. If you're worried you and Patton—"

"I'm not. He hasn't even spoken to me in a few days," I say, wishing the words hadn't left my mouth. There's no hiding it now, though, so I sigh and give her the truth. "We had an argument, Junie. I said crap I didn't mean, and I think he did, too. Not that I can ever read that man's mind."

Arlo's mouth moves sleepily as he rolls over. I decide to let him doze instead of wrestling him into his pajamas.

"Oh, I mean, that's no surprise. I kinda thought you guys were fighting," Juniper nods, tucking a lock of her auburn hair behind her ear. "When he came back here, he just seemed different. Way more protective and guarded, I guess."

My heart sinks.

"That's my fault. I made him think—" I bite back the hurt in my voice. *What's the point of waiting for someone who's so damn scared she won't stop running from the past?* "I don't know what to do. Is he even in town? I couldn't bring myself to ask

Delly." It's a long shot, I know, but I suddenly have the fiercest urge to see him, to hash this out in person.

"I'm sorry. He's on a mission, I heard." Juniper shakes her head slowly.

"Where?"

She shrugs. "I wish I knew. The guys made it clear this was their thing, and I'm trusting they won't screw it up. Feel free to ask Dex if you want, though. Or I'll be happy to do it for you."

I stare at Arlo, the light of my life. He's back to sleeping peacefully and the color in his cheeks looks almost normal again.

Alive.

He's alive and okay, thank God.

I repeat the words in my head as I follow Junie back downstairs, but she stops me before we head into the dining room, where I guess they've all moved for dinner.

"Also, not to make this awkward, but I know about Arlo and Patton," she says softly.

She knows?

Shit.

I stop mid-step and stare. "Patton told you?"

"No. I'm just a good observer, and I'm pretty well acquainted with Rory eyes by now. There's no mistaking that shade of blue with Arlo." She smiles gently. I try to relax before her next words turn me to stone. "But he told his brothers. Accidentally, I think."

"Oh my God, he... he told them? What did they say?"

"Not much. Delly doesn't know, not yet. They decided it's not their place to drop the bomb. They want her to hear it from the horse's mouth. From him, from you, whenever things are less crazy..."

She can say that again.

I don't think I've ever felt so heavy with everything pulling me down.

"I'm not trying to make this harder. I just wanted to let you know that you're not alone. And also that"—her brows draw together slightly—"Patton really loves the boy. There's no faking that."

"I know, I just—" I stop. What else can I say when his words pummel me in the face again?

What's the point of waiting for someone who's so damn scared she won't stop running from the past?

God, he's right, and I'm still living like I'm afraid of my own shadow.

"It'll be fine, I'm sure, even if it feels pretty difficult right now." She pushes the door open to the formal dining room.

Sure enough, Dexter and Archer are arguing again, although their voices hold a little less vitriol than usual. Delly sits at the head of the table like the queen she is, massaging her temples.

I see Colt at the other end of the table. He's checked out of the conversation with his earbuds in, playing a game on his phone.

When they see me, everyone goes silent.

Archer pulls out an empty chair next to him.

"Have a seat," he says, unusually kind. Not that he's ever *un*kind, it just seems extra gentle, coming from a human bear.

Plus, I doubt Archer Rory ever makes being gentle a habit.

I look at Juniper for guidance, but she takes the seat beside Dexter. They exchange a slow, heavy look that feels like an entire secret conversation condensed into a wordless second.

Ugh, I miss that.

I had it with Patton.

He hasn't told his family about our argument, I'm sure. I get the feeling he hasn't said much, even to his brothers, before he decided to disappear.

"Let's say a prayer. We owe it to this family tonight—and to little Arlo," Delly says. I look down at the meal in front of me. It's simple enough, beef brisket and whipped potatoes with some collard greens. I'm in awe that anybody had the energy to cook.

Warmth floods my eyes and I blink rapidly.

She doesn't know.

She doesn't know he's her grandson and she's already giving so much energy to making sure he's safe and happy and comfortable.

Archer pats me clumsily on the shoulder, clearing his throat.

I. Miss. Patton. So. Much.

He knows when to be tender, when to be serious, when to lighten the mood with humor and when I need his stoic, gruff advice. He'd probably hold my hand under the table and mutter some wisecrack.

I'd get annoyed, but I'd also—

A rattle slips out of me, escaping my tight throat. Archer doesn't look at me deliberately.

Thankfully, no one else notices.

I listen in as Juniper and Delly carry on about some art-related project. The conversation turns away from me like the tide, leaving me free to talk to Archer.

Halfway through dinner, I ask him the question I know Junie has been waiting for me to ask.

"I need to know," I whisper. His gaze flicks to me and away again, training it on the fork in my hand. "Where's Patton? He hasn't spoken to me in days and Juniper made it sound like he's gone."

"He was tight-lipped about the details." He swallows, still not looking at me. "Honestly, it's not my place to—"

"Screw that, Archer." My anger boils over, and I struggle to contain it. I've burned enough bridges with this family already. "I need to know."

"It's—"

"My business."

He sighs, knowing I've won.

"All right, dammit. He asked me not to tell you," he growls. "But he went after Evelyn himself. Left a few days ago. He said he was heading to Miami first, and from there, anywhere else he can get a lead on her. And before you ask, no, no one's heard anything."

The shock pins me in my chair, the iciness spreading to my hands. I drop my fork. Holding anything now feels impossible.

Of course he went after Evelyn. I already knew that.

But hearing confirmation hits different.

On the one hand, she's an old lady. He's much younger and he's a Navy veteran. He's strong and he works out regularly. He's more than capable if anything goes horribly wrong.

But Evelyn poisoned Arlo right under our noses without anyone noticing. A horrible feat I'm still not sure how she managed.

If she's capable of poisoning a kid so discreetly, what else could she do?

"He'll be okay. Trust me." Archer nods at Dexter for support. "Last year, this guy took on a whole crime syndicate. We handled ourselves well, even that knucklehead little brother of ours."

Dexter looks over, smirking.

"You make it sound more impressive than it was. I fought

a guy with a broken bottle. I wasn't dodging bullets or anything," he tells us.

I'm not sure that helps.

My eyes rake over him, sizing him up. He's slightly bigger than Patton or maybe it's just the age difference. Everyone in Kansas City heard about the case, the monster of a man Dexter fought.

"He can handle her," Dexter promises. "Don't lose any sleep over him, Salem."

"Yeah. He's not as stupid as he looks—sometimes. She won't trip him up," Archer agrees, though I think he shares my worries about poison. "He'll be on her with the cops right behind him, I'm sure. Pat has more common sense than you'd think in these situations."

I really, really hope he's right.

For now, there's nothing I can do but agree.

* * *

TWO MORE DAYS pass by in a haze of anxiety.

Still no word from Patton, and I'm afraid to reach out to him again. I've already left a half a dozen voicemails apologizing for what I said and how we left things in chaos.

Not quite taking back my fears, but almost.

If he just came home, if he'd *talk* to me, then I could tell him exactly what the situation is, and—well, if he'll listen, I could explain how I've come to my senses.

There are better ways to deal with love than running away to the Ozarks and starting a half-baked boat business.

And I try to will myself into believing I have a shred of courage as the day comes for the meeting I've dreaded.

I chose to meet my parents at the Sugar Bowl, Juniper's bakery, thinking it can't hurt to have a friendly face around.

She doesn't know the whole story, but I know her well enough to trust that she'll step in and help if she needs to.

Not that I think my parents will do anything terrible in public.

I just can't predict what they *will* do.

At three o'clock sharp, they walk through the doors.

Dad looks older than I remember. His hair has receded another inch or two and he's wearing his pointy grey shot beard longer these days.

Weirdly, my mother looks like she hasn't aged a day in five years. I'm sure she's kept time at bay ruthlessly with scalpels and weekly salon treatments, though her hair sports a shiny new shade of black. It makes her skin look oddly colorless by contrast, despite the slight blush.

I suddenly wish I'd worn something smarter. Not this blue blouse tucked into a grey pinstripe skirt. It feels too formal, like what I'd wear to work, but not *chic*.

A shame it's too late to ask Delly for advice.

Mom throws her arms open with an exaggerated grin the second she sees me.

"Salem," she whispers, her voice choked. "Lemmy, sweetheart, it's so good to see you!"

Dazed, I stand up and allow her to kiss both cheeks. She's behaving like she's missed me all these years. Like we don't both know she never tried to contact me once.

Anger flares in my gut. I lean back from her sickly strong perfume.

"You made it," I say neutrally.

"Of course, we made it, honey. And how is he? How are *you*?" She talks like she cares, her eyes searching mine. "We heard about poor Arlo and we came as soon as we could."

"I canceled a business trip for this," Dad adds weakly.

My eye twitches. Probably because I know he's expecting

me to be grateful, like the good accessory daughter they always wanted me to be.

Yeah, I don't have words to express how much they disgust me.

"I didn't ask you to come here," I say. "When he had to go in, I panicked a little, I'll admit. If I'd slowed down, I never would've called."

Mom's brows pull together, her smile vanishing. "You didn't *need* to ask us. We're your parents, even if—"

"If you abandoned me after Arlo was born."

Yep. This is off to a fantabulous start.

"Salem, we assured you our door was always open. We sent you a card with the same note every year for Christmas."

"*Without* Arlo, you mean. You never addressed him by name. Not once. Believe me, I kept track." I'm lucky the bakery is mostly deserted right now. My voice is too loud and shrill.

Juniper glances up from behind the counter, checking in as she wipes down some counters.

I'm sure she has enough money to never work again with Dex, but she's still here, practically every day from what I can tell. She loves this job and making people happy.

I shake my head quickly, quietly assuring her I'm okay.

"You didn't show a speck of interest in Arlo's life or mine. Not after I had him," I say through gritted teeth, dialing my volume back.

The corners of Mom's eyes tighten, fighting the false plumpness that holds her skin in place.

"I wonder, what's changed?" I ask pointedly. "Why did you really come?"

"You think we want to live like this? Separated from our only daughter, our grandson?" She throws herself into a chair miserably. Her nails are fake and long, painted a pale pink coral that matches her jacket perfectly. "Frankly, we

418

want you to come back to California with us. Both of you. We'd like to start over and be a family again."

They want, they want.

They want me to do their bidding without so much as an apology.

Patton flashes in my mind. Before I went and scared him away, I *found* my family. Something real and loving with him and the Rorys, with Delly and Juniper and Archer and Dexter.

I had a future I hope I can still salvage with a man who stood like a rock when he found out he had a surprise son.

"Lemmy, please. Don't tell me that means nothing?" Mom's eyes are big, pleading.

It's almost worse if she's done some real soul-searching, all these years apart.

I wasn't expecting that.

But my voice is granite when I answer. "My home's here now, Mom. You know that. I have a job and a life. I'm not interested in giving it up to live by the ocean in some over-priced neighborhood where people will judge you if you go for a jog without a designer jacket."

Certainly not at your mercy, I almost add, but I hold it in.

"But what do you *do*? I'm sure you can transfer your job to LA." Dad, like always, tries to fix our problems like it's as easy as moving the millions in his retirement accounts. "If you're worried about being stuck under our roof, we can find a place for you and the boy. Do you still pay rent?" He waves a hand dismissively. "Never mind. I'll speak to your landlord and get you out of your lease."

"Dad, no. I'm not moving."

A muscle works in his jaw. "Salem, we—"

Mom places a hand over his. "Careful, Byron. It's been a hectic week for them. Let's all just think about this. *Calmly,*" she stresses.

A tall boy with a shock of sandy hair comes over and sets down coffee and a few small bites for us. I asked Junie to give us whatever she recommended, and she's totally outdone herself. It's a small tower of tiny cakes, bite-sized so we can have as many as we choose.

For a second, my parents shut their mouths and start stuffing them instead.

Good timing.

The only thing I agree on is that we need breathing space, before anyone says something they can't take back.

My participation in this talk is hanging by a thread.

Mom looks at me, the force of her gaze pinning me down.

She always gave me that look when I was a kid and stepped out of line. Right now, it's more like an invitation for me to fall back *in* line.

For me to give up what I've built, what I've lived, and go back to being the doormat she always wanted in a daughter.

Worse, it's the future she wants to inflict on Arlo.

I take a deep breath as I finish chewing my cake. Lemon, with a sweet icing that counteracts the sharpness.

"Look, you can talk all you want about a fresh start," I tell them both. "And you can try to tempt me with money and promises, but I have a life here. I have a *family*. And I have no intention of giving that up. If you'd like to meet Arlo and come back into my life, you'll respect my terms."

Mom's perfectly outlined mouth tightens at the corners. "*We're* your family, Lemmy. Oh, it's been years. Can't we just forget this whole mess ever happened?"

"No. You abandoned me to raise my son alone so you could go chase beaches and your holiday trips to Hawaii." The ire in my voice scrapes them raw with the truth, judging from the way they flinch back. I take a bite of the cake. "Also, I don't need your money or your assistance. I'm co-parenting now."

"With who?" Dad sucks in a sharp breath.

"Arlo's father," I say flatly.

Mom blinks at me as she swallows a gasp. "You—you knew who he was? Not your ex?"

"Not even close. He's a wonderful part of Arlo's life, and mine." There's a secret wish in my words, a prayer that Patton will always be around.

"Who is he?" she demands, drumming her nails on the table.

"His name is Patton Rory. He's smart. He's kind. More importantly, he's always there for us, and I never need to have to ask him twice for anything." There's no point in hiding it now, or the sour little victory I feel at the shock shadowing their faces.

"Rory? As in…" Mom trails off as her face falls.

Dad's expression withers.

Even with their California dreaming, the Rory name hits them like a bullet. That's how it is with Kansas City royalty. Maybe Mom even met Delly while she was here, moving frantically in her lofty social circles.

"One of the Rory brothers," Dad says in disbelief. "Higher Ends?"

"The one and only. The youngest brother, Patton." I don't bother hiding the smugness in my voice. If they thought they could lure me back with money, they're mistaken. Patton Rory earns more in a year than they'll earn in a lifetime.

"Impossible!" Mom hisses. "How could you possibly know them?"

"I didn't, but things change fast. Arlo's actually staying with Delly Rory right now while we have this family reunion."

They gawk at me for what feels like a century.

I'm sure they're waiting for me to back down and say I lied.

No dice.

I don't back down. I meet their gazes with all the defiance Patton taught me, knocking me out of my own head and my fears with every kiss. I wish so badly I'd appreciated it more.

"Arlo's on the mend. He'll be fine, in case you wondered," I say finally, when they don't speak. "You came here because you were worried about *him,* right?"

Dad takes off his glasses and meticulously cleans them on the edge of his shirt before putting them back on. It's a tell he's had forever when he's nervous or at a loss for words.

His eyes are the same watery light-brown glass they've always been, but they can't hide his feelings now.

"Patton Rory," he repeats. "Of all people, she could have at least told us—"

"Byron," Mom snaps, unleashing the anger that's been building inside her.

She's always been the one with the temper. She uses words like swords, but time and motherhood has hardened my skin.

If she wants to stab me in the face, I'm ready.

I'll never let Arlo experience the same awful feelings she inflicted on me, the dread that I was never good enough.

"Salem Hopper, you need to tread lightly," she whispers. Her anger is unsheathed, and the kid working with Junie looks at us. "This is not a game. Men like Patton Rory will entertain you as long as you're pretty and interesting, but that doesn't last forever. Come home before it's too late, before you lose everything."

"Did I say we were dating?" I retort. The color drains from Mom's overdone face. "He's a good man to the end. He's responsible and he's perfectly happy to step up." I stand then, taking one more little cake from the beautifully crafted stand. "It's nice to know it's possible, especially when he's so rich. If you guys want back in my life, you should think about how you want to handle things next time. Think about how Patton treats me. Think *hard.*"

"Salem, wait. Don't you dare walk out. Don't you dare leave us—" Mom says, but I don't turn around. I'm up and moving.

Just like before, we part ways with someone walking out.

Only, this time it's me.

* * *

THIS DAY HAS no chill whatsoever.

I get home to find Kayla waiting for me—the cyanide icing on this awful day.

I just wanted a quick stop to grab a few things before I return to Delly's place to pick up Arlo.

She's sitting on the stairs by the door, her coat hunched around her shoulders, looking like a demented flamingo. She must like the way the fluffy pink draws eyes to her waist.

"Lemmy, where have you *been?* I've been waiting forever."

I don't take her hand. "You never said you were stopping by."

"Um, did I need to? What's with the attitude?" Her bottom lip juts out in a pout that's worked miracles a thousand times before. It's definitely worked me over, before I figured out how to grow a backbone. "I heard about Arlo and I wanted to drop by and give my condolences."

"He's still alive, Kay."

"Oh, wow. Of course he is. Yay?" She gives me a pained smile.

Someone needs to strangle this girl.

Also, it's a weird coincidence to find her here after that toxic meeting with my parents. But this time I don't spiral.

I don't let myself believe I was cursed in a past life and the universe is really out to get me. *I can learn.*

423

"Did you tell my mother about Arlo? Did you ask her to come out?" I ask point-blank.

Her eyelashes flutter at the hardness in my tone.

I know they still talk once in a blue moon. My parents practically worshipped the Persephones and hoped that just being around Kay would make me richer.

And although I know I summoned my mom in the panic over Arlo, I never put her up to coming back to Kansas City. With Kay showing up unannounced, I'm suspicious Mom had encouragement.

"Nope," she says, but she hesitates a beat. "I told my mom, of course, but you know how it is... *She* might have told your mom, but as for me, I—"

"Spare me the excuses."

Surprise flashes on her face, mingled with something else. Hurt?

I'm not sorry.

We've been quasi-friends long enough for me to say something like that without her acting like I just shot her.

Even for this unexpected visit, she's perfectly made up, like the dolls I used to play with as a kid.

Always perfect. Always presentable. Always the *same* selfish brat.

"What do you want, anyway? I need to get back to Arlo soon."

"Oh, right. But did you meet your parents? I heard they were in town," she says, following me up the stairs. "I hope it went okay."

"I didn't tell them I was filing a restraining order, so I guess that's a plus. They have one chance to start behaving themselves. We'll see where we go from there."

"Holy crap. Pretty hardass for you, Lemmy." *What gives?* That's what she really means. Surprise colors her voice. "I thought they might hit you up to go back to California."

"They did."

"Oh. And you said no?"

I turn around and face her, huffing a breath.

"Why, you're trying to get rid of me?" I ask dryly, staring at the water stain on the wall and hoping she notices too. Any hint of mold will send her into a hypochondriac fit. "Or are you just wondering where Patton went?"

"I mean... I stopped by his office today in Lee's Summit. He's been out for a while, according to his secretary, and I wondered—"

"If I know where he is," I finish.

Her eyes widen at whatever the look is on my face. Hopefully bitter rage because that's what's burning through my chest.

How dare she.

How dare she show up and pull this crap, now of all times.

"You decided you'd ambush me while I'm at my most vulnerable. Be honest," I bite off.

"What? No, I—" She flinches back.

"Kayla, you could have visited *anytime* this past week after Arlo was poisoned. You could have called. But you chose the exact second when you couldn't find Patton Rory. So you came sailing over here, pretending to be worried, all so I could bail out your latest boy toy quest. I'm not stupid. You're in luck, I guess, because I have news for you." I walk down a step and she stumbles back a few steps. "Here's the thing, Kayla. He's not going to date you."

"What? What the hell is wrong with you?" Twin red suns flare on her cheeks. "Don't talk to me like that! You don't know him. Guys like Patton always come around."

"Do they?" I laugh harshly. "Because I've figured out Patton Rory's type—me."

The red heat on her face melts into whiteness under her

bronze skin. She grips the banister, not seeming to notice the metal is flecked with rust and grime from years of neglect.

"Y-you? What do you mean? Lemmy, you're talking crazy." She shakes her head. "Are you sure this Arlo situation hasn't gone to your head?"

"No, Kay. Patton Rory is Arlo's father."

Her mouth almost hits the floor.

It would be hilarious if we weren't standing here on a rundown staircase, arguing about Patton, a man I may never see again.

"You're lying!" she yells back. "Do you think I'm stupid?"

"Are you? Let's see. Think about it, Kay, just for a second. I got pregnant from your little party on the casino riverboat. Guess who was there? And you showed zero interest in him then." I tick off the points on my fingers as I go. "And now he's my boss and mentor. We're working together, so thick as thieves you had to come here to find out where he is."

"You—you—oh my God."

"Yeah. Baby daddy. You get it now." I'm growling, my fingers balling up into fists. "Thankfully, he's a way better person than you'll ever be."

It's pure venom, this anger ripping through me now.

I want to hurt her.

To make her feel a sliver of the agony I've lived for the past week.

"But even if that *wasn't* true, and even if he *didn't* have a kid with me, and even if you *were* his equal as a human being… even if you were someone who didn't prey on people's misery…" I take a deep breath, ready for the kill shot. "He told me he'd never date you. He said that himself. In fact, he thinks you're pretty fucking rude."

Her eyes widen, hate and hurt bouncing in her pupils.

Not because of my betrayal, of course—I'm sure she's plenty livid about that—but because she knows I'm telling the truth. We've been friends long enough for her to know when I lie.

"I wasn't going to tell you, not like this... but since you came here trying to capitalize on my grief, why not? You deserve to know everything." She backs up another step as I walk toward her. "I don't want to see you here again, Kayla. Not now, not ever. Life's too short for the kind of *friend* you pretend to be."

After all, just think about what happened to Delly. And she trusted Evelyn Hibbing with her life, her family, until that screwy woman backstabbed her brutally.

The thought makes me sick.

Kayla looks ash-white now, her eyes heavy with tears of humiliation.

I'm surprised she doesn't snap a heel as she turns and flees, the door echoing behind her as she slams it shut.

I stand there, breathing raggedly until I can feel my own body again.

This isn't my home anymore, I realize.

Not since Patton Rory invited me into his life.

I need him back. I need to make this right. I need him reunited with Arlo and his family, and this time with everybody knowing what I just told Kayla.

'Baby daddy' doesn't scratch the surface of what Patton Rory truly means to me.

He's my home.

He's something to fight for, a man who's given me more courage than I knew.

Now, I just have to hope it isn't too late to show him how brave I can be.

XXVI: LUCK BE MY LADY
(PATTON)

*I*t takes me five damn days to hunt down Evelyn Hibbing.

Three days of trekking through Miami and then the Bahamas, talking with police and tracing her steps, following every crumb of information, until I finally stumble across her in Nassau.

The sun feels sickly warm on the back of my neck as I watch the hell-witch who could've murdered my son.

She's perched at a small café overlooking the sea, reading peacefully. It's a near idyllic scene, just an old woman with a book basking in the afternoon shade. You'd never guess there's a thieving, child-poisoning monster underneath.

Just like how you'd never guess she spent all night gambling away thousands of dollars at a casino down the street.

Probably old habits kicking in. A little tip from Archer he heard from Mom reminded me that Evelyn used to come back from Vegas joking bitterly about going broke.

Hell, maybe she's even lost her mind completely, desperately trying to double down on stupid and grow her money before she jets off to another continent.

At least I know where her husband's money went now.

I lean back in my chair and take a long pull from the beer I ordered. She hasn't even thought to look up or check her surroundings. Guess when you're so practiced at scamming, you get cocky.

And it's that arrogance—like giving a slight variation of her real name at the hotel—that told me exactly where she's staying. That's how I found her today, curled up with her book and her coffee, hiding in plain sight and only looking up every so often to smile at the waves as she breathes in the cool ocean breeze.

Salem would love it here. I can just see Arlo running along the beach, too, turning over rocks for shells and tiny crabs.

For a man determined not to think about home, I'm goddamned stuck on it—especially *her.*

I watch Evelyn flip another page in her book.

I force back a groan, turning my gaze away. Here, the ocean stretches on as far as the eye can see, a glinting blue carpet that's perfect for swimming or boating or whatever people do here when they have time and money for fun.

I wonder idly how much Evelyn lost last night.

A metric fuckton, probably.

I kept my distance, watching from the shadows, knowing casino security was too tight to try anything then. She bounced around the entire floor, hitting everything from roulette to blackjack to flashy celebrity branded slots.

She should've known her luck wouldn't last. Winning streaks never do. It's basic math in gambling. What comes up must come down, and it happens much faster when you're pissing away money in games where the house always wins.

429

Eventually, after I've been sitting around for hours, slowly burning to a crisp, she pushes up from her lounge chair, plops her book in her bag, and leaves a few crisp bills on the table for the server. A nice tip she can easily afford with her ill-gotten gains.

Fucking finally.

That's my cue to pack my shit up, too, keeping a careful eye on her as she walks along the road. Back to the hotel, probably, or maybe to the beach for one last walk before sunset.

I pull out my phone and make a quick call.

Thankfully, it isn't busy in the offseason.

As soon as she turns onto an empty street, I pick up my pace, closing on her fast.

She barely has time to turn around before I've grabbed her arm, dragging her into a nearby alley.

It stinks—just like every trash-filled alleyway everywhere—a reminder of the grim reality staring me in the face.

Paradise my ass. Even here, there's plenty gone rotten.

"Patton?" she gasps. Her eyes bug out as they focus.

There's no point in trying to escape. I'm holding her too tightly, and it feels good to dig my fingers in until she gasps.

I hope her squirming leaves a bruise.

I'm not a cruel man, no, but she hurt my son.

"Hello, Evelyn," I clip. From the way her eyes widen, my smile must look as vacant as it feels. "Thought you'd escaped with our money, huh?"

"Patton, please. Think what you're doing," she whispers, her hands fumbling at my grip helplessly.

"I've given that plenty of thought, lady." I slam her against the wall, savoring the fear flashing across her face. She looks like she's about to faint, but I've known her a long time. Evelyn Hibbing isn't the kind to clock out. "Give me one good reason why I shouldn't."

"Oh, dearie, oh God, I… I suppose you must be very angry with me." She shifts back to her usual innocent sounding babble. I wonder if it's always been an act. "Yes, I did you wrong, of course. But I think—if you let me go, maybe it's not too late to get her jewelry back. I'll lead you right to it."

"You read my mind," I snap. "Trouble is, I know you've already sold it, and I also know where. I don't need your help."

"What? Oh, yes, well…" Panic fills her voice as she gives up trying to break my hold and glances down at her bag. "But it's recoverable, Patton. I just know it. If you'll simply let me—"

Enough.

I grab her wrists and pin them to the wall.

The stone feels scalding under my fingers, and her skin feels thin and papery.

"What's in there?" I ask, nodding to the bag. "Mace? Were you going to burn my face off and try to run? Are you that predictable?" I lean in, putting my face too close to hers. She smells like alcohol, some chocolatey liquor that was in her coffee drink.

"Patton, please. You're scaring me."

"*Good.*" I stare at her until she shrinks back. "Listen, I'm not here because you stole Mom's jewelry and fucked her over. I could've let the police handle that." I tighten my grip on her and lower my voice. It's either this or give in to the temptation to roar in her face, but I'm deathly quiet as I say, "But there are no words in the world that will make me forgive you for trying to kill my son."

"Kill him? Oh, no, I—" She stops. Her mouth hangs loosely as she stares at me. I think she's tracing the features Arlo and I share, if she isn't trying to find a flimsy excuse for trying to murder a child. "I wasn't trying to kill him," she whispers haltingly. "Just… enough to make him sick

431

and—and *of course* I hated it! But I needed a diversion, and—"

"A diversion? How?"

I shake her.

Her lips quiver. "His juice! I slipped in the slightest concentrate when no one else was looking. Just enough to cause an upset tummy, his heart was never in any danger, I made sure. I never wanted to hurt the boy too badly, I swear."

Does she fucking hear herself?

It's a living miracle I don't snap her neck like a stick.

"Bull. Shit." I yank her back through the alley, pulling until we're back in the tropical sun. A diversion.

That's all Arlo was to her. Fully expendable.

With the demon's confession, I drag her down the street, making sure I have a firm hold as she begs for mercy. The recording app on my phone will do the rest now, plus a little muscle.

It's hard as hell not to strangle her in broad daylight.

The hardest thing I've ever done.

The Nassau detectives I tipped off this morning are waiting by a scenic overlook.

"Oh, no! Oh, no, no, no. Oh, Patton, *no!*" When she sees them, she starts kicking like a mule, braying loudly enough for people to look up nearby, but I don't give a shit.

As soon as the detectives spot us, they hurry forward.

"Let me go!" she howls, her voice high and unfamiliar. "I'm innocent. I didn't do it. I *didn't do any of it.*"

One of the detectives nods at me.

I nod back.

The timing couldn't be better.

As they haul her away in handcuffs with her head hanging miserably, I take a stroll under the sun, staring at the wide turquoise sea.

It glitters, inviting and warm. There's no denying it's gorgeous here. There's plenty to do on this island, if you want to throw your cares to the wind.

Old Patton, he would've stayed a few days just for the trouble of getting here. But new Patton just wants to get the hell out of here on the first flight home.

I think about Salem and Arlo, how much I wish I had my family here to take the edge off.

Sure, I've been ignoring her messages to stay focused. Mostly so I don't get distracted, but also because I'm at a loss for words.

She let me know he's recovering. He's on the mend, and I let that message go unanswered, too, as much as I hated it.

This isn't just about Arlo anymore. It's about them, knowing how much they belong in my life, now more than ever.

I can't let her go.

And maybe she'll fling it right back in my face, because what right do I have to keep her with me if she doesn't want to be there, but I'm not giving up without a fight.

Not this time.

Not with Salem.

Not without Arlo.

I need to reclaim my family.

And if she'll still have me, I won't mince words.

I'll bring them home forever.

* * *

MOM'S HOUSE looks like it's hosting the entire family when I get back after a sleepless night of delayed flights and layovers.

Arch parked his vehicle slightly crooked on the driveway.

433

Same for Dexter, who's parked neatly beside it, almost like he wanted to make a point about Arch's terrible parking.

The thought makes me grin, though it vanishes a second later.

Before I know what I'm doing, I'm taking the steps to the front door two at a time and barreling inside.

"Daddy!" Arlo comes flying down the hall, his feet slapping the carpet. His face is split by the widest grin and he—

Wait, what?

What the hell did he just call me?

He launches himself into my arms, clearly expecting me to swing him around.

There's a second where I'm too stunned to move, but after a breathless heartbeat, I grab him and press him to my chest. He smells like laundry and fresh cooking and that little kid smell that's distinctly his.

Fuck me, for the first time I can remember, I worry about tearing up.

"I told him," Salem announces quietly over his shoulder. She's standing back a pace, wringing her hands together, barely holding in tears of her own.

Well, hell, at least we make a great pair today.

Arlo has his hands around my neck. I'll be damn happy if he never lets go.

"Delly knows, too. I couldn't wait to tell her, no matter what happens. Even if"—her voice trembles—"even if you never want to see me again."

"Mommy told me you're my daddy!" Arlo says cheerfully. "Does that mean I'm gonna be a superhero, too?"

"Sure thing, buddy." My voice is thick, but I'm past caring. "Sorry I couldn't be around when your mom gave you the big news."

"It's okay. She said you were busy saving the world," he says smugly.

"Yeah?" I look at Salem, who watches me warily with a slight flush on her cheeks.

It hasn't been a full week since I saw her, but it feels like twenty years.

There's nothing I want to do more right now than swing her into my arms and kiss her until she can't remember her own name.

But a lot needs to happen first.

So I just take my sweet time hugging Arlo until he wiggles, then I set him down.

Behind Salem, Mom gives me a knowing smile and holds her arms out. "Come on, little monster," she says. "Colt has some old Legos in the library and he's waiting for you."

"I have Lego dinosaurs," Arlo tells me before he scampers away, taking Mom's hand as easily as she offered it.

I blink at the interaction, letting it soak in, smiling like the biggest idiot on Earth.

The kids must know they're related. They all know about Arlo.

Shit, they know about *me*.

Salem doesn't move, her hazel eyes fixed on my face with the same wariness as before. The egomaniac in me hoped she might throw herself at me in relief that I'm back and everything's sorted. Though I guess she doesn't know it yet.

"I found Evelyn," I say. "Handed her straight to the police. They'll prosecute her soon, and it should be an open-and-shut case with the confession I recorded. There's a chance we might track down Mom's jewelry, too, though the dealer who got it sold some pieces off already."

"What about your money?" The ghost of a frown she's wearing touches her eyes.

"I don't give a shit. I can live without it and so can my brothers. That's not why I went after her."

She swallows thickly.

I take a step toward her, and to my relief, she doesn't bolt away.

Not even when I'm standing in front of her, gazing down into hot honey-brown eyes that haven't stopped haunting me since the day I walked out.

"I did it for Arlo," I tell her. "For you."

I think she's stopped breathing. This would be a fine moment for the conversation we need to have, but if I know my brothers, they're just waiting for the perfect opportunity to burst in and ruin everything.

Privacy isn't their strong suit.

"Let's talk in the garden," I suggest, reaching for her hand, then stopping.

Slow and steady, that's the play here. We need to smooth out the wrinkles first before I can kiss her, even if her lips are constant torture.

And those plush lips part as she takes a breath. Her gaze drops to my hand, a hint of confusion forming before she nods.

We walk together in silence, giving me time to think about how I don't know what to say.

Feelings were never my strong suit.

I can do charm, I can do seduction, I can do grand gestures. But this—talking about what I really want and why it's her—it's foreign as hell when you've always kept a barbed wire fence around your inner self.

Before I can blink, we're in the garden and she's looking up at me expectantly.

I still have absolutely no idea what to say.

Fuck.

I've never had a beautiful woman who means the world looking at me with so much hope welling in her eyes.

"Salem, I'm sorry," I say roughly. "For leaving. For flying

off the handle and going rogue, even if I knew it was right. And I'm sorry for leaving you in the dark."

Her eyes narrow, just enough to send ice down my spine. "Honestly, I wondered if you were coming back at all…"

"I wanted it to be a surprise," I say, an excuse so pathetic I almost smile. Almost. "The fact is, I couldn't say any of this shit over the phone. I had to see you. I wanted—" I stop cold. What I really wanted was to make sure I didn't scare her away. "I wanted to see you."

"Really? You could've fooled me. The way you stormed out that night—" Her throat bobs, proving this entire conversation haunts her as much as me.

And clearly, I still have a lot of explaining to do.

But the stubborn bastard in me folds his arms. I was the prick who left, but not without good reason.

"Can you blame me? After you said you were leaving for the Ozarks? All I ever had on my mind was a future together, especially after Arlo got sick."

She looks away quickly.

"Okay, that *was* a mistake." Her breath hisses out and she backs up a step. "And look, I'm sorry, okay? I should have been more open with my feelings. I shouldn't have talked like I could just freeze you out and run. Deep down, I never could."

Her throat ticks harshly.

"Lady Bug," I growl, moving closer. "That much honesty takes practice. If you can learn to forgive and forget, so can I."

"Yeah, but God, this isn't what I wanted to talk about. I imagined this going differently."

I nod. "There was more kissing involved in my mind."

A fucking jackass comment, maybe, but it makes her look up at me sharply with a twinkle in her eyes.

"Kissing?" I hate how foreign the word sounds on her lips.

Truth be told, I imagined us doing a hell of a lot more than kissing, but that's not the point.

"I came here to tell you I fucked up by leaving. Maybe I still had to, but it could've gone down differently, yeah. I had to chase down Evelyn. I didn't have to freeze you out when we were in the thick of a crisis nobody should ever experience."

Hurt shadows her face.

For a second, I think she'll turn away and run back in the house, which I'd deserve. But then her head tilts and a smile touches her mouth.

Whatever comes next, I know she's not about to dump my ass.

"You mean your big ego lets you admit when you screwed up?"

"My ego allows a damn lot of things. Even when it gets big and overgrown like a weed."

Her smile widens into the expression I've been waiting for, that shine in her eyes that brings out the gold. "Somehow, I don't think you came all this way to tell me that."

"I didn't." I move in, trailing my mouth over her ear, loving the way she shudders and how her breath hitches. "And if you'd stop sassing me for a minute, I might be able to tell you my other mistakes."

"So talk. Spill it," she challenges.

Growling, I take her earlobe between my teeth and pull, not bothering to hide my smug smile. "My first mistake was not staying longer that first night when you asked."

"Would it have prevented this?"

"Don't know, but I should've stepped up for you and Arlo. Turning over the house for proof didn't help much anyway." I turn my attention to her neck, tasting her skin. She grips my biceps, digging her nails in. "Mistake number two—not keeping you chained up in my bed. I never should've let you go home."

"Who said I would've stayed?" Her laugh tickles.

Absolutely no one, but that messes with my narrative, so I ignore it.

"We both know you would have. I might've convinced you then and there to say fuck the Ozarks." I brush my lips over her skin until I feel her pulse, tracing it with my tongue until she shivers. "My biggest mistake was hands down letting you go."

"When?"

"Every single time," I rasp, bringing my lips home.

Oh, shit.

She tastes like new beginnings, all salt and fading sadness and the cinnamon-orange scent of *Salem Hopper*. I don't need some expensive perfume like her friend's company cranks out to get harder than a diamond just from breathing this woman.

I only need her.

Every brittle, broken piece.

If I have my way this time—if I have a second chance—I won't leave her worn. I'll keep her together, safe and whole, complete in a way she's never been. I'll also make her damn tired of hearing how much I love her.

She lets out a small gasp, almost a moan. I practically forget what I came here to do.

As much as I want to sneak back inside before the others notice and fuck her senseless, there's something else I need to say first.

"For the record, I made one more mistake," I whisper against her mouth, pulling away just long enough to see her dark eyes consumed with the same need roaring in my blood. "I should've told you I loved you a hell of a lot sooner."

Her jaw pinches tightly. She trembles in my arms, pushing back so she can read my eyes.

I give her the truth, and nothing but, standing silently until she answers with a smile. "I was a little shocked. I thought you'd never say it."

"We've already established I fucked up, woman. Do you forgive me?"

With a solemn look, she plants her feet against the ground and presses her hands into my shoulders like she's about to say something heavy. I slide my hands to her waist and wait.

"I forgive you, Patton—but only if you forgive me for freaking out and getting scared. It's hard to get past that when it's all I've ever done my whole life."

"Done," I whisper.

"Me too." Her smile sharpens. "I'm done being a black cat. I want this. I want *you*. I even stood up to my parents. They flew in when they heard about Arlo, begging me to move in with them... I couldn't have fought back before. Not before you."

"I'm proud of you," I whisper, leaning down to kiss her again, but she pushes a finger against my lips.

"I wasn't finished. Because I don't just love you back. You... you drive me wild. Some days, I want to strangle you. But despite that, I can't stop thinking about you and the family we could be. I know this won't be easy, but that's also what makes it so, so good. I want to stand my ground. I want to fight for this, Patton, for you and me and Arlo. No more escape attempts or sudden freak-outs, I promise." She takes her hands off my shoulders and cups my face with a sweetness that resonates in my bones.

"Big words. You sure about that, Lady Bug?"

"Yes! I'm positive I can't do anything else," she whispers.

"Because I'm in love with you, dork. Plus, Arlo will kill me someday if he finds out I messed things up with his hero."

I chuckle with a warmth that ripples through me.

That's it, right there.

Everything I hoped for and more—what I was counting on her saying—but hearing it hits different. It's like seeing a painting of a gorgeous sunset versus witnessing the real deal in person.

It turns out, loving someone else and telling them is the strongest drug known to man, and dangerously addictive.

Hearing it with the joy in her voice and the tears in her eyes isn't enough.

I want to hear it forever.

I want to watch the shape of her lips as she speaks every syllable.

I want to whisper it back to her when I'm balls deep inside her, making her look at me before her body convulses.

What started as pure temptation has become a brute need like air and water. But first, there's one more thing.

"Salem," I growl, slipping a hand into my pocket and pulling out the small box I brought home. "Being away from you made me realize how much you mean to me. It also made me hate how much time we've wasted."

Her hands flutter to her mouth as she stares down. "Is that—holy—*are you serious*? Right now?"

"If that's a yes, I am."

"Um. Oh my God. Okay. But I think you need to get down on one knee first," she says breathlessly. She steps back, giving me space.

I don't care that the grass is damp and it'll probably stain my trousers.

A second later, I'm kneeling, popping open that little black box with my thumb.

The ring I picked is white gold with a sapphire stone,

framed with diamonds because it reminds me of her. How she put the color back in my life, and all the money and people and magnetic moments will always be in her orbit, swirling around the true center.

"Salem Hopper," I say, my voice too low. The ring was a spur-of-the-moment decision when I saw the jewelry shop in Nassau, and I'm pretty sure couples usually discuss this sort of thing in advance. If she's not ready, I won't blame her one bit, but I'm also not losing this chance to keep her.

Tonight, we're all in.

"I love you," I say. "I fell for you faster than I'd ever believe. I had it coming, even before I found out Arlo was mine. Fate reached down through years apart and shook me the fuck awake. So I want to do this family thing properly. I don't want to wait. I want you as my wife. I want you where you belong—right by my side, forever."

A painful moment passes.

Seconds feel like days, months, years.

Then she grins, wide enough to bring the sun out through the evening gloom.

"*Yes,*" she whispers, her eyes watering. Her bottom lip quivers. "Yes, of *course* I'll marry you, Grumpybutt."

Music to my ears.

I'm laughing like a madman as I slide the ring on her finger before she can change her mind. It looks like it was always meant to be there, hugging her finger like a promise forged from our worries and doubts, remade into something beautiful.

There's a deep satisfaction in my chest, this greedy caveman thing, seeing her wearing my ring.

She's mine.

She's all fucking *mine.*

Inhaling roughly, I pull her into my arms.

"I might be many things, Lady Bug," I tell her, my lips a whisper from hers, "but I'm no damn grumpybutt anymore."

"You don't kiss like one, I guess. Hard to argue with that," she says, closing the distance.

Time stops cold as I claim her mouth, teasing what I mean to do to the rest of her later, the second we're alone.

I don't give a shit if my brothers are watching and jeering from the windows, or if Mom's looking on with teary-eyed joy.

This is our moment and Salem Hopper finally belongs to me.

My wife.

My son's mother.

My future, my fight, my lady since the day she was born.

My own personal lady luck, and the winning streak that's coming will be one for the ages.

We kiss breathlessly, our hands pulling at our clothes high and low, until thunder rumbles overhead and we're doused in a cool, sudden rain. It's like the universe is urging us to get a room.

Sighing reluctantly, I break away and look up at the sky, then back at Salem. Her swollen lips, her big brown eyes, and the ring glinting on her finger that matches the gold flashing in her gaze.

"We should go tell your family the news," she says.

"Maybe," I admit, tugging her back to the house. "But there's something else I'd rather do more."

"Patton! What if someone's watching, they're probably waiting for—"

"Let them. I want to fuck you, Salem. I want to see that ring on your finger when you grab my cock. I want to feel it on my skin when you're wrapped around me, begging for dear life." I bring her in closer so I can rumble the last part in her

443

ear. "And I want to feel it against my fingers when I'm pinning you down, telling you to come for me. Can you do that for me? Can you wear that pretty ring while I mark you tonight?"

Her lips quiver and she nods slowly, too lost for words.

"Later, yes. But we really shouldn't keep them waiting…"

Smiling, I take her hand, already loving how right that little piece of gold feels on her hand.

It's only right to give her fair warning about what she's gotten herself into.

Judging by the shy excitement in her red cheeks, she doesn't mind at all.

XXVII: STROKE OF LUCK (SALEM)

Months Later

I stand in my wedding dress, staring at my reflection in the mirror.

Behind me, Delly looks on, her eyes warm and her hands clasped in front of her. She's totally bursting at the seams, but she lets me soak in this moment.

And *what a moment.* This dress is everything.

The corset bodice is decorated with diamond-embedded lace, curving around my breasts, equally elegant and enticing. It flares into my waist and over my hips, where the skirt flows in opulent waves to the floor.

Today, I feel like a princess. Amazingly, I look the part, too.

The seamstress even embroidered our initials inside the fabric off to the side, masked by a piece of lace. My little secret. I run my fingers over the letters, tracing them and remembering everything that's happened to bring me here.

Patton's ring flashes on my finger.

I had a matching necklace commissioned as my 'something blue,' and it sits in the hollow of my throat. My clavicle stands in sharp relief as I take a deep breath. Honestly, it's perfect when there's a lot of blue in this wedding.

But holy hell, is it happening for real? In less than an *hour?*

"Is it the heat, dear? You look flushed," Delly says.

"No, I've just been pinching myself about fifty times since I woke up," I tell her with a laugh.

A photographer in the background snaps a not-so-discreet candid shot. I try to remember her advice to forget she's there. We'll want these shots for memories later.

Delly giggles and finally releases her hands. She's wearing a sapphire-blue dress that matches the necklace, regal as ever as mother of the groom.

Patton.

My soon-to-be husband.

He's had three whole months to change his mind, but if anything, he's just been pushing for everything to happen at breakneck speed. There was barely time to book the wedding venue and set up all the moving pieces. Without Delly pulling some strings and calling in favors, I'm not sure if we could've pulled it off.

I can't say I blame him for the urgency.

For us to *be a family* faster.

Marrying this man isn't a trial, though. I'm so over judging him for being gruff and demanding when I know his heart's in the right place.

"Believe it, lovely lady. You two were meant to be," she says. "Fate has a funny way of being pushy until you give in."

That was me, the not giving in part. Patton, to my eternal gratitude, was ready from the start. Or at least from the moment I told him about Arlo after that trip to Utah.

I'm the fool who kept running while he chased.

Thank God he never quit.

"I guess I don't mind pushy," I say absently.

"Well, I hope so. You're marrying my youngest son." She smiles. "Life has a way of making things right in the end."

Delly nods firmly. I wonder if that's as much for her as it is for me.

I don't need to ask to know Evelyn Hibbing still weighs on her mind. And it breaks my heart every time, hating that this sweet lady had to have her best friend turn supervillain.

"*Some things* are meant to be, I should say," she corrects. "But no matter how wild it seems, it'll always be clear with time."

"You're probably right. But there are days when I don't think Patton and I were meant to be at all," I muse, watching my reflection again.

The hotel room is one of the most luxurious I've ever stepped foot in with enormous gold picture frames and a four-poster bed. I thought these beds were almost extinct outside the movies.

Delly shakes her head, her curls bobbing. "Oh, you're right to be nervous. Who isn't on her wedding day? Just as long as you remember, no one else could have infatuated my son like you—and no one could ever capture his entire heart."

My cheeks heat. I touch the embroidered initials on the side of my dress again, feeling them like this security blanket I desperately need.

Later, I'll ask him to find them. It'll be funny, knowing he'll want to shred this dress off me and—

I blink, banishing the vision.

Yeah, let's save that for when his mother isn't in the same room.

"Even when he makes me want to punch him?" I ask.

"That's called love," Delly says without missing a beat.

447

"Even when I feel so unworthy?"

"Even then," she whispers, leaning down to kiss the top of my head. "Give it time. In a few years, you'll wonder how you ever lived before this family."

Wow, she's good.

I think I'm a decent mom, but Delly Rory could write books on it. I wonder if I'll ever turn out a fraction as awesome if we give Arlo a few more siblings?

A lump moves up my throat.

All this talk of love and family makes me think about mine.

My parents are here, yes, after I sent them a belated invitation. We've had phone calls and a brief visit last month where I introduced Arlo since they've been behaving themselves and trying to act human.

But they're not guests of honor.

You don't just move on that easy for a storybook happy ending, not when there's trauma involved.

That's why I'm not having Dad walk me down the aisle. Same reason my mom isn't here with me in the bridal room, where she'd only stress me out before the big moment.

I have Delly, and Junie will be along shortly. So will a couple ladies from The Cardinal, new friends I love going out with for lunch and after-dinner drinks.

Oh, and no Kayla either.

That friendship is charred to a crisp.

I didn't bother sending her an invite. Not that she'd have shown up if I had, although it might have been worth it just to get a bitchy text message back about how atrocious I am for insulting her and stealing 'her man.'

But dwelling on poisonous old frenemies has me thinking about Evelyn again. Her trial date isn't firm yet, but there's no doubt she'll be looking at several lifetime sentences.

The story became a national sensation, especially after a

deeper investigation revealed she murdered her husband on top of her treachery with us.

Poison, made from his own plants, to induce a heart attack. Then she drained his leftover investments in every high-limit room Las Vegas has, gambling herself to doom.

Big surprise, right?

Arlo wasn't her first rodeo using nature's bounty to hurt people.

Although I hate her now with a passion that scares me, the emotion isn't totally uncomplicated.

She's a bitter old woman with an addiction who's set to be locked up for the rest of her life, after the jury finds her guilty. That's a little hard to celebrate, even if I'll still be viciously glad, knowing she can never hurt anyone again.

For Delly, it's different.

When her husband died and her boys grew up, Evelyn took her place as her confidante, her best friend and companion. The news that not only did she steal from her, try to kill her grandson, and fled with her sons' money... It's a freaking lot to process.

I don't blame her for finding it hard to deal with, even today, when we should be so happy it's just a bitter afterthought.

"The honeymoon is only two weeks," I remind her gently. "It was hard enough prying Patton away from work for that long, but are you sure you can handle Arlo?"

"Oh, yes. I'm amazed you managed that. Patton must learn to take a week off sometimes. I just hope you're ready for a spoiled little bird when you get back." Delly smiles, brushing away a tear.

"It was an effort. But we'll be back before you know it and you can call if you need anything." I'm also happy she won't be alone.

She pats me on the shoulder again, smiling fondly as she checks the time on her phone.

"Come, dear. We can't be late for your vows."

Standing, I pull her into a hug impulsively.

"Thank you for being family, *Mom*," I whisper.

"Oh, hush. It's my honor. If you really want to show your appreciation, I'll let you do it with more grandbabies—when you're ready, of course." The impatient note in her voice makes me giggle.

And we laugh together as she pats my hair, styled in long curls, with a clumsy hand.

* * *

I DON'T THINK anyone who ever lived felt more privileged than I do, standing across from Patton, trying not to go numb.

He's in his full princely glory today.

This man is illegally, devilishly handsome in a navy suit that matches his eyes so well it should be impossible.

And when he grins at me, his thumb moving over the back of my hand, I almost detonate.

If I didn't know any better, I might think his eyes are a little shinier than usual.

The riverboat sways gently under us.

What better place for us to say our vows? Here on the water, under the gentle early summer sun, our love comes full circle.

And I hope this evening ends with the same explosive finish as our very first night.

Arlo, giddy with excitement, skips forward with two rings in a tiny wicker basket, handing them to the pastor before he gives me the biggest smile I've ever seen on his face.

His blue suit matches Patton's, complete with a kiddie clip-on tie, a sweet touch that nearly brings me to tears.

Breathlessly, I hold out my hand for him to slip the ring on. His eyes are sharp as his fingers caress mine, sending heat skittering down my spine.

Even as we're getting married, I want him more than I can breathe.

My turn now.

I take Patton's platinum ring, the inside etched with our initials like my dress, and I slide it over his finger, binding us forever.

He's mine.

I'm his.

We belong to each other in every way.

I want to scream it from the rooftops as I stare up into his eyes and see the love, the heat, the softness that waits for me there.

Home isn't a place after all.

It's people, and with him in my life, I'll always have it.

The pastor's words drift over me like surreal music from another world. I'm listening, but not really, too caught in my almost-husband's eyes.

When he says something about kissing the bride, though, Patton doesn't waste a nanosecond.

With one hand on my face, he takes my lips with a claiming fury that curls my toes.

God. It really is 'till death do us part.'

And I cling to him, my hands finding his shoulders and pulling him closer.

Our first kiss as a married couple leaves me in cinders, smoldering with an indecent thrill after he pulls away.

My. Flipping. Husband.

He hits me with one of those grins I know he can't hold inside whenever he looks at me.

"Congratulations, Mrs. Rory." The twinkle in his eye turns wicked. "You just took the most eligible bachelor in Kansas City off the market."

"We're not in Kansas anymore. And you're no Dorothy." Lame, I know, but at least I meet his grin with my own red-faced smile.

"I sure as hell am not." Before he can prove exactly how un-Dorothy he is, I turn back to the cheering guests.

Delly's in the front row, along with Archer and Dexter and Junie. Young Colt sits near the end, watching us. One of the rare times I haven't seen him looking bored out of his mind, but he's a good kid, especially considering who's next to him.

Arlo leans off the chair, laughing and clapping his hands like they're on fire.

My heart swells with pure love for all the folks assembled today, sharing our special moment. Past and present and future melt into one.

Patton slides my hand into his and we walk back down the aisle, through the confetti shower and rowdy cheers, until we're at the other end of the boat, laughing.

He kisses me again with a smidge more privacy, ensuring there's zero chance I'll catch my breath or my senses.

"We have all night you know," I tease.

"Get used to not waiting. I'll be doing this a lot from now on, wife," he whispers.

My skin flares with heat from head to toe.

"Well, okay. Permission granted."

"More reason to celebrate." His next kiss comes slow and deep and that heat rising in my core becomes an inferno. I can't resist running my hands through his styled hair, mussing it up, loving his noise of annoyance that becomes a groan when I nip his bottom lip. "No whining. Do you know how long it took me to get ready this morning?"

"Long enough to enjoy ruining you." And that cocky grin on his face tells me that's a promise.

"Maybe." I lean back and assess his face. "But you have lipstick on your mouth."

"Lick it off," he growls.

Dear God.

For a second, I'm actually a little tempted to tell everyone else to head downstairs for the reception and start the party without us while the boat cruises down the river, but I lean back, both hands flat against his chest.

"Not fair. Our people just want to celebrate with us. Don't we owe them that? Besides, the cake's supposed to be crazy. Junie and her gram worked on it all day."

"The cake, the cake…" His nostrils flare with frustration, but there's a half smile playing across his lips. "Fine. But we're leaving early."

"*If* you behave yourself." I drag my hands down his washboard abs toward his pants and the definite bulge there. "We'll deal with this later. And if you're really a good boy"—I lean in, delighting when he grabs my hand and moves my fingers against his cock—"I'm going to take my sweet time."

"Kill me fucking now," he rasps, but there's humor in his voice, and he releases me. "Do you want this marriage to end before midnight? Woman, I'll be dead."

"Be strong. A little patience, that's a wonderful wedding present."

He mutters something gruff and crude under his breath I can't make out, but I'm definitely snickering.

This man.

His mouth grazes my ear as he links hands and we head back to rejoin the party.

"You're damn lucky I owe you the world, Salem Rory. I'm going to spend the rest of my life carving it up for you on a silver platter." He watches me nod, satisfied, and he gives me another one of his patented smug smiles. "Now, how about that celebration?"

* * *

THE REST of the day blurs by in the sweetest fever dream.

That's what no one tells you about weddings, I guess. Time comes unglued and you spend all day riding such a high that you'll be lucky to remember much later on.

I think I'm starting to understand why those photos are so important.

After the dinner and a heartfelt speech by my husband, thanking everyone for being here to welcome the next chapter of our lives, I tell everyone about how much he's changed my life—the good and bad, but mostly the good—and then the music starts pulsing.

The riverboat transforms into a floating party bus, way fancier than anything I ever dared to imagine on my wedding day.

I dive right into the fun, ignoring how constraining this dress feels for dancing with Patton. I'm seriously grateful for the three dancing lessons Delly offered at her expense. I know Arlo loved them too.

He shows off his moves, yelling at me to watch him as he does the moonwalk, the bust down, and his own wild break-dancing in between. I'm glad when Colt charges in with moves of his own, distracting Arlo long enough so I can enjoy my time on the floor with Patton.

And as I stare into my husband's smoky-blue eyes, I thank the lucky stars we found each other.

Miracle of miracles, we found each other *again*.

We also spend forever thanking our guests, together and separately. We drink champagne and laugh, surrounded by glitter and good company.

It makes this day impossibly bright and too perfect for life.

Just when I feel like my cup couldn't be any fuller, the boat docks back at the marina to let the crowd off and then embarks again with just us and a skeleton crew.

The engines rumble under us as they take us down the Missouri River. Patton and I lean over the railing, just like I did one fateful evening so many years ago.

The orange city lights reflected off the water that night, and I'd eyed the river hard, vaguely wondering whether I should jump in. Now, there's nothing but the hopeful glory of the fading sunset and distant lights spilling across the waters like gold stars.

I'm not alone anymore.

And our honeymoon has officially begun.

"Cheers," Patton says, clinking his champagne glass against mine. "To the rest of our lives."

"Tomorrow and forever," I agree with a smile, turning to face him. "God, I love you."

No lie.

Ever since the first time I said it, I've told him every day, learning how to let myself be vulnerable so we can be stronger. So I can trust Patton Rory.

But now, more than ever, it feels important to say it, to ground us on a night glowing with meaning.

"Salem." Patton turns to me with the very same light dancing in his eyes. Gone is the smirking strongman who's usually there.

Tonight, it's just a man who loves me unconditionally.

He shakes his head, one corner of his mouth curving up in a lopsided smile. "How are you my addiction and my cure? I'll never love anyone like I love you."

"Show me, hubby," I whisper.

I take his face in my hands, feeling the unfamiliar weight of that new band on my finger.

Our next kiss is a slow, gentle storm.

So different from the usual ravenous kisses we share, where every movement fights for dominance, pure possession.

Now, he explores my mouth like we have all the time in the world, slowly simmering me with every movement.

We have all night, at least.

His tongue flicks against my bottom lip, a pointed question.

I open my mouth in answer, granting him access, teasing him back with my tongue.

It's the ebb and flow like the tide around us, this sense of soulful, mingling passion.

If tonight could be forever, I'd never stop kissing him.

The thought makes me smile, and I throw my arms around his neck.

"This would be more fun without clothes," I say. "Unless you plan on fucking me right here."

"Fucking?" He echoes the rough word with amusement, though when he pulls away, his eyes are glinting with total mischief. "Tonight, wife, I won't be fucking you. I will be making love." He trails his hand up my leg. "But you will only be wearing this dress once, and I want to enjoy seeing you in it a little while longer."

"Haven't you been enjoying it all day?"

"Fuck yes," he growls in my ear, reaching up and trailing a finger through the lace on my bodice. "But I'm going to savor this moment, Lady Bug."

So I lean my head back and let him savor.

We kiss like starved animals, my back pressed against the railing, my hands on his broad shoulders, kissing and kissing long into the night.

Eventually, my fingers go to work, tossing away his necktie and unbuttoning his shirt. I never knew how hot a man's collarbones could be until now.

Another molten kiss and he sighs, his hands tightening around my waist. He isn't shy as he grinds his cock against me, though I know he's holding back.

For now.

But he's had his fun, and now it's time for mine.

I lean against his chest, easing him back, looking him over again.

My Patton, my man, with his coppery hair and stark blue eyes and endless capacity to love me. And I'm still insanely smitten with the blue suit, which looks painted on over his muscles.

But one day of seeing him in that suit feels like plenty, and I'm sure he'll agree. Time to say a fond goodbye.

"My turn." He raises a hand to help me and I shake my head.

It's painstaking, my progress.

Shucking his jacket off, then working off the open shirt underneath, I let my knuckles graze him as I work, silently worshiping every inch of bronze skin coming into view.

"You approve?" His eyes heat when they meet mine.

"You already know I do." I press my palms on his chest, loving how his muscles tighten under me.

"Then let me help you out of this thing."

I turn my back to him, blushing as he slowly undoes the buttons at the back of my dress. I'm thankful he hasn't had too much to drink—they're finicky at the best of times. But he doesn't struggle, not for more than a minute or two.

Freedom!

Cool evening air teases my skin as I step out of the wedding dress piled on the floor. Underneath, there's just the lingerie I bought for this occasion.

A red and black lace bra, showing off more than it conceals, and matching panties with polka dots. No need to complicate it with anything more elaborate when it won't be staying on for long.

"Fuck," he rasps, his voice gritty. "You've made this ladybug shit next level."

I smile. "You're just saying that because I'm almost naked."

"Like hell. I'd think you were hot as hell even if you were wearing an old granny sweater."

I twirl around on the spot. "So you're saying you *don't* like my panties?"

"Fuck no." And the greedy way he embraces me proves it.

One hand finds my breast while the other caresses my stomach with a silent promise of where it may go next. Warmth pools between my legs.

As one hand toys with the lace of my bra, his other hand draws lazy circles against my stomach, sweeping lower, lower, before he trails a finger down the front of my panties.

I can't hold back a moan.

And I feel his deep laugh more than I hear it as he turns his attention to my thighs.

"Someone's in a hurry," I tell him, wiggling my ass against the hardness behind me.

"Woman, I don't have infinite patience," he growls.

"But you're going to spoil my fun," I whine.

"Lying brat. You'll have plenty."

There's no denying it as I grind against him again, grinning as his hips thrust against mine, the movement almost involuntary.

He circles my nipple in retaliation and slips a hand under my panties, one finger brushing my slick center.

I bite back a gasp.

Pleasure, overwhelming.

My nerves tingle, primed after being teased by his kisses,

his wandering hands, the heady anticipation of what's coming next.

My whole being cries out.

More, more, more.

And his fingers grow more insistent, grazing my clit.

I buck into their movements, urging them inside me, faster and deeper.

He happily obliges, sliding one finger in, and another as my ass rubs against him again.

"I married one demanding lady," he whispers, amused lust in his tone.

I can only moan in reply.

This spot is private enough, near the back of the ship. There aren't many crew around, and they're mostly up in navigation, but you never know.

Anyone could see us, but I don't care.

I'm too close to the edge.

Sighing, I throw my head back against his shoulder, my body tight in his arms as he brings me to the brink with practiced ease, plucking all my strings.

"Bite down on this hand when you come," he whispers, pushing the meat of his palm against my mouth.

That's it.

Undone.

I come so hard the night becomes streaks of gold and flicking shadows.

I lose myself to his embrace and the deep storming curses he breathes into my ear.

I melt into him the same way I always will, like the world itself folds into just us, two beating hearts given over to our own special madness.

I love how he's coming apart, too.

His breath turns sharp and ragged as his fingers pump inside me, rubbing me down from my high with demanding need.

"Do you like it, hubby?" I gasp. "Seeing me like this?"

"Yeah. Just not as much as I like you mounted on my cock." His voice is corrupted with desire, the roughness driving me into a deeper frenzy.

I barely see the passing water, even when my vision clears, or the dark shadows of the silhouetted trees on the far shore as the city fades into the distance.

It doesn't matter.

All I need is him.

And the hunger in my veins builds until I can't stand it, turning to face him.

"Not here," I plead. "We're already risking so much in the open, why press our luck?"

For a second, I think he'll push me back against the railing and take me anyway.

But in one smooth movement, he relents, throwing me over his shoulder.

I wrap my legs around him, and each step, each strike of friction, sends more pleasure shooting through me. At this rate, I might come again before he's in me.

"Be glad you married a jealous man. Only reason I didn't take you back here was the thought of anyone else feasting their eyes on my wife on our honeymoon."

"The least I deserve on my wedding night, right?"

"No argument." His lips curl against my skin as he nips my flesh.

Finally, we reach our cabin and the large double bed that's waiting.

Rose petals cover the sheets in a messy heart shape that's swiftly broken by Patton tumbling me down across them.

I'm about to complain when he lowers his body over mine and kisses me again.

This is so familiar, but so deliciously new.

I fight his pants off, and he hurries to help, tossing aside the belt, shoving down his bottoms until he's free, angry and pulsing and pressed against my entrance.

"Can you take it, good girl? Can you take all of your husband's cock tonight?" he asks sweetly.

And it hits me. He asked a slightly different question the night we met.

I was younger and drunk, but I'd been so sure I could.

Now, I'm unshakeable.

"Fill me," I whisper, and he smiles.

His blue eyes never leave mine as he slides inside me, one slow inch at a time.

Filling me.

His eyes are electric as he looks down, admiring what he sees, our bodies joined in the most intimate way, just like our new lives.

"I love you so much it's obscene," he says, moving his hips.

I dig my nails into his shoulders and meet his thrusts.

As his speed picks up and our breathing quickens, I sink deeper into the zone.

But before I'm gone, I push gently against him, urging him on.

Soon, we're twisted around so he's sitting on the edge of the bed, and I'm perched on his lap.

The first time we did this, I had no idea what I was doing.

I let him take me and I loved every second.

But now, I have a lot more experience, and tonight I want to ride Patton Rory to the explosive end.

I stroke his thick hair back and push down on him.

His groan leaves my soul in flames.

"Love you more," I whisper, bracing my hands on his shoulders. His hands find my hips, guiding me as his eyes meet mine with so much passion. "Do you feel how much I love you?"

"Shit, Salem." He kisses me again, biting my bottom lip.

He's so close to losing control, I smile, working my hips to leave him on the edge of insanity just a little bit longer.

I grind against him as he groans, his thrusts becoming truly punishing now.

Close.

So, so close.

"Come with me," he mutters, one hand pinching my breast as his strokes come faster, harder. "You're so beautiful. *Shit.*"

I'm close, too, another climax beckoning. Less like the edge of a cliff and more like a shaft of light. I just need to feel his warmth. I need—

"Salem," he says. *A warning.*

I shred the last of my self-control, writhing on him as my pussy clenches him so tight.

My head snaps back and I chase my pleasure, demanding his, too.

His fingers dig into my hips as he tips his head back, eyes wide with delight, and we're gone.

The fire finally consumes us.

We finish together with his big hand pressed to the small of my back, holding me against him, our gazes clashing, fusing together.

It's the eye contact that makes this so perfect.

By far one of our most sexy, intimate moments ever.

And my heart sings when I realize it's only the first of many.

Later, we flop down and roll in the rose petals, basking in the afterglow.

"What's on my wife's brain?" he asks.

"I was thinking about boat businesses again. Maybe I don't need to go to the Ozarks after all to chase a dream...

What do you think the market's like for rental cruises? This is the only ship in town I could find for a wedding."

"The market? Hmm, that's tough." He frowns, holding me tighter. "I think it's whatever you decide to make it. If you're serious about this, I'm already behind you. We'll figure it out."

I grin, knowing he'd say that. I also know this is a tomorrow conversation, not really fit for pillow talk on our wedding night.

But that's not what steals my breath away.

Here we are on a boat that feels familiar, yet so very different from our first night together.

Here I am with a husband I still can't believe I've won.

If this is where bad luck brought me, it wasn't so terrible after all.

And as I kiss him again and he groans in my mouth, I know things are looking up.

Patton Rory has altered my luck forever, and you'd better believe I'll enjoy every crazy, giddy, awesome bit of it.

FLASH FORWARD: ONE LUCKY FAMILY (PATTON)

Years Later

"*P*urple honey, huh? This is what you're doing with your life these days?" I turn the jar over in my hand with a sneer.

Archer flips me off.

"Fuck you, man," he growls. "We worked our asses off to get this stuff sourced right and branded. Are you really going to shit on my wife's work?"

I set the jar of odd, almost glowing honey down and hold up my hands. "Relax, bro. I wouldn't dream of it. Honestly, it's a nice touch. I think the happy couples who decide to get hitched here will love this stuff. Very generous to hook us up with your miracle honey." I purse my lips and lean closer to his ear, whispering. "Does it really make your dick three times bigger and cure skin tags?"

"You really are an idiot." Archer pushes me away. I make a

big show of windmilling my arms and flop back against the railing.

We settle in to stare across the water. In just a few weeks, this old refurbished riverboat will be hosting its very first events with the most regal floating ballroom, bar, and dining hall to ever set sail on the Missouri River.

I put up the money as an angel investor, yeah, but how could I say no after my beautiful, whip-smart wife worked her soul out?

"She's smarter than you. Don't ever forget it. Wish I'd thought of this whole party boat thing," Archer grumbles.

I give back an exaggerated yawn. "Tough talk from a guy with a woman who makes magic honey. Also, I'm convinced she's the nicer one. More patient, more worldly, definitely more social and—"

"Enough," he clips. "How about you shut your mouth and enjoy the view, Pat?"

For once, I can't argue with his ornery ass.

If marriage made Dex and me softer, it hasn't sanded down my oldest brother one bit, but I don't have the heart to keep pulling his tail.

Not with a view this magnificent, the city glimmering in the background with summer all around us. The silver spires of Kansas City throw off so much light.

How did I get here again?

Married man. Father. And soon to be husband of the happiest wife on ever when we christen this floating baby with a bottle of champagne and launch her latest business.

The last pieces of life are sliding into place way too easy.

If anything, it's hard to find time to slow down and enjoy the view. Every time I blink, my kids are a little older, their childhood slipping away as the days go by while we tour the future.

Blink again and I'll see Arlo in college. Probably some

expensive damn place just dripping prestige and flung far from home, honing his artistic muscles into lethal weapons.

I shouldn't assume too much, though. He's only heading into second grade.

And as for little Winter—fuck.

"Remember to breathe. Dex is going to give you more shit than I will if you come dragging in for his anniversary party looking like you did that time you went commando in the Bahamas."

"Never again." I snort, slowly turning to look at him and straightening up. "Tell me, Arch, does it ever get easier with Colt? Thinking about the future, I mean?"

For a few heavy seconds, he's quiet, leaning one big arm on the railing. Then he looks at me.

"Easier, no. The older they get, the more complicated your worries. You've got a lot of sleepless nights ahead, little brother." He slaps me on the shoulder. "Here's the good part —it fucking gets better. If you're raising your kids right, they'll learn. They'll do you proud. And even when the time comes when you can't do shit but stay up till sunrise worried sick, you'll know they can hold their own. Colt got that from me. Keep going, and you'll look like father of the year."

That wins a smile that cuts across my face.

"Wow, thanks. When's your parenting podcast dropping? Think I'd subscribe."

Chuckling, he flips me off again. We start walking off the boat together, back to the dock.

There are actually days when I appreciate this giant asshole, especially when he reminds me I'm not alone in playing family man.

And with Archer's advice still ringing in my ears, I speed home, feeling lighter than air.

* * *

"PATTON, TIME TO GO!" Salem calls from downstairs.

I look down at Arlo, slouched in my chair in front of the aquarium.

He's in the zone, razor-focused on sketching the octopus, which is oddly on full display today. My talented son takes advantage of the scene, working to get the perspective and shadowing of its legs right, his tongue sticking out the corner of his mouth in deep concentration.

"Keep going," I whisper when he looks up. "You're almost done, little man. Bring it home."

Arlo frowns at his paper. "But I've got two more legs to go, Dad…"

His pencil flies across the page, desperately sketching. I ruffle his hair as I push myself to my feet to meet the soft pad of the approaching footsteps.

"I'll hold her off. Finish up as fast as you can, okay?"

"Hmph." He glances up at me and grins.

Damn.

The smile makes him seem older, too much like yours truly. Where the hell does the time go?

I never thought I'd miss the cheeky kid who caused a new crisis weekly so much, but eight years old is world of difference from five.

Arlo's getting *sensible* for his age. Probably his mother's influence.

Speak of the devil. I meet her in the doorway, positioning myself to block her view.

"Are you trying to break records today? You're looking gorgeous," I say, giving her the slow, lazy smile I know she can't resist. "Thankfully, your date's not half bad."

"My *date* is flipping full of himself." Laughing, she whacks me on the arm playfully.

I reach over to take Winter out of her arms and press a

kiss to my baby daughter's face. She's such a bouncy little girl, but when she's sleeping, she's all cherub.

And she blinks at me now, her eyes wide and owlish. She's got her mother's eyes, thank God, and adorably soft dirty blonde hair. Salem is sure it'll darken over time.

Apparently, Salem was almost blonde as a kid. But I secretly hope little Win never changes. The family could use a little color in its hair.

"Look what your mama's saying about your old man," I croon, winking at Salem. "I'm blaming you, peanut. You're the whole reason my head's gotten bigger than a boulder."

Salem's mouth twitches into a smile, but she shakes her head, chasing it back. "Where's Arlo? We're going to be late!"

"Give him a minute. It's a matter of octopus-related life or death," I say, glancing back in the room. "Isn't that right, Arlo?"

"Yeah! Death!" he yells back.

Salem wrinkles her nose. "What's more important than showing up in time for Dex and Junie's anniversary?"

"The octopus, for one. My brother making kissing faces can wait." I love the way her face tightens into an amused frown. Time keeps aging her like a fine wine, and maybe Winter has given her a few wrinkles, but I love every single line.

"Patton, be serious."

"Salem," I mimic, "why?"

When I hear her annoyed sigh, I slide my free hand around her waist and pull her in for the close. Despite her irritation, she doesn't fight my kiss.

Every bit of her melts under my lips, and soon I'm the clown who's annoyed because I don't want to stop.

Later, I promise silently. *Later, when we're alone, I will do bad things.*

With Winter nestled between us, she doesn't fully press

against me, but she sighs against my mouth with a heat that says she knows.

"God, you can't just do that every time you want to win an argument."

"When it works so well? Would Batman give up his secret weapon? Maybe let Arlo weigh in on that one." My thumb strokes her cheek as Winter wakes up with a giggle.

She grabs a tuft of Salem's hair, pulling with silly baby strength.

It's cute enough now, but if we don't break that habit in another year or two, my wife will be on track for a wig.

"I'm ready when Arlo is," I promise.

"We're not having our schedule dictated by an octopus." Huffing a breath, she reaches up and slides a hand behind my neck. "Grab him and get me to this party," she breathes against my skin. "If you're quick, I *might* make it up to you later."

Oh, shit.

Desire ripples through me, just like she knew it would.

"You're a cruel woman—and you're lucky as all hell I trust you."

"Are you guy being gross again?" Arlo demands, stomping up behind us.

Spell, broken.

Without missing a beat, he holds up his latest drawing and waves it impatiently. "I finished! Take a look. Thanks for buying time, Dad."

He claps a hand over his mouth.

I smile sheepishly.

Salem glares at us, her mouth dropping. "You guys conspired to make us late to the party so you could draw the octopus?"

"But look at it this masterpiece" I say, twisting the paper so she can see more clearly.

Honestly, I don't know how Arlo was bit by the art bug—my mother, maybe, because it's sure not from me—but there's no denying he's got it in fucking boatloads.

It's just a quick pencil sketch, but he's nailed perspective, the lighting, everything. I'm sure there's room for improvement, even if I don't have an eye to see it, but in a few more months? A few years with the right teachers and plenty of time to practice?

My boy will put Leonardo da Vinci to shame.

"See? It's worth letting Dex grumble at us for a few minutes," I tell her.

"That's the best part," Arlo says with a disarming smile, "we can give it to Uncle Dex. As a present."

I smile.

The kid knows exactly how to play his mother. Unlike his art chops and impressive maturity, I like to think he got that skill from me.

"Great idea, bud." I pull him closer, giving Salem another peck on the lips for good measure. "Better get moving now, though, or we'll be late enough for it to matter."

"I hate you," Salem hisses affectionately.

But there's no hiding the smile curving her lips.

"Tell me that again later," I mutter back.

Of course, I'm rewarded with a flash of glowing gold heat in her hot brown eyes. There's no guarantee Winter will sleep tonight either, but usually we can steal away a few minutes for ourselves.

I thought a second kid would be a huge adjustment.

It hasn't been half bad.

Guess I've caught on to this family gig naturally.

Our family.

I thread my fingers through hers, an unexpected bolt of emotion stabbing through me. We've spent a lot of time working, figuring out what a life together means, but right now, it feels like we've finally sorted it out.

"Patton?" Salem stops in the doorway, her dark hair edged with amber stripes in the sunlight. Her burgundy dress hugs her curves, laying flatter after Winter's birth eight months ago, tempting my hands to roam.

I have to keep them on a tight leash.

Winter gurgles in her arms, drifting off to sleep again. On her other side, Arlo looks back at me with a frown. He's a mini-me, growing into the lanky little beast he is, crowned with dark russet hair.

Shit, I don't think I've ever loved my little tribe as hard as I do right now. The emotion hits so hard I have to blink at the hot, biting sensation in my eyes.

"You guys go on ahead," I say, glad my voice stays steady. "I'm right behind you."

Salem's mouth quirks like she can sense every thought as she pulls little Winter up in her arms. Then she puts a hand on Arlo's shoulder, ushering him along.

"Come on, sweetie," she says, steering away. They disappear into the sunlight at the end of the hall.

After a few seconds where I'm just staring like a frozen moron, she comes back child-free. She probably strapped them in the car and parked on the driveway.

Her smile is soft and slow as she cups my face in her hands and looks at me.

"I know that look," she says matter-of-factly, her thumbs smoothing over my cheekbones. "I feel it, too."

I chuckle deeply, grabbing her hips and pulling her closer.

This weird need to have her close, to taste her, overwhelms me.

No, I can't bring myself to give a damn about the time.

"I love you, Lady Bug," I tell her fiercely. "Goddamn, I love you."

"Love you, too." Reaching up, she presses her mouth to mine, and my hands slide down her waist. When she pulls away, her eyes are lined with moisture, too. Fucking emotions. "Now can you make your legs work? Your family's waiting and Winter will freak if we leave her waiting too long."

"*Our* family," I correct, and her smile widens.

"Our family."

It's tempting as hell to stay here longer, but like any good wife, she's right.

We start walking with Salem's little hand tangled in mine.

When we step outside to the sunny driveway, I'm beaming so hard it might split my face in two.

ABOUT NICOLE SNOW

Nicole Snow is a *Wall Street Journal* and *USA Today* bestselling author. She found her love of writing by hashing out love scenes on lunch breaks and plotting her great escape from boardrooms. Her work roared onto the indie romance scene in 2014 with her Grizzlies MC series.

Since then Snow aims for the very best in growly, heart-of-gold alpha heroes, unbelievable suspense, and swoon storms aplenty.

Already hooked on her stuff? Visit nicolesnowbooks.com to sign up for her newsletter and connect on social media.

Got a question or comment on her work? Reach her anytime at nicole@nicolesnowbooks.com

Thanks for reading. And please remember to leave an honest review! Nothing helps an author more.

MORE BOOKS BY NICOLE

The Rory Brothers

Two Truths And A Marriage

One Big Little Secret

Bossy Seattle Suits

One Bossy Proposal

One Bossy Dare

One Bossy Date

One Bossy Offer

One Bossy Disaster

Bad Chicago Bosses

Office Grump

Bossy Grump

Perfect Grump

Damaged Grump

Dark Hearts of Redhaven

The Broken Protector

The Sweetest Obsession

The Darkest Chase

Knights of Dallas Books

The Romeo Arrangement

The Best Friend Zone

The Hero I Need

The Worst Best Friend

Accidental Knight (Companion book)*

Heroes of Heart's Edge Books

No Perfect Hero

No Good Doctor

No Broken Beast

No Damaged Goods

No Fair Lady

No White Knight

No Gentle Giant

Marriage Mistake Standalone Books

Accidental Hero

Accidental Protector

Accidental Romeo

Accidental Knight

Accidental Rebel

Accidental Shield

Stand Alone Novels

Almost Pretend

The Perfect Wrong

Cinderella Undone

Man Enough

Surprise Daddy

Prince With Benefits

Marry Me Again

Love Scars

Recklessly His

Enguard Protectors Books

Still Not Over You

Still Not Into You

Still Not Yours

Still Not Love

Baby Fever Books

Baby Fever Bride

Baby Fever Promise

Baby Fever Secrets

Only Pretend Books

Fiance on Paper

One Night Bride

Grizzlies MC Books

Outlaw's Kiss

Outlaw's Obsession

Outlaw's Bride

Outlaw's Vow

Deadly Pistols MC Books

Never Love an Outlaw

Never Kiss an Outlaw

Never Have an Outlaw's Baby

Never Wed an Outlaw

Prairie Devils MC Books

Outlaw Kind of Love

Nomad Kind of Love

Savage Kind of Love

Wicked Kind of Love

Bitter Kind of Love

Made in the USA
Coppell, TX
12 December 2024